Sins and Needles

Needlecraft Mysteries by Monica Ferris

CREWEL WORLD
FRAMED IN LACE
A STITCH IN TIME
UNRAVELED SLEEVE
A MURDEROUS YARN
HANGING BY A THREAD
CUTWORK
CREWEL YULE
EMBROIDERED TRUTHS
SINS AND NEEDLES

Anthologies

PATTERNS OF MURDER

Sins and Needles

Monica Ferris

BERKLEY PRIME CRIME BOOKS, NEW YORK

THE BERKLEY PUBLISHING GROUP
Published by the Penguin Group
Penguin Group (USA) Inc.
375 Hudson Street, New York, New York 10014, USA
Penguin Group (Canada), 90 Eglinton Avenue East, Suite 700, Toronto, Ontario M4P 2Y3, Canada
(a division of Pearson Penguin Canada Inc.)
Penguin Books Ltd., 80 Strand, London WC2R 0RL, England
Penguin Group Ireland, 25 St. Stephen's Green, Dublin 2, Ireland (a division of Penguin Books Ltd.)
Penguin Group (Australia), 250 Camberwell Road, Camberwell, Victoria 3124, Australia
(a division of Pearson Australia Group Pty. Ltd.)
Penguin Books India Pvt. Ltd., 11 Community Centre, Panchsheel Park, New Delhi—110 017, India
Penguin Group (NZ), Cnr. Airborne and Rosedale Roads, Albany, Auckland 1310, New Zealand
(a division of Pearson New Zealand Ltd.)
Penguin Books (South Africa) (Pty.) Ltd., 24 Sturdee Avenue, Rosebank, Johannesburg 2196, South Africa

Penguin Books Ltd., Registered Offices: 80 Strand, London WC2R 0RL, England

SINS AND NEEDLES

This is an original publication of The Berkley Publishing Group.

Copyright © 2006 by Mary Monica Kuhfeld writing as Monica Ferris.
Cover art by Mary Ann Lasher.
Cover design by George Long.

First edition: July 2006

Berkley Prime Crime hardcover ISBN: 0-425-21003-0

This book has been cataloged with the Library of Congress.

PRINTED IN THE UNITED STATES OF AMERICA

10   9   8   7   6   5   4   3   2   1

Acknowledgments

The idea for this book came from Todd Warner, of Mahogany Bay in Orono, Minnesota. I can't tell you more about it here, because that would give too much of the plot away. I would also like to thank Marge Scheftel and Jean Deggerdorf, who live on the Big Island of Lake Minnetonka. And Tanya Dee Smith for looking just like someone else I know when the sun is at her back. Oh, and Luci Zahrey, Texan.

One

❖ ❖ ❖

IT was mid-June, and the sun was at its northernmost position in the sky. Its beams filled the big front window of
Betsy Devonshire's needlework shop, Crewel World, drown-
ing the careful effects of the lighting inside, especially near
the front.

Betsy was sitting behind the checkout desk, shielding
her eyes from the glare with one hand while going down a
list of customers signed up for a knitting class. Most were
beginners who had knitted all the simple scarves in exotic
yarns they could possibly use and wanted something more
challenging.

So Betsy had hired Rosemary Kosel to teach her famous
beginner sweater class, and her store manager, Godwin, to
teach the fine art of knitting socks. Rosemary's class, already
full, was to begin the last Thursday of next month, but Godwin's was starting in a few days, and he needed another student to make the class pay for itself. Instructors were worthy
of their hire, but Betsy could not afford to pay for instructors
out of shop profits. Godwin was charging forty-five dollars for

three ninety-minute sessions. In that time, quick students would have one sock finished and everyone else would know how to finish it.

Betsy checked the mail to see if there was another registration. There was, but it was for Rosemary's class. She sighed and went over the list of both classes to see that she had the mailing address, phone number, and e-mail address of each student. Well, Mrs. Shipman had no e-mail address; she wouldn't even have a computer in her house. Betsy was about to put the stack into her desk drawer when the door chimed. She looked up to see who was coming in.

With the strong sun behind her, the woman was barely more than a silhouette, but Betsy recognized her sturdy outline and the blond tumble of curls around her shoulders. "Well, good morning, Jan! That twenty-eight count Laguna fabric came in. Do you still want a piece?"

The woman entered the shop, speaking in a Texas drawl. "I'm not Jan. I'm Lucille Jones. Remember me, from Trinity Church on Sunday?"

Betsy's eyes widened. "Why, of course, Mrs. Jones! I'm so sorry! But you wore your hair up on Sunday—even so, funny I didn't see how remarkable the resemblance is."

Now she remembered Lucille Jones and her husband— what was his name? Robert, that's it. The first words out of his mouth over coffee after the service, spoken in an even more pronounced drawl than his wife's, had been, "Call me Bobby Lee. Everyone who knows me does." He was tall, deeply tanned, good looking, and he'd worn to church what every good ol' country Texan does: stiff new jeans, a western shirt, cowboy boots, and a clean black cowboy hat, held in one hand. It was probably rude of Betsy to be so surprised to learn he was a surgical nurse at a prestigious hospital in Houston.

His uncommon costume and disarming manners drew

her attention, which was another reason she hadn't paid close attention to his wife.

Lucille was standing at her checkout desk right now, waiting for her to stop woolgathering. When Betsy's eyes came back into focus, Lucille smiled. "I take it this Jan is a regular customer?"

"Oh, yes, she's in here a lot."

"But you still thought I was her." Lucille had a twinkle in her blue eyes. "I must look a *whole lot* like her."

"Well, I can tell the difference now that you're not outlined by the sun coming in the window, but you do look alike." Both were in their forties, had sturdy builds, curly blond hair, and DMC floss color 996 blue eyes.

"They say everyone has a twin somewhere in this world, so maybe she's mine." Lucille looked around without moving. "This is pretty nice. You told me about your shop, and I came to see what you have in knitting yarn. I'm looking for something fancy, maybe that kind that looks like fur? I want to knit one of those twirly scarves for my goddaughter, who's going into high school this fall."

As she led Lucille toward the yarns, Betsy said, "Well, I don't have as large a selection as Three Kittens or Needlework Unlimited, but I do lean toward the exotic. What color are you after?"

"Something mixed, you know, three or four shades of a color. Sydney likes green or turquoise. Oh, this one is pretty!" She took a fat skein of yarn from Betsy's hand, a dense plush in shades of medium and light green. Then her eye was caught by a group of skeins in a basket. "Say, you've got eyelash yarn. I just love it. Do you think it would look nice knit together with this?" She held up the plush skein.

"Yes, I do," said Betsy.

A few minutes later, Betsy was ringing up a sale that included two skeins of the plush, two eyelash, two of a beautiful merino wool, a book of patterns, three pairs of bamboo needles in the larger sizes, and a fabric knitting bag to carry it all. Lucille handed Betsy a credit card and said, "This Jan you said I look like—what's she like? Is she nice?"

"Well, like you, she's a knitter. But she goes to the other end of the scale from you. She likes size zero or even double- and triple-zero needles. She knits teeny little beaded bags and lace. She also does counted cross-stitch. Her latest project is a Persian rug stitched on silk gauze, sixty count."

"I like counted cross-stitch, too, but give me a nice eighteen-count linen. What eyes she must have!"

Betsy laughed as she handed over the receipt for Lucille's signature. "She has excellent vision, but she also has a Dazor light." The Dazor featured a big magnifying glass surrounded by a full-spectrum light; looking through it was like sitting in a window full of sunlight with Superman eyes. Used by advanced cross-stitchers working on high-count fabric, it was also a godsend to stitchers over forty.

"And she looks like me?"

The insistent question made Betsy frown just a little, but she obediently considered Lucille's face and acknowledged, "You could be sisters."

"What's her last name? Where does she live?"

Starting to feel really uncomfortable, Betsy said, "I'm sorry, I don't give out customers' addresses."

Lucille seemed instantly abashed. "No, no, it's all right," she said hastily. "It's me who should be sorry. But let me explain. My mama died a year ago February—Daddy died about five years before that. I was their only child, and as I was going through their papers, *I found adoption documents!* Well, I was sure floored! I had no idea! But after I picked myself up, I thought about it and finally decided to search for my biological roots. I found out I was left at an orphanage in Minneapolis, but it was like hitting a brick wall trying to get further than that. I finally told Bobby Lee—he's my husband; he was with me on Sunday—"

Betsy nodded.

"I told him we were spending our vacation in Minnesota." She smiled in a way that showed she had had to overcome some objections on his part. "But you know something?"

"What?" asked Betsy.

"I *like* it up here. It's really different from Houston, but it feels . . . I don't know . . . right. It's like I've come home, even though I've never been here before. Do you think that means my biological parents really are from here?"

Betsy didn't believe in genetic memory, but she said politely, "I suppose it could mean that. How did you end up in Texas? Were your parents originally from here, too?"

Lucille laughed. "Oh, my, no! My mother was a proud Daughter of the Confederacy, and my father's great-great-uncle died at the Alamo." She leaned closer to confide in an amused undertone, "Though there's a rumor that his wife's brother fought with Santa Anna."

Betsy laughed.

Lucille opened her wallet to put her credit card away. "I know my birth date, so I've been checking at hospitals, but so far I haven't found any record of an unmarried woman giving birth on that day."

Betsy's eyebrows lifted. "Maybe—" She hesitated.

But Lucille broke in, her tone inviting, "What? Tell me. One of the ladies at church said you're like a female Sherlock Holmes, so detect for me."

Betsy, wondering vaguely which of her friends had spilled those beans, said, "Well, this isn't detection, it's more like deduction. Maybe your mother was married but died in childbirth. Sometimes a father feels overwhelmed and can't deal with a newborn."

Lucille stared at her as if Betsy had said something

ridiculous. "No," she said firmly. "My biological mother is *not* dead."

Betsy did not, of course, want to start an argument, but Lucille must have read something in her eyes, because she said, touching the center of her breast, "I can *feel* it, right here. She is alive, she's around here somewhere, and I'm going to find her."

Two

BETSY said she was not angry, and she wasn't. But she *was* aggravated.

"It's your own fault," said Godwin. "If you had told me about her, I wouldn't've told her about the class. But I needed one more person, and she's a knitter, and I didn't know.

"Anyhow, what harm can it do?" he continued, his stronger tone indicating a frailer argument. "She's interested in meeting her twin. I'd be, too, if someone told me there was this person who looked just like me." He drew himself up and turned sideways. "As if!" he added, sure there was not a handsomer profile anywhere.

As usual, Betsy was amused at his vanity, which got her past her annoyance. "Oh, you're probably right. And it wasn't as if she seemed angry or confrontational. She's just curious. Anyway, she's only here on vacation, so even if she turns out to be a nuisance, pretty soon she'll go home, and it'll all be over."

But her own rationalizations didn't entirely ease Betsy's mind, so she decided to sit in on the first class to see how Lucille behaved toward Jan Henderson—and how Jan took it.

The class was scheduled to begin at six thirty. Godwin stood in the back, tugging at his light blue polo shirt, clearing his throat, smoothing his hair, buffing his shoes on the back of his khaki Dockers, preparing to make an entrance.

It was Betsy's role to unlock the front door—the shop had closed at five—and let the students in.

First to arrive, at six fifteen, was Doris Valentine. She had the least distance to travel, as she lived in an apartment on the second floor of the building that housed the shop.

But she was followed in short order by Katie Frazier, a redhead with hazel green eyes in a sleeveless maternity blouse, and then by Jan, Katie's aunt. After Jan came Phil Galvin, a senior citizen in jeans and a chambray shirt, the pocket of which held his four double-pointed bamboo knitting needles. In one gnarled hand he held a big ball of green lightweight yarn. "Good evening!" he said, in a loud, hoarse voice.

Last came Lucille, entering shyly, unsure of her welcome. Her bright hair was pulled back with a scrunchie. She wore a dark blue T-shirt with a loon painted on it, and she carried a lavender Crewel World plastic bag. Her blue eyes flashed to the table, then fastened on Jan.

Jan was talking to Doris, so it was Phil who first noticed her. His eyes opened wide. He looked across at Jan, then back at Lucille. He leaned a little sideways and poked Doris on the arm and said in what he probably thought was a murmur, "Lookit over there!"

Doris looked at Lucille and, with eyebrows raised, smiled in pleased surprise. "Now that is *amazing*!" she said to Phil.

Jan also looked at Lucille. "Hello," she said, frowning a little at her.

Lucille stood captured in shyness, her fair complexion pinking under the stares of the others. Betsy took pity on her and said warmly, "Lucille, welcome! Come on over, there's plenty of room!"

Lucille smiled gratefully at Betsy and came to the table. She took a seat across from Jan, next to Kate.

Phil said, "Say, Lucille—is that your name?"

"Yes, sir," said Lucille in her western drawl, pulling out a chair. "Lucille Jones."

"Jones—does that mean you aren't related to Jan here?"

"I don't think so." Lucille studied Jan for a few moments. "But we do look alike, don't we?"

"You sure do!" said Doris.

"Yes, I suppose so," said Jan.

"Suppose so?" said Katie. "Aunt Jan, what's the matter with you? Can't you see it's like you're twins?"

"Do you really think so?" Jan, like most people, couldn't see the resemblance between herself and this other person.

"Oh, not twins," said Lucille quickly. "But—well, sisters, maybe?"

Jan smiled. "A secret sister—there's a concept you don't hear much about."

Lucille chuckled. "Actually, I don't think I've ever heard of it. Unless you're adopted, too?"

"Nope. I'm my own mother's daughter, and I think she would've told me if she gave one of her other children away. I mean, what a great threat: 'I gave your sister away, and if you don't straighten up, I'll give you away, too!'"

"Almost as good as, 'I brought you into the world and I can take you out of it.' Ah, for the happy days of having little ones in the house," Lucille said.

Kate was scandalized by Lucille's comment. "You never in your life said that to a child of yours!" she said.

"No. But I came close a couple of times."

"Me, too," said Jan. "I still might use it. My younger one is only sixteen."

Phil, who'd been listening to all of this, spoke up. "You're not from around here, are you?" he asked Lucille. "The way you talk and all."

"No, I'm from Texas. But you know something?" She looked around the table. "Actually, I think I look more like people up here than back home. I mean, I never saw so many natural blondes in my life before!"

A chorus of soft laughter swept the table. Kate was a natural redhead, but Jan's streaky blond hair, without the aid of her hairdresser, was mostly gray. Doris's elaborate blond hairdo was probably a wig. Phil's hair was silver, but his dark eyes suggested that he had been a brunet when he was young. Betsy went to the same hairdresser Jan did.

Godwin chose that moment to make his entrance.

The renewed grins and chuckles that greeted his entrance surprised him—he, too, was a chemically enhanced blond. But he took his place at the head of the table as if he had no idea what they were so amused by. "Good evening, good evening," he said. "It looks like we're all here. Has everyone got at least one skein of lightweight yarn and a set of number three double-pointed knitting needles?"

Everyone had.

"Good. Now, before we begin, how about we go around the table and introduce ourselves? I'm Godwin DuLac, your instructor. I'm also Vice President in Charge of Operations of Crewel World, Incorporated, and Editor in Chief of *Hasta la Stitches*, its newsletter. Your turn, Phil."

"I'm Phil Galvin, retired railroad engineer. I do counted cross-stitch, but I had to wait until I retired to admit it in public. Then last year my mother died, and as I was closing her house, I came across a knit scarf. It was wrapped around a letter my dad had written from a hospital in England. He'd been shot in the leg and both shoulders during the Battle of the Bulge, and the nurses had set him to knitting as . . . whaddayeh call it? . . . physical therapy. He'd knit that scarf as a present to my mother, and she'd kept it all those years. I was gonna try a scarf, but then I heard about this sock class and thought I'd rather have a pair of socks."

"Gosh!" said Godwin, impressed. "Okay, next!"

The young pregnant woman said, "I'm Katie—well, Mary Katherine O'Neil Frazier, really, and Jan is my aunt, and she persuaded me to take this class. I already knit a little, and I do counted cross-stitch and needle lace, and now I'm hoping to knit socks, too." She smiled at Jan, who smiled back.

"I'm Doris Valentine," said Doris in her deep, breathy voice. "I'm new to needlework, but I really like it. I especially love counted cross-stitch, and I wish I could afford some of those wonderful needlepoint canvases. All kinds of needlework are domestic, but knitting a sock is like the most domestic thing you can do, next to baking bread. I did factory work all my life, and I never married, but now I'm retired and have the time to do some traditional women's work, and I'm really grateful." She blushed at being so open about her feelings and hurriedly began to pry open the clear plastic envelope of her double-ended needles with her bright red fingernails.

"That's really nice. I'm glad for you," said Lucille, smiling. "I'm Lucille Jones, visiting from Texas, but you already know that. I'm here because Mr. DuLac said someone who looked a lot like me signed up for it, and I was curious about her. I can knit and purl, but I've never made anything before except scarves and booties."

Godwin said, "Does everyone know how to cast on? Good. Cast on sixty-four stitches—except you, Phil. With your big feet, you cast on seventy-two. Then divide them onto four of your five needles, sixteen—Phil, eighteen—apiece.

Doris started the slow, beginner's way of casting on until Godwin said, "Here, let me show you a faster way." It involved taking a length of yarn and pulling it into a V between her left thumb and forefinger, then lifting first one side then the other into a simple knot on the needle. "Now, pull it tight and do another—no, not that tight."

Phil said, "You didn't say what you do back home, Lucille."

"I'm a lab tech. How about you, Jan?"

"I'm a registered nurse."

"Why, my husband's an RN, too," said Lucille, surprised and pleased. "He's a surgical nurse at Methodist Hospital in Houston. They do a lot of heart surgery there, and the doctors just love him. They ask for him when it's going to be tricky in the OR."

"I thought about being a surgical nurse, but it's very stressful work."

"Yes, it gets to Bobby Lee sometimes, too, but he says he loves it too much to try something else." Lucille knit a few more stitches then turned in her chair to smile at Betsy. "Aren't you going to introduce yourself?"

Betsy said, obediently, "My name is Betsy Devonshire. I own Crewel World, and I already know how to knit a sock."

Godwin said, "After you've cast on, start doing knit one, purl one, using the fifth needle. This will make the cuff. Begin at the place that will join the ends together."

Lucille had already cast on. She began dividing the knitting evenly onto the four needles, struggling a bit with so many needles all apparently wanting to help. That done, she started to knit.

"This is harder than I thought it would be," she grumbled after a few minutes of knit and purl, winding her yarn carefully through the forest of needles. "I don't see how you do it so slick," she added, watching Godwin's nimble fingers build his cuff with amazing speed.

"Experience," said Godwin. "It's hard for beginners, but once you get even just half an inch done, things settle down. You'll find you can concentrate on just the two needles you're using, and the other needles won't get in your way so much."

Lucille frowned doubtfully.

"You're right that it's hard, Lucille," Jan said. "But

Goddy's right, too. This is my second try at learning to knit a sock, and I can tell you that that once you get past that first inch, it seems to get a lot easier."

"Well, if it gets easier, why are you having to come back for a second try?"

Jan laughed. "I got the cuff all right, but I couldn't get the part about turning the heel. I mean, I did it the first time, when my teacher was right there to talk me through it, but when I tried to do the second sock, it just wouldn't work. So here I am again, with a different teacher, to see if I can cross reference the instructions and internalize them."

Lucille leaned sideways for a closer look at Jan's work. "What you've got so far looks pretty good from here."

"Yours looks good, too," Jan said. "I like the color of the yarn—did you buy that here at Crewel World?"

"Yes, I found it in the sale basket. Fortunately, there were two skeins, so I can make a pair." Lucille had selected a lightweight wool-blend yarn in graduated shades of dark and light blue. She knit another couple of needles' worth, then asked Godwin, "How many inches long is the cuff?"

"It's up to you," he replied. "I like just the top inch and a half most of the time, but sometimes I get crazy and do the whole first part as cuff, right down to where I start turning the heel."

"Well, I don't like baggy socks, so I guess I'll do the top all cuff."

"That's a good idea," said Jan. "I'll do it that way, too."

"I can knit, knit, knit faster than I can knit, purl, knit, purl," said Katie, "so I'm going to make a cuff just at the top." She set off, her fingers moving her pink yarn with slow deliberation, lips just noticeably pursed.

"At that rate, you'll have one sock finished by the time the snow flies," drawled Lucille, then smiled at her.

Jan giggled, and Katie smiled, first at Lucille, then at Jan. "You're probably right."

"So long as you're sitting here with us," Godwin said to Betsy, "why don't you join us?"

"No, thanks. I've knit a few pairs of socks, but they take too much time—especially when you can buy them so cheap."

"If you can knit socks, why aren't you teaching this class?" asked Phil.

"Because while I can follow a pattern to knit a sock, I'm not good enough at it to teach. I know a little bit about a lot of needlework, usually just enough to know what my customers need."

"I think it must be just the greatest thing in the world to own your own business," sighed Doris.

"Oh, I don't know," said Katie. "My dad has tried all his life to get one started, and it's not easy."

"Maybe he's lucky he hasn't succeeded," said Betsy. She pointed to a needlepoint model on the wall behind her. " 'The only thing more overrated than natural childbirth is owning your own business,' " she said, reading it aloud.

"Maybe," said Katie.

Phil said, "My parents owned a grocery store right here in Excelsior, and they worked all kinds of hours. So did I *and* my two brothers and three sisters, as soon as we got old enough to pick up a can and put it on a shelf."

"Three boys and three girls?" said Lucille. "I'd say they didn't work *all* the time. Not in the store, anyhow."

"Unless . . ." said Godwin slyly, then added all in a rush, waving his burgeoning sock as if it were an eraser, clearing the air of that word before it could become offensive, "No, no, never mind; that was back in the fifties, and such things *never* would've gone on in Excelsior shops in the *fifties* . . ." He leaned forward and added in a low, confidential tone, nodding as he did so, "Even in the back rooms."

"Oh, Goddy, you are the *limit*!" said Jan, amid the general laughter.

Everyone knit for a while. Then Lucille said, "You mentioned children, Jan. How many, how old?"

"I have two. Reese is a pre-law senior at Carleton—he got a full scholarship. Ronnie just turned fifteen; he wants to design the first really workable artificial heart." Jan's head lifted in pride at her two children. "How about you?"

"I also have two. Wanda is about finished with her veterinary internship at Woodhull Animal Hospital. Glen is an airplane mechanic at Dallas/Fort Worth International. Mine are six years apart. Yours are at least that much, sounds like."

"They're seven years apart." Jan's smile was bittersweet. "Mama always said I should space my children, but . . ."

"I lost a couple in between, too," Lucille said quietly.

"Oh, that's so sad," said Doris. "I'm sorry to hear that. I couldn't have children, but losing one is even worse than not having one at all, I think."

"How . . . interesting that you know you couldn't have children," said Lucille. "I mean, since you said earlier that you never married."

"Oh, for heaven's sake!" said Godwin, hoping to lighten the mood that was rapidly darkening his class. "Hasn't anyone told this poor woman the facts of life?"

Phil choked back a laugh, and Lucille said, in a high, innocent voice, dripping with Texas honey, "Why no, my mama never sat me down for that li'l ol' 'talk' I hear other girls whispering about. Maybe you could give it to me some time?"

Godwin widened his blue eyes at her. "My dear, if you think *I* could be a mother to you, no amount of talking will do you the slightest good."

Phil burst out laughing. "Godwin, you *are* the limit!"

"Why, Phil, you say the nicest things!" said Godwin. "But I'm sorry to say, you just dropped a stitch."

"I did? Well, dammit to hell. Now what do I do?"

Godwin showed Phil one use of a number 5 crochet hook in picking up the dropped stitch and restoring his knitting.

The class went on until Godwin called a halt, promptly at eight. His "homework" for his students was to lengthen the sock to the point of "turning the heel," which he would show them next week.

Katie signaled to Jan, and they both lingered after the others left. "Who is that Lucille person?" Katie demanded of Godwin.

"Why, just what she said, a visitor from out of town."

"What's your problem, Katie?" Jan asked. "She seems nice enough."

"She was very nosy about you. Didn't you notice?"

"Of course I noticed! But she wasn't nosy, she was curious. I was curious, too, once I realized everyone seriously thought we looked a whole lot alike. Actually, this isn't the first time this has happened. I guess I'm a 'type.' Why, only last winter I was at a medical convention and some people were asking me if I had a twin. I didn't get to meet her, so I don't know how close the resemblance was. So why make such a big deal out of this?"

"Money, is why. M-O-N-E-Y. She wants to be a long-lost relation so she can get in on the money Great-aunt Edyth is going to leave you. I should think you'd be—"

"Now how on earth could she know about Aunt Edyth?"

That stopped Katie in her tracks. "Well, I guess I don't know."

"She could have Googled you," said Godwin.

"What?" said Jan.

"Googled you. Put your name in the search engine Google to see what pops up. Edyth Hanraty has been in a couple of newspapers and magazines because of her beautiful house. Maybe Lucille found out about her that way."

"Putting her name in a search engine won't link Aunt Edyth to me," said Jan. "Nor will putting my name in one."

"Oh," said Godwin.

"So that's that," said Jan. "Well, we'd better get going. This has been fun—you're a good teacher, Goddy. See you next week."

Jan smiled at Betsy, frowned at Kate, and went out.

But Kate followed her. "Wait a second, wait a second," she said. Her aunt stopped with a sigh and turned to let her catch up.

"Now she's here, she can find out about Aunt Edyth," said Katie.

"And so what if she does? In fact, so what if it turns out she is a relative? If it was about the money, she'd have to be related through the female line, and we'd know about that if she was. Mom's the only descendant through the female line, and I'm the only girl child she had."

"But Uncle Stewart—" started Kate.

"Is your father, and a man, as I'm sure you've noticed. If he went off sowing wild oats and Miss Lucille is the result, so what? Great-aunt Edyth's will leaves her money only to the descendants of her sister Alice. through the female line."

"What if she doesn't know that?" asked Kate.

"Then someone will tell her, if it even gets that far. I don't see what you're so upset about. Since you aren't in line to inherit, it's no money taken from you; your connection to Grandmother Alice is through your father." She grimaced. "I don't mean to sound as if I approve. Great-aunt Edyth is a strong and wonderful person, but she's coldhearted about some things. I've tried to talk to her and failed. She likes you, so keep going to visit her—I wish you luck with her."

Katie raised one finger, a prophetess making a prediction. "If that Lucille Jones finds out about her, you can bet she'll try even harder."

Three

❖ ❖ ❖

BETSY was online checking her newsgroups, answering e-mail, noting that an order for some of Kreinik's new metallics had been shipped, when her phone rang. The ID display on the phone said it was Jan Henderson.

"Good morning, Jan," she answered.

"Good morning. Hope it's all right to call you this early."

"Certainly. I've been up for hours. What can I do for you?"

"Could you tell me where Lucille Jones is staying? I want to talk to her."

"Just a second—let me think . . . yes, she's staying at the Minnetonka Cabin Resort—you know, that little row of cabins with the different-colored doors."

"The Nickelsons' place."

"Yes. Hold on, I've got the number here somewhere. Why do you want to talk to her?"

"Just nosy," Jan said.

* * *

THEY met for lunch at The Waterfront Café. Jan recommended the BLT on whole wheat toast, and they each ordered it. "It's like before the cholesterol scare in here," Jan said, inhaling happily. "Their BLTs have real bacon and lots of mayo."

"I suppose it's better that we know about such things," Lucille replied. "But sometimes I wonder. It's taken all the fun out of eating."

Jan nodded in sincere agreement and took a drink of her water.

Lucille cocked her head sideways and looked all over Jan's face. "I thought it would be like looking in a mirror, but it isn't."

"I know. Everyone at that sock lesson was amazed at how much we look alike, but while I can see a resemblance, I don't think it's quite that pronounced."

"Me, neither. Still, there must be something to it, if everyone around us can see it."

"I guess so. When were you born?" Jan asked.

"August twelfth, 1959. You?"

"June twenty-first, 1964," replied Jan. "That makes us five years apart. You have two kids, I have two kids—but that's not unusual. And mine are both sons, you have—"

"A son and a daughter, yes. I married an RN, you married a doctor. My oldest is going to be a veterinarian, your oldest is going to be a lawyer. My youngest is an aircraft mechanic, your youngest is going to build a mechanical heart."

Jan thought that was stretching it a bit, but she nodded. "We both like needlework. I enjoy knitting, counted cross-stitch, and needlepoint."

"I'd like needlepoint if I could afford it—those canvases are kind of pricey!"

"I agree. I don't do a lot of them. I probably have three in my stash."

"Where do you keep your stash?"

"I used to keep it in an old chest of drawers my mother gave me."

Lucille's jaw dropped. "Well, isn't that strange. That's where I kept mine, until it overflowed into my closet and then into the garage. When Glen moved out for good, I converted his bedroom into a sewing room. When Wanda moves out, Bobby Lee can have her room for a den."

"I've converted Reese's. When Ronnie goes, Hugs—that's what I call my husband, Harvey—gets his den."

"I tell you, we've been living parallel lives."

"Oh, I don't know. Every stitcher does that as soon as a kid moves out," Jan said.

"Okay, what do you like to do besides needlework?"

"Well, we used to go camping. But one night the four of us got washed out of our tent and had to spend the night in the car, sitting on plastic bags so we wouldn't ruin the upholstery. The next day we found that a bear had gotten into our food, and what he didn't eat, he scattered. I decided that was enough, and I refused to go again."

"I loved desert camping for years. You would not believe the stars at night out there. Bobby Lee and I used to make the kids get up in the morning and start the fire—it gets cold out on the desert once the sun goes down. One year both kids were in school, so it was just the two of us, and we'd zipped our sleeping bags together to help us keep warm. The second morning, I woke and thought Ronnie was feeling frisky, tickling my tummy, then I saw he was sound asleep with his back to me. I wasn't sure what was sharing my side of the bag, but I slid out of that sleeping bag in one motion, and—I don't know how—without unzipping it. That woke Bobby Lee, and I whispered at him to lay real still. I unzipped my side as slow as I could—" Lucille demonstrated, reaching as far out as she could with one hand, fingers extended, head half turned away. Jan giggled with excitement. Lucille continued, "I turned the top back verrrrrry carefully—and there, big as my arm, was a big ol' rattlesnake!"

"No!" said Jan, horrified. "What did you do? What did Bobby Lee do?"

"Nothing. We just froze, like statues. And after a while, its wee little brain realized the cold morning air was chilling its scales and it slithered off, and that was the last time I went camping."

"Whew, I don't blame you! That's worse than our bear! Ronnie still goes off to the Boundary Waters for a week every summer with his friends, but none of the rest of us has been back, not even Hugs."

"Where did your husband get that nickname?"

"He was a very affectionate little boy, so that's what his grandmother called him, and when he found out that Harvey was the name of an invisible rabbit in a Jimmy Stewart movie, he decided Hugs, bad as it was, was better than his real name. One reason it stuck was that he was a wrestler in high school and college and famous for his grip." Jan smiled. "Plus, he's still very affectionate."

Lucille laughed. "That is *adorable*! So what do you do instead of camp?"

"Well, boating runs in the family. We have a boat, and so does my brother. Mother sold her powerboat when Dad died, but she kept a canoe and recently bought a kayak. This is Minnesota, after all. When they said 'Ten Thousand Lakes,' they underestimated. We fish and water-ski and just putt around Lake Minnetonka all summer."

"You water-ski? Why, so do we! We have friends, Mickey and Jacki Morris, who have a boat with this huge motor, and they take us out six or eight times a year. We have a little boat of our own, but it's way more fun on Mickey and Jacki's boat. Can you ski on one ski? I can."

"No, but Hugs can. He can even ski barefoot."

"Bobby Lee tried that and took four bad spills before he gave it up. Maybe your husband can tell him how it's done."

"Maybe he can—but personally, I think the secret is in the feet. Hugs's shoe size is twelve, extra wide."

"Bobby Lee's is only nine—but my son Glen's is fourteen. I'm telling you, I was about to study how the Chinese did that foot-binding thing when Glen was in high school. He was going through shoes like I go through embroidery floss."

"I'm glad I didn't think of it. I might've tried it with Reese. His feet are even bigger than his father's."

Their sandwiches came at last, and after a few bites and exclamations of pleasure, Jan took her courage by both hands. "Lucille," she asked, "did you Google me?"

"I beg your pardon?"

"Did you use the Google search engine to see if you could find out about me?"

"No. Why, should I have? What would Google have told me about you?"

"I don't know. I've never Googled myself."

"Do you have a Web site?"

"No."

"Me, neither. I wonder what Google would say about me?" Jan asked thoughtfully, "What would you like it to say?"

Lucille took a bite of her sandwich and thought that over while she chewed. After a few moments, she said, "That I hope no one thinks I love my mama and daddy less because I'm trying to find my biological family."

JAN came into Crewel World the next day, Saturday, to buy some tatting thread. "I'm going to knit a bed-spread," she said.

Betsy held up the single ball of thin white thread Jan was

buying. "With number three thread? That should take you a few years. And I don't think this single ball would be enough to knit even an edge on a bedspread."

Jan laughed. "No, it's for a dollhouse bedspread. A friend at the clinic bought a dollhouse for her daughter, but now she's caught the bug herself and won't let Chloe anywhere near it. This will be a birthday present for her."

"Do you need a set of needles, too?" People in business for themselves quickly learn to never pass up an opportunity to make a sale.

"No, I've already got four pairs of double-zero steels." As Betsy opened her cash register, Jan asked, "Has Lucille been in today?"

"No, I haven't seen her. Are you still thinking you're twins separated at birth?"

Jan smiled. "You know, I almost could. It's weird how alike we are. Like, we both *used* to love camping, but wouldn't go now for a million dollars. We both love swimming, water-skiing, and fishing—though where on earth you can find a lake big enough or a river deep enough to ski on in all of Texas, I don't know—and we both love it when we can mix a conference or seminar with pleasure travel to make it tax de-ductible."

"Now that last one really is a peculiar coincidence!" Betsy said.

Jan's smile turned a little odd. "I know. You know what's even odder? She tells great stories, just like my uncle Stew-art. And she knows it. Her eyes twinkle just like his when she tells one. Betsy, what do you think? Could Lucille and I be related?"

Betsy didn't know what Jan wanted to hear, so she fell back on the truth. "I don't know. Is there a mystery in your genealogy? An uncle who was suspected of having an affair? An aunt who disappeared for, oh, say, nine months?"

"Not that I know of. Well, except the man part. I mean, how long does it take to father a child? Part of an evening? Shoot, a coffee break will do for some of them."

Betsy grimaced. "But that would mean . . ."

"I know. And there's never been a hint of anything like that."

"Yet, you two look so much alike that it's hard not to think there's a genetic link in there somewhere. I'm sure you've heard about those cases of identical twins separated at birth who turn out to have a lot of traits in common. But we're not talking about identical twins here, are we?"

"No, of course not. For one thing, she's nearly five years older than I am." Jan cocked her head sideways. "And that would mean Uncle Stewart, if he is her father, became a father at the age of twelve." She snorted. "Not very likely."

Betsy hesitated, then said, "Could your father . . . ?"

Jan immediately shook her head, then the movement slowed as she thought about it. "I don't think so," she said. "It would have happened when they were dating, before they got married." She counted on her fingers, eyes rolled upwards. "Of course, he would have been seventeen, which *is* old enough. And unwed mothers back then put their babies up for adoption, didn't they?"

Betsy nodded. "That could account for it."

"Still, it's hard to think of my father doing something like that and never mentioning it."

"Why would he tell his children about it?" asked Betsy. "If he told anyone, it would be his wife."

"Well, Mother never said a word about it." Jan grimaced. "But why would she?" She put her change into her wallet. "I'm having lunch with Mother today," she said. "I'm going to ask her."

*   *   *

JAN met her mother for lunch an hour later at Antiquity Rose, a combination tearoom and antique shop. "Mother, I want to ask you something," she said over the house salad.

"Certainly."

"There's a woman visiting here from Texas. She came into Crewel World, and Betsy mistook her for me. Mother, she looks enough like me to be my sister. Now, I know both Jason and I look more like Dad than you. Is it possible that he . . . you know?"

"No, it is not possible!" She looked indignant at the very idea.

"Well, is there something you haven't told me about the rest of our family?"

Her mother stared nonplussed at her for as long as it took to take a breath. Then she said, "Certainly not! Anyway, no one in our family ever went to Texas."

"She wasn't born in Texas. She discovered she was adopted after her parents died and has been trying to find out something about her biological roots. She says she came from a Minnesota adoption agency, but she can't find any records of her birth parents." Jan smiled. "I wasn't one of a pair of identical twins, was I?"

Recovered, her mother smiled back. "No, I think I would have noticed if you were. So this person is your age?"

"She says she's a few years older, though she doesn't look it. But it's the oddest thing: we not only look alike, we *are* alike, in a lot of ways. We have so many things in common! If she's not yours, or Dad's, I wonder where she came from?"

"Well, it wouldn't surprise me in the least if there were children with a family resemblance scattered all over the place, thanks to your Uncle Stewart!"

"*Mo*-ther! How can you say that?"

Her mother offered a pained smile. "Oh, you're right, of course. His two most obvious faults argue against that. First, he is possibly the laziest human alive. Anyone lazier couldn't be troubled to breathe or blink, and so wouldn't have survived. Second, he drinks. And as a nurse, you know what drink does to male, er, capability. Who was it who said, 'Liquor enhances desire while diminishing performance'? So even if he fell over a willing female, or one fell over him . . . no." She shook her head with a regretful smile.

"He has four daughters, so . . ." Jan boggled at getting even more specific. "And anyway, he's not an alcoholic, not really!"

"Well, it's true that I don't remember seeing him drunk until he got into high school." Jan's mom gave her daughter a sardonic look as she took a drink of her Arnold Palmer— half iced tea, half lemonade, an Antiquity Rose specialty.

"Oh, Moth-*er*!" said Jan again.

"You sound just like you did when you were fourteen," Susan said, amused.

"I do? I was imitating Ronnie." Jan's younger son was at a tiresome stage of teendom.

Her mother raised her eyes to heaven. "It's a mother's hope come true: I often wished you'd have children who would give you the same grief you gave me."

"Oh, Moth-*er*!"

"It's never as funny the third time."

"You're right, you're right," sighed Jan. "It's even less funny the twenty-fifth time."

Her mother cast her amused eyes heavenward again but didn't say anything.

"Katie thinks she's after our money."

"Who's after whose money?"

"Lucille, our Texas visitor. After Aunt Edyth's. I think Lucille is not well off, and Kate thinks she might have heard about Aunt Edyth and decided to see if she could cut herself a piece of that pie."

Jan's mother snorted. "I wish her luck trying. She's not mine, and, thanks to DNA testing, people can't play tricks like that anymore, no matter how much they look like a member of the family. With your medical training, you must know that."

"Yes, I do." Oddly, the thought made her a little sad.

After lunch, Jan went across the street to the parking lot, a hollowed-out space in the center of the block, surrounded by the backsides of stores. She walked into the center and paused. As usual, she wasn't sure just where she'd left her car. She finally spied it farther down a row than she thought she'd put it. It was a cranberry red PT Cruiser, an eminently spottable car, and she hurried to it. She put the key in the door lock, but it wouldn't turn. Then she noticed the pair of fuzzy dice hanging from the rearview mirror. She stepped back, hoping no one noticed her trying to get into someone else's car and saw her own in the next row, about six cars nearer the lane that led out.

"Hi, Jan!" came a woman's voice, her Texas accent making it sound like, "Hah, Jee-an!" She looked around and saw Lucille in a deep orange sunsuit waving at her. With Lucille was a tall, deeply tanned, attractive man with curly silver-and-black hair, and a very white grin.

"Hi, Lucille!" called Jan, waving back. She trotted toward the pair. "Having trouble finding my own car," she noted as she came up to them.

"This is my husband, Bobby Lee. Bobby Lee, this is Jan Henderson, a fellow stitcher."

"How do?" said Bobby Lee in a drawl even more marked than Lucille's.

Lucille said, "I saw you admiring my car. Are you thinking of buying a Cruiser? They're super fun to drive, and"— she grinned—"they're easy to find in a parking lot."

Jan turned to look again at the red car. "That PT is *yours?*"

"Sure! Why?"

"Because that one right over there is mine." Jan pointed at her own cranberry red vehicle, and the pair turned to look.

Lucille exclaimed, "No, that's too much, that's way too much, that's *insane!*"

"Well, ain't that a kick in the head," said Bobby Lee. "Luci here has wanted one ever since she saw it on the Internet. And it had to be that color red, too."

"When I saw one on the Internet," Jan said, "I thought it was a concept car, and I was so excited to find they were actually going to build them. This is my second one. My first one was black."

"Did you put a bullet hole in it?" asked Lucille.

"A bullet hole?" echoed Jan, wondering if that was some strange Texas custom, for luck or something.

"You know, those decal things. I put just one, in the back passenger door, down in the corner, so hardly anyone can see it. A lot of Cruiser owners do that, for a joke."

"No, it never occurred to me," said Jan, relieved to find one difference between her and Lucille. She'd changed her mind: being too much like another person was scary—and, in an odd way, suffocating.

"I think I have another one back home I can send you."

"No. No, thank you. I'd better get home. I've got a lot to do."

BOBBY Lee watched Jan go down the row to her car and get in behind the steering wheel. "What do you think?" he asked his wife.

Lucille watched Jan start up and drive off. "So far, so good," she said.

Four

J AN came up to the beautiful carved walnut door of the old house and paused—as she often did—to admire the pattern of leaves and flowers carved into it, before pushing the doorbell. After a minute, she pushed it again. Still no answer, so she got out her copy of the old-fashioned bronze key. The house was big, and Aunt Edyth was slightly deaf, so sometimes she didn't hear the bell. Aunt Edyth's housekeeper had a key for the very same reason.

Jan was met at the door by Lizzie, Aunt Edyth's miniature fox terrier. The little black and white dog shot past her, across the porch and lawn to her favorite shrub, where she squatted with a look that could only be interpreted as relief.

That was odd. Aunt Edyth was always good about letting the dog out. Jan paused in the big entrance hall, waiting for Lizzie to come back. Meanwhile, she cocked her head, inhaling and listening. It was almost nine o'clock—she was here to take Aunt Edyth to church—and she was surprised not to smell coffee. Her aunt was an early riser in any case and enjoyed a cup of coffee first thing "to get her blood stirring," as she put it. Jan enjoyed sharing that pre-church cup of the rich, dark brew.

But there was no welcoming smell, or even the small clatter of someone in the kitchen preparing it.

And poor Lizzie was still tinkling, an indication that she hadn't been let out last night, either.

Perhaps Aunt Edyth was ill. Though clear-minded and physically active, her great-aunt was, after all, ninety-seven. Starting to feel anxious, Jan went slowly up the stairs to the second floor. The windowless corridor was dim and creepy; she flipped on the ceiling lights. There were rooms on either side, their doors all shut, except one—the bathroom. Its open door laid a splash of light across the narrow carpet. At the end of the hall, facing Jan, was another door, also shut. Like all the woodwork in the house, it was made of oak so hard it hurt her knuckles when she rapped on it.

"Aunt Edyth? Are you in there?"

There was no reply. The open bathroom door meant she wasn't in there; the lack of coffee smell meant she wasn't in the kitchen; the anxious dog meant she hadn't gone out. Feeling frightened now, Jan opened the door.

On the tall wooden bed, which stood against the center of the wall, lay a thin figure. She was on her back, the covers draped evenly across her, head turned away, toward the window. Jan could see the white hair, thick and abundant for someone her aunt's age, pulled into its usual bun, half hidden by her big feather pillow.

"Aunt Edyth?" called Jan, loud enough to penetrate deaf ears. But there was no response; the figure lay perfectly still. Fearing the worst, Jan went around the bed for a look. Aunt Edyth's features were unnaturally pale and frozen into a look of surprise. Her chin was lifted. Her eyes and mouth were open, as if startled by Jan's appearance beside her pillow. "It's just me," said Jan—then she realized that Aunt Edyth wasn't looking at her. Or at anything. Jan stretched out her forefinger to touch the wrinkled skin: cold.

"Oh, dear," said Jan, pulling back her finger hastily. Then, feeling she ought to say something more sympathetic, she managed to murmur, "You poor thing." Then it hit her: this was Great-aunt Edyth, who had loved her and bullied her and admired her—but would no more. She choked on a sob. As a nurse, she'd dealt with death, but never the death of a loved one. What should she do? From the chill of the body, it seemed clear that this must have happened early last night. Her sympathetic heart wanted to close her great-aunt's staring eyes, but something else kept her from it. Something that wasn't quite right. No, that was silly. She gave herself a rough shake. It was because she had begun to believe that Aunt Edyth would never die, that she would always be there, expressing a sharp opinion, telling uproarious stories, loving her dogs, ordering people about. That, and only that, was what was wrong.

Aunt Edyth, ever contrary, would have to pick a time when her housekeeper was out of town, leaving her body to be found by Jan. And yet it was nice to have had it happen quietly in bed—the bed covers were not disturbed, meaning there had been no struggle. She probably was gone before she got beyond that first look of surprise.

Jan rubbed her forehead to stop her rambling thoughts and went to the phone on the little bedside table to call 911. This wasn't an emergency, obviously, but she knew the rules. When someone is found dead at home, government officials have to be notified. Never mind that Jan Henderson, RN, knew a dead body when she saw it. Aunt Edyth wasn't really dead until the county's medical examiner declared it so. The operator said she'd send the police—no matter what the emergency, the first responder arrived in a squad car. Then Jan went downstairs to let Lizzie in and give her breakfast while they waited.

She was sitting with the dog on the front porch steps when the squad car pulled through the twin brick pillars that marked the entrance to the house's curving drive. No siren or lights, which was fine. And all the nice young police officer did was call the medical examiner's office, which is what Jan expected to happen. Funny, though, how the bureaucrats couldn't take even a policeman's word for it that Edyth Hanraty was dead but had to come for a look their own selves.

While they waited, Jan made the policeman a cup of tea, made one for herself, then sat down by the kitchen phone. She called her mother first. "Mother, bad news. I'm at Aunt Edyth's house—I said I'd take her to church this morning, you know—and she's . . . she's dead."

"Oh, my dear, how awful! What happened? Did she fall?"

"No, she died quietly in her sleep."

"Well, that's a blessing. The poor old thing, I suppose we should have been prepared for this, but it's still a shock."

"Yes, it is. The police are here, and they've asked someone from the ME's office to come by, and I have to stay until that's finished. Could you call Jason and Uncle Stewart? I'll contact Reese at the university, and I'll tell Ronnie when I get home. Meanwhile, there's a list she had all drawn up of people to notify. I'll call her doctor and that Excelsior mortician she decided on, Huber's, to let them know they have a customer to take care of. She had a prepaid arrangement with them. It says on the list to remind them of that—wasn't she something? And her attorney, and Pastor Garson."

"Give me those last two numbers. I'll call them for you."

"All right. There are some other names here, too. Friends, I guess. I'll call them. Bless her for that list. This will make things a lot easier."

* * *

Susan was sitting in her kitchen, lingering over her lunchtime cup of tea and considering mortality. Aunt Edyth had been an old woman when Susan was a child and had seemed to live in a kind of time warp, never growing any older. Susan had started to wonder if she would outlive everyone.

But right now, this minute, Susan's brother Stewart was at Huber's Funeral Home waiting for the arrival of Aunt Edyth's body. It appeared Aunt Edyth was mortal after all. She had gone from a determined, opinionated, cranky old woman to a mere body.

If a body meet a body . . . That weird song began to run through her head. When she was a child, she thought it a very scary song about dead bodies meeting in a field. *If a body kiss a body . . .* Ugh!

She remembered when her mother died. It had been explained to her that a dead body turned into a piece of property. So now that Aunt Edyth was dead, her body didn't belong to her anymore. Mortal remains belonged to the next of kin—as if anyone could think of doing anything with a dead body but burying it as quickly and decently as possible! But Aunt Edyth, bless her, was still maintaining control, having previously selected Huber's in Excelsior to handle "the arrangements"—an odd term. She had also set out the order of her funeral and sent copies to everyone last spring after a bad cold had turned into a mild case of pneumonia and frightened her. In that same letter, she had reiterated the terms of her peculiar will, which had reignited Stewart's old campaign to make her change it.

Even so, Stewart, to Susan's surprise, had proved surprisingly amenable to driving to Huber's Funeral Home to sign papers and get that process started. Susan would have done it herself but had found herself caught up in a sad weakness over all this. She'd been relieved when her brother—usually not one to step up to the plate—said he would handle it. Perhaps he understood that Susan had been genuinely fond of Aunt Edyth, even though she could be exasperating.

Only a couple of weeks ago, Aunt Edyth had complained to Susan that Stewart was trying, again, to make her think he was fond of her, too. He had come over several times, ostensibly to run errands, but in fact to hint ever so heavily that he had four daughters, and since Aunt Edyth liked girls so much, how come she wasn't willing to remember them in her will?

But Aunt Edyth wasn't to be swayed by the arguments of a male, particularly this one. She was sure he only wanted his daughters to be given some of her property so he could wrest control of it from them, and sell it. She had filled Susan's ears with her angry complaints and had threatened to sell off some of the items herself to stop his annoying hints.

The sad thing was, Susan mused, Aunt Edyth was undoubtedly right, both about his motive and his clumsiness in acting on it. Stew certainly would have guilted his daughters into sharing any property or money they came into possession of—and just as certainly have wasted it on improbable schemes.

He had the attention span of a housefly, and the work habits of a dead possum.

So Stewart's efforts were unavailing—and now there could be no more of them.

She looked down at the notepad beside her coffee. A lifelong list maker, she had started this one as soon as she finished talking with Jan. It was a to-do list, of course. It started with "phone Stewart" and "phone Jason." There were check marks after each. Stewart hadn't been home when she called, but Katie was there. She had been shocked and was in tears before they hung up, which rather surprised Susan. She hadn't realized that Katie actually had been fond of Aunt Edyth. Jason's reaction had been, "Oh, really? Man, I thought she'd never die! I'm sorry, Mom, but seriously, didn't she seem, like, immortal?" Susan had been both shocked and amused that his reaction was so much like her own, if more boldly expressed.

Next on the list, "Funeral." That was pretty much taken care of. St. Luke's Lutheran—whoops, she'd better call Pastor Garson again. He should be home from church by now. He would call her back, he said, after consulting his calendar, to arrange a date and time for the service. She'd already left a message with the attorney, Marcia Weiner, and Dr. Phyllis Brown.

Next on the list, "close house." She remembered how sad and creepy it was going through her mother's things after she had died. This would be different: Aunt Edyth was so distant there wouldn't be that Peeping-Tom feeling. Besides . . . Susan tried but failed to suppress the thought.

Aunt Edyth's house had been built by her father early in the twentieth century. It was large and full of wonderful things. Susan allowed a guilty little thrill of anticipation to run through her. Going through that house was going to be . . . well . . . fun.

ON Monday morning, Jan was soothing a frightened child before Dr. Hugs came in to look at an infected thumb. Another nurse came in and said, "I'll take over here, Jan. You have a phone call, line three. It's your mother, and she says it's urgent."

Jan's mother rarely disturbed her at work; that she felt it necessary to add that it was urgent made Jan go immediately to an empty exam room. She touched the button beside the blinking light and said, "Yes, what's the matter?"

"Jan, dear, I just got the strangest call. It's from a

Dr. Wills, who works in the medical examiner's office. He says Mr. Huber at the funeral home notified him that—well, he says—" Her mother paused, whether to gather her strength or her vocabulary or her courage, Jan couldn't tell.

"Is this about Aunt Edyth?"

"Yes, of course. He says Mr. Huber was, er, arranging the body to prepare it for, for embalming, when he cut the finger of his glove—his rubber glove, presumably—on something stuck in Aunt Edyth's head."

"Something stuck in her head?" Jan echoed. "What does that mean? A hairpin?"

"No, not a hairpin! Something actually stuck into her head, like a needle. Stuck right into the bone."

Jan just sat there for a few moments.

"Jan? Are you there?"

"Yes. A needle, he said?"

"*Like* a needle, or a pin. And . . . and so, the medical examiner says they're going to do an *autopsy*."

"I see." A perfectly dreadful thought was forming in Jan's mind, although she fought against it with all her strength.

Susan continued. "I said, 'But what about the funeral?' And he said he was very sorry, but we will have to put off the funeral."

"Oh, yes, of course. Oh, Mother, do you know what this means?"

"Well, I'm sure there must be some innocent explanation. I mean, didn't you say she died peacefully in her sleep?"

"Yes, I did." But now Jan was remembering that staring look of amazement, and again that feeling that something wasn't quite right.

Her mother's voice interrupted her thoughts. "If someone came and tried to stick a needle into my brain, I'd struggle with all my might."

"Well, of course, so would anyone."

"So that can't be what happened, don't you see? Maybe

she did fall, and there was a needle in the carpet, and she didn't realize what happened but just went to bed with a headache. That *must* be the explanation."

Jan took a breath, then let it out. "Of course, I'm sure you're right." Her head was starting to ache. Conversations with her mother often made her feel like that. "Will you call Pastor Garson about the delay in the funeral service?"

"Yes, as soon as I talk to Stewart and Jason."

"Fine. I'll tell Hugs." Jan hung up and closed her eyes. Aunt Edyth's death had been a surprise, though Jan also thought it a blessing, going like that, quickly, without a protracted illness. Now . . . this was really, really scary. She needed to talk to someone levelheaded about this, someone whose nickname described what she also needed from him. Her dear, patient, kind, strong husband.

Five

SERGEANT Mitchell Rice didn't like autopsies. Like many police detectives, he was tall and burly, with dark hair, very thin on top, and an unstylish tie worn so tight it looked as if it were strangling him.

An autopsy is sort of like an operation, only a little rougher, and without the anesthesiologist. And the surgeon takes photos of his progress, which Mitch was pretty sure didn't happen in an operating room. Normally there are no non-medical people in the operating room; but if an autopsy is for the purpose of collecting evidence for a criminal investigation, a representative from the police department must be present.

Finally, autopsies are a grim reminder of mortality, something Mitch didn't need; and while he tried to be professional and distance himself from the process, he couldn't get far enough away to remain undisturbed.

Maybe if he went to more of them . . . now there was an ugly thought. He was not one of those cops who liked action. In fact, while he enjoyed his work, he was also grateful to be a cop in a community where murder was a very rare thing.

He was startled back to the present by the sound of something metal falling into a little pan. The medical examiner gave a grunt of satisfaction, and Mitch said, "Got it?"

"Yes." Using his tweezers, the ME poked at what he'd retrieved. "Looks like a piece of wire. Steel, maybe." He picked it up, rinsed it in a jar of water, then held it out to Mitch, who reluctantly came closer. It was about two inches long, shiny and pointed at one end. The other end was snipped off, not smoothly.

"That's not a piece of wire," Mitch said.

The ME lifted it up to his own eyes, squinting behind the clear plastic mask that covered his face. "You're right." He held it closer, then touched the pointed end with a rubber-gloved hand. "Dull point, but doesn't seem from wear."

"What do you think?"

"I couldn't say for sure. It looks machined, not ground or cut, except at the other end. Shiny, so stainless steel? Maybe it's a part off something."

Mitch, intrigued now, held out his hand for the tweezers. The piece of metal didn't look cut or filed to its point, but polished or rolled. There were no scratches on its gleaming surface. It was very thin—thinner than most nails. He very gingerly felt the pointed end and agreed that it was not very sharp. The other end, when touched, felt rough on the tip of his finger.

"Which end was the end inside her head?" he asked.

"The pointed end, up to about the last eighth of an inch, barely visible to the naked eye. And something else," the ME went on, "there are a couple of small puncture wounds very near where I found this. In my opinion, someone made several tries to insert this in order to cause the deceased's death."

Mitch frowned. "That can't be true. I have a report that the decedent was found in her bed under undisturbed blankets, as if she'd died peacefully in her sleep. If someone came into my bedroom and started poking me in the back of the head with something pointed, I'd kick up a fuss. Maybe the other injuries are because she was out in her yard with the mosquitoes."

"They don't look like mosquito bites to me," said the ME, who had photographed them. "Unless it was a mosquito with one hell of a proboscis."

Mitch handed the piece of metal back. "So it's your expert opinion that we're talking homicide here?"

"Oh, I'd say so. I don't see how she came by this injury any other way. This was done by an individual who knew where to insert this pin or whatever it is, but was inexperienced in doing it." He looked across at Mitch's baffled face and clarified his remark. "The puncture wounds say the murderer poked around a bit. Not a brain surgeon, in other words."

"Oh. Okay. But what do you mean, insert it? Is there a place, an opening in the skull?" The thought that the human brain pan was not a solid round of bone was startling to Mitch.

"Where the base of the skull meets the first vertebra of the spine is a layer of—well, call it gristle. Shaped sort of like a disk—you've heard of slipped disks? There are disks between the vertebrae, and one on top, where the spine meets the skull. This piece of metal wasn't driven through the bone—it was slipped through that tissue and up into the brain stem."

Mitch, not big on clinical detail but swift at methodology, asked, "If it could be pushed in, why couldn't it be pulled out again?"

"Probably because the woman, in a dying spasm, threw her head back and pinched the space closed. This piece of metal was once longer than it is now, though how much longer is anyone's guess. The roughness of the cut would indicate it was done with a dull blade—that's why the mortician cut himself on it."

Mitch nodded. "Good thing for us that criminals generally make mistakes. This one thought the old woman's hair would hide it. And it almost did," he added, without sympathy for the ME's rookie representative who hadn't found it before sending the body to that mortician in Excelsior, and who would get soundly rapped on the knuckles for that error.

Mitch thought some more, reaching for his notebook. The murderer would very likely not have brought wire clippers along and would have had to go looking for them. And then, not wanting someone to notice them missing, he probably put them back. Mitch wrote that down. Maybe there were fingerprints on them.

He'd go search the house today.

S USAN was scrubbing down the kitchen cabinets when the doorbell rang. In good shape for a woman in her midsixties, she hopped nimbly off the little step ladder, wiped her hands on a dish towel, and hurried through the dining room to the front door. From habit, she looked around before opening the door. All was in order; she kept a very clean house.

She glanced through one of the leaded lights beside the door and saw a tall, heavyset man with dark hair. He wasn't carrying an attaché case, so he wasn't a salesman. And his suit was too ill-fitting to belong to an attorney. Not a mortician—that was all taken care of. That left one choice, and her heart sank. A police detective had called earlier to see if she would be home. This must be him.

She opened the door. "Yes?"

Sure enough, he reached into a side pocket and produced a photo ID and badge in a worn leather folder. "Mrs. McConnell?"

"Yes?"

"I'm Sergeant Mitchell Rice, Orono Police. I called you earlier. Is it all right if I come in?"

She hesitated, but it was too late to say no without a really good reason, and she didn't have one. "All right."

She turned and led the way into her living room. It was a good-size room for such a small house, done in pastel shades of green and cream, with touches of pink. Not fluffy, but definitely feminine. He paused a moment, then chose the pale upholstered chair; in his dark suit he was like a june bug on a buttercream birthday cake. He offered her a business card printed with his name, phone number, fax number, even an e-mail address, plus the round Orono city seal.

She couldn't think what to do with it, so she held it in her hand as she went to sit on the couch. "I assume you're here about my aunt," she said.

"I'm here about Edyth Hanraty. She was your aunt, right?"

"That's right—my mother's sister."

"Huber's Funeral Home contacted the police when Mr. Huber found evidence that Ms. Hanraty's death occurred under unusual circumstances."

Susan nodded. "Yes, I know."

His eyebrows lifted in surprise. "How do you know that?"

"The medical examiner's office called me to say Mr. Huber found something little and sharp, like a needle, stuck in the back of her head. He said that the funeral should be put off because there was to be an—an autopsy. Has there—have they finished it already?"

"Yes, and we have the preliminary results. I'm very sorry, but it appears your aunt was murdered."

Susan leaned back in the chair. "I was afraid you were going to tell me that. But are you absolutely sure? I was thinking that maybe she fell. You know, and a nail or a needle was in the carpet, and she fell on it, and—and she didn't know it was serious. And she went to bed with just a headache and died in her sleep."

"No, ma'am. For one thing, it wasn't a nail, or a needle. For another, it went right into her brain, killing her instantly."

She blinked at him, shocked.

He held up a hand to forestall a response. "I'm sorry. But what that also means is that she didn't suffer. There was no evidence of a struggle, and the medical examiner told me that it happened very quickly, between one breath and the next. A little poke, and she was gone."

"Oh. I . . . I see." Susan swallowed and clenched her hands shut, surprised to find one of them crumpling the card. She began to smooth it out with her fingers. "Still, it's so horrible. And you think it might be murder? I don't see how—I mean, who would have done such a thing? And why?"

"Well, that's where I come in. I'm going to see if I can figure it out. And I'm hoping you can help me."

He seemed in earnest, so her response was sincere. "Of course, if I can."

"First of all, I'm trying to understand the family. Who's who, and how they're related. May I ask you some questions about that?"

"All right, I'll tell you whatever I can."

"Good, thank you." He reached into an inside pocket and came up with an absurdly tiny notebook and a ballpoint pen. "Your aunt never married, is that correct?"

"Yes, that's right," she said.

"So she left no children?"

"Of course not! I mean . . . I suppose in this day and age that's not an impertinent question, but it certainly was in hers. My goodness, to think of Aunt Edyth——" Susan had to pause a few moments, torn between indignation and laughter, before she could continue. "Her only immediate relative was a sister, Alice, who died nine years back. Alice was my mother."

"And your father?"

"Was Dr. John O'Neil, also deceased. They had three children, a daughter named Margaret, who died very young, me, and a son, Stewart." She spoke slowly, watching the detective write this down in his tiny notebook. "My husband was David McConnell, and we had three children: Jason, Julie, who died young, and Jan. My brother, Stewart, married Terri Pepperdyne, and they have four girls: Katie, Alexandra, Bernie—Bernadette, but no one calls her that—and CeeCee—Cecilia. My daughter, Jan, is married to Dr. Harvey Henderson. They have two boys, Reese and Ronnie. My son, Jason, is currently divorced and has no children. The oldest of Stewart and Terri's children is married to Perry Frazier; that's Katie, who just turned twenty-one."

"And all these people except your parents are alive?" asked Sgt. Rice.

"No, my husband is also deceased."

"I'm sorry to hear that."

"Thank you." Susan gave a grave nod. Though it had been nearly ten years since Dave had collapsed at the office, she still sometimes felt the pain of loss.

Perhaps the detective caught the fleeting look of distress in her eyes, because he gave her a moment while he looked around the room. "I see you do counted cross-stitch," he said, nodding toward a framed trio of Marc Saastad roses on the wall.

Susan, pleasurably surprised, said, "Yes—and how interesting that you know what it is. Most men just say sewing, or embroidery."

"My wife does counted cross-stitch, too."

A penny dropped. "Well, my goodness, is your wife Lizzy Rice?"

He nodded. "Yes. Do you know her?"

"Of course! She and I have taken I don't know how many classes together over at Crewel World in Excelsior!"

"She loves those classes. And they must do her good; she wins a lot of ribbons at the fair."

"Yes, I know. Not that she brags. It's Betsy, the owner of Crewel World, who is always bragging about her. Well, isn't that interesting, you being Lizzy Rice's husband! She never told me she was married to a policeman!"

Sergeant Rice shrugged, his head cocked a little to one side, and gestured with his notebook. "A woman can't always help who she falls in love with," he said, almost straight-faced.

Susan laughed, just a little, but felt more comfortable now that she could place this man within her own circle. Lizzy was a gentle-mannered, intelligent woman; no husband of hers could be a bad person. "What else do you want to know?" she asked.

Now Sergeant Rice looked a little uncomfortable. "Well, I've been out to Miss Hanraty's house, and this house you have here is very nice, but it's not exactly in the same category. I've done a little research, and it seems that your grandfather left his fortune to Edyth. Did your mother have some kind of quarrel with him?"

Susan bridled a bit. "*First* of all, it wasn't so great a fortune to begin with, though it *was* a lot of money in its time. Aunt Edyth was a clever investor. She ran her inheritance up all by herself." She felt herself smiling; she couldn't help it. "Actually, it's an amusing family story."

"What's an amusing story?"

"How it came about. You see, my grandfather was what was called back in the twenties a capitalist. Instead of entering a profession, he played the stock market and speculated in land and was able to build that beautiful house that Aunt Edyth grew up in. He realized early on that she was never going to marry—it was as if she never got over that stage where girls think boys have cooties. Her sister, Alice, was different—she married a doctor with an established practice. And Grandfather, seeing Alice was well taken care of, decided to give Edyth the house and settle a great deal of money on her as well. He had this notion—common in his day—that a woman needed either a man or a big bank account to take care of her, you see."

Sergeant Rice smiled at this old-fashioned notion.

Susan continued. "It turned out that Edyth inherited her father's eye for a good investment, and she turned the six hundred thousand dollars he settled on her into twenty million. But she never got over her intense dislike of the male sex and—" Susan stopped.

Sergeant Rice looked up from his notebook. "And what?" he asked, prepared to be further amused.

"Is all this pertinent? Do I need to tell you?"

He grew serious. "You don't have to tell me anything. But it really helps me to understand the family dynamics, if for no other reason than I will understand if I need to look outside the family for the person responsible for this."

A chill went down her spine. "Do you mean you are looking at me right now as a suspect?"

"No, no, not at all! I have no reason to think you murdered your aunt!" He looked sincerely startled at the idea.

"I'm glad to hear that. Though you may change your mind when you hear about Aunt Edyth's peculiar will. You see, she made no secret of it; we all knew what it said. And all of us thought it was very unfair, even me—and by its terms I inherit a good deal of money."

"You mean she didn't distribute the money among family members evenly."

"I mean she disinherited my brother entirely."

His eyebrows rose high on his forehead. "Why?"

"Because he's a man."

"Seriously?"

"Very seriously. She left a considerable sum to the University of Minnesota to be used for scholarships for women wanting to major in business or science, and the rest was to be divided equally among the female descendants of her sister, Alice, *through the female line*. You see, that cut Stewart and his daughters right out." Susan watched while Sergeant Rice wrote that down.

"So these female descendants get all the—what do they call it?—the rest and residue?" he asked. "Who are they?"

"There are only two of us—me and my daughter, Jan. My son gets nothing, nor does my brother Stewart—or any of his four daughters."

"That seems unfair to those girls."

"Exactly!" Susan gestured angrily. "We all thought that was particularly unfair."

"Surely someone must have tried talking to her about this."

"Of course we did! I did, Stewart did, even Katie went to her. It was no use. She was the sort of person who, once she makes up her mind, won't change it. Plus, she had this unfortunate mind-set about men."

"But his daughters—I don't see how she could do that to them."

"Well, they're young. The youngest is only fourteen. I'm sure Aunt Edyth was concerned that Stewart might take control of the money and use it to start a business."

"And this would be bad because . . . ?"

"First of all, it wouldn't have been his money."

Sergeant Rice made a note in his little book. "Do you believe your aunt had an accurate estimation of Stewart's character?" he asked.

When Susan didn't reply, he looked up at her with a pleasantly inquiring expression. A silence fell on the room. Susan grew more and more uncomfortable, but his expression didn't change. "All right," she said, "Aunt Edyth may have disliked all men, but she had a pretty good estimation of Stewart."

"Has he ever taken money that didn't belong to him before?"

"Oh, heavens no! He isn't a thief. That isn't what this is about at all!"

"Then what is it about?"

"Well, she was probably afraid he'd lose the investment he'd've made on his girls' behalf. He's bright enough, he gets good ideas for a business or an invention, but he loses interest fairly quickly. He hasn't got Aunt Edyth's drive to squeeze every nickel of profit out of a business." She sighed. "I don't think I would have minded so much, but—well, Katie's going to graduate from college next year. But Alexandra is only a sophomore, and there's Bernie and CeeCee to be sent in a few more years. And besides, Katie would like an MBA—she got a dose of the Hanraty genes."

"Did Aunt Edyth put any conditions on your inheritance?"

"Conditions?"

"Once the money is shared out, you can do whatever you like with it?" said Rice.

"Yes, of course. But it seems unfair for those girls to have to depend on me and Jan—especially since Jan has two boys of her own to provide for."

"Who's the executor of her will?"

"Aunt Edyth's attorney, Marcia Weiner."

Rice made a note of that and began looking back over what he'd written. Feeling again a need to fill the silence, Susan said, "I want you to understand that Jan and I will be glad to help Stewart's girls. And, naturally, I'll give a large portion to my son."

Rice paged forward again and then asked abruptly, "But not a portion to your brother?"

"Well, no. Aunt Edyth didn't want him to have any of her

fortune." Rice did not remark that Aunt Edyth also didn't want Jason to have any of it, either, but he did look quizzically at Susan, who continued defensively, "Anyway, Stewart's not a young man anymore, so I think he's pretty much used up all his chances at building a fortune from any investment I might make in him."

Rice cocked his head at her. "How old is he?"

"Fifty-seven."

"Your older brother, then."

She drew an indignant breath—she didn't like false flattery—then saw he was making a joke, and let it out with a smile. "No, as a matter of fact, he's nearly ten years younger than I am."

He did look authentically surprised by that. Susan smiled. Genuine flattery she did enjoy.

He smiled back, then went back two pages in his notebook. "Now Alice, Edyth's sister, your mother. She's deceased, you said?"

"That's right, and my father as well. He was a doctor, well-known in the cardiac field, so it isn't as if we've been sitting around impoverished and impatient to get at Aunt Edyth's money. My late husband did very well for himself, and my children are doing well also."

"But not your brother Stewart."

She jumped at this opportunity to say something nice about him. "Oh, it's not as if they're living in a slum or anything like that! It's—it's more like in comparison. He and his wife own a nice house, and she's a high school principal, so they're doing just fine. Stewart always did march to his own drummer, and he seems happy, so . . ."

"So?"

She blurted, "So there's no need to go looking in his direction for a suspect." He looked surprised at the strength of her assertion, and she smiled to soften it. "You're going to have to do what you said, look outside the family." She grimaced.

"Funny, talking about the family made me almost forget this is a murder case. How awful. I hope you catch whoever did this."

"I do, too." He made a final note and closed his little tablet. "I want to thank you for your cooperation," he said, rising.

She showed him to the door and then hurried to the phone to tell her daughter not to worry about the policeman going around asking questions.

Six

THE receptionist came back to the exam room to give Jan a jolt of déjà vu: "Your mother is on the phone. She says it's urgent."

"Thanks, Char. I'll be in Doctor's office."

Though the office belonged to Jan's husband, she used the traditional nurse's term, calling him "Doctor" as if that were his first name.

She retreated to Hugs's tiny private office, with its stacks of paper, books, file folders, X-rays, medical advertisements, and other detritus, then dug out the receiver on a half-buried phone and punched line 2. "Hi, Mom. What's up?"

"A policeman was just here," said her mother, but instead of sounding alarmed, she sounded mildly excited, as if she had good news.

Jan felt enormous relief. "What did he want?" she asked.

"Well," sighed her mother, "that's the bad news: Aunt Edyth was murdered."

Jan fell into her husband's desk chair. "You mean the mortician was right? From the way you were talking I thought the policeman came to say it wasn't so! So what *did* he want?"

"He's investigating, of course, trying to find out who might have done such a dreadful thing. He was very nice to me, a nice man altogether, which brings me to the good news: He's Lizzy Rice's husband!"

As was not unusual when talking with her mother, Jan felt her brain begin to spin. "So what?" she blurted.

"Well, don't you see? He actually knew my Marc Saastad roses were counted cross-stitch!"

The spinning continued. Jan gripped the receiver as if it were the single solid object in a too-fluid reality. "I'm afraid I still don't understand."

"Darling, he's one of *us*! He understands that we're nice people, people who don't go about murdering one another. He really *understands*."

"Oh. That's good. I'm so glad you had a meeting of the minds."

"That's exactly *right*," declared her mother, oblivious to Jan's sarcasm. "He was so easy to talk to, he realizes how upset we were over Aunt Edyth's peculiar will. He even understood about Stew."

Jan's brain stopped whirling the instant her heart sank into her shoes. She asked in a voice that only vaguely resembled her own, "What did you tell him about Uncle Stewart?"

Suddenly aware of Jan's tone, her mother became defensive. "I only said what Aunt Edyth used to say. That he's not good with money, and that if his daughters were given a share of her money he would find a way to take some of it and lose it on bad business ventures."

"Did you say that as if you agreed with her assessment?"

"But I *do* agree with it! You know very well—"

Jan interrupted her as a new thought intruded. "So he knows Uncle Stewart doesn't get any of the money."

"Yes, I think so."

"Did you tell him how much money was at stake?"

"No, because nobody knows how much the total will be."

"But you told him it was substantial."

"I . . . I don't remember." She was definitely beginning to sound defensive now.

"What else did you tell him?"

"Well, he wanted to know about the family, so I gave him a kind of genealogy. I told him everyone's name and how they were related—you know, you and Hugs and the boys and Stewart and Terri and the girls. You can't find any objection to that, surely. And yes, that's right, I did tell him that Stewart couldn't possibly be a suspect because he was not in Aunt Edyth's will." Amusement crept back into her voice. "I asked him if that meant he would be looking slantwise at *me*, and he said of course not—he has no reason to think I'm a murderer."

"What did you say about me?"

"What about you?"

"Well, you told him that the two of us are sharing the part of Aunt Edyth's fortune that she doesn't give to the U of M, right?"

"Well," Susan replied, "I explained how strange and unfair Aunt Edyth's will was, and yes, that of all the family, only you and I would share the money she didn't give to the university."

"So if he agrees that Uncle Stewart has no motive and he's sure you didn't murder her for her money, that kind of leaves *me* twisting in the wind, doesn't it?"

"Janice Margaret McConnell Henderson!"

"Yes?" Jan replied in her sweetest voice, tinged just the merest bit with acid.

"Why—why on *earth* do you think I would for one second allow the police to suspect you, my own daughter, of *murder?"*

"I don't think you did it on purpose. I think you were just so enchanted by this policeman's being one of us that you weren't thinking very clearly."

"I didn't do it at all! Your name just didn't come into it!"

"But he will deduce that! Oh, Mother, because he had nice manners and is married to a friend of yours, you forgot he is a police detective looking for a murderer. You thought that because he could identify cross-stitching when he saw it that he was on your side. He's *not* on your side, Mother."

"But darling, he said he would be looking outside the family for suspects, not at us."

"In so many words?"

"Yes, in exactly that many words. I don't see why you're in such a snit over this."

"Oh, I don't know, either, I guess. It was so awful finding her dead, I think I'm still upset over that. And then to find she was actually murdered—!"

"I understand. It's enough to frighten anyone. But take a minute, dearest, and just breathe quietly. Let your mind settle. You'll be all right. Everything will be all right."

This was the kind of language Mother used when Jan would waken from nightmares as a child, and it soothed her now to hear her mother's quiet voice.

"All right, I'm feeling better now. Thank you, Mother."

"Call me later if you start feeling anxious again."

"I will." Jan hung up and sat down to weep quietly for a few minutes.

Half an hour later the little receptionist came by again to report another urgent phone call.

"Is it my mother again?" asked Jan.

"No, it's your uncle Stewart."

Jan sighed and went back to Doctor's cluttered little office.

"Do you know your mother called me to say Aunt Edyth was murdered?" Stewart demanded, almost squeaking in his distress. Since his normal voice was a baritone, this squeak nearly moved Jan to laughter. But she took a calming breath before replying, "Yes, I know. She talked to me, too."

"I don't understand. Why do they think it's murder?"

"The medical examiner found some little thing in her head, something metal."

"What are you talking about, something metal?"

"I think they don't know what it is. Or maybe they do. Mother wasn't very clear. A pin, maybe, or a nail. Why don't you call her and ask? The police were just over there."

He said plaintively, "I can't call her. You know Susan and I don't get along! You're the one who found her—you *must* know more about it! When was this 'murder' supposed to have happened?"

"Well, I went over there Sunday morning before ten, but she'd been dead for hours. They did the autopsy yesterday, and today the police are going around asking questions."

"Have they talked to you?"

"Not yet."

"What will you tell them?"

"How do I know until I hear the questions?" Jan was starting to feel abused.

"I don't understand about the pin. How can a pin be used to kill someone? Oh, wait, you mean it was stuck in her ear? I think the Mafia used to kill people by sticking piano wires in their ears."

"No, I heard it was stuck in her skull somehow. Like a nail, except it isn't a nail."

"What? He saw it sticking out?"

"No, Mother said the undertaker said he felt it under her hair when he was doing something with the body. So he called somebody—the police I guess—and they ordered the autopsy."

Jan worked her shoulders to stop the chill flickering between them like summer lightning. Aunt Edyth on a mortician's slab, with a stranger's gloved hands on her; Aunt Edyth being cut open by a medical examiner. Jan had attended an autopsy as part of her nurse's training, and it was one of the most difficult things she'd ever endured. The thought of him opening poor Aunt Edyth's head—ick, ick, ick!

"Uncle Stewart, I can't talk anymore. I'm at work. I've got things to do. I suspect the police will be calling on you pretty soon. Maybe you can ask them to explain it to you."

Jan hung up and took several calming breaths. Uncle Stewart was going to be a terrible nuisance until this was over. She wished—as she had wished before—that he and her mother could get along. It would be nice to sic him on Mother. There were times when he was a real pest.

But as her annoyance faded, she began to smile. Annoying as he could be, she'd adored Uncle Stewart all her life, from the day he'd sneaked her off to the circus when her mother had expressly said she wasn't to go. She'd come home with a balloon and a tummy ache, thrilled to the core from all the exotica she'd seen and the forbidden sweets she'd eaten.

Stewart had been a charming but naughty little boy, then a charming but naughty adult, and now he was turning into a charming but naughty old man. Apparently, he'd been devoutly wished for by Grandmother and Grandfather and arrived only after years of yearning—interesting that miscarriages ran through the family, thought Jan, wandering into a sidebar. Mother had lost babies, Jan strongly suspected, and so had she. But one result was that Stewart's youth had been spent in a cocoon of indulgence that had left him unprepared for the cold, hard real world. He was a college dropout who had never held a job for more than a few years, and he had mooched shamelessly off his sister until, in despair, she had slammed the door on him—literally, according to both of them, though in very different versions. Mother had been hoping he would finally grow up. Uncle Stewart had seen it as a betrayal of an unspoken agreement.

The problem was, by the time the door slammed, it was too late; nothing could change his behavior. Soon after, he'd married a woman he'd been halfheartedly courting. He had thought she was wealthy and indulgent—and she was—a dangerous combination to a man of his boundless ability to squander. She, too, had finally closed the spigot, but only when they were down to a few income-producing investments and a nice lakefront house that she kept adamantly in her own name. Fortunately, she had a good job as a high school principal, which kept them solvent. Stewart made a very good house husband, though Jan sometimes wondered if Terri liked her job as bread winner.

But maybe she was content. Jan had never heard her complain.

There was something sweetly helpless about Stewart that made his friends, especially the female ones, muffle the alarms that sounded when he came asking for yet another loan. He was always cheerful about loans; asking politely and, in this new world of less cash in the pocket, willing to walk around the corner with his victim to the ATM machine, telling a funny story on the way. And unlike most moochers, he hung around after, grateful and ever ready to do favors. He would fetch and carry, clean up, or jury-rig—he was, not surprisingly, talented at making an old car or toy or piece of furniture serve one more turn. One thing he rarely did: repay the loan.

Jan was as susceptible as anyone to her uncle's charms. She loved his deprecation and self-aggrandizing, even when she knew both were often merely strategy. And too often she had succumbed to his hints that she should forget the laundry, abandon her husband and sons, and go fishing with him—using her boat, her gas, her bait.

Even now, past his midfifties, there was something elfin about him. He'd shrug up his shoulders, wink, and look around as if for eavesdroppers, then suggest they sneak off for a drive, maybe stop for a sandwich and beer at this out-of-the-way place he'd heard about.

Jan smiled to remember all the crimes and misdemeanors they'd committed together. As recently as two weeks ago, he'd come around needing "one of those yuppie food-stamps," meaning a twenty, because he'd gotten a bargain on cold cereal and what good were half a dozen boxes of Frosted Flakes without milk? She'd long gotten past expecting him to repay any of the money he'd gotten off her, nodding at his usual earnest declaration that one day he'd pay her back all he owed. They both knew better.

But now there was a new element. Jan didn't know the total of Aunt Edyth's estate, but she knew it was millions of dollars, with maybe as much as ten million to share with Mother, even after her other bequests. As soon as it was hers, Uncle Stewart—the man with his hand ever out—would be right there. And this time he'd want a lot more than a couple of yuppie foodstamps.

STEWART was at home with his youngest daughter, CeeCee, fourteen, when the police came calling. Actually, it was just one police officer, a six-foot man probably in his forties, wearing a baggy suit and too-tight tie. He was about Stewart's height and probably thirty pounds lighter—Stewart had once come across the arch term *embonpoint* to describe a certain plumpness of person, and ever after used it to describe himself. This man was more big boned than a man of embonpoint.

The cop was polite: "Good afternoon, sir. I hope I'm not taking you away from something important." Or was that an insult? Hard to tell—his eyes were shiny flat surfaces and his mouth an unexpressive line. He showed an ID card and a badge, which Stewart only glanced at.

"No, nothing important," Stewart said. Nothing at all, in

fact, but an old movie he'd been trying to use as a distraction from the terrible news about Aunt Edyth. It was just starting to work when the doorbell rang. "Come in, come in," he said quickly, remembering his manners. "Don't mind the mess."

"Not at all, and thank you," said the detective, his eyes darting all around the big living room with its several windows looking out at the lake. It was a beautiful room, in a beautiful house, even if the furniture was rather shabby. The scattering of belongings were mostly Stewart's: an old shirt, his slippers, his box of Lorna Doone cookies, his boating magazines, his big bunch of keys that gave a satisfying jingle when carried in his pocket. He made a hasty stack of the magazines on the coffee table, then went to turn off the TV.

"CeeCee," Stewart said, "why don't you go out in the yard and play for a while? I need to talk to this man."

"Okay, Dad." CeeCee, a leggy, long-haired blonde with deep blue eyes, cast a speculative look at the detective and departed.

"Won't you sit down?" Stewart said to the detective.

"Why, yes, thank you." The man took the upholstered chair, the one with little bits of stuffing coming up through one arm—their late cat had loved that chair. But it was a comfortable chair, nonetheless.

Stewart sat at one end of the couch and said, "I suppose you're here because of the death of my aunt, Edyth Hanraty."

"Yes," said the man.

"May I—I'm sorry, I didn't catch your name," confessed Stewart.

"I'm Sergeant Mitchell Rice," said the man, reaching into a pocket inside his suit jacket and bringing out a business card, which he handed to Stewart. "Orono PD," he added.

Stewart looked at the card, which had a lot of information on it that he couldn't read without his glasses. He rubbed it with a thumb—not embossed, he noted—and put it into his trousers pocket. "May I get you a cup of coffee or a soft drink?"

"No, thank you."

"Well then, what can I do for you?"

Rice went into a side pocket and produced a ballpoint pen and the smallest notebook Stewart had ever seen. "An autopsy performed on Miss Hanraty has shown that her death was not from natural causes," he said. "It is the opinion of the Hennepin County medical examiner that her death is a homicide, brought about by a human hand."

Stewart looked into Sergeant Rice's inexpressive brown eyes. "You mean she was murdered."

"Yes, sir."

Stewart looked away, wiping his mouth with his fingers. "That's just about too awful to think about," he said, coming back to look at the man. "I mean, who would want to murder her? She was just an old woman who never did anyone any real harm that I know of."

"How well did you know her?"

"Pretty well. She was my aunt, my mother's sister. I used to go to her house a lot when I was a kid. I still go out there—well, I guess it's I *used* to go out there, now—to run errands, help around the place. She was pretty rude to me—she didn't like the male gender; anyone who knew her can tell you that—but she liked the things I could do, lift and haul, minor household repairs, you know the drill. She wouldn't always thank me pretty, but she never ran me off the place with a shotgun." He laughed.

"Was she involved in a quarrel with anyone that you know of?" Rice asked.

Stewart widened his eyes in surprise as he shook his head. "Not that I know of. I doubt if you'll find any sign of a quarrel. She didn't go out much anymore, didn't have many visitors outside of the family. She had a housekeeper named Fran March—been there a few years. She was one of a series that started when Aunt Edyth was in her late sixties and couldn't do for herself anymore. Fran may know if she was mad at someone or someone was mad at her. But I'll bet you no one was." He grimaced and dared to ask, "Are you really sure she was murdered? It seems so damn unlikely."

"The medical examiner says so, and I have no reason to doubt his conclusion." Sergeant Rice wrote a brief note and then asked, "Where were you last Saturday evening?"

Stewart jumped as if he'd been shot at. "I beg your pardon?" he asked, and instantly cursed himself for being an idiot.

"I'm sorry, sir, but we have to ask."

"Oh. Well, I suppose you do. But I should tell you, I don't in the least profit by her death."

"No, sir, I understand that. Still, could you tell me where you were?"

"Certainly. Here at home."

"Alone?"

"Yes. My wife took our daughters out to dinner and a concert. One of those girl-bonding things they like to do. I'm not all that fond of Asian food and I don't like Bach, so I played like a bachelor and fixed my own little dinner, watched a ball game on the television, and went to bed early."

"I see."

"Now hold on a minute. My wife called me at least twice, and I was here to talk to her. You can check with her to confirm that."

"What time did she call?"

"Let me think. About seven the first time and somewhere around nine the second."

"So your wife was with the four girls, and you were here, but in touch with her by phone."

"Yes, that's right."

"Cell phone or landline?"

"What? Oh, cell phone. We don't have a—what d'ya call it?—a landline anymore. Ever since we went wireless on our computers, we couldn't see the use of it."

Rice nodded. "How old are the girls?"

"Well, Katie's just turned twenty-one. She's married and out of the house, but she comes home a lot now she's pregnant. And Lexie is nineteen, Bernie's sixteen, and CeeCee, who you just got a glimpse of, is fourteen."

Rice wrote it all down. Then he asked, "What is your occupation?"

"I beg your pardon?"

"What do you do, sir?" asked Rice, a hint of impatience showing in his voice.

"Oh. Well, at present, I'm a house husband. You know, take care of the house and the kids. I used to be an office manager at Markham and Sons. They run a pair of big excursion boats on Lake Minnetonka." Stewart tilted his head toward the windows overlooking the lake. "But they decided to give the job to their daughter, so out goes me." He let the grimace slide into a wry smile. That had been one of his favorite jobs. It was not in the least difficult, and he got to schmooze with the public, mostly while selling tickets, though once he even got to help plan a wedding reception on the *Lake Minnetonka Empress*, the bigger boat. It wasn't his fault they invited too many people.

"Is your wife employed?"

Stewart, ruminating on the job, almost missed this question. But he got the last two words—enough to know what the man wanted.

"Yes, she's the principal of Lincoln High in Wayzata."

"Do any of your children go to Lincoln High?"

"No, Katie and Lexie are in college, but Bernie and CeeCee decided to go to Orono. They're all good kids. We're proud of them."

"I can believe that," said Rice. He went back a page in his little notebook and studied something.

"I don't understand about how Aunt Edyth died," Stewart

said to fill the silence. "I talked to my niece, and she said something like a pin was stuck in her head?"

Rice nodded and closed his notebook. "Yes, that's right." He stood, but looked at Stewart as if waiting for another question or comment. Stewart held his tongue, and Rice said, "Thank you, Mr. O'Neil, you've been very helpful."

"Well, I hope you catch whoever did this."

"Me, too."

Stewart showed him to the door and watched him walk out to his car.

The moment he closed the door, Stewart went to pour himself a stiff whiskey and water—hold the water. After the first big gulp, he drank the rest slowly, going over the conversation in his head. Should he have asked him the piano wire question? No. Never volunteer you know something about murder to the cops. He'd done all right, he was all right, everything was going to be all right.

Seven

IT was quitting time, but Mitch never paid much attention to the clock when he was on a case. The first forty-eight hours after a murder were the most important to an investigator—several television shows had made everyone aware of that—but he hadn't even gotten this case until after that golden window had closed.

Still, he'd collected some useful information. And when he'd seen those counted cross-stitch pieces on Mrs. McConnell's wall, a lightbulb had gone on inside his head. That piece of metal—not a wire, not a screw, not a nail—resembled, he was pretty sure, a tapestry needle with its eye cut off.

He'd gone back to the medical examiner's office to ask for a photocopy of the murder weapon and found a small stack of photocopies already waiting for him. The ME had thought to put a little flat ruler beside the thing so you could see the size of it. One copy Mitch posted in the station house with a note:

WHAZZIT? TELL MITCH. WINNING GUESS WINS A
SAWBUCK.

He stuck another copy in the file folder he'd started, and
he put one in his pocket.

Then he did go home. There, he sat down to a late dinner
with his wife and all four of the kids—for a change—then
helped get the kids ready for bed. He came downstairs to sit
with his wife, who was doing some needlepoint. "Hon?" he
said.

"Yes, dear?" Funny how still, after all these years, her
calling him dear was almost painfully pleasant.

"Can I see your box of needles?"

"Certainly," she said, putting down the canvas after tucking the needle into it. "May I ask why?"

"Believe it or not, it's for a case I'm working on."

She handed over a gray-blue plastic box about four inches
long, two wide, and half an inch deep, with a twist-snap
closure. He opened it and found a white magnetized surface
scattered with blunt-pointed needles of varying sizes. He
selected the biggest and compared it to the photocopy, gri-
macing as he tried to get them both in focus.

Without a word, she handed him a pair of magnifying
glasses. He used the glasses without putting them on, looking first at one, then the other.

"Huh," he grunted after a minute, disappointed.

"What's the matter?"

"Oh, I had a notion this thing might be a tapestry needle. But it isn't."

"May I see?"

"Sure." He handed over the needle, the photocopy, and
the magnifying glasses.

She put the glasses on, slid them down to the end of her
pert little nose, and compared the needle with the photocopy.

"Oh, I see what you mean," she said. "The needle forms its point right at the tip, while the point on whatever this is starts back almost a quarter of an inch."

"You got a good eye, Liz." He reached for the paper and refolded it, careful not to form a crease across the object.

"You know what it might be?" she asked, putting the needle back in its box and nodding at the paper in his hand.

"What?"

"A knitting needle."

"Go-wan, it's too thin to be a knitting needle." Liz knit, so he'd seen lots of knitting needles in many sizes, but none even approaching this slenderness.

"It is not! There are people who knit lace and doll clothes and baby sweaters with needles as thin as triple zero."

"Triple zero?"

"Just when you think you can't get a size smaller than one, they come up with zero, and then double zero, and even triple zero. Steel ones, usually, because wood is awfully fragile when ground down that thin."

Mitch unfolded the paper again. "You really think this could be a knitting needle?"

"Possibly, but just the end of one. They're generally about seven or eight inches long."

"Yes, this one was snipped off."

"I see." She picked up her canvas and pulled the needle out of the corner where she had tucked it in. She didn't ask for any more details, so he didn't offer any. But before he went to get their evening glass of wine, he kissed her very tenderly.

IT was time for another sock lesson. As before, Doris came first, her lavender sock bristling with needles at the top and hanging down about seven inches from her hand. Phil was next, his sock in an opaque plastic bag, the needles making tiny peaks from inside. "How're ya, Ms. Doris?" he shouted in his rough voice.

She shied, then saw him smile and managed a smile back. "I'm fine, Mr. Galvin."

"Call me Phil!" he ordered, then smiled sheepishly when she winced. "Sorry," he said, much more quietly. "Y'see, I'm a little deaf."

"It's all right—Phil," she said. She raised her own voice, and held up her sock as a further aid. "Did you get your sock's cuff done?"

"Oh, yeah, yeah, sure," he said, holding out the bag. "You?"

"Yes." Doris was a little shy and couldn't think how to continue the conversation, and after a moment she bowed her head and went to sit at the table.

Phil looked at her for a few seconds, crestfallen and baffled, then went into the back to look at counted cross-stitch patterns.

Lucille came next, with the smile of someone who has successfully completed her homework. She went to sit across from Doris and engage her in conversation. They got their socks out to compare progress.

As the start time approached, Betsy began to worry that Jan and Katie might miss the class. Then they came in together. Katie seemed protective of Jan, looking around at the others with a "don't start something" expression on her face.

Which Lucille ignored. She stood and asked, "What's the matter?"

"Nothing!" snapped Katie.

"Oh, don't be ridiculous," said Jan. "Everyone will know. It'll be on the news tonight."

"What will?" asked Godwin, entering with Phil from the back of the shop.

Jan stopped and heaved a quick sigh. "You know that my Aunt Edyth died?"

"You mean Edyth Hanraty?" asked Doris. "I didn't know she was your aunt! I'm so sorry."

"Well, she was—my great-aunt, actually," said Jan. "And it seems she didn't . . ." She hesitated, unsure how to continue, and finally blurted, "She was murdered."

Everyone gasped and stared at her except Katie, who touched her on the shoulder comfortingly.

Jan looked down as if ashamed. "I know, I know, it's too terrible, it's so horrible I can hardly believe it. The Orono police are investigating. And although they say they don't suspect a member of the family, I think they do. And as one of the two family members who stands to inherit some money, I'm high on the list!" She seemed more angry than frightened about it.

"Oh, for heaven's sake, Jan, don't be silly. They can't seriously think you're a murderer!" Katie stroked Jan's shoulder.

"Maybe I should just go home. I'm so upset over this."

"No, no!" said Godwin and Lucille, almost in chorus. They looked at one another and smiled.

"Please don't go," Godwin went on. "Sometimes a class like this can be a break from trouble."

Lucille added, "We're your friends here. Maybe we can help."

"Help? What could any of you do that would help?"

"Um," said Godwin, casting a sideways look at Betsy, who nodded. "One of us really can help. Some of you know what Betsy did for me."

Hope flared in Jan's eyes as she looked at Betsy. "That's right, it was your doing that got him out of jail, wasn't it?"

Lucille looked at Godwin, scandalized. "You were in *jail*? What for?"

"Murder."

Lucille went from scandalized to horrified and saw Phil and Doris backing up Godwin's serious nod with nods of their own.

"But I didn't do it, and Betsy proved it," he said.

"Betsy is amazing," said Doris. "She can solve crimes just like Miss Marple."

"Well, dip me in glitter and call me a Christmas tree ornament," said Lucille. "I had no idea!"

Phil stared sideways at Lucille. "Dip me in glitter?"

"It's just an expression," she said impatiently. "The thing is—" She looked at Jan. "How seriously do the police suspect you, and can Betsy, here, help?"

"Oh, never mind," said Jan. "I mean, they haven't even talked to me yet, so I can't believe I'm in real trouble. I'm just upset, that's all. It was a shock when Aunt Edyth died, so unexpected."

"How can you say that?" said Katie, sharply. "She was older than dirt!"

"Mary Kate!" scolded Jan.

"Well, she was. Rude, cranky, and unfair, too. Come on, let's sit down." She went to the table.

After a moment's hesitation, Jan followed. "Mary Katherine, I can't believe you'd speak ill of the dead," she said.

"If she were alive, I'd say it to her face," said Katie obstinately.

"So, your aunt was old," said Lucille with the air of a peacemaker. "Was she sick?"

Jan said, "No, that's why her death surprised all of us. I—I'm the one who found her. Her housekeeper had gone to help out her daughter with a new baby, so I went to check on her, take her to church. It was kind of a shock, but she was in her bed, and it looked as if she'd had a stroke or something in her sleep."

"So how come they now think she was murdered?" asked Godwin.

"I don't know all the details. Mother called to say the mortician found something like a pin or needle stuck in Aunt Edyth's skull." She touched the nape of her neck. "So they did an autopsy, and the medical examiner said it was murder."

Lucille touched the nape of her own neck and looked thoughtful. Phil asked, "You can kill someone by sticking a little pin in the back of their head?"

"Oh, yes," said Jan, nodding. "If you stick it in the right place."

"Oh, ick!" exclaimed Katie. "Stop talking about it! I can't stay if you're going to talk about it!"

"All right, all right," said Betsy. "Katie's right. If we're here to give you two a break from it, then let's do that. Goddy, are you all set to start them turning the heel?"

Godwin wrenched his attention to business with a visible effort. "Sure. Did everyone get their cuff done?"

Everyone sighed, some from relief and others from disappointment that such an interesting topic was finished. Everyone held up his or her sock. Katie's pretty pink one had just the top inch or so as knit-purl cuff. The rest of the leg was just knit. Lucille's blue and white and Jan's dark red were knit-purl all the way down. Phil and Doris had done three and four inches of cuff, respectively. Phil's light green sock was several inches longer in the leg than everyone else's. "Don't like them mingy short socks," he said.

"You'd better pick up another ball of yarn, then," said Godwin.

"Already did."

"No, I mean a third ball. Not only did you make your legs longer than the directions call for, your feet are big, so you'll need more yarn than average."

Phil turned in his chair and stuck out an ancient work boot of considerable size, which he contemplated for a moment. He said loudly, "Y'hear that, Betsy? I need another ball of this green color." He held up his sock; with his foot also lifted, he looked as if he were performing a circus stunt.

Betsy, who had been doing her books, rose promptly. "I'll

get it right now," she said, and went to the bin of sock yarn. A not infrequent consequence of classes was the student who saw something she wanted or who needed to buy more materials for the class.

Godwin said, "Phil, I think I remember telling you to cast on seventy-two instead of sixty-four, right?"

"Yep." He turned back around and prepared to knit.

"Good. Last week I had the instruction sheet but forgot to give it out. So here it is—" He handed them around. "Put this on the table in front of you and find the part about turning the heel."

The instruction sheet was printed on two sides of a yellow sheet of paper and laminated. A color picture of a striped sock was in the upper right-hand corner. Everyone nodded when he or she found the place.

"First," said Godwin, "divide what you've got onto three needles, half onto one needle and a quarter onto each of the other two needles. That's thirty-two stitches on one needle and sixteen apiece on the others."

Phil anticipated Godwin by saying, "Thirty-six and eighteen for me and my big feet. Got it."

"Good. Now the heel is a flap that wraps around the foot, and we're going to work it first. Make sure your sock is right side out." He paused while his students checked, and Jan, with a little exclamation, righted hers. "The flap is the bigger section. We start with it. Everyone ready? Okay, slip one stitch." He saw Doris's confused look. "Just slide that first stitch off the needle onto your working needle." He watched Doris slip the needle into her lavender yarn carefully. "Got it? Now, purl across."

Everyone's hands got busy. Godwin, of course, was fastest, and as soon as he was done, he went around the table to make sure all of his students were on the right part of their segmented socks and had slipped the first stitch. Doris, despite her big, clumsy-looking hands and lack of experience, was nevertheless doing well with her lavender sock. Lucille, narrowing her blue eyes in concentration, was making good progress on her white-flecked blue sock. Jan, squinting identically, was swiftly purling on her red sock. Phil, lips pursed, was stoically progressing along the green row. Katie, still unhappy, was making sharp movements with her needles on her pink sock.

"Well done," Godwin said when they were all finished, returning to his seat and picking up his own sock again. "Now, slip the first stitch of the next row, and knit to the end. When you're halfway across, put one of these on the needle." He pointed to a little pottery bowl that held a dozen tiny plastic circles, each one jointed so it could be opened and closed. "Just slide it on the needle and keep going. It'll mark a place so you can find it later."

They did the slip-stitch thing for twenty-nine rows—thirty-three for Phil—and then Godwin said, "Okay, here comes the tricky part. Everyone just finished a purl row, right?"

They all nodded, except Doris. "No, I've just finished a knit row." She smiled and blushed. "But my feet are kind of big from all those years of standing at the factory, so an extra row or two couldn't hurt."

"Your feet are just the right size for you," Phil said, managing to keep his voice down, and Doris, despite a blush, pretended she was concentrating too hard to hear him.

The rest of the class exchanged secret smiles as they waited for her to complete another row.

"Now," said Godwin, when she had finished, "for this row, slip one, knit sixteen—eighteen, Phil—then we do what the instructions say is 'SSK.' Slip two stitches, then put the *left* needle into the front of these two stitches and knit them together." He went around the table with his own sock, SSK-ing for those who didn't understand, un-knitting it between students. Back in his own seat, he said, "Knit one, and turn the knitting around."

"But I'm not at the end of the row," said Doris.

"I know, it's all right."

"Okay," said Doris doubtfully. She obediently turned her knitting.

"Now, slip one, purl three, and purl the next two stitches together, purl one, and turn."

Phil, his tongue just showing in one corner of his mouth, gamely followed instructions. Then he grinned encouragingly at Doris, who was groaning softly.

"Slip one, purl three, purl two together, purl one, turn."

Row by row they worked, until the fourteenth one. "Slip one, purl fifteen, purl two together, purl one, turn," intoned Godwin, his fingers flashing as he followed his instructions.

"Well, I'll be dipped in glitter," said Doris as she stared down at her sock. "Look, it made kind of a pocket!" She held it up. "Isn't that cute?"

Godwin said, "Very well done! Phil, you have to do two more rows—"

Phil said, "I bet I knit sixteen on the next row, and purl seventeen on the last."

Godwin chuckled. "Very good! It's always nice to find a student who can extend—" He turned and looked at Betsy. "Extend? Is that the right word?"

"Extrapolate," said Betsy without looking up. "But 'extend' works, too."

"Extrapolate a concept," he said to Phil, then looked around the table. "You should all have twenty stitches on the heel needle." He waited a bit anxiously while they counted, but each of his students nodded.

Phil, after all this practice, going much faster than at the start, gave a great gasp of triumph and said, "Hah, done!"

"Great! And we're done for this class, which was the difficult one—the hardest part of knitting a sock." He checked his watch. "*And* in less than the hour allotted, so you are really doing well! Those of you who understand picking up stitches can follow the instructions and continue down the instep. The rest of you can wait until the next class, our last one, to tackle that. But—" He lifted a slim forefinger. "All of you, every single one, can now turn a heel. This is not a common accomplishment. Congratulations."

As she did after the previous class, Katie signaled Jan to stay behind. Then she turned to Betsy. "Is what Godwin said true? That you helped him when he was accused of murder?"

"Yes," said Betsy, nodding.

"Can you help my aunt?"

"We don't know that I'll need her help," objected Jan, but not too strongly.

"*You* told me," said Katie, slowly emphasizing her words by thrusting a forefinger at her cousin, "that *your* mother told the police investigator that *my father* had no motive, and the policeman told *her* he didn't think *she* did it. And that therefore *you* were the most logical suspect, because you are an heiress under Great-aunt Edyth's will."

"Strewth! Is that true?" asked Godwin.

"Well . . . yes," admitted Jan. "But I didn't murder her. She was ninety-seven, for God's sake! I wasn't in any hurry for her money. Don't you think I should trust the police to find that out?"

"No," said Betsy and Godwin together. They looked at one another and smiled.

"Well . . ." hedged Jan. "Do you charge a lot for your services?"

"No, I don't charge anything."

"Jan, I thought you were an heiress," said Godwin.

"I am, but so what? That's not why I'm asking, all right?"

"All right," said Godwin with a shrug, trying not to intercept the quelling look Betsy was sending him.

Katie said, "Does the person have to be arrested before you'll help her?"

"It's been a him, often as not," Godwin pointed out.

"No," said Betsy, giving Godwin another look. "You said the police haven't talked to you yet."

"Yes, that's right," said Jan.

"Well, then, maybe you are worried over nothing. If they talk to you and you realize you really are a suspect, call me. I'd love to help if I can—but remember, I'm an amateur."

"Yeah, but an amateur with a terrific track record," said Godwin.

"All right. Thanks."

After Jan and Katie left, Godwin said, "Well, what do you think?"

"I don't know what to think. You look about to explode with an idea. What is it?"

"I was thinking she may be in the exact position I was—looking guilty because of a will made by a not-nice person. I bet when the answer's known, it won't be about the will at all."

Eight

❖ ❖ ❖

JAN was in the kitchen fixing Ronnie's bag lunch, putting an extra-thick slather of the honey mustard he loved on his ham sandwich. She gave him two trail mix bars so he could have a midmorning snack—sixteen-year-old boys are all appetite—and meanwhile watching *The Morning Show*, where a political figure she had never heard of was being interviewed. His tone was reasonable, and he was very articulate, but his opinions on health care had her pink with indignation. She reached to shut off the television just as the phone rang.

"Hello!" she said more brusquely than she meant to. "I mean, hello?"

"Mrs. Henderson?" asked a deep male voice she didn't recognize.

"Yes?"

"This is Sergeant Mitchell Rice, Orono Police. I was wondering if I might talk with you some time today."

Her fingertips tingled with alarm. She said, "I don't think I can. I have to work. We have a very crowded schedule today, and I'm head nurse at my husband's clinic. There seem to be a lot of allergies showing up this time of year." She realized she was nattering and bit her tongue to stop it.

"It will only take a few minutes," he persisted.

"Can you hang on a minute?"

"Certainly."

She put the receiver on the table and went to find her husband, who was lathering up to shave. "Hugs, there's a policeman on the phone."

"What does he want?" Harvey—he hated that name, hence his acceptance of the marginally less offensive nickname—put down his razor and looked at her with steady, hazel green eyes.

"To talk to me."

"About what?"

"He didn't say, but his name is Sergeant Rice, and that's the name of the man who talked to Mother about Aunt Edyth."

"Well, then of course you have to talk to him. Are you afraid of what he might ask?"

"No, of what I might say. You know me, when I'm nervous I just can't stop talking."

"And you're afraid you might say . . . what?"

"I don't know." She smiled suddenly, realizing that she couldn't think what she might say that could harm her. "Never mind, I'm worried about nothing. And who knows? I may be able to say something useful."

"Want me to come along?"

She recalled the full schedule waiting at the clinic and said, "No, and I don't want him to come to the clinic and disrupt things. I'll ask him to come here."

"All right. But if you're at all nervous, maybe we should get our attorney to sit with you."

"Well . . . no, because then he'll think I'm guilty."

"You sure?"

She hesitated, then said firmly, "Yes." After all, he was Lizzy Rice's husband. And Mother had said he was nice.

"All right. But make sure Ronnie isn't here when he comes. He can be a terrible wise ass."

"Ronnie's going fishing after his summer classes. He won't be home till dark."

"Fine. Call me as soon as he's finished with you."

She went back to the phone to negotiate a time for the sergeant to come over. He wanted to come over now; she wanted him to come over at four, near the end of the workday. They settled on one thirty.

Jan went back to the bathroom to tell Hugs she'd work till noon and might or might not come back after the interview, depending on how tough he was. "Of course, I might call you from jail," she joked.

"That's not funny," he said, and his eyes were so worried she went to him for one of the hugs he was famous for, and got shaving cream in her hair.

B ETSY had barely more than unlocked the door when a customer came in. He was a burly man with dark hair and a thick neck cruelly restrained by a white shirt and dark red necktie. He looked around like someone who'd seen this sort of place before, but not with a stitcher's real interest. Betsy pegged him as the husband or father of a stitcher.

"Do you have zero or double-zero knitting needles?" he asked. "Steel ones?"

"Yes, sir, I do. They're right over here." She led him to a spinner rack of knitting needles. He glanced at the rack and chose a flat packet of four Skacels. Then he pulled out a piece of paper and seemed to be comparing it with the needles in the plastic pack. Thanks to LASIK, Betsy had a good pair of eyes, so she drifted a little closer and looked around his elbow. What she glimpsed was a black-and-white picture of part of a needle with a short ruler beside it.

The man must have sensed her near him; he turned

abruptly and caught her peeping. But he only smiled and folded the paper. "I'll take this, please," he said, handing her the packet, and followed her to the checkout desk.

She punched code numbers into her computer and, screwing up her courage, asked, "Are you from the Orono Police Department?"

His eyebrows climbed his forehead in surprise. "What makes you ask that?"

"A customer of mine is taking a knitting class and she told us that the police suspect her aunt was murdered in Orono. She described the murder weapon as a pin or nail and she touched herself here"—Betsy touched the nape of her neck—"as the place the weapon was used."

The man looked thoughtful. "Huh, your customer did that?" he asked.

Betsy nodded. "Now you come in and somehow I don't think you do needlework, and you have a sheet of paper with a printout or photocopy of a steel knitting needle on it and you buy a set of steel double-zero knitting needles."

"Maybe my wife sent me for the needles."

"She'd've written a note saying she wanted Skacel double zeroes, not sent you with a picture that could be any brand and any size from one to triple zero."

The man smiled suddenly. "I bet you're Betsy Devonshire."

"You win. But how do you know?"

"My wife comes in here a lot. Liz Rice? Plus, there's a cop here in town who complains about this amateur crime-solver."

"Oh, my gosh! You're Lizzy Rice's husband? Well, isn't that nice!" Betsy put out her hand. "How nice to meet you!"

He took the hand in a warm, slightly-too-firm grip. "Nice to meetcha," he said. "Was this customer Susan McConnell, by any chance?"

"No, her daughter, Jan Henderson. Have you talked to her yet?"

"No. So she's a knitter, is she?"

"Yes, among other things. Most people who stitch do more than one kind. But you know that; Lizzy knits, does counted cross-stitch, free embroidery, and needlepoint. She's thinking about tatting or needle lace, but she's waiting for a good class on it."

His eyes twinkled. "Yes, I know." He paid for the needles, tucked the receipt into his wallet, and left.

R ICE pulled into the driveway of Jan Henderson's home just as the minute hand arrived on the half hour. He'd just had lunch with Sergeant Malloy of Excelsior PD, whose opinion toward Ms. Devonshire seemed to have mellowed a bit over the past year. He had recommended that Rice pay attention to her conclusions but not even think about her methods. "She's one of those one-of-a-kind people, y'know?"

"Yeah, there's one of them in every crowd."

"You said it," Malloy had said fervently—then saw how he'd been suckered and laughed.

Rice shut off his engine and climbed slowly out of his car. The Henderson house was nice-size, not new, a Cape Cod or saltbox, he couldn't remember which label to apply; white clapboard with black shutters, two stories. Well maintained. Fireplace chimney up one side. Maybe three blocks from the lake. He paused to inhale the sweet, warm air. June in Minnesota made a lot of people forgive Minnesota's version of March.

As he walked up to the little porch that marked the front door, he saw a woman standing in a window, watching for him through lace curtains. He lifted a hand in greeting, and she twitched the curtain shut. A moment later, the front door opened.

She was dressed in medical-clinic scrubs, baby blue with

cartoon songbirds printed all over them. He recalled that her husband was a pediatrician. "Ms. Henderson, I am grateful you took time off work to see me," he said.

"No problem. Come on in."

He stepped into a living room cooled by air conditioning, made to seem even cooler by the use of pale green as the main decorating colors—the same color her mother used—interesting. There was even framed needlework on the walls, like at her mother's house. On the couch sat an amazing purple needlepoint pillow. It had silver threads, fancy stitches, and big tassels.

She saw him looking at it and said, "Your wife saw me at a local needlework shop having a fight with it and taught me how to do the interlocking wheat stitch."

He smiled. "I keep running into people who know my wife," he said. "The common denominator seems to be Crewel World."

"It's a wonderful shop," said Jan. "Just about everyone who stitches in the area goes there. Won't you sit down?"

"Thank you." He took an armless upholstered chair and got out his pen and tiny notebook. Jan sat on the couch. She picked up the pillow and held it on her lap with both forearms, as if it were a pet and could comfort her. Or a shield that would protect her.

He began by gathering basic information, some of which he already had—but asking again helped establish whether people were being truthful or not. Her answers checked out, and she seemed only about as nervous as anyone would be in her situation. As she spoke of the murder victim, something in her tone made him go deeper into that subject.

"Tell me about her," he said.

"I loved Aunt Edyth, even though she was cranky and peculiar."

He smiled. "If she was cranky and peculiar, why did you love her?"

"She wasn't like a lot of people today, all full of contradictions. There was something about her that was . . . all in one. She said what she thought, and, much as I disagreed with her on some things, she was consistent. All of a piece, the expression is. And never dishonest."

"You mean she never told a lie?" He let a little doubt show in his voice.

"It wasn't like that; I'm sure she told fibs, maybe even a whopper or two. It was more that she paid her debts in full and never broke her word. She was rigid, but in the really floppy world we live in today, that was kind of refreshing."

He nodded, making a note. "I agree, very refreshing. Was she religious?"

"Yes, church every Sunday, rain or shine." Jan thought a bit, then said, "Believe it or not, she was very kind—at least she was kind to me, always. She listened to me, even when I was just a kid, which is an enormous favor, you know. She was fair with her employees, who were loyal to her. She expected them to do their work, but she was good to them. And she had a great sense of humor. She was fearless and didn't care what people thought of her. She used to ride a motorcycle back when that was considered not just dangerous but unladylike. And she rode that stinky old machine well into her sixties. Never had an accident, either."

"Interesting," he said, amused at the thought of a skinny old woman tearing up the asphalt on a Harley.

"Back when she was still driving, she always drove too fast, but I was never scared, because she was so good. She had a speedboat, too. It was her father's, one of those old wooden ones, but it could go really fast. I never got to ride in it, never even saw it, but Mother told me about how she would take her and sometimes her brother all over the lake. And she would give Mother rides on her motorbike, too, until Grandmother put a stop to it. Said Aunt Edyth would break her neck on that old thing one of these days and didn't want her to take someone else with her." Jan smiled. "She didn't take Mother anymore, but she continued to ride herself. She was not one of those helpless-female types at all."

"Do you know why she never married?"

"Hah, she never even had a boyfriend. She had some kind of twitch about men, though I don't think she was a lesbian." Jan paused. "I tried talking to her about it from time to time, but she'd just say there was nothing anyone had ever shown her about the male sex that could hold her interest for more than three seconds. They were 'untrustworthy scoundrels' in her book and 'not worth the powder it would take to blow the lot of 'em to hell.' Those were her exact words." Jan was smiling more broadly now. "And she wasn't easily moved to profanity. So, see? Opinionated and not to be moved, in a world full of people scared to death of being called judgmental."

Rice made a brief note: *Liked Edyth Hanraty.* "And her will reflected that judgment," he said.

Jan hesitated. "Yes. I used to be really upset about that. She never made any secret of it, and I think every member of the family tried to talk her out of it, but she had made up her mind long ago. Then one day I thought, well, it's her money, she can do whatever she likes with it. I mean, if it was my money and someone kept bothering me to leave it to an organization dedicated to—oh, I don't know—taking away the right of women to vote, I'd stand as firm as Aunt Edyth in refusing to change my mind."

Rice pressed her a bit. "And, of course, if she had changed her will, you wouldn't be inheriting as much money."

Jan smiled ruefully. "That's true. And having a lot of money is nice—if only because I can leave big hunks of it to my two sons." Her smile thinned with stubbornness, and Rice reflected that here might be a chip off the old block, as determined to give money to her male heirs as her aunt had been determined to deny it to them.

"May I ask you to show me something?" he asked.

Her eyes widened the least bit. "What is it?"

"Your collection of knitting needles."

"Why would you want to see them?" She seemed genuinely puzzled.

"I want to compare them to something."

"All right." She rose and left the room, but returned promptly with what looked like a roll of thick cloth in one hand. The roll was held closed with a narrow cloth band tied in a bow. He smiled; his wife had one of these, too. Needle cases, they were called.

She pulled the bow loose and unrolled it, a double-thickness of light blue cloth with clear plastic pockets sewn onto one side of it. In the pockets were an assortment of knitting needles, the thickest at one end, dwindling by size to very thin at the other. The pockets shortened down the row so the tops of the needles always protruded. "Is this what you wanted to look at?"

"Yes," he said, and pulled the thin packet of Skacels from an inside pocket. "Do you have some of these?"

She leaned forward to check the size printed on the packet. "Certainly." She went to the second-smallest size and pulled out the little handful, frowning as soon as she touched them. "That's funny."

"What?"

"I thought I had six of these, but there are only five." She counted them quickly. "That's right, there are only five here. How odd."

"Are you using some of them?" he asked.

"Yes, one pair. I buy the same brand as you have in your hand, Skacels, which come four in a packet. I had two sets of four, and two needles are currently in use, so that means there should be six here. I can't imagine where the one missing might have gone."

"Suppose I told you it was a knitting needle like one of these that killed your aunt?"

"It couldn't be. Look at them—they're eight inches long. It would have been noticed."

"Noticed?"

"Sticking out . . ." She gestured. "Behind." He could feel her revulsion in talking about this.

"Maybe it wasn't stuck in behind, but, say, in an ear. Or up her nose."

She looked at him, wanting to challenge him, but not sure if she should.

"What?" he asked.

"Please don't play games with me." She looked about to burst into tears.

He put on his most disingenuous smile. "Games?"

She stood. "I think this conversation is over."

He leaned back, looking up at her. "All right, okay. I'm sorry. The reason I think the weapon was one of these knitting needles is because they look very much like a fragment that was recovered from your aunt's body."

"You mean from her head."

"Yes."

"It was put into the back of my aunt's head just above the first vertebra."

"How do you know that?" he asked, a trifle too sharply.

She sat down. "Because my mother told me."

"Who told her that?" the detective asked.

"The medical examiner."

Rice mentally cursed the ME and said, "He told her it was stuck in the back of her head?" He reached back to touch his head just below the crown.

"He didn't say just where, but I pithed more than a few frogs in college, so I know where the needle goes. You can't stick it through the solid bone, and if it had gone into an eye or ear or nose, someone would have seen it. Mr. Huber found it when it scratched his finger, which means he didn't see it, either." She shrugged casually, but she was well aware of his intense interest. "I figure the murderer didn't pull it out for some reason, but perhaps bent it back and forth until it broke, or ruined a pair of scissors cutting it off. In any case, it didn't break off flush with her skin. He thought her night braid would hide it—and it did, until Mr. Huber scratched his finger on it. So I conclude it was pushed into Aunt Edyth's brain stem. Which would call for some medical knowledge." She looked away, but continued bravely, "And here, heir to a great deal of money in Aunt Edyth's will, sits Jan Henderson, RN."

"Did you murder your aunt?"

"Great-aunt. No, I did not."

"Have you any idea who did?"

She sighed. "No."

"Might your mother have done this?"

"No, of course not!"

"How about your uncle, Stewart O'Neil?"

"He's not a doctor. And anyway, why would he? He gets zip from Aunt Edyth."

"Your husband?"

She smiled. "No, not Hugs, not for all the money in the world. I think it must be someone outside the family."

"Like who? Who had a grudge against your great-aunt?"

"I don't know. She never said anything—but she wouldn't. She was not one to complain or explain or gossip."

"Where were you last Friday evening?"

"Here at home. But I was in my sewing room with strict instructions no one was to disturb me. I didn't realize how tired I was and fell asleep in my chair and didn't come to bed until around two a.m."

He made another note, *check braid*, and rose, this time

with finality. "I won't keep you any longer," he said. "Thank you for your cooperation."

JAN called Hugs and told him the interview was over, but she wasn't coming in. "I'm too upset to come in. Oh, hon, he thinks the murder weapon was a double-zero knitting needle, and there's one missing from my kit, and I can't explain why."

There was such a long silence on the other end of the wire that at last she said, "Are you still there?"

"Yes, darlin'," he replied. "You don't have any idea where you lost the odd one?"

"Not the least idea. You know how careful I am of my needles."

Again a long silence. Then a gusty exhalation. "I don't like this."

She wailed, "Well, neither do I! I can't explain it, I can't think how it happened! What are we going to do?"

"What did he say?"

"Not much. He didn't seem, you know, *focused* on me."

"All right, maybe that's good. But still, I'm calling George tonight. I think it's time we got some legal advice."

George Markasite was the family lawyer. "All right."

After she hung up, Jan walked around the house, top to bottom, touching familiar things and trying to think. But it was no good. There was really nothing to be done right now. She called her best friend, Martine, who wasn't home, and left a message, then decided to try her new friend from Texas, Lucille. "Are you busy?" she asked.

"I'm on vacation, remember? I'm trying to knit with that flame yarn, and it's really hard, because you can't see what you're doing. If you're offering me a reason to quit, I'm yours."

"I need a break. I had a disturbing conversation a little while ago, and I want to not think about it for a while. Can you come get me and not ask me any questions for an hour or two?"

"I guess so."

"No, no guessing. Promise we'll just go shopping and talk."

"But since I don't know what disturbed you, how will I know what not to say?"

"If I say, 'enough, friend,' change the subject."

"Sure, I can do that. See you in fifteen minutes."

Nine

IT was nearly two. Betsy was, Godwin knew, over at Antiquity Rose finishing her half-sandwich and a cup—not a bowl—of soup. This was so she could have a slice of pie for dessert. She would bring Godwin a turkey sandwich with potato chips and a length of pickle. His stomach responded enthusiastically to that thought, the greedy, impatient old thing.

The door sounded its two electronic notes, and Godwin came out from the back of the store, where he'd been putting a model of one of John Clayton's beautiful young women on the wall. He saw a short, chesty man, whose big white sideburns flanked a face trying, not very successfully, to look cordial.

"Well, Joe Mickels!" exclaimed Godwin. "I haven't seen you in here for a long while!"

Mickels's grin was as false as his teeth. "Well, Mr. Du-Lac," he said, "the very person I was looking for."

"Me? What did you want to see me about?"

"I was hoping to buy you lunch."

Godwin was speechless for a moment. Mickels, a very wealthy man, had gotten that way by never spending a dime more than desperately necessary. "You're kidding!" Godwin said before he could stop himself.

Mickels scowled. "Why would I kid you about that?"

"Well, I'm not the owner here, and to my knowledge, you have never tried needlework, so what are you trying to get on my good side for?"

"I'm not trying to get on any side of you. I'm trying to do us both a favor. I want to talk to you about the money you're taking in."

"What, you mean here?" Godwin looked around the shop. Some years back, when Joe owned the building Crewel World was in, he had made a serious attempt to force the closure of the shop, intending to tear down the whole place and put up a high-rise. Thwarted, he ended up selling the building to Betsy. Collecting rent on the other two stores, and rents from the other two apartments upstairs (Betsy stayed in the third herself), Crewel World, Inc., was making just about enough to pay Godwin's salary, plus upkeep and taxes.

Joe said impatiently, "I'm talking about *you*, son. Have you thought about taking the money you inherited from your attorney friend and making it work for you?"

"Oh. That money."

Mickels turned his head a little sideways. "What, didn't you get it yet?"

"Oh, yes, probate's all finished now." Godwin couldn't help smiling, now that he knew what Mickels was after. He broadened his smile. He wondered what story Joe would tell. Would it be a chance to invest in a South American gold mine? An African diamond mine? An Idaho oil well? Florida real estate? "Betsy is bringing me my lunch today," he said. "How about tomorrow?"

Joe checked his watch. "I already had my lunch today. I was thinking tomorrow. You always eat this late?"

"Sure. We often get customers on their lunch hour, so we eat afterwards."

"All right, I'll pick you up here tomorrow at two on the dot." He turned and walked out.

G ODWIN was so cock-a-hoop when Betsy came back from lunch that he was nearly incoherent. It took her a minute to understand what he was so pleased about.

"Why is it good news that Joe Mickels is taking you to lunch tomorrow?" she asked.

"He wants me to come in with him on some kind of deal."

"You aren't going to agree to it, surely!" said Betsy, alarmed.

Godwin said loftily, "I don't know. It can't hurt to listen, can it?"

"When the proposal is coming from Joe Mickels, it might!"

"You still don't get it, do you? He won't stay interested— the income from my trust fund isn't enough to interest Joe!"

"So why is he courting you?"

"*Courting* me?" Godwin stared at her, then began to laugh. "Oh, that's too rich! If anyone heard you say that— Oh, that's too funny!"

"Goddy . . ." Betsy said in a chilly voice.

Godwin understood that tone and brought his amusement under control, though his eyes still twinkled. "You see," he said, "Joe doesn't know I have a spendthrift trust." Godwin, an eternal grasshopper, spent all he earned. He could not access the principal in his trust fund and received the interest on it in the form of a monthly check. He continued, "All Joe knows is that I inherited a chunk of money from John. He sees poor, little, ignorant, *trusting* me with a pocketful of cash and wants to 'help' me invest it where it will do both of us a lot of good. He wants to talk to me about it over lunch. I'll go, and I'll listen, and I bet I can get him to buy me dinner, too."

"Don't do that. He'll be angry when he finds out—"

Godwin interrupted. "So what? I can take it. Serve him right, thinking he's so smart. You did it to him, but that was a while ago, and another serving of humble pie will be good for the old fellow."

Betsy didn't think so. She tried to convince Godwin but was making no progress doing so when the door sounded its two notes. Jan and Lucille came in together, deep in conversation.

Betsy knew they were speaking English because they used words like *for, the,* and *can,* but she couldn't understand much more than that. *Mitochondrial* and *autosomal dominant* and *karyotype* were only some of the terms they used, but they were deeply interested by whatever they meant.

In fact, they came into the center of the shop before Lucille stopped short and said, "Why are we here?"

Jan laughed. "Because you wanted to show me those Lucci yarns you almost bought the other day."

"Oh. Yes, that's right."

Godwin led them to the display of exotic yarns that had been ordered at the Columbus Market a few weeks ago.

"Oooh, look at this!" said Jan, taking down a skein. It seemed at first to be pastel-colored ribbon yarn, but was, in fact, thin nylon braid with "tags" of pastel-colored ribbons fastened at intervals.

"And this!" exclaimed Lucille taking down a fuzzy black yarn whose "fuzz" was extra long and curly. "It's called ostrich feather. Isn't that cute?" She turned it over twice and blew on the fuzz. "You know, I bet a boa made of this really would look like ostrich feathers."

But Jan had taken down a skein of what looked like miniature rickrack in a dense yellow. "Hmmmm," she murmured, "this would make a darling sweater and cap for Katie's baby.

It's due in six weeks. I can finish a project like that in that amount of time."

"*It?* Don't they know if it's a boy or a girl?"

"No, they decided they didn't want to know. Her doctor did an amniotic test and found no genetic problems. Of course the test also tells the gender, but they asked him not to tell."

Godwin would have stayed to help, or at least continue to eavesdrop, but Shelly came in right then, wanting to see if the new Brenda Franklin charts had come in. Godwin had been working on a big pattern by that designer, and Shelly wanted to work it, too. He was trying to get Shelly to teach a class using one of her smaller designs. He took out the yellow lab and Egyptian sampler charts and sat down with Shelly at the library table in the middle of the shop to discuss it.

So Betsy came to where Jan and Lucille were fondling the yarn and found it easier to overhear the rest of their conversation.

"Have you ever noticed a pattern of heritability to spontaneous abortions in your patients?" Lucille was asking. Then she noticed Betsy. "I'll take this," she said, handing over three skeins of the ostrich plume yarn.

"Sometimes," said Jan.

"See, I'm paid to find a genetic reason for that. Plus, I've had several myself," Lucille said as a shadow passed over her face.

Jan said, "Actually, I know my mother lost several babies between my brother and me, and from the way my grandparents spoiled Stewart—and the years of difference in age between him and my mother—I'm pretty sure my grandmother had the same problem. They never talked about it in front of me when I was young, of course, so when I started having late and painful periods every so often, I thought I was developing endometriosis, and even Hugs was surprised when my doctor told me it was early stage spontaneous abortions. So it runs in my family; that's why Hugs insisted Katie's doctor test her fetus. I'm so lucky I got my two boys." She paused to hand Betsy four skeins of the yellow rickrack yarn. "I'll take these, thanks."

"This way, please," said Betsy, leading the way to the checkout.

"You know," Jan said, as she followed Betsy, "one reason I became a nurse was because Mother had another baby, a girl, after me. I was about four when she was born, and she had all kinds of problems. My earliest memories are of being warned to be very careful around Julie because she was frail. She was born with a cleft palate, but even after it was repaired, she didn't really thrive. She lived to be three, but she never learned to walk or talk, and every time she caught a cold, she ended up in the hospital. I wanted to take care of her, but I didn't know how, and that pushed me to become a nurse, so I could learn how to take care of sick, frail babies."

Lucille put her arms around Jan. "You are the sweetest thing!"

Jan pulled back and snorted. "You think so? You've never seen me with a child who won't let Doctor look in his ears!" She looked away, her face pensive. "My mother learned a lot about taking care of frail babies, poor thing, so she was pleased when I went into nursing. We used to talk about what I was learning. Our talk even influenced Uncle Stew; he took some pre-med classes but quit when he had to pith his first frog."

"Ugh. That's what kept me out of nursing! All that messing around with innards. I can take stinks, and even blood, but I hate insides!"

Betsy hated to interrupt, but Shelly looked to be winding things up with Godwin, who would want to use the cash register. "That will be seventeen fifty, please, Mrs. Jones," she said. "And Jan, yours comes to twenty-four dollars even."

Jan opened her purse. "Have you ever been tested to see if it's a genetic problem?" Lucille asked her.

"Well, of course it's genetic, if it runs in the family," said Jan with an air of stating the obvious.

"No, I mean to see what the problem is, specifically. Like, I don't know, a balanced translocation or something."

"No, why? Is there anything that can be done?"

"Well, if you can afford in vitro fertilization, they can check the embryos before they implant and only use the healthy ones. That's called pre-implantation diagnosis, and it wasn't even possible until after my daughter was born. By the time she starts having problems, I hope they will have found something easier and less expensive." Lucille handed a credit card to Betsy.

"Is that what your problem is? A 'balanced translocation'?"

"Yes. Not that we could have afforded the test ourselves. But when I was in school, we performed all kinds of tests, and I was using my own blood when we ran a cytogenetics test. And it turned up a balanced translocation on eight and nine. My teacher said it didn't mean anything bad—well, except I might have problems carrying babies to term. And I sure did."

"Isn't that odd how you found out?" remarked Jan. "I wasn't as lucky—though when I was in nursing school, I always thought I had whatever disease we were learning about that week. My med-school husband got really tired of that—until it turned out I really did have mono."

They laughed and signed their credit card slips, then left, still talking medicine.

THE next day featured a fine mist driven by a sharp wind from the north. The temperature at opening time—ten a.m.—was sixty-three degrees. Betsy hustled around, rearranging stock, putting out the new "When I Am Old" sam-

pler with its gorgeous flowers and red hat border, starting
the coffeemaker. Betsy offered free hot coffee to her customers, and she suspected many more than usual would take
her up on it today.

Godwin came in shivering, shaking water off his khaki hat
out the door behind his back, then doing the same with his
beautiful Burberry raincoat. "Global warming indeed!" he
growled, and went to stand impatiently by the coffeemaker.

Betsy had barely gotten the radio going, tuned to a soft
jazz station—NPR was playing music as gloomy as the
day—when the door sounded, and she rose to greet Lucille.

"Betsy, honey, can I talk with you?" The wheedling tone
in Lucille's voice was overlaid with concern.

"Certainly," said Betsy, aware this was something more
than a worry about knit socks or flame-colored yarn. "But if
you need privacy, you'll have to wait until I go to lunch."

"No, no, this can't wait. It's about Jan."

"What about her?"

"There's a policeman who thinks she might be . . ." Lucille hesitated, as if the notion were too mind-boggling to
be expressed in mere words. She took a breath and said in a
low voice, "A murderer."

"Jan? Oh, no, you must be mistaken."

Lucille shook her blond curls. "No, I'm not mistaken.
Jan told me her very own self. I knew she was upset about
something while we were shopping in here yesterday, and
she finally told me that a police investigator came by and
talked to her. She wouldn't say what was said, but she talked
to a lawyer last night, and he told her not to talk to that policeman anymore without his being there to hold her hand."

"Oh, dear. It's gone that far?"

"What do you mean, 'gone that far'? Were you expecting
this?"

"Not exactly. But that police investigator came in here
yesterday and bought a set of double-zero steel knitting

needles. Jan said the other night that the medical examiner found a nail or pin in her great-aunt Edyth's skull. And Jan knits with needles that thin."

Lucille's blue eyes widened. "You don't think—"

"No, I don't. I know Jan, and I can't imagine her doing such a terrible thing."

"I can't, either. Can you help?"

"I can try."

"Is there anything I can do?" Lucille asked.

"Will you answer just one question first?"

"Of course, if I can."

"How sure are you that you're related to Jan?"

Ten

❖ ❖ ❖

ATTORNEY Marcia Weiner was a little uncomfortable with this whole situation. First of all, her client had been murdered. That had never happened before, to her or any of the other lawyers in the firm—well, Janice had her suspicions about poor Mr. Wilson, but nothing was ever proved. In the Hanraty case, unfortunately, there was no doubt at all.

Worse, it seemed likely that the murderer was a member of the family. And Marcia, as executor—excuse me, *executrix*—of Edyth Hanraty's will, had to deal with them. It was very uncomfortable, trying to answer questions and make pleasant conversation with any member of a group of people when one of them might be a murderer.

Otherwise, the family was a respectable one, middle and upper-middle class, its members citizens of good reputation. She had met some of them, notably Susan McConnell and Jan Henderson, in person. Edyth Hanraty spoke of the other members of her extended family often enough that Marcia felt she knew them.

To make sure of the relationships, she began to sketch out a family tree.

Edyth, of course, had no direct survivors. Her sister, Alice, and Alice's husband, John, both deceased, had two surviving children. The older was Susan McConnell, a trim little widow still active in her midsixties. She had two adult children: Jason, a twice-divorced attorney whose sweet, shy manners belied a lecherous eye; and Jan, an RN married to a pediatrician. Jason was childless; Jan had two sons, Reese, a junior in college, and Ronnie, still in high school.

Susan had a brother, Stewart—how fortunate that this family mostly followed a charming custom of giving their children names that began with the same letter! Alice's Susan and Stewart, Susan's Jan and Jason, Jan's Reese and Ron. Stewart was an exception. About ten years younger than Susan, he was the sort of lazy, charming ne'er-do-well that tail-end boy babies inevitably become—according to Miss Hanraty, who was enormously prejudiced against the male sex, with a particular dislike for this specimen. Stewart was married to a high school principal named Terri, and they had four daughters: Mary Katherine, called Katie, twenty-one, married, and pregnant; Alexandra, called Lexie, nineteen, a freshman at the University of Minnesota; Bernadette, called Bernie, sixteen and a genius at science, taking college-level classes in high school; and Cecilia, called CeeCee, a cute and funny fourteen.

Edyth Hanraty was born in an era when women were considered to need a man to complete them and to take care of them, but she had flouted convention and remained defiantly single all her life—even long after the necessity to be defiant was gone. She declared that no woman should ever find herself dependent on a man and decided her fortune would enrich only women. She made a will that left most of her considerable fortune to the University of Minnesota to set up a scholarship program for female students majoring in business. The rest was to be divided equally among the female children of her sister, Alice, and their female descendants.

That meant, out of all those people, only Susan McConnell and her daughter, Jan Henderson, were heirs.

This was, Marcia privately opined, grossly unfair. Katie, Lexie, Bernie, and CeeCee were left out, and they were not only female, they were the members of the family who were most in need of a windfall. As Edyth had loved to point out, Stewart's many business schemes had never panned out, and Marcia knew a high school principal's salary only went so far. But while dictating the terms of her will, Miss Hanraty had declared that Terri had made her bed by marrying the feckless Stewart and must lie in it, along with her daughters.

Marcia had privately hoped for a change in Miss Hanraty's heart when Katie got a degree in business. And Miss Hanraty *had* been delighted—but then Katie married Perry Frazier right after graduation and, worse, got pregnant on her honeymoon. Even Katie's earnest desire to go back to school for her MBA had not re-softened Miss Hanraty's heart.

"Ruined! Ruined!" scolded Miss Hanraty, "She'll never get her MBA, not with a baby to raise! The best we can hope for is that Bernie doesn't follow her example!"

Three months later, Edyth Hanraty had been found dead in her bed. Marcia had been shocked to learn the death was not natural, that someone had managed to insert a thin knitting needle into her brain while she slept.

Marcia's mind went off on a tangent. How was that possible? Surely she would have wakened and struggled! But Edyth had been found in a peaceful pose by her great-niece, Jan, and might have gone quietly to her grave had not a mortician felt something while he was poking around, arranging her hair.

Now that the funeral was over and the family was starting to make inquiries—Jan had called, and so had Stewart—she decided it was time to call a family meeting.

One thing Marcia was grateful for—when it came time to select a law firm to work for, she had chosen Bailey, Farwell, and Winston. Mainly it was for the same reason Edyth had called on it to represent her: all its attorneys and support staff were female. Marcia was no longer the ardent feminist she had been back when her law degree was new, but she still enjoyed working in an all-female atmosphere. Yet there had been other pleasures she'd discovered after joining the firm, not least of which was an efficient staff. All Marcia had to do was tell her secretary she wanted a two-hour meeting with Edyth Hanraty's family as soon as possible. Her secretary checked Marcia's schedule and began making phone calls. By the close of next day, the meeting was set for two days later, in the big conference room, beginning at ten a.m.

So this was the day. And while Edyth's will had been both interesting and distressing to draw up, it was going to be merely distressing to talk to the family about it.

But Marcia had been in the law business for a long time; she had been in distressing situations before without letting it show. Her job was to follow her client's instructions, not to divert or second-guess them.

The meeting was held in Conference Room A. It was painted a rich cream with a cream carpet, dark green drapes on the one big window and matching green leather cushions on the chairs. The table was some exotic wood with a distressed and bleached finish coated with plastic to make it smooth again. Thermos jugs and porcelain cups with the firm's logo on them waited on a sideboard.

"Anyone who wants coffee will find it here," said Marcia, pouring a cup for herself.

Stewart took a cup, ostentatiously putting an envelope of imitation sugar in it and stirring piously as he went halfway down the far side of the table and sat next to his wife with her cup of plain black coffee. Susan took a cup, and so did Jan—who doctored hers with real sugar and cream.

When everyone was seated, Marcia rose from the head of the table to speak. "This is a sad occasion. My client, Edyth Hanraty, is dead, and we are about to begin the process of distributing her estate in accordance with her wishes, which were expressed in a will signed five years, three months, and seven days ago. I have asked you to this meeting to discuss that will and what it means to each of you."

She opened her attaché case and lifted out a legal-size document, its pages stapled at the top to a blue back. "This is the original copy of the will. If anyone feels a need to read it, it is here for that purpose, and I have photocopies of it for anyone who wants one."

Jan raised a hand, and so did Stewart. The others shook their heads, if tentatively. Marcia suspected some would ask for a copy later.

"Rather than read the whole thing, how about I outline the contents pertinent to you all?"

The family sighed lightly, relieved not to have to listen to yards of legal language, and settled back to hear Marcia's synopsis.

Marcia began, "Edyth Hanraty gave instructions that her estate was to be liquidated and the proceeds divided after her bills were paid. I have only begun the search for assets and liabilities. However, the estate is likely to total at least fifteen and possibly as much as twenty-two million dollars."

The listeners could not help brightening at this.

"Under the terms of the will, 65 percent of the net money realized is to go to the University of Minnesota to establish a full business scholarship for one or two women a year." She took out a yellow tablet on which she had written some figures. "That will likely mean a scholarship fund of somewhere between almost ten and a little over fourteen million dollars. Of the rest, she has left three hundred thousand to her church, a hundred thousand to various charities, and minor bequests to her housekeeper and her veterinarian.

The 'rest and residue,' as they say—somewhere between four and eight million—is to be divided equally among the living descendants in the female line of her sister, Alice O'Neil." Marcia looked up from her notes. "That is, to Susan Mc-Connell and Susan's daughter, Jan Henderson."

"No codicil?" asked Stewart.

Marcia blinked at this legal term. "I beg your pardon?"

"I'd been talking to her the last few months of her life," explained Stewart, "and I thought I had her convinced to leave a little something to my daughters. She didn't even need to write a whole new will, I told her; all she had to do was make a codicil, a kind of amendment."

Marcia shook her head. "I'm afraid she never mentioned that to me."

Stewart sat back glumly. "Oh. Well, I hoped she would. I know she was particularly fond of Katie, here." He gestured at his daughter, who blushed faintly.

"Oh, Daddy, I hope you didn't bother her too much about that," she said. "She gave up on me when I married Perry—and I put the cap on it by getting pregnant on our honeymoon." A young man, who might be handsome once he finished growing into his nose, took her hand. She looked at him, a warm smile forming. "I was sorry to disappoint Aunt Edyth, but we're doing just fine without any help from her."

"Still," said Stewart, "I think another thing we're all aware of is how unfair this will is. Surely, now that the money is going into Jan's and Susan's hands," he said, "they can correct this injustice by redistributing the money."

"The estate is far from being closed, Mr. O'Neil," said Marcia, "so I don't think it appropriate at this stage to talk about what is to be done with any monies your sister or niece might end up with."

Terri O'Neil, Stewart's wife, said mildly, "Of course, you're right. Stew, would you please let Ms. Weiner finish telling us what we need to know?" Terri was a stick-thin woman, not tall, but her experience as principal of a public school gave her an unmistakable authority; and though her tone was pleasant, Stewart immediately sank back in his chair with a shrug that dismissed the whole matter.

But then, perhaps feeling the censorious thoughts directed at Stewart, Terri spoke to the whole table. "I'm sure you all understand Stewart's anxiety about this. We're all agreed that Aunt Edyth's will was grossly unfair to the girls."

The girls, all four of them, squirmed uncomfortably in their chairs along one side of the table. There was a similarity of delicate features among them, though their hair ranged from flaming red (Katie) to pale blond (CeeCee). They had their mother's slender build but their father's light coloring.

CeeCee said abruptly, "I don't want any of the smelly old woman's money."

"Hush, CeeCee," said her mother.

"But I mean it! I *don't* want it!"

"Be happy then!" snapped Bernie. "Because I don't see anyone at this table offering you any!"

Susan turned to Marcia. "Is it possible Aunt Edyth wrote one of those codicils all by herself?"

"It's possible, but I don't think so. I feel I was entirely in her confidence, and I would have been pleased to do that for her, or even draw up a new will."

Stewart said, "How long will this search for assets take? Not long, right? From what I know of her, I'm sure she kept very careful records."

"She did. She had a wonderful head for business," said Marcia, nodding. "But some of the assets need to be valued. The house, for example. It's a beautiful example of the Craftsman style, and in a prime location. I've been in it twice, and it seemed to be very carefully kept up."

"Yes, it was," said Stewart, sitting forward again. "I was out there just a couple of days before she died. That house is in perfect condition, inside and out." He smiled around the table. "And it's full of antiques." He raised and lowered his eyebrows at them, as if sharing a jolly piece of gossip.

Marcia said, "It does contain some interesting things. Was Miss Hanraty a collector?"

"Yes," Susan said, "she had exquisite taste in antiques. She was buying them when I was a child. I remember watching her bid once by telephone. She would say 'thirty-five' and 'thirty-seven,' and I was dancing with excitement. Only afterwards did I learn she meant thirty-five and thirty-seven thousand dollars. I was quite shocked that someone would spend that much money over the telephone." She smiled at the memory.

"She had many years and all the money in the world to indulge in her passion," said Stewart. "Our grandparents were collectors, too. The house is full of top-drawer things."

"Hmmmm," said Marcia. If they were right, the estate was even more valuable than she'd thought.

Katie spoke up. "She has the most beautiful silver service. It's not that complicated Victorian style, but it's not modern, either. It's . . . willowy. I thought it was Art Deco, but Aunt Edyth said it's Art Nouveau. I think it's beautiful. If there's going to be an estate sale—" Suddenly she turned to her mother. "Do you think Perry and I could buy it, Mama? It's huge—a service for twenty at least, so we could share it. Or if it's going to cost a lot, could you come in on the sale with us? If you don't want any of it, Perry and I will buy out your share, no matter how long it takes, I promise. Mama, please?"

"Now, darling," said Terri, obviously preparing to say no.

But Katie became agitated, and her eyes filled with tears. "Oh, don't say no! You don't understand! I admired her so! She was so strong, she wasn't afraid of anyone! And this service is kind of like her, not . . ." She made a gesture of frustration. "You know how lace and hoop skirts are feminine, but then there's female without the fluff? Oh, it's hard to explain!

Aunt Edyth wasn't fussy-female but she was, so . . . womanly. I guess that's the word. Not like some kind of man, not—not butch. And somehow that's how that silver is, not fussy but not plain. It reminds me of her. She was brave and I wanted to be like her, and I know she *liked* me! I'm so sorry I disappointed her. I tried to make her understand how much I love Perry, and I thought she'd see it was all right, but she didn't. Oh, how I wished she loved me just a little bit more, then she might have put me in her will, and I could use the money to buy that silver! But can we anyway? How much would it cost?" She turned to Marcia, her eagerness like a naked flame. "How much would something like that cost, do you know? I mean, maybe not so much, right? 'Art Nouveau,' is that an important style? If it is, there are so many pieces, maybe it could be divided in half, and then maybe we could afford it." She looked at her parents beseechingly.

Susan said, "Katie, I'm afraid it might be very costly, since it's not only antique, it's real sterling."

Katie groaned. "I was afraid of that! Maybe something else . . . But oh, I *want* the silver!" She didn't cry, not quite, but her husband put a comforting arm around her.

Stewart put his elbow on the table, holding his hand up, calling for permission to speak. "I have an idea," he said.

A little current passed through every member of the family. Marcia suspected Stewart was a Man of Ideas—not all of them good.

"I understand how we have to follow Aunt Edyth's wishes as expressed in her will. And why not? It was her money, after all. I'd do as I pleased with it, if it was mine. But"—he let his hand fall onto the table's smooth surface—"the rest of us are family, too, and some of us over on this side had a fondness for the old b—uh, bird ourselves." His eyes twinkled at his near miss. "So how about we say that each of the girls can buy one item from the house—at a discount? Katie, here, has been visiting her aunt since she was eleven or twelve, and I'm sure you at least, Jan, know the two of them got along like a house afire until recently. Every time I went out there, she'd ask about the girls. I know she was pleased at how well Bernie's doing in her science classes."

Jan looked at her mother. Maybe this wasn't so terrible an idea.

Susan said, "If Jan agrees, I think that each of the girls should be permitted to choose one thing from the house."

"I think that's a grand idea," Jan said.

"Well, then, what about Jason?" asked Stewart.

"What about me?" asked Jason, surprised.

"If my girls can buy something, I think Jason should be allowed to do that, too."

Jason threw up his hands. "I don't want anything."

"She has some first editions," said Susan temptingly.

"Yeah?" said Jason, his eyes kindling, then threw himself back in the chair. "No fair, no fair!" he grumbled.

Jan laughed. "Gotcha, brother mine!"

"And how about Terri?" asked Stewart. "She's at least female."

Marcia spoke up. "Hold on, Mr. O'Neil. It seems as if you're trying to get this privilege for every member of the family."

Stewart winked at her. "And so what if I am? I think it's a damn good idea! 'Fair's fair' is fair for all!"

Susan asked, "What kind of a discount?"

"What?" Stewart frowned at her.

"What kind of a discount?" she persisted. "Are you saying half price? Less than half price?"

Stewart threw up his hands. "I don't know," he said, looking puzzled at being asked. "I was just throwing out the idea. It's up to you to decide how much to charge." He scratched under his chin rapidly, then his fingers slowed and he began to smile. "A dollar!" he announced. "You know that legal sentence, 'a dollar and other good and valuable'—whatevers."

When Susan glowered at him, he said with patently false innocence, "Well, you asked!"

Jan said, "I think it's a wonderful idea. I've been feeling very guilty at mother and me getting so much money and everyone else getting nothing at all."

"There are others getting money—getting most of the money, in fact," noted Marcia. "You and your mother are dividing only about 25 percent of it."

"Yes, but none goes to them!" argued Jan, gesturing to her family members around the table. "Actually, I had been thinking about giving everyone something, a kind of souvenir from the house, but I like this much better, that everyone can choose for herself, and himself, what he wants."

"What, *everyone?*" asked Stewart, giving her a challenging look.

Before Susan could draw a breath to object, Jan said, "Everyone." She smiled at her Uncle, who smiled back, satisfied. Marcia suddenly thought, *That's what he was after all the while—and Jan not only knows it, she approves.*

"Ms. Weiner, is this legal?" Susan asked. "Can we do this?"

"You two are the heirs. You can do what you like with your inheritance."

Jan looked at her mother, who cocked her head sideways for a few moments, then surrendered with a nod. "All right, everyone," Susan agreed.

Stewart laughed aloud in pleasure. "That's great! That's just great! Thank you! What do you say, girls?"

Katie's eyes filled with tears. "I guess you don't have to wonder what I'm going to pick. This is so great. Thank you so much!"

CeeCee said, "I was only at Aunt Edyth's house one time. Do we get to go look at what's there? Or do we have to say what we want now?"

"Of course you get to go look, honey," said Jan.

"I think I remember there were statues of horses in one room," said CeeCee.

Marcia smiled. The child was fourteen and, of course, mad about horses.

"I'll arrange for a key to be given to you on the day you decide to go for a look," she said. But as she wrote up some notes on the meeting and composed a letter to be sent to family members confirming the arrangement, she reflected on how cleverly Stewart had brought up the subject and, starting with his children, had managed to get himself in on the deal. She wondered how familiar he was with the house—by his own admission, he'd been going out there lately. She decided she'd better get out there first and have a look around. And she'd bring someone with her who had an eye for antiques.

B ETSY sighed as she looked at the beautiful but complex Tapestry Tent canvas Jill Cross Larson had brought in. Jill was buying far fewer needlepoint canvases since she had quit her job. The reason was in her arms: Emma Elizabeth Larson, aged six months.

Jill had meant to take a few weeks of maternity leave then return to her desk job in the police department. As a sergeant, she was earning more than Lars, so it seemed a reasonable thing to do.

But when the time came to return to work, she took a week's vacation, then used up her accumulated sick leave—Jill was never ill, so that gave her another three weeks—and at the end of that, she'd reluctantly concluded there was no way on earth she could leave her daughter for work. The decision surprised everyone, Jill perhaps most of all. But once the decision was made, she'd settled into homemaking with utter content.

She was also digging into her stash of unfinished projects. She'd come up with the hand-painted canvas and was seeking advice along with the wools and silks she'd need to stitch it.

"Well, it's got an awful lot of detail," said Betsy. The canvas was a Christmas stocking, with Santa in a gold-embroidered red suit standing in front of a shadowed Christmas tree covered with small, cat-themed ornaments. The floor around him was full of cats of every description; he was stroking a cat on one shoulder, and there was a cat in each coat pocket. Everything was subtly shaded; it would take infinite patience to indicate the shading without making lines.

"Maybe blended stitches here and here?" asked Jill, touching Santa's rounded belly and bent arm.

"Maybe," nodded Betsy, studying the canvas. "But you know, this may be a place for shadow stitching. Have you heard of it?"

Jill frowned. "I think so. It's a technique that lets the colors show through, isn't it?"

"That's right. You use one strand of wool instead of three, for example, or silk or DMC cotton instead of needlepoint wool. Do complex stitches in the appropriate colors, but let the shadings come through. I have a chapter of Amy's book *Keeping Me in Stitches* that's pretty good on it, I hear—though I haven't tried it myself."

Keeping Me in Stitches was a set of loose-leaf chapters on various elements of stitchery; a person could choose among them, buying only the chapters she was interested in.

"May I see it?"

Betsy brought one from the box shelves. Jill looked the chapter over and decided she'd try it. "If it doesn't work, well, I'm used to frogging." Jill was never unwilling to rip out stitching that didn't satisfy her.

"If you don't like it, bring it back. If you do like it, will you write a review for our newsletter?"

"Deal," said Jill. After paying for the chapter and some Kreinik silks, she said, "Have you found out anything help-ful for Jan Henderson?"

Betsy smiled. Jill didn't need to be working as a cop to know about this; the Excelsior grapevine was available to any-one with ears. "I hear Sergeant Rice went to the funeral but didn't arrest anyone."

"No," said Jill, "he wasn't there to arrest anyone. He was there to see how everyone was behaving."

"You mean, to see if someone was snickering at the eu-logy?" asked Betsy with a smile.

Jill smiled back. "Well, sometimes it's a little more subtle than that. Have you got any ideas about who our perp might be?"

"No. I think it's going to hinge not on who owns a set of double-zero steel knitting needles—anyone can walk into a needlework shop and buy a set for a few dollars—but on who knows how to use one as a murder weapon."

Eleven

❀ ❀ ❀

Two days later, the family met again, this time at Edyth Hanraty's house. They came in several cars: Susan riding with her son, Jason, in his classic Corvette convertible; Jan and Hugs and their son Ronnie in their Chrysler LeBaron (Reese, still away at school, had opted out); Stewart with his wife, Terri, and daughters Lexie, Bernie, and CeeCee in their three-year-old SUV; Katie with her husband, Perry, in their five-year-old Saturn.

The house stood on a low, broad slope across the road from Gray's Bay of Lake Minnetonka. It was fronted by a stone wall with a wrought-iron gate—now, as rarely during Edyth's life, standing open. The grounds were dotted with well-tended flower gardens, shrubs, and big trees.

The house was large, of course, but severe in shape. It had been built in the Craftsman style, with a low-pitched roof that overhung the walls. It was two stories high with a single-story, many-windowed addition on one side and a porte cochere on the other. All the windows were vertical rectangles, proportionally identical. The porch was large, with a roof that echoed the pitch of the house's and featured square wooden pillars.

Susan had the house key. She paused a moment, as had her daughter on the morning Edyth's body was discovered, to admire the floral pattern carved into the quartersawn oak door before unlocking it. Then she turned to make sure everyone who wanted to be there was present. Eyes shiny with anticipation, they all crowded close as Susan inserted the key.

The front entrance hall was large, with a light-oak staircase rising on the left. A set of windows faced the stairs, casting golden lights on the risers. Another window on the landing helped fill the hall with light, illuminating a magnificent red, yellow and navy blue Navajo blanket mounted in a large shadow box.

"Wow!" said Jason.

"I forgot about that blanket," said CeeCee. "It's real, isn't it? I mean a Navajo woman wove it a long time ago."

"That's right," said Katie. "Your great-grandmother bought it on a trip to the Southwest in 1901." Katie had been in the house more often, and more recently, than her youngest sister and had heard many stories.

Susan said, "Great-grandfather used it on camping trips. It was Aunt Edyth who discovered how valuable it was and had it mounted for display." She led them to the right, into the big parlor, a symphony in brown and plum, down to the Berber carpet.

Lexie, who hadn't been in the house since early childhood, pointed to the huge, boxy couch with its high wooden sides and dusty plum cushions. "I remember this! Did Great-aunt Edyth make it herself?"

"It is kind of homely," agreed CeeCee.

"But it isn't homemade," said Bernie, walking around to look at it from a different angle. "It's some kind of style, I think." She turned to Susan. "This isn't Art Deco, is it?" she asked.

"No, it's called Mission or Craftsman."

Jan said, "Believe it or not, this sort of thing is very collectible right now."

"I'm afraid I don't think much of the Craftsman style," said Terri, who had never been in the house at all.

"Then you probably won't want any of the furniture in the place," said Stewart, stroking her absently while looking around.

"Now, wait a second, look at that. That isn't Craftsman." Katie, one hand on her swollen belly and the other touching the side of her face, nodded toward a small, four-legged pedestal, with some kind of animal head marking where each leg fastened to the square top. It was delicate and very beautiful. Equally delicate was the lovely object sitting on it. Shaped rather like a jack-in-the-pulpit, it was a vase made of golden-sheened glass.

"Oh, my," breathed Terri, reaching as if to touch it, but drawing her hand back.

"That little table used to be in the guest bedroom until Aunt Edyth caught me putting a cold drink on it without a coaster," said Susan. "It's a hundred years old. She bought it in New York during the Depression for almost nothing. But the vase on it is Tiffany, which was expensive even when it was new. It's an early example, so it's particularly valuable today." She looked around at the people staring at it. "Any takers?"

After a long silence, Jan—who had been waiting to give everyone else a chance—said, "I'll take it."

"Good for you, Jan," said Stewart. "Now the ice is broken. Anybody else see anything they like?"

"Oh, look at those chairs!" exclaimed Katie.

Over by the set of rectangular front windows was a pair of wooden chairs with round seats bracing a potted palm. The high backs partly surrounded the seats and were made of slats that went all the way to the floor, an echo of the design of the couch. The seats were padded with cushions worked in a green and white William Morris pattern of acanthus leaves.

"Are those Craftsman, too?" asked Jan's son Ronnie.

"Yes. And those as well," replied Jan. They turned back to look at two big, deep easy chairs with purple leather seats and wooden arms slouched near the stone fireplace.

They looked at Katie, but she had made her choice a few days ago, and it lay waiting in the kitchen.

"But *that* isn't," said Katie's husband, Perry, pointing to the large painting over the fireplace. Framed in unstained oak, it was a messy piece, done in shades of blue, red, yellow, black, and green on white canvas. Wild streaks of color curved across it, with here and there a vertical stroke, and, in two places, what looked like a dribble. There was nothing recognizable in it, no hint of a human figure or landscape.

"I guess that's what you call an abstract painting," said Stewart dismissively.

But Bernie said, "Ooooh, I *like* it!"

"Now, don't be sarcastic, Bernie," said Susan to her niece.

Bernie's pale eyebrows lifted in surprise. "I'm not being sarcastic. I really like that, it's like . . . like Aunt Edyth on her motorcycle, going really fast."

Ronnie snorted.

Bernie ignored him and asked her father, "Do you think I should choose that as my one thing?"

He twisted his eyebrows and looked askance at her. "If you bring that home, it has to stay in your room."

Lexie said immediately, "Only if she hangs it in the closet."

"Now, Bernie," said her mother, "you shouldn't go asking for the first thing you see that you like."

"But I really *like* it! Honest!"

"Oh, Mama, she doesn't want that, she's just being perverse—" began Lexie.

"We can pick anything we want, and I want that painting!"

"That's enough, Bernie," said Terri. "Let's just say for now you have dibs on that painting, all right?" She looked around. "Unless someone else wants to claim it?"

There was a chorus of hasty denials, and Bernie beamed at them.

Terri asked Susan, "What's next?"

"The dining room, I suppose."

The dining room was too large for the round wooden table and six chairs crowded around it. The table was on a very thick pedestal. Stewart said to Susan, "Do you know how this works?"

"I sure do." She came to help Stewart pull the chairs away, then each grasped a side of the table and pulled. The table top pulled open into three slice-of-pie parts. A triangle shape rose from the center of the pedestal. Then Stewart leaned in to the center of the table, reaching in to push sharply downward into the open space. Loaded on springs, a board leaped up. He repeated the operation twice more, and the three boards were laid into the open spaces of the table top. A gentle push brought the table together in a new shape, that of a rounded triangle, and now the six chairs were merely sufficient.

"Oh, that's *so* clever!" exclaimed Terri, coming to rub her hands on the shining surface. "And *such* a beautiful table. I just love the shape!"

Stewart said, "Well, my dear, why don't you claim it?" He smiled warmly at her.

She smiled back, liking the idea, then looked over at Susan. "All right?"

"Of course. It's lovely, and it's good that it will stay in the family," said Susan.

"So it's ours? Brilliant!" said CeeCee, coming for a look. "I just love the way it goes together!" She bent over the shining surface to trace the seams with a forefinger, then ducked to look at the underside.

Lexie came for a look at the chairs. "I thought all the furniture in the house was Craftsman, but I don't think these are. For one thing, they're not oak, like all the other furniture."

Susan said, "You're right, Lexie. This isn't the dining room table I remember from my childhood."

From under the table came CeeCee's voice. "It says *Hovby* on a label down here. And *Made in Denmark*."

"Did Aunt Edyth ever visit Denmark?" asked Ronnie.

Stewart and Susan looked at one another, shaking their heads. "Not that I'm aware of," said Susan.

"Vell, it's not like you can't findt Svedish vurniture in Minne-soooo-ta, you bet," said Jan, with a singsong Scandinavian accent. The others laughed.

"Anyway, thank you very much," said Terri, and she stroked the table again.

"I believe the kitchen is next," said Stewart.

The kitchen was large but without a center island. The appliances were old but in excellent repair; the cabinets were painted white with hammered-copper handles. Katie went straight to the walk-in pantry to open the silver-cloth-lined drawers that contained the enormous silver flatware collection. She lifted out a ladle whose bowl was shaped like half a poppy flower and two tablespoons with stylized leaves clinging to the handles. "Oh, I claim this, I claim this!" she exclaimed and began counting the rest of the tablespoons noisily. ". . . Nineteen, twenty, twenty-one, twenty-two, twenty-three, twenty-*four*! Wow!"

Then her bright smile faded as she paused for a few seconds, thinking. She came to a conclusion and turned to put the pieces back, closing the drawers, pausing again, head down, before coming out of the pantry to face them. "I looked up this style of silverware on the Internet yesterday," she confessed, "and Art Nouveau silver really is very valuable. It can easily cost ten thousand dollars to buy a set as big as this. I don't think I should take it all. It's a service for twenty-four, and I'll never have two dozen people over for a sit-down dinner. I want to claim half."

Stewart said, "Now wait just—" But his wife gave him a look that shut him up as easily as if she'd flipped a switch.

Then everyone looked at Susan and Jan. "Come on." Jan sighed and took her mother back into the dining room, out of earshot of the others. "Well, we knew when we agreed to this that she'd pick the silver. On the other hand, it's sterling, a service for two dozen with all the odd extra pieces, like salad knives and ice cream forks. Art Nouveau is a desirable style to serious collectors, and it may even be one of the most expensive things in the house. Should we take her up on her offer to claim only half of it?"

Susan said, "Are we going to help her with her college loans?"

Jan frowned at this sudden swerve in the conversation. "I had certainly thought to do that. Why?"

"Because she can sell half the silver and pay them off—and pay for her master's degree, too, probably. That set isn't just Art Nouveau, it's an extraordinary set, worth far more than ten thousand—I talked with an expert in Chicago yesterday about it. Katie says she'd be satisfied with half the set. Fine. I think we should let her take the whole set and sell half of it. It's obvious that while she's feeling guilty about taking something so valuable, she really loves it. It's not like I want it— I'm not that fond of Art Nouveau. How about you?"

Jan shrugged. "It's attractive, but I've got the Henderson silver already, and this certainly doesn't match it—the Hendersons went for Georgian."

"Jason always hated polishing our silver, remember? He doesn't even want mine when I'm gone—says it's too much maintenance. That means if Katie doesn't take Aunt Edyth's silver, it will be sold out of the family. Which would be a shame."

"Not to mention that if we say she can't have it, it will

look as if we're going back on our promise, which doesn't seem very nice."

They looked at one another and nodded. Susan led the way back into the kitchen. "The whole set is yours, Katie."

"Thank you, thank you, thank you!" Katie came to hug them both, then ran to kiss her father loudly on his cheek. He returned the kiss and grinned hugely. Katie exchanged tiny but sincere screams of joy with her sisters, then, almost as an afterthought, hurried to hug her mother. Then, still beaming, she went to lean on her husband, who smiled and put his arm around her, having endured all this in gentle silence.

Stewart said to Jan in a teasing voice, "Maybe you and your mother should reconsider that promise. We've got pretty good taste, you know. It may turn out that painting Bernie likes so much is even more valuable than the silver."

"Oh, shut up, Stew!" said Susan, but not angrily. "Come on, let's keep moving or we'll be here all day."

The library had two glass-fronted cabinets placed where the sun could not get at the books in them. Both were full of first editions, one by men, the other by women, further evidence of Aunt Edyth's strange opinion of the male gender.

Jason, a bookworm, noticed a first edition of Hemingway's *The Old Man and the Sea* and pulled it gingerly from the cabinet. "Wow!" he murmured. "This was the first adult book I ever read, and I just loved it." He opened it and said, "Gosh, it's *autographed*!"

Stewart reared back a little and said, "Ladies and gentlemen, I believe we have another winner."

Jason laughed. "You know me too well." He put it down on a side table but immediately picked it up again when he saw a sunbeam strike it. He put it back into the cabinet.

CeeCee said, "I *knew* there were statues of horses in this house!" She was standing in front of a table under a pair of windows, smiling at a Remington bronze of a horse nearly throwing his rider while shying at a rattlesnake. She turned away from it, only to have her eye caught by another horse sculpture under another window, this one of five young stallions galloping full tilt over a rocky rise. "Ohhh, this one's *really* nice!" She turned toward Stewart. "Daddy, which one should I pick?"

Stewart came to look at the two statues. "How about that one, over there?" he said, pointing to a Lladro porcelain of a leggy foal. She looked at the statue, then at her father, and, seeing he wasn't serious, shyly shook her head no. "So, it's between these two, is it?"

She nodded, a smile starting to form.

"Which one do you like best?"

She pointed to the five galloping horses. He came for a closer look, bending to read the name on the piece. "Candace Liddy," he said.

"It's got five horses," CeeCee said. "The other one is bigger, but it has only one. So should I pick this one?"

"You'll take your old father's advice?" His tone and face underlined the importance of the question.

She nodded. "Yes."

"Pick the Remington." He took her by the pointing arm and turned it so it was aimed at the rearing horse and rider. "Keep it for a while, then if you still want the Candace Liddy, sell the Remington and hunt down the person who bought the Liddy and buy it. I'll wager you can do that and still have money left over to pay at least for your first two years of college." He looked around, caught Jan's eye, and winked.

She shook her head at her uncle's bold statement of avarice but didn't object. After all, he was right. An authentic Remington was a real find.

"All right," said CeeCee, "I pick the Remington horse."

The others laughed. Susan looked around the room. "I think that's a Tiffany lamp over by that window," she said. But no one spoke up, so she led the way out.

Back in the hall, Susan asked, "Isn't anyone going to claim the Navajo blanket?"

Jan said, "Perry, you haven't made a choice."

He looked at Jan, surprised. "I'm not family, not really," he said. "Besides, after the pick my wife made, I don't think I'm entitled to so much as a potted plant."

"But don't you have a Native American ancestor?"

He nodded. "Yes, I'm one thirty-second Lakota. But they have absolutely nothing in common with the Navajo."

Lexie spoke up. "May I have it?"

"Where would you keep it?" asked her mother.

"I'd store it until I finished school—I don't have to take the case, too, do I?" Lexie was a freshman at the University of Minnesota.

Terri looked at Stewart, who shrugged. "I guess we could keep it for her, if that's what she wants," he said.

Lexie looked at Jan and Susan. "All right?"

"Of course," said Susan.

Jan said, "Wonderful, a good choice, Lexie. Any reason we should visit the conservatory?"

Katie peered past the stairs and sniffed the warm, humid air coming from the foliage. "I don't think so," she said.

"Wait, I think I hear a fountain," said Lexie.

"There's one in there," said Stewart. "It's got a pitcher plant growing in it."

"What's a pitcher plant?" Ronnie asked.

"A carnivorous plant. It draws flies by smelling like dead meat and eats any foolish enough to land on it."

That did it. No one wanted even to go into the room.

"Come on, then," said Jan. "Upward and onward."

They trooped up the oak staircase to the second floor and stood a while at the top, undecided where to begin. Then Susan said, "This room was originally the nursery," and opened a door. The room was painted a very chilly pink, though the trio of windows on the other side poured with sunlight. Jan went to look out the windows at the front lawn, the highway and the lake beyond it, sparkling in the sunlight and dappled with sailboats. She turned and halted, her head cocked sideways. The slant of sunlight was such that faint shadows could be seen under the paint on one wall. "Look, I think that's Humpty Dumpty," she said, pointing to one of the shadowy figures.

"Hey, I think she's right!" exclaimed Lexie, moving to stand beside her and cock her head the same way. "And there, isn't that Bo Peep?"

"Yes, you're right," agreed Jan. There seemed to be a sheep-like sort of shadow beside it. The shadows were child-size, elusive—the original colors could not be seen—or perhaps they had been silhouettes.

Hugs said, "Say, Susan, when you came here as a kid, were they painted over then?"

"No," said Susan. "I'm the one who painted over them. They're silhouettes. This was to be my room when I stayed here, and on my first visit I was brought up here half asleep and put to bed. I woke up before dawn, and the full moon was shining through those windows, and I thought some people were standing around my bed. I about screamed the house down. Aunt Edyth moved me out, and a few years later I tried to sleep in here again—there's a wonderful view of the lake out those windows—but I had a bad nightmare about being chased. Aunt Edyth could be very understanding, she really could, and she let me paint the walls. They're not the least scary in the daytime, but I felt like a conquering hero covering them with paint. I was nine and made an awful mess in here, but Aunt Edyth never scolded me about it. And I never noticed that you can still see them under a strong light. I probably only did one coat." She hadn't moved from her place near the door. And she wasn't looking at the walls but at the one piece of furniture in the room—a bentwood cradle standing in a shadowed corner. The cradle was suspended from a bentwood frame.

Following her gaze, Jan saw the cradle and made a low exclamation: "Oh, how beautiful!" She went to it and touched it to set it rocking. "This looks old."

"I'm sure it is," said Terri, coming to still its movement with a hand. "Do you suppose—?" She turned to look at Susan. "Was this possibly Edyth's cradle? Susan?"

Susan came blinking back from wherever her thoughts had taken her. "What? Yes, she told me it was. Hard to believe she was ever a sweet little baby herself."

"You got that right!" said Stewart with a hard laugh.

But Susan went to stand beside Terri. "You know—I think I'd like this. Or do you want it, Lexie?" She didn't look at Katie.

"No, I don't think so," said Lexie.

Jan said, "You take it, Mother. Perhaps a great-grandchild will sleep in it some day."

"What a lovely thought. Yes, I claim the cradle. Katie, your child can sleep in it when you bring her for a visit."

"Thank you, Aunt Susan."

They went to the next bedroom, which also had a trio of windows, these overlooking the side yard.

"Wow!" said Ronnie, walking ahead of the others to the antique four-poster bed. "I bet this sleeps six!"

Susan walked to it. "It's older than the house. I remember Aunt Edyth bidding for it over the phone years ago. She was very pleased to get it, and she paid an awful lot for it—it's late eighteenth or early nineteenth century. "Would you like it, Stewart? It's pretty valuable."

He came over to put a hand on one of the pillars. "I don't think our ceilings are high enough for it." He looked at his wife. "Right, Terri?"

She smiled. "Yes, I think you're right."

CeeCee walked to the windows that looked over the side lawn, where squirrels frolicked in the shade of the big elms. "Was this Aunt Edyth's room?" she asked.

"No, her room was at the back of the house," said Susan. "Quieter back there, she always said."

"Quieter than what?" said Jason scornfully. "I haven't heard a thing since we came in here but our own voices."

"Well, she liked a window open all year round, and you can hear cars passing out on the road," said Susan.

Bernie had gone to a door in the opposite wall and opened it. "Take a look at this bathroom!"

It was a large room, walled with sea green tiles dotted here and there with stylized patterns of frogs or water lilies or fish in high relief. The small rectangular window was filled with stained glass in a many-angled pattern of green and gold.

"I think it's beautiful, in an old-fashioned way," said Terri.

"But not completely original," noted Susan. "I can remember when she had the old white tiles taken out and replaced with these green ones. Those ornamental tiles were old. I don't know where she got them, but I think the style is from the thirties. The tub is original, though it's been recoated." It was an enormous claw-foot bathtub.

"Is this great or what?" said Stewart, pointing to it. "It's big enough to swim in!" He made backstroke motions. "Three laps and you're clean!" CeeCee giggled and began to "swim" around him.

"Are you saying this is the thing you're choosing from the house?" asked Susan. "The tub matches the sink, so you can have it, too. How about the tiles, do you want them as well?"

Something in her tone made Stewart turn to stare at her, and the temperature in the bathroom went down about fifteen degrees. But he took an ostentatious calming breath, and said, "No, of course not; we already have a bathtub." He put on a smile. "Anyway, neither of our bathrooms is big enough for this tub."

Jan came up behind her mother. "For heaven's sake, Mother!" she muttered in her ear. "Lighten up!"

Susan turned on Jan, her eyes bright with anger, her lips twisting to scold. Then she closed her eyes and imitated Stewart's calming breath. "All right." She turned back to her brother. "I apologize."

"For what? We're just having some fun here. Come on, let's see what the next room has."

The next room was Edyth's. Her big old bed had been stripped, but that only reminded them of what had happened here. They stood in a double crescent around the bed, heads bowed, for nearly a minute.

Then Susan said, "All right, look around, everyone."

The room was large, rectangular, painted a soothing shade of blue with a deep blue ceiling and even darker blue paint on the trim and doors. There was a big gray overstuffed chair in one corner with a reading light behind it. A fat oval rug was on the floor, its colors of blue, white, wine, green, and yellow making an abstract pattern. The bed was oak, very plain in design, with thick square legs and the head- and footboards made of broad planks framing slats. A matching bedside cabinet held an old-fashioned alarm clock, and there were a chest of drawers and a vanity, also of identical design, against the walls.

There was also a modern cabinet, head high and about five feet long, made mostly of glass, and in it were small figurines, some of age-yellowed ivory, some of clay, some of metal—and some of the metal was gold. There was no theme to the pieces. They apparently came from every continent. The only thing they had in common was their diminutive size.

"Some of this stuff is made of ivory," said Bernie.

"Oh, no, the poor elephants!" cried CeeCee.

"It wasn't always illegal to collect figures made of ivory," said Susan. "Once upon a time piano keys were made of it."

"No!" said CeeCee, who took piano lessons.

"Yes," said Susan. "And billiard balls, too. That was back when there were more elephants on the earth than anyone knew what to do with. No one could imagine there might be a shortage of elephants one day."

"Interesting," remarked Ronnie, going for a closer look. His face was reflected in the glass doors of the cabinet. He was a quiet young man, with his father's craggy bones but his mother's fair coloring. "Say, look over here, Dad." He tapped on the glass with a forefinger.

"What is it, son?"

"There, bottom shelf, in the back. Isn't that Hippocrates?"

Hugs came to stoop and peer into the cabinet. "Where— oh, I see it. Hmmmmm." It was a small bronze statue, pitted and battered, of a bald man wrapped in ancient Greek costume, one shoulder bare. In his right hand was a scroll. The statue was fastened to a small wheel of dark wood. "I believe you're right."

Jan came for a look. "Where's his snakes?" she asked.

"That's Asclepius, god of medicine, who carried a staff with snakes on it," said Ronnie, who was going to be a doctor. "This is Hippocrates, a real human being who lived around five hundred B.C. He invented some surgical procedures and figured out how to reduce fractures."

"That's right," said Jan. "And he made up the Hippocratic oath."

Hugs and Ronnie recited together, " 'I swear by Apollo the Physician and Health and Panacea, etcetera, that I will use regimens for the benefit of the ill in accordance with my ability and my judgement, but from what is to their harm or injustice I will keep them.' "

Stewart said, "I thought the oath said, 'I swear by Apollo that first, I will do no harm.' "

"No, that's not in the real oath," said Hugs.

"This would look nice in your waiting room, you know that?" Jan said.

"You think so?" He smiled up at her. "Are you hinting I should ask for that?"

"Yes."

"All right, I claim the little statue of Hippocrates."

"Good for you," said Stewart.

"Anyone want something else from this room?" asked Susan.

"Craftsman cabinet matches the craftsman bed," noted Jan. "I bet this set is worth a lot."

"I don't care how much it's worth," said Bernie with a dismissive gesture. "It's not pretty, and anyway it doesn't look old enough to be antique."

"That's because Aunt Edyth took good care of her things," said Katie.

Jan said, "The Craftsman style started in the late eighteen hundreds. The house was built—when, Mother, do you know?"

"Around 1910, I believe," said Susan. "And this is the best furniture you could buy from that period. It was a reaction to the Victorian style, which thought that every surface should be ornamented."

"I think they went way too far in the other direction," said Lexie, looking around.

"Oh, I don't know," said her mother. "That chair over there looks very comfortable."

"Let me see." Katie went over and sat down with a sigh. "Oh, it is *very* comfortable!"

Bernie said, "Well, look over there on the wall—a photograph I've seen before! You have this same picture in your house, Aunt Susan!"

The photograph was taken in the late nineteenth century. It depicted a young couple standing side by side. The man

had an enormous dark mustache and a light gray or blue
suit that looked too tight. He might have been smiling, but
it was impossible to see his mouth under that mustache. In
any case, one eyebrow was slightly lifted, giving him a dryly
amused expression, and he had a frivolous straw hat resting
on the inside of his cocked forearm, held in place with his
fingers. His other hand lay on the shoulder of a beautiful
young woman in a square-necked white dress with half an
acre of lace trimming on the bodice. The skirt, gathered,
ruched and ruffled, came just to her ankles, exposing
pointy-toed white shoes. Her sleeves were full but ended in
a ruffle of lace just below the elbow. Her hair was up and
tendrils of it were in front of each ear. She looked proud and
amused.

"Yes, that's your Great-grandfather George and Great-
grandmother Harriet Hanraty, on their honeymoon in At-
lantic City in 1908."

"Were they happy, Aunt Susan?" asked Katie from the
chair.

Susan looked at her, surprised. "I suppose so. Why do you
ask?"

"I don't know."

Jan said, "They look so young."

"What a silly mustache!" exclaimed CeeCee.

"Well at least he could shave it off without leaving a scar,
unlike young people today with their tattoos and piercings,"
said Jan.

"Oh, old people always hate what the kids are doing," retorted Bernie, touching herself around the navel with a secretive smile.

"Onward," declared Susan, starting out the door.

"Oh, gosh," sighed Katie and held out her arms for Jason
and Ronnie to lift her to her feet.

There was one more bedroom on the second floor. It was
spacious and airy, its walls painted a soft lavender. The bed

was a different sort of Victorian antique; the head- and foot-boards were curlicues of brass connected at every crossing by flower-shaped pieces, the coverlet a white confection that looked hand crocheted. The floor, like the others made of wide planks stained some light color, was mostly covered by a white plush rug making a fat oval centered under the bed. The pillows on the bed were edged in purple crocheted lace. On one wall was a pair of "psychedelic" posters, carefully matted and framed. "Oh, wow!" exclaimed Jan when she saw them.

"What are they, paintings?" asked CeeCee going closer to peer at them.

"No, posters," said Susan. "That one you're looking at is by Peter Max."

"Who's Peter Max?" CeeCee asked, staring at the green, yellow, orange, and pink paper with its vaguely Pre-Raphaelite head of a woman and the big blue word *LOVE* painted in fat letters.

"An artist from the sixties and seventies," said Susan. "He kind of set the mood for that era."

Katie shook her head at the peculiar tastes of people back then.

Ronnie went to the other poster. "Is this another Peter Max?" he asked. It depicted a black man, except he was green and orange and yellow with flames exploding from his hair and hands.

"No, that's a Martin Sharp. He was a lot edgier than Peter Max."

"They don't exactly go with the décor of this room," noted Lexie. "Are these your posters, Aunt Susan? You're from that era."

"No, when these were popular I was an old married woman with two children and not coming out here to stay any more," said Susan.

"Mom, are these yours?" asked Ronnie.

"No, I never had a room out here," said Jan, who remembered that era from an early-teen perspective. "Besides, I was in elementary school when Jimi Hendrix was huge." She looked at the posters again. "These must have been bought by Aunt Edyth. I guess she was wilder than we knew."

"Naw!" growled Jason. "Aunt Edyth was never wild!"

But Susan, remembering Aunt Edyth's motorcycling days, smiled. "I wouldn't be too sure about that," she said.

Ronnie said, "Can I have this?" He was touching the narrow frame of the Martin Sharp poster.

Jan said, surprised, "Are you sure?"

"Yes. I like it. I like it better than anything else we've seen in this whole house."

Stewart said, "You have an eye, my boy. Those posters are worth about two grand apiece."

They all turned to stare at him. "How do you know that?" asked Susan, narrowing her eyes at him.

"Because I looked it up," he said smugly. "I was out here a few weeks ago, helping out around the place—you know that. I've told you all that—and I came in here and saw them, and I was kind of surprised, but I figured she had them for a reason, and I checked them out on the Internet."

"Uncle Stewart, you never fail to amaze me," said Jason. "I bet you've looked up a lot of things from this house on the Internet."

"I resent that," Stewart said with a frosty glare, but Jason merely met it with a look of his own. To everyone's surprise, Stewart backed down first. "Oh, what the hell. All right, I looked up a few things. If I was to choose the most valuable thing in the house, it would probably be that bed in the front bedroom. It's worth close to a hundred thousand dollars."

There was a collective gasp, then Susan demanded, "So why didn't you—"

"Because if I did, and you found out its value, you'd be all over me for a gold digger, that's why! So I made up my mind that I'd pick something I liked."

"Well, we're about done going through the house. What do you want? What's your choice?"

"I don't know. I want to think about it." He looked at his watch. "Let's go eat."

"But we haven't looked in the attic yet," said Jan. "From what we've seen down here, there are probably some amazing things in the attic."

"Have you ever been up there?" asked Katie.

"Well, no."

"I bet it's hot, and dusty, and full of discards," said Katie. "I agree with Dad. I think we should eat lunch, then tackle the attic."

But Susan said, "I think we should at least take a quick look. Not more than ten minutes. If Katie is right, then we won't have to come back."

Everyone sighed but followed as Stewart led the way to the back bedroom, where the let-down ladder to the attic was hidden in the ceiling of the closet.

"How did you know about this?" demanded Susan.

"Aunt Edyth sent me up there with a broken rocking chair a few months ago."

"I suppose you took the opportunity to look around there, too?" suggested Susan heavily.

"Oh, yeah, naturally. But I didn't see anything interesting. Of course, I wasn't really looking." He gave her a wide grin, and went first up the ladder.

Stewart fumbled around for a couple of minutes, muttering to himself, before he found the switch. Three 40-watt bulbs came on, casting a gloomy light down the center of the long, broad, but low-ceilinged attic. The air was still, dusty-smelling, and very hot.

In the middle of the room were three big chests made of rough boards gone gray with age, a female dress form distorted in the way a severe corset deformed a woman's torso in the late nineteenth century, suitcases, a free-standing oval mirror with a crack across the bottom, an oddment of mismatched chairs, and a rocking chair whose wicker seat had been worn through.

"See?" said Stewart. "Nothing of interest up here."

But Susan didn't like being told "See?" and so she went determinedly to the nearest wooden box and lifted the lid. Inside were neatly folded cloth winter coats and out-of-fashion wool dresses and suits, all smelling strongly of camphor. Undaunted, Susan dropped the lid and went to the second box. Inside were hats, lots of hats, some with feathers. She picked up a particularly large purple one with ostrich plumes drooping off one side of its brim. She made an exclamation of pleasure and went to the mirror to try it on. She turned this way and that, by turns mugging and serious. The hat, while ridiculous, was also magnificent and gave her a certain air.

"Let me try it!" demanded CeeCee, dropping the golf club she'd found back in a corner.

"Get your own hat," said Susan, though not without affection.

CeeCee hurried to the box. "Whoa, there's a whole lotta hats in here!" She came up with a bright yellow brimless one decorated with a red bow. She tried it with the bow in front, in back, and to the side, then tossed it aside for an ice blue cloche with a tarnished silver stripe running front to back. Susan traded the purple for the yellow, and Jan came to select a cone-shaped hat entirely covered with a pheasant's breast feathers. Bernie came to try on the purple hat, and soon everyone was laughing and handing hats around. Even the quiet Perry was persuaded to try on a big straw picture hat with a plaid ribbon band.

"Oh, Mama, look at this!" It was CeeCee, who had quickly become bored with hats and gone off to throw back the top of the third chest. It was full of dolls, teddy bears, and books.

"Oh, I remember some of these!" exclaimed Susan, coming to look. She was wearing a black felt hat ornamented with what looked like a cardinal's wing. "This old chest was in the nursery when I was a child. Look, here's Old Stiffy!" She held up a worn teddy bear with long arms and legs.

"May I see it?" asked Jan. She took it with her to stand under the nearest lightbulb. "Look, it has a button in its ear—it's a real Steiff!"

"What's a Steiff?" asked Lexie, coming to look at the bear.

"It's a German manufacturer, very famous. If this bear is as old as it looks, it's worth a lot of money."

"It is?" That was Stewart, coming for a look. "How much?"

"I don't know. Possibly thousands of dollars."

"It was an old bear when I was a child," said Susan.

"Wow, all that money for a funny-looking old bear!" said Bernie.

"Ma-*ma*!" said a new, high-pitched voice. They turned to see CeeCee holding a baby doll in a drop-waist dress and golden long curls. The doll was bowing deeply over CeeCee's forearm, and when CeeCee made it bow again, it repeated the sound.

"Isn't this cute?" she said. "I love her dress."

"And look at it," said Jan, taking it from her. "It looks brand new."

"That's because it wasn't in the toy chest when it was downstairs," said Susan. "It must've been Aunt Edyth's," she continued. "Bought for her before her parents discovered she didn't like to play with dolls."

"Why not?" asked Bernie, coming to take the doll from CeeCee. "I mean, I know she didn't like men, but this is a girl doll."

"Because playing with dolls is how little girls practice to be mothers," said Susan. "And Aunt Edyth wasn't going to have any children, because she didn't want to get married."

"Poor thing," said Katie, touching her belly tenderly.

"Look, a wedding dress for the doll!" said CeeCee, holding up a long white garment heavily ornamented with tucks and lace. The dress was split vertically in several places.

"I don't remember that, either," said Susan. "May I see it?" CeeCee handed it over. "This is very old silk—see how it's split? That's called shattering." She held the dress up to the dim light overhead. "But isn't it lovely? Oh, that lace! CeeCee, this dress is older than that doll, I think. And it's not a wedding dress. It looks more like a christening gown."

"What's a christening gown?"

"It's like the beautiful dress you wore when you were baptized. You've seen that picture of yourself in it."

"Oh, yes! Did they baptize dolls back in the olden days?"

"No, darling. But they sometimes dressed baby dolls in fancy clothes to make them even prettier. Is there another baby doll in there?"

CeeCee obediently rummaged in the box. She found a jack-in-the-box, a flat basketball, more books, a Raggedy Ann doll with a torn apron and hardly any hair, a child-size baseball bat, but not another baby doll.

"Maybe it got broken," suggested Katie.

"Yes, that's probably what happened," agreed Jan, speaking heartily. She was impatient now for lunch. "Dolls back then had china heads or even papier-mâché and were easily broken."

"Can we go to lunch now?" asked Stewart plaintively.

"Yes, yes, let's go eat!" agreed Ronnie.

The vote was carried by everyone's feet, as they turned nearly in unison to march down the steep, narrow staircase that led out of the attic.

Twelve

❈ ❈ ❈

L UNCH was a picnic on the grounds. Jan, Susan, and Terri each had brought an ice chest and a basket or shopping bag. Cold roast chicken, potato salad, cherry tomatoes, lime Jello with diced celery suspended in it, half a ham, a plate of smoked salmon, wheat crackers, bread and rolls, lemonade, beer, wine, and a couple of pies were brought out of the ice chests; three kinds of plastic tableware, paper napkins, a chess set and a Frisbee came out of the basket and bags.

"The basement is all but empty," said Stewart. "Nothing down there but an empty freezer chest and a furnace that'll need to be replaced."

"Is there any room in that house you haven't gone poking into?" demanded Susan.

Stewart's helpless grimace told her the truth before he could deny it. So he got defensive. "Well, so what? I'm nosy. Everyone knows that. I didn't take anything, I just looked."

"And valued a few things here and there," said Jan, dryly.

He smiled at her. "Yes, I did. What's the use of looking if you don't know what you're looking at? It's another part of being nosy. I suppose you never looked around when you visited out here."

Jan said, "Of course I looked, but only at what Aunt Edyth invited me to look at."

"She never invited me to look at anything," he said, "so I guess you can't blame me for showing some initiative and looking for myself."

Susan sighed heavily, but Jan said, as she had on many similar occasions, "Now, Mother." She continued, "Besides, I might have ducked into the library on occasion, just to find something to read while she took her after-lunch nap." Jan had only done that once—but Jan liked Uncle Stewart.

Stewart smiled and winked at her.

"Are we done looking at things?" asked Jason.

"No, there's the garage and that big shed out back," said Susan.

"Do we hafta?" whined CeeCee. "Everyone's picked what they want, haven't they? I'm supposed to go swimming with Natalie and Abbey this afternoon."

"Yes, we 'hafta,'" said Susan. "For one thing, we need to give your father a chance to make up his mind what he wants before we leave."

"Do I have to say what I want today?" asked Stewart, surprised.

"Yes, you do," said Susan. "The executrix wants to get started setting up an estate sale."

"'Two executors and a steward make three thieves,'" quoted Jason.

"What?" barked Stewart indignantly, and Susan laughed.

"It's just an old saying, Uncle Stew," soothed Jason. "I learned it in law school. Dates to Chaucer's time, if not earlier. A steward—and your name is, in fact, a corruption of that title—functioned like a foreman on a ranch, except the steward ran a lord's estate. Or served a king over the whole kingdom. It was pretty much expected that these people would help themselves if they could."

"Do you think Marcia Weiner is a crook?" asked Katie.

"No, of course not. I was just making a joke."

"Not a very funny one," said Hugs, frowning at him.

"I apologize. Now, can we go look at the garage?"

"You all go ahead," said Susan. "Jan and I will pack up here."

"I'll help," said Terri.

"Thank you, by the way," said Jason, "for a really excellent picnic."

There was a guilty chorus of agreement from everyone who had forgotten his or her manners as they set off for the garage.

It was a lovely day, with temperatures in the midseventies, low humidity, and light breezes to make the flowers bob and the trees whisper. Jan, Terri, and Susan worked quickly, putting leftovers back in the ice chests or garbage and putting paper plates and plastic utensils into tall white plastic bags that Susan had brought.

"I'm glad one of us had the sense to bring these," said Terri, stuffing a wad of used paper napkins into a bag.

"Mother," Jan said, "why are you so down on Uncle Stewart? I mean, more even than normally?"

"Because he's up to something, I just know it," she replied.

Terri bristled. "Susan, you always think Stewart's up to something."

"That's because he generally is," she replied without rancor.

"He is not!"

"Hush, both of you," said Jan. "Uncle Stewart is just being himself, partly because he can't help it—and partly, Mother, because he knows it annoys you no end."

Terri laughed. "You are undoubtedly right," she said.

"Well . . ." grumbled Susan. "All right, he's getting my goat, and he knows it."

"So just ignore him," advised Jan. "There, are we done?" She looked around.

"Looks like it," said Terri. "Where are they? In the garage still?"

"Yes," said Jan. "Come on, let's see what they've found."

They walked around the side of the house to the small wooden garage with its twin, pull-open doors. CeeCee was sitting behind the wheel of a huge Cadillac probably thirty-five years old, deep blue in color, with one flat tire. The roof and hood were coated with dust and bird doo. "Honk, honk!" she shouted, and then the rich sound of the horn really sounded. She squeaked in alarm and got out. "Sorry," she said.

"That's all right, hon," said Jason, grinning.

"Must be some life in the old battery yet," said Stewart.

"Want to claim it, Stew?" asked Susan as she approached with Jan and Terri.

"Naw," he said. "But take a look at what's right here beside it." He edged in sideways and pulled an ancient tarp off something leaning against the wall.

"It's a motorcycle!" exclaimed Bernie. She turned to her Aunt Susan, grinning with excitement. "Is this the one Aunt Edyth rode on?"

"Why, yes, it is. She must have kept it out of nostalgia."

Stewart supported the old machine by holding on to its handlebars, straddling the front wheel. Both tires were flat. It was painted a khaki color and had a large headlamp front and center.

Jason approached, whistling in appreciation. "My God, it's an *Indian*!" He came for a closer look, rubbing dirt off the gas tank. "I wonder if we could get it started."

"Don't even try!" said his mother. "It would probably catch fire and burn you to a crisp!"

"That's my mom!" said Jason, laughing. "Still—" On the right handlebar was a cylindrical object with a stem on top of it. He reached out impulsively and pushed down on the stem. It resisted, then moved in jerky stages, emitting a kind of crunching sound. He kept working it, pulling it up and pushing it down, and as the movement smoothed out, the crunch became a kind of rough bark or growl.

"Stop it. You're breaking it!" scolded Jan.

"No, he's not," said Susan. "That's the sound it's supposed to make. It's instead of a bell or horn."

"Too weird!" said Katie.

"Enough, enough!" ordered Stewart, who was standing right over it. Jason obeyed, stepping back, but he still was grinning from ear to ear.

"Can I change my mind?" he asked.

"What, you *want* that old thing?" asked Susan.

"Sure, it's worth more than the Cadillac, probably more than the Hemingway book."

"You're kidding, Jason," said Katie, looking askance at the rusty, oily object.

"No, he's not," said Hugs. "The Cadillac isn't nearly as old as the motorcycle, and old Indians are very valuable."

"Aunt Edyth rode that thing until she was fifty years old," Susan said. "She had a World War I pilot's leather helmet and goggles and didn't give"—she raised her hand and snapped her fingers—"what anyone thought of her. She could go pretty fast, too." Susan was smiling in remembrance.

Jan said, "I think Stewart should have first refusal, since he hasn't claimed anything yet."

Stewart looked the motorcycle over with interest—he was pretty good with old engines—then shook his head. "I'd be scared to ride it. You take it, Jason."

But Jason was having second thoughts. "Tell you what, Ron, you give the poster back and take this instead, and I'll help you restore it."

"You will do no such thing," said Jan, in words that had thorns and icicles all over them.

Ronnie rolled his eyes and gave a big, helpless shrug.

"Oh, all right, never mind. I'll take the bike anyway." And he looked fondly at the ancient motorcycle.

Susan sighed. "Well, on to the last place we have to look through."

The shed at the back of the property probably had started life as a two-horse stable. Its double doors were the Dutch kind, with top and bottom halves that can open separately. Hugs saw that the padlock had been left unfastened. He pulled the top half of one door open.

"Whoa!" he exclaimed, stepping back. The opening was jammed nearly to the rafters with a huge old dismantled dining room table, faded and chipped lawn furniture, and sun-ruined hammocks.

He opened the door all the way and then the other one—which was also blocked with rolled-up rugs, two pedal cars, three tricycles, a paint-spattered stepladder, a golf bag holding both clubs and croquet hammers, and assorted smaller items such as tennis and badminton rackets.

"Why is that table out here instead of in the attic?" wondered Hugs.

"Can you imagine hauling it up that ladder?" asked Stewart.

"Oh. I see."

"I learned to ride a bike on that old thing!" Susan said, pointing. "And see that? We invented a game combining croquet and golf! Oh, I had such fun with the Hamblin twins!" She put a hand over her mouth, trying not to cry.

Jan went to her mother and put an arm around her shoulder. "Such good memories," she said, squeezing.

"Yes, yes," her mother replied, nodding. "Good memories."

"Well, how are we supposed to look at whatever is in here, when we can't get in?" asked Bernie, very sensibly.

CeeCee spoke up. "It's empty in the back," she said.

Stewart turned quickly to ask, "What do you mean, empty? How do you know?"

She took a step away from his sharp expression and said, "I just went to look through the back window, and it looks like everything is just piled up on the side with the door in it."

"Oh. I thought you meant you tried to crawl through this stuff." He gestured at the heap blocking the door. "Might've pulled it all down on yourself."

"Dad, I'm not an idiot!"

He smiled. "Glad to hear it. Come on, let's move some of this out so we can see what's back there." He suited action to words and began quickly hauling table parts out onto the grass.

A few minutes later, looking at the table leg in his hand, then around at the quartet already on the grass, he asked, "What is this, a spare?"

"No," said Susan. "The original table had five legs. One was in the center to support the leaves when they were put in."

"Oh." He nodded. "Yeah, I think I remember that. Have we found all three leaves?"

"Right over here," said Perry, putting the last one down beside the other two.

"Look, there's a Stickley label here on the underside," said Jan, looking under the tabletop.

"So?" said Bernie.

"Stickley invented the Craftsman style, and his name on a piece raises its value tremendously."

"How come you know all this stuff about antiques?" asked Jason.

"I'm a big fan of *Antiques Roadshow*. You should watch it sometime. It's not only fun, it's educational."

CeeCee, meanwhile, had found an opening in the heap of items still in the doorway and gone inside the shed. "Hey!" she shouted. "There's a big old *boat* back here!"

"CeeCee, where are you?" demanded her mother.

"In here," she said, more quietly. "With the boat."

"Didn't you listen when your father warned you not to go in there?"

"But there was a path through, and I was careful not to bump anything. You want me to come back out?"

"No!" Terri, Stewart, Jan, Hugs, and Susan all spoke with one voice.

"What kind of boat is it?" called Hugs.

"I don't know. Like a great big motorboat, all made of wood. But there's no motor on the back. And it has a steering wheel. And a windshield."

"Oh, my God, it's the *Edali*!" said Susan. "I thought she must have sold that old thing by now."

"What's the *Edali*?" asked Katie, trying to peer through the pile of stuff.

"A powerboat. Gosh, Grandfather bought that during the Depression for a few thousand dollars, and it came with the house to Aunt Edyth. We used to go for rides in it. It could go really fast." She turned to her brother. "Remember, Stew?"

He had a big smile on his face. "Boy, do I remember! It had a tremendous engine—made a heck of a racket—but it was the fastest thing on the lake."

"I thought Aunt Edyth never allowed boys on her property," Hugs said.

"Oh, once in a while she'd let me come for a visit," said Stewart. "Sue would insist that it wasn't fair to keep me away, and the old lady would give in and let me come for a day. Once I stayed for a weekend, but it was a good thing the weather was nice, because I had to sleep in that hammock out in the yard."

"Now, you wanted to," Susan reminded him. "You said it was like camping out."

"All right, I did volunteer to sleep out," admitted Stewart, his grin broader. "But she didn't like me. Remember how she only let you drive the boat, not me?"

"That's right," said Susan, smiling now herself. "And I was pretty good, too."

"Yeah, you only nearly swamped us one time." Stewart began hauling stuff out of the way faster than before. "Gosh, I wonder what kind of shape that old boat is in?"

It only took a few minutes more to clear a proper passage. The light inside was not the best, because the windows were clouded with dust and spider webs, and the bulb in the ceiling fixture was apparently burned out. Hugs and Jason kept clearing things out of the doorway so more light could get at the boat.

"Wow, there she is all right!" said Stewart, his eyes big and shining. He walked up and took a big swipe at the side of it with his hand, revealing a rich, red brown color.

The boat—it had to have been at least thirty feet long—sat in a wooden cradle fastened to a four-wheeled cart. All four tires were not only flat but decayed. The boat's finish was bubbled and crazed under a heavy layer of dust and bird dirt. A tiny breeze began to stir the heavy, hot air of the shed. Alexandra sneezed.

On the back of the boat, in dust-clogged, gold-leaf letters, was the name. "*Edali*," read Susan, her tone fond.

"What a funny name," Bernie said. "Do you know where it came from?"

Susan said, "It used to be the custom to name your boat after your daughter, or, if you had more than one, by combining syllables from their names. This boat was named after Edyth and Alice, Grandfather Hanraty's two girls."

Hugs, having put the last bicycle out, came closer in for a look. "Oh, wow, look at her!" He sounded impressed.

"Yeah, what a mess!" said Jason, in a disappointed voice. "They put a tarp on the Indian. Why didn't they cover the boat? Look at all the crud on her! And her finish is ruined. If that's how they treated her, I bet her bottom is rotted through."

"Let's have a look," said Stewart. He went back out for the stepladder and set it up beside the boat.

But the ladder looked so rickety that he hesitated at the foot.

"Let me!" said Bernie.

"No, me!" said CeeCee. "I'm the littlest!" After some discussion, CeeCee was helped up the ladder. "There's a place where you're supposed to step into the boat—it's black," instructed Stewart, holding her hand over his own head.

"I see it. It says Baby Gar on it."

"Who's Baby Gar?" asked Katie.

"Beats me," said Jan.

"Maybe it was the original name of the boat," said Ronnie.

"No, it's the brand name," said Jason. "See how the step is a part of the boat?" He had gone up a couple of steps behind CeeCee and could read it.

"Too bad it's not Chris-Craft," said Stewart. "There's a giant club for collectors of old Chris-Craft boats. Go ahead, CeeCee, climb in."

"Shall I go in the front or the middle?" asked CeeCee. The boat, in fact, had three compartments, but the ladder was well forward of the rearmost one.

"The front," said Stewart.

CeeCee said, "Good thing these are my old jeans. It's very dirty in here." She plopped down on the front seat behind the steering wheel, stirring up dust, which made her sneeze, then laugh. "Brummmmmm, brummmmm," she said, moving the wheel. "This is nice!" She looked down between her feet. "And hey, Jason, there isn't any hole in the bottom! I wish this boat was on the lake. We could wash it off and go for a ride!" She waved an invitation to her father and said, "Come up, Daddy!"

"By God, I think I will!" he said, laughing, and climbed the ladder, which squeaked and trembled but held. CeeCee moved over, and he climbed in the front compartment to sit beside her. "Now this was a luxury boat!" he declared. "The leather's not in bad shape," he added, running a hand over the seat, which, as the dust and dirt were moved aside, proved to be a deep burgundy color.

"Gar Wood, Marysville, Michigan," said Bernie from under the boat.

"What, honey?" said Terri.

"There's a label here on this thing holding the boat that says 'Gar Wood, Marysville, Michigan.'" She came out from under to look up and call, "Dad? Have you ever heard of Gar Wood?"

He pulled a forefinger down his cheek, thinking—and leaving a dark streak in the perspiration there. "Yes, I think so. Not nearly as famous as Chris-Craft, of course. And this is a Baby Gar, so I guess the other Gar Wood boats were even bigger."

"Well, it would probably cost what it's worth to get it into running condition," said Susan.

"At least," said Jason.

"Oh, I don't know," said Hugs. "It would depend on what it's worth—and if the motor is still in it." He moved the ladder to the back of the boat and started climbing.

Lexie said, "Still, it's like from one of those old thirties movies. I can see William Powell and Myrna Loy driving around in one of these." She was smiling, head tilted as if wearing a ridiculous Myrna Loy hat.

"Holy cow, look at this!" Hugs had gotten into the last cockpit, from which he'd opened the double folding doors covering the engine compartment forward of it.

Jason immediately climbed up to get in beside Hugs. "What the hell kind of an engine is that?" he asked, leaning over it.

It was huge, with a lot of pipes coming off it. Hugs began counting aloud. ". . . Four, five, six, my God, it's got *twelve* cylinders!"

"Aunt Edyth always said it was an airplane engine," said Susan.

"That's right," said Stewart. "What kind of shape is it in?" he asked, kneeling up on the front seat and craning his neck, trying to see.

"Can't really tell, not for sure," said Jason.

"Let me see!" Ronnie said, climbing the ladder so he could peer into the engine compartment.

Hugs, looking for labels and finding one, said in an awed voice, "You know what? Aunt Edyth was right. This is a *Scripps aircraft engine*. Twin carburetors—look at the size of them!"

"I told you it was noisy!" said Stewart, tilting wildly as he stood on the seat, trying to see.

"Pick this, Daddy!" CeeCee shouted. "Pick the boat!"

"Hush, CeeCee!" scolded Terri, looking with distress at her husband, who was, in fact, climbing into the middle cockpit with a gleam in his eye.

"You may have a good idea, CeeCee," he said.

Terri threw her arms in the air and left the shed, and, a few seconds later, Katie hurried anxiously after her.

Susan would have followed them, but CeeCee shouted, "Hey, Aunt Susan, look at this!" She had found a storage compartment from which she had extracted a raggedy object that might once have been a pillow.

"Oh, for heaven's sake, CeeCee, give that to me!" Susan scolded, coming up to the side of the boat, snapping her fingers. "Right now!" she added, and CeeCee obediently dropped it into her open hands, then turned to rummage some more.

"What is it?" Jan asked Susan.

"It *was* a pillow. Now it's a nest for mice!" said Susan, holding it at arm's length. "Phew, it stinks, too!" She marched out of the shed with it. Jan got a glimpse of coarse weaving—or was it knitting?—on the front of it, wine, gray, and blue stripes, with yarn hanging loose from the bottom.

"Look, a thermos!" called CeeCee, holding up a silver object and shaking it. It rattled.

"Broken," diagnosed Hugs. "Throw it away, too, honey."

"Awww, I want something I can keep," grumbled CeeCee, tossing the thermos overboard. Ronnie reached for it, but missed. CeeCee climbed into the center compartment and opened another storage cabinet. This time she found a yellow silk scarf with white stars printed on it, also badly mouse-chewed and smelly. That was thrown overboard with no urging. But the last item was an old pair of red-framed sunglasses with the eyes shaped like a sunburst. She immediately put them on and said, "Can I keep these?"

"Sure you can, sweetheart," said Hugs, pausing briefly in his conversation with Stewart and Jason about the engine.

CeeCee climbed into the front cockpit, resumed her seat behind the wheel, and began making engine noises again. Ronnie moved the ladder so he could come up and get in beside her. Jan went over to pick up the scarf and thermos.

"You know, I bet with a little bit of elbow grease, I could get this old baby running again," Stewart was saying.

"Oh, I don't know," said Hugs. "This is a really old boat, and it's been sitting for a long, long time. I mean, look at it. It's a mess. I bet the seams have given way. It'll leak like a sieve."

"And it'll probably cost you a fortune before you realize you can't afford to get it back in shape," Jason added.

"Yeah, maybe you're right." Stewart closed the engine compartment and sat down on it. "But you know something? It was running fine in the fifties. I can remember riding across the lake in it. What a rush!" He fell silent for a few seconds, a smile playing around his mouth.

Then he turned around, looking for someone. "Where's Terri?" he asked.

"Outside somewhere," said Jan. "Why?"

"Because I want to tell her I think I've found what I want to claim."

Jan felt a rush of dismay. The *Edali* was far beyond even the cynical definition of a boat: a hole in the water into which you pour money. It would take thousands of dollars just to get it to the point of making a hole in the water. "Oh, Uncle Stew, not really! Terri doesn't want it, she said so. Didn't you hear her?"

"She did?" asked Stewart, frowning. "Why? This boat is terrific!"

Jan went to the door of the shed. "Aunt Terri?" she called. "Can you come here a minute?"

But behind her she could hear her uncle saying, with the usual supreme confidence he displayed before making a disastrous mistake, "I can talk her around. Because I know it for sure. This is my choice."

Not wanting to be present at an unpleasantness, Jan left the shed to take the scarf and thermos over to the large white plastic bag that held the discarded remnants of the picnic. She pulled the drawstringed top open to toss them in—then saw the pillow in there, nestled against a plate smeared with Jello salad. She started to reach for it, then, for a reason she could not have articulated, looked around to be sure the coast was clear before pulling it out. She held it down, away from her nose; it did indeed smell, not just of rot but also of incontinent mice. About a foot square, its face was knitted in a U.S. flag pattern, faded to pinky wines, dull grays, and dusty blues, raveled along two sides. It was leaking furry stuffing.

Something about the field of stars looked wrong and she frowned at it—then saw it had seven rows of seven stars. Forty-nine? How peculiar. Who had made this? Aunt Edyth, in an early showing of a failing mind? Except Aunt Edyth had seemed in full command of her faculties only a month or so ago.

No, wait a minute, there had been a year when there were forty-nine stars, back in the fifties. Alaska had been admitted to the union a year before Hawaii. This thing was probably made then.

Maybe it was knit by Susan, who spent many a summer weekend up here in her youth. No, Jan's mother had stopped coming when she got into high school, which was before Alaska—wasn't it? And anyway, this was knit rather competently; no pre-teen did this. So it was probably knit by a friend to give as a gift. Jan nearly tossed it back into the bag.

But, said her brain, and she paused, waiting for the rest of the objection. *But what if Aunt Edyth had in fact knit it?* Her thumb rubbed the nubbly front of the pillow.

Suppose this really was the work of Aunt Edyth's hands, now stilled forever? She went to the basket she had brought to the picnic, selected a new plastic bag, pushed the pillow all the way to the bottom and wrapped it up tightly before putting it in the trunk of her car.

As she slammed the lid down, she became aware of raised voices coming from the shed—Terri and Stewart.

"It's no good like it is, and we can't afford to fix it!" Terri was shouting.

"It won't cost much to fix," Stewart argued, "because I can do the work myself!"

"You'll try, and you'll fail, and the thing will sit on our front yard like a . . . like a junker car! Stewart, I won't allow that! Pick something else. Pick the Stickley table, or that Indian motorcycle. Pick the antique four-poster—something worth the money we can badly use! But not the boat; I won't allow that boat on our property!"

Jan started reluctantly for the shed, where Stewart could be heard saying, "Fine, I'll keep it in Jason's garage!"

Jason said, "Now, hold on a second. I don't want to be put in the middle here!" Jan felt a sad empathy for her brother. No one wanted to be involved in a family train wreck.

"Hold on, Jason, you already said I could!" Stewart objected.

"That was before I knew Aunt Terri was going to raise hell about it!"

"Oh, she'll come around when she sees how nice the boat turns out—won't you, sweetheart?"

Jan stopped at the door to the shed. Terri, white and shaking, was close enough to Jan for her to touch but didn't seem to know she was there. "No, no, *no*! This is too much! I am not going to permit you to get involved in another scheme that only uses up money we don't have to spare!"

CeeCee said, "We can sell my Remington horse to fix the boat! I'll give you my horse, Daddy."

"That's awfully sweet of you, pet." Stewart turned to his wife. "See how CeeCee believes in me?"

"You would actually permit her to make that sacrifice, wouldn't you?" said Terri in a terrible voice. She turned and walked away.

"No, of course not!" called Stewart, but Terri kept going. "I wouldn't take money from her. I only said it was sweet of her to believe in me!" When Terri still didn't turn around, he muttered, "Unlike my own wife, God bless her."

"Uncle Stewart," said Jan, "why do you want that boat so much?"

He turned to her, mouth opening to reply, then shut it again. He heaved a huge sigh. "You'll understand one day, Jan. I promise you, you'll understand."

Thirteen

❖ ❖ ❖

ALTHOUGH the shouting appeared over, the tension remained, and everyone began looking for an excuse to
leave—not hard to do, since the exploration of the property
was over. Stewart tried to jolly them all into a more comfortable mood; they were having none of it.

But when CeeCee whined, "Can we go home now?"
Stewart took her out under a big cottonwood tree, stooped
down, and began whispering in her ear. In about a minute,
she began to giggle. He whispered some more, and she
whispered something back, and the two came back to the
door of the shed with identical smug smiles on their faces.

"All right," said Jan, "what's the big deal here?"

"No big deal," said Stewart, his smile instantly replaced
with a surprised and hurt look. "I was just sharing a joke
with my beloved youngest daughter."

"Yeah," said CeeCee, her smile refusing to go away.

"By the way, Jan, may I speak to you in private?" Stewart
asked.

"What about?" she replied suspiciously.

"Oh, it's not urgent or anything. Maybe some time in the next few days?"

"I guess so."

Stewart bowed. "Thank you." He turned to Susan. "And you? May I speak to you?"

"Certainly. How about right now?"

"Now?" He looked disconcerted. "Well, uh, certainly, all right. Where shall we go?"

"How about that same tree beneath which you talked with your beloved youngest daughter, CeeCee?"

"All right." Still looking disconcerted, he led his sister to the big cottonwood. There, out of earshot, he made some kind of pitch while the others watched. Susan became stiffer and stiffer until she folded her arms and began shaking her head. The more earnest Stewart grew, the more firmly she shook her head. Still, he never lost his temper. Nor did she. Finally, the two came back together, both breathing deeply and not even looking at one another.

Now the gathering really did break up, to a chorus of good-byes and car-door slams.

Jan, closing her mother's car door, said through the open window, "What did he want?"

"Three guesses."

"Money?"

"Of course, money. What else could he possibly want?"

"What for? To repair that wretched boat?"

"Oh, no, the boat's only the beginning. He also wants me to finance the opening of a tourist fishing-guide operation. He's spent so many years fishing on Lake Minnetonka that he's convinced he knows all the best spots and that he can rent boats and take fishermen out and simply *coin* money. It would only take several hundred thousand dollars of start-up money, and he's sure he could pay me back out of the profits in a few years."

Jan stared at her mother. "Is he serious?"

She shrugged and started her engine. "He sounded serious."

"You aren't—" Jan recalled Susan's folded arms, her head shaking back and forth, beneath the big tree. "No, of course you aren't."

"And neither should you, when he approaches you."

T HE next day, Jan came into Crewel World holding a white plastic bag. "Hi, Betsy," she said. "I think I have a job for Sandy here." Sandy Mattson was Betsy's "fix it" stitcher; she could take raveled knitting or poorly done needlepoint and mend it invisibly. At a price, of course— but one many stitchers were willing to pay.

Jan opened the bag and rolled it down to reveal the terrible remains of the pillow found in the old boat. "Gosh, it didn't smell that bad when I packed it!" she said, as both she and Betsy stepped back, waving their hands in front of their noses. "Sorry, I'm sorry!" Jan, blushing, stepped forward to grab the bag, hold it up, and put a long twist in it.

"What do you want done with that, besides to deodorize it?" asked Betsy.

"Never mind. I'll take it home and try to get the stink out."

"Well, no," said Betsy. "I have some connections in that area. And methods of my own, for that matter. What is it, anyway?"

"It's a pillow with a knit cover. I think my aunt Edyth made it, so I was hoping to get it restored. Obviously, mice have been living in it, plus I think it once had mildew—it was found in a storage cabinet in an old boat. If you want to have a go at taking out the smell as well as restoring it—the knitting is badly raveled along two sides—I'll be very grateful, and I'll pay whatever it costs."

Betsy nodded. "All right. Let's write it up. Are you in a hurry? I'd like to talk to you about something else. It's important."

"You sound serious."

"I'm afraid it is serious."

"Then of course I can stay."

Betsy wrote up the work order and had Jan sign it, which she did with a little flourish. "Now, what's the matter?" she asked, as she handed the pen back.

"I had a long talk with Lucille. Do you know she really thinks she's your sister?"

Jan smiled. "No, that's kind of a game we're playing—"

"No, she has what she thinks is a good reason to think she is actually your sister."

Jan stared at her. "You're joking!"

"I am not. She collected the evidence a few years ago in Houston, at a medical conference you both attended."

"We did?"

"Certainly. You said something about it to me, about being accused of attending under two names? Or was it having a twin?"

"Was that in Houston? Well, I suppose maybe it was. But what does—oh, you mean Lucille was the other person?"

"That's right. She had just found out she was adopted and was beginning her search for her biological parents when her laboratory sent her to the conference—it was in her home state, remember."

Jan said, "I don't remember talking to her there."

"No, you never spoke to one another. But she stole your hairbrush from your room. The maid let her in—she thought she was you. The maid, that is."

"She stole my *hairbrush*? Why?"

"So she could have a DNA test done on the hair caught in it. If you hadn't brought a hairbrush, she was prepared to steal your toothbrush."

"She faked her way into my room in order to steal something?" Jan's nostrils flared, and an angry frown was forming.

"Yes. She was feeling pretty desperate."

"I guess so!"

"She was probably in that same state of mind Molly was in last year." Molly was a mutual friend who had recently discovered that her big sister wasn't her big sister at all, but her mother. Molly had gone through stages of denial and anger for months before arriving at acceptance.

Jan looked thoughtful. "All right, all right, I can see that. And finding out you're adopted only after both parents have died would be worse. You can't talk to them about it. So I guess some people would go a little crazy." She thought some more. "So *that's* why she was talking so much about DNA the other day when we went shopping! She wanted me to catch her hint! I thought we were talking medicine because I warned her I was in a funny mood and there were other things I didn't want to talk about."

Betsy nodded. "She was setting you up to talk about your DNA and hers."

"But you can't prove two people are siblings with DNA. She knows that."

"Yes, she does. But do you remember why Lucille had a problem carrying babies to term?"

"Yes, we talked about that, too. She has a balanced translocation on two genes."

"And I remember you mentioning at the sock class that you'd had pregnancies end without warning. Lucille was there, too, remember?"

Jan grimaced. "Gosh, you'd've thought I'd've caught the hint!"

Betsy smiled. "She was certainly hoping you would. She told me this particular translocation doesn't cause much of a problem in the person it happens to, except that it makes the carrier more likely to have early-stage spontaneous abortions."

Jan's eyes closed, then opened. "I was so focused on the pattern I was going to knit I just didn't pay attention."

Betsy nodded. "When she started a search for her genetic parents, she found that she was born in Minnesota, but the trail stopped at the St. Paul hospital where her newborn self was dropped off, apparently by a sorrowful mother who could not care for her. She couldn't get beyond that. Then, about a year ago, her company sent her to a medical conference in Houston."

"You know, I would have talked to her if she came up to me. Why didn't she approach me?"

"She was afraid to approach you without more knowledge. All she had was your looks and where you were from—and a big dose of wishful thinking."

"Still, I wish she had said something. It would've been fun to discover this together. I would have given her some of my hair, or a swab from my mouth."

"Would you? A perfect stranger walks up and says, 'I think I'm your sister. May I borrow some of your saliva?'"

"Oh. Well, she may have been right. I mean, you hear all the time about people about to come into money besieged by formerly unknown relatives."

"Or estranged ones wanting to make up," nodded Betsy, whose ex-husband had made a determined effort to win her back when he heard of her own inheritance. "But you see the real problem here. Given that you both were born in Minnesota and that you look very alike, the DNA results improve the odds tremendously that you are natural sisters. And if you are, that is going to complicate the inheritance situation enormously."

"I suppose that's true," said Jan. "No, if it's true, it means our inheritance is cut by a third."

"She has a daughter, you know."

Jan's eyes closed. "My God, you're right. It cuts it in half. Oh, this is . . . amazing."

"Yes, but it gets worse. If she did know about the inheritance, she becomes a very likely suspect in Aunt Edyth's murder. She was up here when it happened."

Jan went white. She grabbed a chair as if it were a lifeline, pulled it out, and sat down. "Oh, my," she said. "It seems I have a sister . . . who may be a murderer." She looked at Betsy, her blue eyes huge and blank. "Does she know about the inheritance? Oh, of course she does. We talked about it at the sock lesson, and it's been in the papers because it's such a strange will. But she might not have known before she came up." She touched her forehead with her fingertips. "But wait, if she is my sister . . . when? She's five years older than I am; Mother would have been—" She calculated, eyes half closed. "Fifteen—no, sixteen. That's old enough. But I asked Mother if anything had happened she never spoke of, and she said 'No.' She didn't sound as if she was lying, but she must have been. I always wanted a sister, and now I have one—a big sister. How odd. This is disturbing. This is amazing. Lucille is my *sister*. And oh, I'm an aunt again, because she has two children, a son and a daughter. I can't even remember their names. But what if Lucille knew, if she came up here because she knew about Aunt Edyth? Then maybe she did it. I don't *want* that! My head is just spinning, and why can't I stop talking?" A cup of tea appeared on the table in front of her, and she picked it up and took a hasty sip—then sucked air over her tongue, because the tea was too hot. But it stopped the nattering.

Betsy sat down at the table beside her. "The next question is, what are you going to do?"

"Oh, I think the first thing to do is tell Mother! She may be able to explain how it can't be true. Or, if it is, why she lied."

"You'll need to do another DNA test on her, you know; that will prove one way or the other if she is your mother's daughter."

Jan said, "And if it proves she is, we'll have to tell Sergeant Rice."

"No," said Betsy, "we'll have to tell him now. Because true or not, Lucille believes it and may have acted on that belief."

Fourteen

J AN went straight from Crewel World to her mother's house. She rang the doorbell rapidly three times, her usual signal of arrival, then walked in—Mother never locked her door when she was at home.

Susan was in the living room, working on a counted cross-stitch piece, a square magnifying glass leaning out from her chest on two cords. She looked up and smiled. "Hello, dear," she said.

"Mother, I have something to tell you." Despite her effort to speak calmly, Jan's tone was almost frightened, and her mother immediately put her needle into a corner of her framed fabric and took the magnifying glass from around her neck.

"What's the matter?" she asked.

"Remember that woman from Texas I told you about? The one who looks like me?"

"Yes, Lucille somebody. What about her?"

"Lucille Jones. She has proof that she's related to me."

Her mother frowned. "What kind of proof?"

"You know how both you and I had problems carrying babies to term? So did she. And the reason for her problem was a translocation on two of her genes. She found the same translocation on the same genes in me, and that makes her think we may be sisters or cousins or something."

Her mother turned her head a little sideways. "And just how did she discover this same genetic translocation in you?"

"It's kind of an involved story." Jan sat down on the couch and explained about the medical conference, the stolen hairbrush, and the genetic test performed on the hairs found in it. "One thing the test could have done was shown we could not be siblings, and it didn't do that."

Her mother's eyes had been growing wider and wider during Jan's story. "So if she's telling the truth—which you don't know—she's a confessed thief!"

"Oh, for heaven's sake, a hairbrush—that's not important! She was afraid to talk to me directly, because she didn't know what kind of person I am and because she didn't have any evidence that we were related. But she was desperate to connect with her genetic relatives. And she was afraid that if she just walked up and asked me to help her find out, I'd think she was some kind of nut." Susan raised a hand, wanting to interrupt, but Jan said, "Just listen one more minute, please. She's adopted, and now that she's found out I have the same genetic flaw she does, on the same two genes, she suspects we're related. There's a high probability that we are. Mother, am I adopted?"

"No, of course not! Why on earth—"

"If I'm not adopted, then is she right? Are you her mother?"

"No, I am not!" So fierce was Susan's denial that she looked close to tears.

"She is absolutely sure she's related to me—and to you, because of this translocation thing. So where did she come from?" Jan felt her face squinch up as she fought tears of her own. "She just wants to know—and she's got me wondering. I do have the translocated gene—"

"Lucille *says* you have the translocated gene."

"You think she's lying?"

"All I know is, *she is not my daughter*. You say she looks like you, and she says she likes a lot of the same things you do. Well, good for her. I have no doubt there are a great many blondes in Minnesota and Texas who like to stitch and ride in boats and take business trips, and not one of them is related to you, or me, or anyone else in the family." She gestured in a spiral upward. "For all you know, she may be lying about liking those things, just as she may be lying about that translocated gene business. Has she shown you any documentation about it?"

"No, she hasn't."

Susan made a dismissive sound and added, "I think you should talk to your brother the lawyer. Ask him what we need to do to protect ourselves. Because I foresee a lawsuit that can tie things up for years if we don't cut this off right now."

Jan was hurt at this assertive dismissal of her trust in Lucille, as if she were a naïve child. Jan had worked with the public for many years and considered herself a shrewd judge of character. And Lucille had seemed perfectly sincere and honest. "Well, suppose she's not lying?"

"Fine. Then she's got the proof. Ask her to show it to you."

"And if she does? Then what? Her next step will be to ask that you be tested. Would you be willing to have a DNA test?"

"Certainly, and thank God there is such a thing to disprove her claim once and for all."

*   *   *

STEWART was in the kitchen preparing lunch. Lexie, Bernie and CeeCee were weeding the gardens—vegetable and flower. Minnesota's growing season was short, but there were already lettuces, radishes, and green onions for the salad he would make. The cucumber he was slicing was store bought; the garden wouldn't offer cucumbers until July.

The phone interrupted him, and he grabbed the receiver, laying it on his shoulder and holding it in place with his chin while he cut up leftover chicken to add to the salad. "Speak to me," he said in a cheerful tone.

"Stew, it's Susan."

He closed his eyes briefly, took a breath and said in a good imitation of that same tone, "Hello, Sis! What's up?"

"Jan just left me. She came by to talk about that new friend of hers, Lucille Jones."

"I don't think she's told me about Ms. Jones."

"Well, brace yourself, because we're probably going to hear a whole lot about her. She's from Texas, and she's up here trying to prove she's related to us. In fact, she wants Jan to think she's my daughter."

The telephone jumped out from under Stewart's chin, and he had to drop the knife and grab it before it hit the floor. "Wait a minute, I don't think I heard you right. Did you say there's a Lucille Jones who wants Jan to think that she—Lucille—is your daughter?"

"Yes."

Stewart began to laugh. He couldn't help it. "What does Jan say about this?" he managed after a bit.

"She says that Lucille got access to some of Jan's hair and had a DNA test performed on it that seems to indicate they are siblings."

That killed the amusement, stone dead, instantly. "Holy cow! So Jan believes her, then?"

"I don't know if she still believes her, after the talking-to I administered. I think at least now she has some doubts. She

likes this Lucille person. They've become firm friends. It is
my opinion that Ms. Jones is a liar and a con artist. Jan asked
me if I'd submit to a DNA test, and I said of course I would."

"Can you pass it?"

"Why does everyone keep asking me that?"

"All right, all right, calm down. I guess we ask because of
what it means. If this woman can prove she's your daughter—
I don't know how; can these things be rigged somehow?—if,
as I said, she can prove she's your daughter, then she's going
to cut herself a slice of Aunt Edyth's fortune."

"She can try, but she won't succeed," said Susan grimly.
"If we do the test, I want it photographed, recorded, sur-
veyed, supervised, and overseen by an attorney every step of
the way. I won't have a cuckoo in our nest. Not if I can pre-
vent it."

SERGEANT Rice was at lunch when his cell phone rang.
He sighed and pulled it from a pocket. "Rice here," he
said.

It was a colleague from the Orono Police Department.
"Sarge, you got two calls, one from a Ms. Devonshire at
Crewel World in Excelsior; and the other, marked urgent,
from one Stewart O'Neil. He's very anxious that you should
call him back right away."

Rice took both numbers but finished his tuna on rye before choosing which one he'd call back first. "Mr. O'Neil?"
he said, when the phone was answered. "Sergeant Mitchell
Rice, Orono PD, here. Is there a problem?"

"Sergeant Rice, I'm glad you called me back so promptly!"
came the genial voice. "I've got some interesting news for
you. It's about the case you're working on, you know, the
murder of Edyth Hanraty?"

"Yessir," said Rice, preparing to be patient with a foolish
citizen.

"Well, it seems there's this woman in town—in Excelsior, really—who came up from Texas, came here on purpose to make the acquaintance of my niece, Jan Henderson, and she's trying to convince Jan that she's a long-lost sister, so she can cut herself in on the inheritance."

Rice managed to confine himself to a snort of disbelief. Long-lost heirs already? Miss Hanraty was barely settled in her grave. Anyhow, claims like that were becoming rare with the advent of DNA testing. "What kind of story is she telling?" he asked.

"I don't know," said Stewart, "or not exactly. Something about transplanted genes and a test done on a stolen hairbrush. No, not transplanted, something else, some kind of trans thing. Anyway, this woman has that kind of genes and Jan has them, too, and she thinks that proves they're sisters."

"Is it possible?"

"Hell, no! I talked to my sister, and she says absolutely not. But it seems this woman believes it. She's been up here for a couple of weeks, making friends with Jan. And she knows about Edyth being Jan's great-aunt. I mean, that's obviously the real reason she's up here. Her name is Lucille Jones. Can you go talk to her?"

"Oh, yes, I am definitely going to go talk to her."

Rice asked some more questions, thanked him, and hung up. So not some idiot who hadn't heard about DNA, then. Some other kind of idiot. Or worse.

He called Betsy Devonshire next and was amused to find she had the same information to share with him. Better, she had the phone number where the Joneses were staying—they'd opted to rent a cottage.

So they'd been here for several weeks already and knew on arrival they'd be here a while—cottages were rented by the week or month, not by the day. They'd been here since before Edyth Hanraty had been murdered. So very likely,

Stewart O'Neil was right—they knew before they got here about the wealthy old woman. Why else try the con?

But were they responsible for her death? That was the question.

THE cottage was one of four in a row set behind two ordinary houses on adjoining lots. They all were tiny, made of white boards with dark red trim around the doors and windows, but each had a different color door. The Joneses were staying in the cottage with a pale orange door, second from the one nearest the lake. The color reminded Lucille of Dreamsicles, her favorite summer treat when she was a child.

But she and Bobby Lee were not talking of Dreamsicles over lunch. "What if Jan's mother won't agree to a DNA test?" he asked.

"She will. There's too much at stake for her not to agree."

"What if it proves she's not your mother?"

Lucille smiled. "I don't see how that's possible. There's no one else in that family it could be."

"Sure there is. Jan's father."

She considered that briefly while she nibbled on a potato chip—they were having chicken salad sandwiches, chips, and milk for lunch. "I suppose that could be," she said. "But Jan told me her mother had the same problem bearing children, so the link is more likely through her. Though she did say she looks more like her dad than her mom."

"Hell, I look more like my stepdad than my dad. I'm sorry to keep bringing up the negative, but I just can't help thinking something is gonna go wrong here. It pretty generally does for us, you know."

Lucille sighed. Bobby Lee was right—but things wouldn't go wrong so often if they could just get ahead of the money flow. And they could get ahead if Bobby Lee would stay away from the casinos.

"Have you called to see if there's a GA in the area?" Gamblers Anonymous meetings were everywhere. Bobby Lee was supposed to contact one up here—that was their agreement.

"Not yet," he mumbled, and took a big bite of his sandwich.

She got up and went to the phone. "I'm going to call the landlady and tell her we're leaving at the end of the week," she said.

"Don't do that!" he said, his words barely understandable around the mouthful of food. He stood, chewed fast, and swallowed hard. "You don't want to do that," he said, more clearly.

"No, of course I don't." She turned and saw the bright relief on his face. She erased it by saying, "But I will. This is much, much too important for you to mess it up by going on a gambling binge."

"Darlin', I promise, I'll call them this afternoon."

"No, you'll call them right now." He studied her for a few moments, and she let him see that this was not negotiable.

He wiped his fingers on his paper napkin, making a job of it while he looked at her, a smile slowly building on his face. Only when she began to smile back did he put the napkin down and go to gently push her aside and lift the receiver.

Because he was eager to get back into her good graces, he found a meeting starting in half an hour and so was gone when someone knocked. Lucille put her knitting down and opened the door to find a tall, stocky man with dark hair and a collar squeezed tight by a dark blue tie. He had a small leather folder in his hand that he flipped open to show a gold badge and photo ID. She felt her heart close in a grip as tight as his collar.

"Y-yes?" she faltered.

"My name is Sergeant Mitchell Rice, Orono Police. May I come in?"

"Is this about Bobby Lee?"

"Who is Bobby Lee?"

The look of relief on her face surprised him.

"I thought something had happened to my husband," she explained. "We're not used to the roads up here, all curving around that big lake—and the curves hidden by big ol' trees."

He smiled. "I have friends who come up here from Arizona, and they say it's like being suffocated in greenery up here."

She smiled back. "Really? I like it. It feels right to me. My husband is more like your friends, I guess. Come in," she added, stepping back.

As he did, he glanced around the small room, which featured walls and furniture in shades of tan with oxblood trim on the window frames. "Sad, isn't it?" she said. "But rents up here are scary."

"It gets better the farther from the cities you get," he said.

"Well, we needed to be here, so here's where we are."

"Will your husband be back soon?"

"In an hour or so. He's . . . at a meeting in Wayzata."

He looked curious about her hesitation, but she held her tongue. Then he said, "I want to talk to you about Edyth Hanraty, Jan Henderson, and Susan McConnell."

She had gathered that when he said Orono—that was where Edyth had lived. "All right. Won't you sit down? Would you like something to drink? We have Coke in several flavors."

"No, but thank you."

"That chair over there isn't too awful." She pointed to one upholstered in a pale tan fabric, then went to the loveseat— the room was too small for a regular couch. It was upholstered in a tan buzz-cut fabric, with random curving lines carved into the nap. It made the backs of her legs itch, so she tucked one leg under her.

"What do you want to ask me?" she inquired.

"Let me get some basic information first," he said, and pulled out his notebook, in which he wrote down her full name, date of birth, Dallas address, occupation.

"Why are you asking me all this?"

"Standard procedure."

She doubted that but didn't want to object. "You know Edyth Hanraty was murdered?" he asked.

"Yes, but what does that have to do with me?"

"I have information that you believe you are an heir to the Hanraty estate under the terms of her will."

"Where did you hear that?" she asked sharply.

"So it's not true?"

"Well, I'm not sure whether or not I'm an heir. I don't know much about that part of things. I came up here—my husband and I came up here together—because I'm trying to find my birth parents. I'm adopted, you see. I saw Jan Henderson at a medical conference and, well, people thought we were twins or something, because we look so much alike, and I went home and started up my computer. The Internet is just wonderful for things like that. I didn't want to say anything until I was sure, but we had some vacation coming, and so we came here. And Jan and I met at a knitting class, and it's weird how many things we have in common, it's like, you know, 'twins separated at birth,' except we aren't twins, of course. I didn't know anything about her aunt—her great-aunt, isn't it?—until she told me. And I was *so shocked* when Jan said she'd been murdered, I just don't understand how someone could do that! But now I don't know what to do. I mean, should I just withdraw from this whole thing and go home, or what?"

Sergeant Rice rubbed his nose hard to hide a smile.

"I'm telling you the *truth*!" she said.

"I believe you," he said sincerely. Now he was smiling openly.

"Well, then what's got you so tickled?"

"Ma'am, I understand you are telling people you think you are Ms. Henderson's sister."

"I do—and so what?"

"Well, you might want to call me as a witness if anyone doubts your claim."

Lucille couldn't think what to make of that. "Why?"

"Because both you and Ms. Henderson tend to run off at the mouth when you're feeling stressed."

"Jan does that, too?" Lucille smiled broadly, she couldn't help it. "You know, I just may ask you to be a witness," she said.

He said, "Now, if I may continue: what is your husband's full legal name?"

"Robert Lee Jones."

She answered the same set of questions about Bobby Lee that Rice had asked about her. He was fifty-three, his address and phone were the same as hers, he was employed full-time as a nurse.

"He's an RN?" Sergeant Rice asked.

"Yes," she nodded. "A surgical nurse."

He looked impressed and made a note. "Good for him! Does he like the work?"

"Yes. It's stressful, but he really likes the way the surgeons rely on him."

"You said you're a lab tech. What kind of lab?"

"It's called Advent Medical Laboratories. We do all kinds of medical tests."

"Would that include DNA?"

"Oh, yes. We get samples from all over the country."

"Do you perform some of these DNA tests yourself?"

Lucille smiled. She knew where he was going now. "Yes, I do."

"Did you take, without her permission, a hairbrush from Jan Henderson?"

Put that way, it didn't sound as much like a lark as she liked to think it was. "Yes," she admitted.

"Did you subsequently perform or have performed a DNA test on some of the hair from that brush?"

"Yes. I had it performed by a friend at another lab."

"Why did you do that?"

"I didn't want my employer to know about it."

"Why not?"

Worse and worse. Lucille almost broke into tears, but she didn't, because this man didn't look like the type to be moved by them. So she took a deep breath and told the truth. "Because I couldn't afford to pay for the test. It's an expensive one. My friend owed me a favor; I've done a couple of tests for her."

Kindly, he didn't flinch or frown. "What was the result of that test your friend performed?" he asked.

"First, there was nothing to show we couldn't be sisters. Second, there was a translocation of two genes that matched identically a translocation I have. That doesn't prove we're sisters—you can't do that with DNA. But one result of the particular translocation we share is a problem carrying babies to term. Both she and I had that problem—and so did her mother and grandmother. So this is not a new translocation—it's something handed down several generations. It's not perfect proof, but it's pretty indicative."

"But a test of Mrs. McConnell could prove she's your mother."

"Yes."

"Have you asked her to submit to a test?"

"Not yet. Jan said she would talk to her."

He made another note. "Did you ever meet Edyth Hanraty?"

"No."

"Did you try?"

"No. By the time I found out about her, she was . . . dead."

"Did you murder her?"

Even though she half-expected the question, it shocked her. "No!"

He made a lengthy note, then in an abrupt segue, he asked, "Do you knit?"

She said "yes" before she noticed he was looking at the ball of yarn on the cushion beside her. What, did he think Bobby Lee was a knitter? That sent a whole cascade of possibilities tumbling down the corridors of her mind.

"Have you ever knitted with very thin needles?"

Oh, *that*. She said, too quickly, "I tried it one time, but a few minutes of trying told me I don't have the eyes for it. That was four or five years ago, and I don't even know what I did with the needles." The laugh she forced after that statement sounded even more phony, so to steady her nerves, she resorted to good manners. "Are you sure I can't get you a Coke or something?"

"No, thank you." He again consulted his notebook. "How did you find out the name of this mysterious 'twin' at the medical conference?"

"Her name tag. We all wore name tags."

"I thought you were afraid to approach her."

"I didn't have to come all that close. They gave us these huge tags in big square holders we wore around our necks on elastic cords. Big black lettering, name and hometown, an inch high."

He nodded and made a note. "How did you find out you were adopted?"

"I didn't know until very recently, when my mother died. I'd lost my father ten years earlier, so when my mother died, we had to go through her papers and things, get the house ready to sell and all, and I found some documents that revealed the adoption. I was born in St. Paul—or rather, I was abandoned at a hospital in St. Paul by my birth mother. That was in 1959, when it was still a shameful thing to have a baby out of wedlock. Or maybe she died, and my father couldn't care for me, so he brought me to the hospital. Whoever did it didn't leave a name. So when I learned about this woman from Minnesota who looked a whole lot like me, well, naturally I was curious."

"So curious you stole her hairbrush and had a DNA test performed on it."

She nodded. "That's right. That's not weird when you think about it. You've heard the saying, 'when all you have is a hammer, every problem looks like a nail'?"

He nodded.

"So I know DNA. Nowadays, when someone wants to know for sure if he's the daddy, the first thing they do is run a DNA test. So I find out I'm adopted, and I see someone who looks a lot like me, I want to walk up and run a swab around the inside of her mouth. I couldn't do that, so I took her hairbrush."

"You were very determined to do the test."

"Yes, it was like God had given me this great big hint, and I wasn't going to just ignore it."

"I guess that makes sense."

"Sure. Oh, and I think the fact that she's in the medical field like I am encouraged me to think she's related to me. That sort of thing runs in families, too."

"Too?"

"Like being in law enforcement. We—my husband and I—know this guy, Lenny Marx. He's a cop in Houston, and his dad's a state trooper, and his brother's a deputy down at the jail. His granddad was a Texas Ranger, and his great-grandfather was sheriff of Kaufman County. This guy says that's really common."

"He's right. It is."

"Well, Jan's grandfather was a doctor, one of her sons is taking pre-med courses, and one of her nieces wants to be a nurse. No one in my adopted family was into medicine, but it's all I ever wanted to do, and my daughter is going to be a veterinarian."

"And your husband is a nurse."

"Like calling to like." Lucille nodded. "Jan married a doctor."

"So she did." He checked something in his notebook. "Can you tell me where you were late afternoon and evening the Saturday before last? That would be June twenty-second."

Lucille paused to think. "I think we went out to dinner at that Chinese restaurant on Water Street—the Big Wok or something like that. Then we came back here and watched television before we went to bed."

He wrote that down and closed his notebook. "Well, I guess that's all for now. Thank you, and good afternoon."

Lucille hurried around him to open the door. "I hope you don't suspect me."

"Of what?" said her husband, caught in the act of reaching for the doorknob. He saw Sergeant Rice and took a step back. "Who are you?" he asked sharply.

"It's Detective Sergeant Mitchell Rice, Orono Police," said Lucille, before Rice could say anything. She semaphored with her eyebrows at him.

"Oh?" he said, coming forward so Lucille had to step out of his way. "What do you want?" he asked belligerently, ignoring his wife's signals.

"I'm investigating a murder, and I was hoping your wife—or you, now you're here—might be able to help me." Rice had his ID folder out and open now.

"Well, we can't. We don't know anything about a murder. We're just up here on vacation."

"Your wife says you came up here to meet and talk with

Jan Henderson and to persuade her mother to take a DNA test to see if she's your wife's mother, too."

Bobby Lee shot Lucille a glance full of meaning. "I don't think the purpose of our coming up here is any business of yours."

"It is if it involves Edyth Hanraty or any of her heirs."

"Who's Edyth Hanraty?"

"Jan Henderson's great-aunt. And a victim of a homicide."

"If you're thinking we had anything to do with that, you're nuts."

"I don't know who had anything to do with it, but if your wife is correct—that is, if she is Susan McConnell's daughter—she is in line to inherit a great deal of money."

"Really? How much money?"

Lucille sighed; any mention of money could turn her husband's mind in an instant.

"That has yet to be determined. On the other hand, you might be aware that a person responsible for another person's demise cannot inherit anything from the decedent."

"Well, we're not responsible. Okay? And that's the end of the story, as far as I'm concerned. I'd like you to leave now." He went to the door, which Lucille had closed, and opened it again.

Rice gave him a long, considering look, but then went out. Bobby Lee slammed it shut and turned on his wife. "How much did you tell him?" he demanded.

A T closing time, Godwin picked up the plastic bag that held the stinky pillow Jan had brought in. "What's this?" he asked.

"Something a customer wants restored," said Betsy. "No, don't look at it. It smells to high heaven and probably has fleas, among other mouse leavings, all over it."

"Oh, ish!" He put it down hastily. "What are you going to do with it?"

"Take it down in the basement and put it in that big chest freezer for a couple of days. That'll take care of the livestock and most of the smell. Then we'll see."

Fifteen

❖ ❖ ❖

RICE climbed into his car thinking, *Lucille Jones was lying to me, but Bobby Lee Jones has an attitude problem.* Rice knew that the difference between people in need of an attitude adjustment and people with felony problems was not always immediately apparent. He would know more soon enough. He'd already made a note to contact Houston PD to see if either Jones had a record.

After a quick lunch at McDonald's, he stopped at Excelsior PD and sat down with Sergeant Mike Malloy. Malloy worked out of a little office he shared with a fellow detective, who was out somewhere, so Rice took his office chair. "This Hanraty case may involve two more people in Excelsior than Jan Henderson," he said, over a cup of coffee that he'd raised from awful to merely bad with two teaspoons of sugar and a big dollop of milk.

"Yeah, who?" Malloy asked, taking a gulp of his coffee without even wincing.

"A husband and wife, up from Houston. Lucille and

Bobby Lee Jones. Lucille is trying to convince Ms. Henderson that she's a long-lost sister."

Malloy snorted. "I think I once saw a silent movie with that plot."

"You probably did," nodded Rice. "But this claim has a modern twist. Ms. Jones says she has DNA evidence that backs her claim."

Malloy put his mug down, surprised. "Jones really is Henderson's sister?"

"That has not yet been proved beyond a doubt. When I took a family history from Ms. McConnell, she never mentioned a daughter she gave up. But there's a rare genetic twist in Jones's genes that she shares with Ms. Henderson. And Ms. Henderson is going to ask her mother to submit to a DNA test that could disprove the connection for sure."

Malloy nodded. "All right, that's sensible. So what's the big deal that's got you interested?"

"Miss Hanraty wrote a will dividing her estate among her female relatives, but only those descended from her sister's daughters and their daughters. So her nephew, Stewart, gets zilch and so do his four girls. But this woman, if she *is* Susan McConnell's daughter, gets a full share, and the amount may be in the millions."

Malloy's full attention was captured now. "Is there some way to fake a DNA test?"

"I don't see why you can't forge one, or put someone else's name on the results of a test you like, but you can bet the parties involved in this upcoming one will be watching the process like hawks. Lucille Jones claims she never knew about Edyth Hanraty until after the murder, but she and her husband arrived here before it happened, and her alibi is as thin as tissue paper. Plus, the murder weapon appears to be a very thin knitting needle, and Ms. Jones is a knitter."

Malloy made a whistling shape with his lips. "You like her for this?"

"Yes, I do. She's had medical training, and she didn't know Edyth Hanraty as a person like these other people do. Murdering a stranger for a couple million is a lot easier than murdering an aunt who used to give you boat rides on the lake."

RICE went straight from the cop shop to Crewel World. There he found Betsy deeply involved in a discussion of gauge for knitting felted slippers, so he turned to her employee, a medium-short male with very light brown hair and pale blue eyes that lit up when he saw the detective. Rice became left-handed long enough for the man to get an eyeful of his wedding band, and the twinkle died.

"May I help you?" asked the young man.

"I am Sergeant Mitchell Rice, Orono Police—"

"Oh, you're investigating Edyth Hanraty's murder! How interesting to meet you! I'm Godwin, Betsy's Vice President in Charge of Operations here at Crewel World, Incorporated."

Rice grinned, he couldn't help it. "Nice to meet you."

"I assume you want to talk to Ms. Devonshire," he said in a confidential tone.

"Why would you assume that?"

"Well, you certainly don't want to talk to me—do you?" The twinkle was back.

"No, I don't. Unless you can tell me if she's been conducting her own investigation."

Godwin started to say something but changed his mind. "I think you should talk directly to her. Hearsay and all that." He nodded wisely.

"Fine. When she's finished with her customer."

It was nearly five minutes before Ms. Devonshire ushered

her customer to the door. "I don't care," the woman said as she departed. "No more felting. This time, my husband can wear the slippers I made for myself, so I'm glad I didn't knit them in pink."

Betsy laughed, then turned to look at her latest visitor. "Sergeant Rice," she greeted him. "Are you here to buy another set of knitting needles?"

"No. I've just come from talking with Lucille Jones and her husband. I was wondering if you'd been talking with her."

"Yes, I have."

"About what?"

"About why she believes Jan Henderson is her sister."

"Did she show you any proof of that?"

"No."

"Do you believe her?"

"Yes. That is, I believe she had a DNA test performed that proved, to her own satisfaction, that Jan is her sister. Whether that is true, I don't know."

"When did you first see Lucille?"

"Two—no, three Sundays ago. She came to my church and we shook hands. But it wasn't until the next morning, when she came into my shop and I mistook her for Jan Henderson that I saw the resemblance." Betsy frowned. "She had her hair up on that Sunday, and Jan is a Methodist, so Lucille was . . . out of context, I guess is the best way to describe it, so I didn't notice then how much the two of them look alike."

"Jan is a regular customer?"

"Oh, yes. In fact, I was expecting her that morning."

"You know Sergeant Mike Malloy?"

"Yes, I do."

"He told me you sometimes conduct amateur investigations and that you are often successful."

Betsy looked both surprised and pleased. "How flattering of Mike to say that. He doesn't approve of amateurs, of course."

"Of course," agreed Rice, rather more warmly than he meant to. Amateurs were foolish, dangerous, and disruptive. "But he said you get results. I was hoping you could tell me something helpful about the Joneses."

"I don't know much, not yet."

"What do you make of her?"

"She's very likable—but she wants to be liked. She hopes she belongs to the McConnell family, so she's grabbing onto every sign that she and Jan share more than just physical traits. It may merely be that she's eager to belong to this family. Of course, there is a lot of money to be had if she *is* Susan's daughter. I just don't know. I feel sorry for her; it must be hard to learn the people you thought were your blood parents aren't." The look in Ms. Devonshire's eyes was thoughtful and compassionate.

"Have you met Mr. Jones?"

"Just briefly, not long enough to form an opinion."

But there was something in the way she said it that made him ask, "Still, what do you think?"

"Well, I hope you aren't confining your investigation to Lucille. As her husband, he has a lot to gain, too. He is a surgical nurse, so I assume he, even more than she, might know where to put a thin, pointed steel wire so it would stop someone's heart."

Rice thanked her and left. He had already made a note to see if either Lucille or Bobby Lee Jones were known to the Houston police, but that was because Bobby Lee had been hinky as a cat with a feather in its mouth back there at the cabin. Funny that Betsy Devonshire had come to that same conclusion—and not in a haphazard way at all.

B ETSY'S freezer was a holdover from when her sister Margot had owned the shop and lived in the apartment above it. It was enormous; God knew what Margot kept in it. Betsy put her Christmas goose in it and the occasional roast or leg of lamb too big for her freezer upstairs; but mostly she kept it for the use of her tenants.

And this. She lifted the freezer's thick lid and pulled out a big blue plastic box, which contained the white plastic garbage bag with the damaged pillow. Betsy put a layer of newspapers into the deep sink and opened the bag. The bad smell was all but gone. She lifted out the pillow. It wasn't big, about fourteen inches long by nine or ten inches high. The top was a knitted pattern of a flag, but the colors had washed to a dull blue, a pinky maroon, and a dingy white. The pillow had been about four inches thick, its sides and back made of cotton duck, once perhaps light blue or even white, now a dull gray color. The bottom and one side leaked batting from large, ragged holes.

Betsy went into a pocket and pulled out the rubber gloves she kept in her kitchen. She grasped some of the batting and began to pull. She cleared a hollow inside the pillow but was reluctant to reach too far inside, where there were likely tiny corpses of fleas and who knew what else? Maybe bigger corpses of baby mice. She went back to her apartment for a seam ripper.

The thread that had been used to sew up the seams was tough but old, and soon she had opened all of one narrow side and half of an adjoining longer side. When she emptied the batting onto the newspapers, she was glad she hadn't put her finger inside. No baby mice, but lots of their leavings. With a grimace of distaste, she wadded up the newspapers and pushed them into the plastic bag the pillow had come in.

Then she turned the pillow inside out. It had a fabric lining, but the maker apparently had chosen to use some old embroidery because there was a good amount of freehand stitching on it. Whether it was a practice piece or something else was impossible to tell, because the front was facing the flag. The back of the cloth was like a web of floss made by a drunken spider, a sign of a careless or novice stitcher, who had carried the thread over to another area to be done in the same color, rather than tucking it into nearby stitching and cutting it off. Betsy smiled at this very personal evidence of a stitcher's method. But what was on the other side? The edge of the lining had come loose when Betsy ripped open the seam, so she turned it inside out.

Protected all these years from light, the colors of the threads on the fabric were bright and fresh. The piece appeared to depict a seashore scene as seen from the sky. There were waves indicated by upside down blue Vs and dashed lines of green to show a grassy shore. A tiny sailboat and larger powerboat plowed through the Vs. There were a few buildings along the shore—hold on, here was a building Betsy recognized: The Lafayette Club. This wasn't a view of a seashore, but of Lake Minnetonka. Not the entire lake, just a portion. Near the bottom was Excelsior, marked by what was probably supposed to be a roller coaster—this map must be from back when there was an amusement park along the shore of Excelsior Bay. So over here was the Big Island, with details too small to make out.

Betsy took the emptied pillow upstairs, into her apartment's living room. She turned on her Dazor magnifying light and held the stitched map—for so she now thought of it—under the powerful rectangular magnifying glass. There was a square-built house along the Crystal Bay shore that Betsy thought she remembered seeing from the road. Was that the Hanraty mansion?

And there were two cottages stitched on one side of the Big Island. Betsy knew there were more than two families who lived out there. Personally, she thought they were crazy, because there was no bridge to the shore. Residents had to use a boat in the summer and a snowmobile in the winter—but in the spring and fall, when the ice blocked boats but was too thin to support even foot travel, they were castaways.

Well, except that nowadays there were cell phones and television sets and radio and the Internet.

Holding her breath, Betsy bent over her Dazor lamp and saw, along a broad path—or perhaps it was a road—a red heart done in tiny, perfect satin stitches. The road continued past one of the cottages near the shore—a miniature dock was indicated, with a brown triangle indicating a boat tied up to it. A curl of smoke came out of the cabin's chimney.

The stitching on the map was clear but hasty, with uneven stitches and mismatched colors. And they'd run a bit—Jan had said the pillow was found in an old boat, so doubtless the pillow had been wet on occasion. But the artist was sure of her topic.

Around the edge of the map were small letters. On two sides they were partly hidden by the seam of the pillow, and on the third side, mice had chewed them away. Betsy's careless hand with the seam ripper had damaged the writing on the fourth side. Holding her breath again, she put the pillow under the magnifying light and turned it back on. ". . . there will your . . ." read one segment, and here, ". . . will your hear . . ." No, not hear, heart. She straightened a bit, took a deep breath, and bent over the light again. ". . . where your treasure . . . will your heart . . ." No good, no good! She let her breath out in a sigh of exasperation and tried again. Okay, it was something repeated, because the same phrases kept turning up. The chewed edge had almost no letters, but gently pulling at the sewed edges gave her some more letters. Yes! *Where your heart lies, there will your treasure be also.*

Deep in thought, Betsy took the pillow back down to the basement. She plugged the deep sink and ran cool water into it. She added a little Orvus—a horse shampoo taken up by stitchers as a gentle detergent for needlework—sank the pillow into it and stirred the water for a minute. The words were a transposition of the Biblical verse, "Where your treasure lies, there will your heart be also." There had been a tiny red heart stitched near that tree on the Big Island. Which raised the obvious question: What was buried under the heart?

Sixteen

❖ ❖ ❖

WEDNESDAY was Betsy's day off, so it was kind of a shame that it was also a water-aerobics day. Three mornings a week, she went over to the Courage Center in Golden Valley for an hour of jumping jacks, twisting, leaping like a frog, and other exercises, beginning at six thirty. In the morning. In the pool. It was the only exercise program she'd found that she'd stuck with, mostly because there wasn't anything else going on at that hour of the day to give her an excuse not to go. And besides, by now she was friends with her fellow sufferers and enjoyed being with them.

Wednesday was Vicki's day to lead the group. Music always pulsed in the air to encourage movement during these classes, and Vicki liked salsa. So, although it was an unholy hour to begin moving briskly when Betsy and the others waded onto the level floor of very warm water, the salsa rhythms made her feel chipper. She couldn't understand the words, but the *chicka-boom* was insistent; she went to the platform where the water was just over waist deep and began a fast walk. Vicki was already in the water, a dark-haired woman in her late forties, slim and amazingly flexible. "All right," she called out from her place in the water, "let's side step, stretch it out."

Each of the other Early Birders had her continuing story: Ingrid was moving rather gingerly as she recovered from a broken hip; April was yawning because she was taking night classes toward a library degree; Barbara was cross with the inefficient builders putting an addition on her house; and Mary was excited about a forthcoming trip to Thailand. Even Vicki had a life outside the pool. She and her husband maintained a big sailboat up on Lake Superior, and she often livened up the sessions with funny stories about her adventures in sailing—and the endless work it took to keep the craft seaworthy.

But today Betsy let the conversation flow around her all but unheard. She was planning a day of detective work.

She had talked to Stewart last night on the phone, and he had agreed to meet her for lunch. He knew she was an amateur sleuth—Jan had talked to him a time or two about her friend's strange ability to prove the innocence of falsely suspected people. Now, offered a chance to help his favorite niece by helping her friend, he was very willing.

But first, Betsy was going to meet Susan at the Hanraty mansion. Betsy had heard about the interesting visit paid there by Edyth's family and the selection of memorabilia.

But Susan had said something else when she'd come into the shop with a counted cross-stitch piece to be finished. "Nobody took what I expected except Katie. The strangest was Bernie. She picked this abstract painting nobody else even liked."

Betsy had remarked lightly that there was no accounting for taste. "Well," Susan had said, "sometimes there is, and the accountant's name is Stewart." Betsy had heard about Stewart trying to change his aunt's mind about her will by visiting her and doing odd jobs around her place. Which meant, of course, that he had several chances to look around. Everything was still there; the *executrix*—such quaint terms the law had!—hadn't completed her inventory yet.

This was going to be a very interesting tour, thought Betsy, doing the grapevine to her left: right foot over left, step left, right foot behind left, step left, and reverse to cross the other way. It made her feel graceful and accomplished.

As she stepped, she thought about old houses, either properly restored or never altered, and how wonderful they were at giving modern people a glimpse of lost times. This house would tell her something about Edyth Hanraty—and perhaps offer a clue to the person who could not wait for this very elderly woman to die.

Then, after lunch with Stewart, she had arranged to meet Lucille and Bobby Lee, ostensibly to get support in her quest to prove Jan innocent, but in reality to explore their personalities. Could one or both of them be the kind so eager to get rich they would resort to murder?

After riding around on foam plastic noodles in the deep end for fifteen minutes, the group paddled down to the shallow end to stretch out, and class was over.

Betsy showered, changed into pink clam-diggers and a pink gingham sleeveless top, and headed out for Orono. The air was already hot.

It was eight forty when she pulled in the driveway of Edyth Hanraty's mansion, ten minutes after the arranged time. There was no for-sale sign up yet, but the wrought-iron gate was open.

The house had a solid look that took the preceding Victorians to task for frivolity. Betsy went all the way up under the porte cochere, a little surprised not to see Susan there or in back. She got out and started around to the front door, then saw a little hybrid Honda coming up the drive. Susan's.

Susan got out, a little breathless. "Sorry to be late. Mrs. Beekman from church called, and I just couldn't seem to get

off the phone." She looked up at the big front porch. "Shall
we go in?"

They went up the front steps together. From a distance,
the simple design had made the house look ordinary in size;
now, up close, it could be seen for the mansion it really was.

"When will your family members be able to pick up the
items they've claimed?" asked Betsy.

"After tomorrow, I think." Susan unlocked the carved-
oak door. "The attorney for the estate said she was having
the items valued this week, and she called last night to ask
if she could talk to me this afternoon, so I think that means
she's done it. Katie's champing at the bit; she bought a chest
to store her silver in—Aunt Edyth kept it in a special drawer
lined with silver cloth in the pantry."

Betsy nodded understanding.

"But some of the others won't get their things right
away; they have to arrange for a place to keep them—Jason's
one, there's no room in his garage for the motorcycle. And
God knows where Stewart is going to keep the boat he
chose." Susan opened the door, and they went into the hall.
Betsy noted at once the Navajo blanket in its glass case.
"Oh, how *beautiful*!"

"Yes, isn't it?"

"Is this one of the very valuable items you believe Stewart coached his daughters to pick?" asked Betsy.

"Yes. Lexie—Alexandra—Stewart and Terri's second-
oldest daughter, is going to take that. Stewart and Terri will
store it for her until she finishes college."

"Help me out here," said Betsy. "How valuable is it?"

"Well, I did what Stewart probably did. I Googled
'Navajo blanket' and found nothing exactly like this one,
and only a few similar ones—and they seem to run between
sixteen and twenty thousand dollars."

"Oh, my!" said Betsy, turning for another look at the blanket in its glass case.

Susan went into the living room, flipped on the lights, and sank down on the timber and plum-cushion settee. She looked around and thumped a fist on the wooden arm. "Damn my conniving brother!"

Betsy followed her. "But after all, why are you so upset?" she asked. "You and Jan agreed to the arrangement that they could pick whatever one item they wanted from the house."

"You don't understand. I think Stewart will ask them to sell their choices so he can have the money to start up that new business he wants!" Susan stood and walked around the room, twisting one fist into the other hand. "That man has started enough businesses to have made six fortunes, but he's ruined every one of them! He's lazy, that's his biggest flaw. He loves the idea of big money, and his schemes match his ambition—but when it comes to the daily struggle, he just can't do it! He's a great talker, he gets people all excited, and they invest in his schemes—then he loses their money. And then they let him get away with it because he sounds so plausible when he starts making excuses. What has me angry is that while he was right to get the girls a share in the estate, he'll take the money they could have realized and will waste that, too!"

"Do you really think he'd take the money from his children?" Betsy asked. "That's a terrible accusation!"

"You don't know how terrible he is. All his life he's believed that what he wants is the most important thing in the world—and everyone has catered to that belief. Even I did it, for years and years."

What an awful thing to do to someone, thought Betsy. How destructive and cruel. But she didn't say so, because it wouldn't help, not now. She did say, "Isn't Katie an exception? She's married and has her own home to worry about. She's going to have a baby, and she's got college expenses ahead. Surely she's not going to allow herself to be talked into selling that silver flatware to satisfy another one of her dad's pipe dreams."

Susan came back to lean on the settee. "You may be right there. After all, she's seen enough of them collapse. Plus, she really seemed to want that service. You should have heard her raptures about it at the lawyer's office—" Then her expression changed. "No, no, it was Katie's little speech that gave Stewart the opening to ask that his girls be allowed to take one item from the house. And I can't believe he came up with that on the spot. No, that was a setup. He came in there all primed to do that. Katie started the ball rolling, that's all, so she must be in on it! He is *so slick.* He makes me sick!"

"I don't think I'm clear on just what happened," said Betsy.

"We all met at the attorney's office—"

"What's her name?" interrupted Betsy.

"Marcia Weiner. She explained the will and said that its terms stipulated that Aunt Edyth's estate was to be liquidated, with most of the money going to start a foundation to give scholarships to women studying business. The rest was to be divided equally between me and my daughter, Jan. Well, that started a discussion about the house and its valuable contents. I don't think Ms. Weiner understood that Aunt Edyth was a very astute collector of art. Katie asked if family members might buy something at the estate sale and said she'd like to buy the silver. Well, she can't afford it. It's Art Nouveau and sterling, a service for twenty-four. Its value is tens of thousands of dollars. And Stewart jumped in and said we all knew the will wasn't fair, and couldn't his daughters each take just one thing from the house? And we agreed that would at least make it a little more fair. And somehow, I don't remember how, it turned into every family member could take one thing. We agreed to meet here at the house so everyone could get a look at the things inside it and decide what he or she wanted. And right here in this room, Bernie surprised us all by saying she wanted that painting." Susan pointed to the abstract over the fireplace.

Betsy went over for a closer look. To her, it looked at first like one of those paintings that zoo elephants did, just colored streaks applied slapdash, mostly horizontal with a vertical here and there. Then, as she continued to gaze at it, it seemed to turn into a vague expression of a horse race, with the vertical streaks being jockeys.

"I kind of like it," said Betsy. Then she asked, "How old is Bernie?"

"Sixteen," Susan said dryly.

"Maybe she has an artistic nature?"

"No, not Bernie. But I remember something Stew said in the kitchen when we were concerned about how valuable the antique silver service Katie wanted was. He said, as if he was teasing, that maybe Bernie's painting was the most valuable thing in the house." She looked at Betsy. "He was wrong. It's the second most valuable thing. There's an eighteenth century four-poster bed upstairs that's the most valuable, then this painting, then Katie's silver."

"*This* painting is very valuable?" Betsy tried to keep the doubt out of her voice.

"Yes, it's an early example of Joan Mitchell's work. I described it to someone at the Walker Art Museum, and she said it might be by Joan Mitchell, so I looked her up on the Internet. I found this exact painting, and it said 'in a private collection.' It didn't give a value, but some of the prices of her other works about took my breath away."

"Who claimed the bed?" asked Betsy.

"No one. Stew said he would have, except then we all would have called him a gold digger."

"What made you suspect this plot of Stewart's, anyway?" asked Betsy.

"What happened was, he slipped up and mentioned that two framed posters on a bedroom wall were worth several thousand dollars, and I asked him how he knew, and he admitted he'd looked up a few things."

"Would you have called him a gold digger?"

"Yes, indeed."

They walked through the house, Susan pointing out various items—the Hovby dining room set, the silver, the Remington horse, the autographed Hemingway first edition—and explaining who had chosen what.

"What did Stewart pick?"

Susan laughed harshly. "Nothing in the house. He picked Aunt Edyth's old motorboat we found out in a shed. It's a mess. It's going to cost a lot of money to fix up. He wants to use it as an advertising gimmick in the fishing business he wants to start." She told Betsy about Stewart approaching her for a loan to restore the boat and get his business up and running. "I told him no, of course. And I warned Jan that he'd be coming after her next."

"If he needs money to start a business, you would have thought he'd at least not pick something that was going to cost him money," said Betsy.

"That's our golden-haired boy all over," sighed Susan. "His boating business may be a really good idea—and if he did have the money, he could do worse than have that boat as part of the business. It used to be kind of famous out here on the lake."

"Why? Is it steam powered, like the *Minnehaha*?"

"No, it's not that old. It's a runabout from the twenties, made of wood, with an inboard motor. And it's big—more than thirty feet long. I'm sure there are people who'd get a thrill out of riding in it, some of them people who would remember seeing it on the lake when they were kids. But he couldn't charge them enough to make up for what it's going to cost to repair."

"Maybe it's not going to cost as much as you think."

"Oh, it's a real mess. Would you like to see it?"

"Sure."

"Come on. It's out back."

They went downstairs and out the back door from the kitchen. "Looks like that building used to be a stable," said Betsy.

"It was. Aunt Edyth and my mother had ponies when they were young."

The padlock wasn't closed. Susan pulled it out of the hasp and opened the big doors to let the light in. The stuff that had formerly blocked the doors was piled up on either side, leaving a clear view of the boat.

"Golly!" said Betsy. "It *is* big!" She went closer. "Is it a Chris-Craft?"

"No, it was built by someone, or a company, named Gar Wood. The engine is a World War I aircraft engine."

"Are you serious? An aircraft engine? Where would you find a mechanic who could work on it?"

"Exactly," said Susan with a dry tone. "Where indeed?"

Betsy smiled. "I bet it used to just tear up the water."

"It sure did," said Susan, a smile flickering across her face. "Nothing on the lake could keep up with it."

"You've ridden in it?"

"Yes, I have, lots of times. Aunt Edyth was still driving it on the lake in the early sixties. But look at it now—the finish is destroyed, the seat covers are shot, and after all these years of sitting, no doubt it leaks like a sieve." She walked up to it, reached as if to touch it, then turned with an angry gesture. "Let's get out of here."

Susan stalked to her car, said a brief good-bye, and left. Betsy stood awhile, thinking, then looked at her watch and made a little exclamation. She hurried to her own car, drove out through the pillars and turned left, heading up Highway 15.

Weaving between the bays of Lake Minnetonka, she followed Highway 15 until, near Wayzata, it connected with Highway 12. At this point Twelve still thought it was I-394, but a couple of miles west it went around a sharp bend and became a two-lane highway, and soon after that ran along the south side of Long Lake, where Billy's Lighthouse Restaurant was. Billy's was well-known—it appeared to be just a shaggy roadside place, as much bar as restaurant.

Betsy had barely found a parking place when she saw Stewart crossing the lot, heading for the front door. He had made a reservation for an indoor seat—there was a large deck out back, facing the lake and its surround of trees, but the weather was too hot and sticky to dine *al fresco.* The indoor dining area was faced with tall windows that gave the same view, unleavened by mosquitos and humidity.

They both ordered the walleye, the most popular fish in Minnesota—lutefisk might be more famous, but it certainly wasn't the best tasting. Billy's walleye was fresh and came with a white wine and grape sauce that was fabulous.

Betsy found Stewart a charming luncheon companion. He told stories about Lake Minnetonka she had never heard before and described catching fish in a way that made her decide she really needed to try for a "lunker" herself some day soon.

"You know," he said, "you have the quiet, sensible attitude of a good angler, and I really look forward to showing you some of the places that have rarely failed me."

"Thank you," said Betsy.

"In fact, I wish you were more of an angler, because I'm working on a business deal that could earn you a lot of money, if you wanted in—but you have to understand the lure of the lake—" He stopped short and began to laugh. "My best pun in a long while!" he said. "Maybe I should name my company Lure of the Lake!"

"What company?" asked Betsy.

"It's an idea I've been working on, ironing out the kinks and all. You know, if you really understood the powerful attraction that fishing holds for Minnesota residents and tourists, you'd know how valuable a business catering to that might be."

"If you're about to begin a pitch for an investment, I'm going to ask you to contact my investment advisor, Marty Kaplan. I do nothing without his recommendation."

"May I call you about contacting him as my plans mature?"

"Certainly. But can't you persuade your daughters to invest in this plan?"

"They haven't got the kind of money it would take." He looked surprised that she would suggest such a thing.

"They may now. Didn't they each pick items of considerable value from Edyth Hanraty's house?"

His eyes went frosty. "Who told you that?"

"Susan. More, she said you at least suggested to each of them what to pick with an eye toward getting them to invest in your new company."

"Well, damn her!" He scowled and took a breath to continue. "All right, since you got the distorted picture from her, let me tell you what I really did. I did everything in my power to convince Aunt Edyth to leave a share to each of them—and then when she wouldn't budge, I asked her to leave each of them something from the house, as a memoriam. She didn't seem to think that was such an awful idea, and so I went on the Internet to do some research. I picked the most valuable items I could find the value of and told Lexie, Bernie, and CeeCee about them. I said that I would try to get permission for each of them to pick something, and if I succeeded they weren't to get all sentimental but to pick from the list I gave them. That way, they'd have something more like a share in what should have been their inheritance. So Susan is right, I coached the girls—all but Katie. She knew she wanted the silverware and wouldn't think of picking anything else. But then I found out what it was worth, and thought, *attagirl!* Now even Susan will agree the will was unfair, so why she's all mad about this now, I don't know. She and Jan were okay with them picking something. I just wish this could've been done by the old woman herself. I'm so angry she was murdered! What a stupid waste! I hope that police investigator finds out who did this."

"So you didn't tell Katie to pick the silver," said Betsy.

"No, she's wanted that silver ever since she first saw it—when she was about ten years old. I told her to register the pattern for a wedding present, but she couldn't find anything like it. Then I told her to ask about buying it at the estate sale. And then I brought up my idea that each of the girls should get to pick something, and when they didn't jump all over me, I decided to expand the request so that everyone got a chance to grab something. I wouldn't have done it, except it's not like Jan or Susan are hurting for money."

"Susan seems rather down on you, but Jan doesn't."

He nodded. "Jan's a good sport. If she were mine, I'd say she was a chip off the old block—but for her to be mine I would've had to've gotten married before I started shaving." He grinned.

"Did she know your Aunt Edyth well?"

He considered that. "Pretty well. When Jan started nursing school, the old woman asked to see her—there was a bit of a rift between Susan and Aunt Edyth over Susan's marrying so young, and visits really slacked off. But Aunt Edyth liked Jan. Not Jason, of course. I don't think he's been out there more than four times his whole life. But Jan's kind of a regular."

"Did they ever quarrel that you know of?"

Stewart shook his head. "Not that I ever heard of. And I think Jan would've told me. She and I are buds from way back. I used to take her fishing when she was just a tyke, back before I started having my own set of girls."

"So Jan was quick to approve your proposal to let your daughters pick an item from the house?"

Stewart nodded. He was using a wad of bread to soak up the last of the delicious sauce on his plate.

"And this proposal wasn't a scheme to get your hands on items of value to fund your fishing business?"

"No, it wasn't." He dropped the bread on the plate and looked at Betsy. "Do you have children?"

"No."

"Too bad, because then you'd understand how I love my girls and want to give them everything they need to get a good start in life. I've never been a good provider. I just can't get the hang of it somehow, so I couldn't give them the finer things myself. But I wasn't going to pass up a chance for them to acquire something of real value. They may have to sell those things, but the money will be theirs, to pay for college or whatever they need." He said it very firmly. Betsy nearly smiled to think Stewart was confessing that his latest business scheme wasn't the surest way of building a secure fund for his daughters.

Since she was paying for the lunch, she got to ask if he wanted dessert.

"They do a terrific cherry cobbler," he said promptly.

So Betsy ordered some, too. After it arrived, she continued. "Susan said she quit going to her Aunt Edyth's house when she got into high school, but I'm wondering if she didn't spend a last summer there later than that. I know she's quite a bit older than you—"

Stewart smiled a little sadly. "Ten years isn't as big a gap nowadays as it was when we were kids."

"That's very true. Do you recall what year it was when Susan last spent part or all of a summer at the Hanraty house?"

Stewart looked up at the ceiling while he calculated. "I was going into third grade, I think. No, fourth. The summer before I had gone out there a couple of times with Suze and got to ride in the boat, but for some reason that summer she got to stay out there the whole vacation and I wasn't allowed to go at all. Susan was being a typical teenager, full of angst and very touchy. Mama said she'd come home happier, but she didn't. I was upset about not getting another boat ride, I remember—but I did get to go see the place decorated for Christmas."

"What year was that?"

He thought for a moment. "That must have been the summer of 1959."

Betsy smiled. "That was the year Alaska was admitted to the Union."

"Was it?" He looked at her, surprised. "You may be right. But don't you mean Hawaii and Alaska? Didn't they come in together?"

"No, they made Hawaii wait until the next year, 1960."

"The things you know," he said admiringly.

"But you're sure 1959 was the year Susan spent the summer with your Aunt Edyth?"

"Yes. She hadn't gone out for a long stay the year before, but she went the whole summer that year. And that was the last time. She never went on even an overnight trip out there after that. Of course, she got married right out of high school, so she must've been dating Dave by then. Aunt Edyth was very disappointed about her interest in boys, so I bet that summer was a long one for Susan, with Aunt Edyth trying to talk Susan out of getting serious over Dave. I can remember our mother saying the letter she wrote to Susan after the wedding burned the fingers of anyone who touched it." He smiled. "I think that was the first figure of speech I ever really understood."

"Did she ever express direct hostility to you?"

"Not to *me*, no. As a representative of the male sex, you bet. You started her on the subject, and she'd give you a real stem-winder."

Betsy was still thinking about Stewart's last comment when she got home from lunch. She was in the middle of straightening up the apartment when the phone rang. It was Jan, very distressed. "Where have you been?" she demanded. "I've been calling and calling!"

"I'm sorry, I just got home a little while ago, and I forgot to check my phone messages. What's the problem?"

"That police detective, Sergeant Mitchell Rice, came over to our house last night with a *search warrant*! He went into my needle case and counted my Skacel steels—and the one that was missing is *back*! I told him I didn't replace it, but I'm sure he doesn't believe me! He took all of them away with him, and I'm sure he thinks I'm a murderer! Betsy, I don't understand why there was one missing and now it's back. I didn't replace it! What am I going to do? I'm sure he thinks I murdered Aunt Edyth. What will I do if he comes and arrests me?"

"Where are you?"

"I'm at the clinic, of course! Can he just walk in and put handcuffs on me?"

Betsy tried for a soothing tone. "I don't think he will do anything like that, at least not right now. It's not illegal to lose and then find a knitting needle."

"But I didn't lose it. That's what's really scary!"

"Then someone else took it and either replaced it or brought it back. Who's been in your house since you first noticed it missing?"

"Who knows? People can walk in any time they want!" Jan's voice had risen perilously high.

"Jan, Jan, calm down. Are you saying you usually leave your doors unlocked? Come on, think, talk to me. This may be important."

"Yes, okay, I understand. All right." There was the sound of a breath being taken. "All right," she said again, in a quieter voice. "No, I don't leave my doors unlocked when no one is at home. Let me think. Lucille and Bobby Lee came to supper night before last. Katie came over earlier that afternoon to borrow a knitting pattern. Uncle Stewart brought her. He was taking her out to lunch, I think."

"Did any of them have access to your sewing room while you weren't right there with them?"

"Gosh, let me think." After a few moments, Jan said, "Well, I guess any one of them could have. Bobby Lee asked to use the bathroom—I think he really likes our bathroom. That's the second time he's been in the house, and both times he's gone up to use the bathroom. I don't think Lucille did. I sent Katie up to look for the pattern by herself. And I left Stewart alone when I went to make coffee for them. That's not much help, is it? I mean any of them could have gone up there."

"Did Sergeant Rice ask you about someone else having access to the needles?"

"No—and I didn't think to tell him. Oh, Betsy—"

"Now Jan, don't panic. If you're really scared, call an attorney. And if you do get asked to come to the police station, don't tell anyone anything. They'll give you that spiel about your right to silence, and you say, all right, I won't talk without a lawyer present. And stick to that."

"Oh, my God, you do think he's going to arrest me! You think I'm guilty!"

"No, I don't—" but she was speaking into a dead phone. Jan had hung up.

Seventeen

BETSY decided she'd better check her phone messages. Besides two frantic calls from Jan, she found a message to call the shop. "Betsy," Godwin said when he answered, "Mrs. Halloway was here a little while ago. She wants to return the knitting needles she bought last month. She's got the receipt and everything, but the needles aren't in their original packet. She says she didn't realize right away they're the wrong size. I told her I'd have to ask you."

Betsy, savoring this chance to do something mundane and shop-related, thought a few moments. "What do you think?" she asked.

"I think she only had one project to knit on size fours and doesn't intend to have another. And I'm a little tired of her using us as a rental store."

Betsy smiled at this confirmation of her own opinion. Mrs. Halloway was a great one for returned lightly used items, from books to gadgets. "Offer her half the purchase price, and if she takes it, put them in the table bin." Betsy kept a wide-mouthed vase on the library table filled with items customers could try out.

"Gotcha," said Godwin and hung up.

As Betsy went back to making her apartment presentable, she got an idea. She called Sergeant Rice at his office in Orono, but he wasn't there, of course, so she left a message asking him to call.

She had barely hung up when her doorbell rang, and she went to buzz in Lucille and Bobby Lee. They walked in with that attached-at-the-hip pose common to newlyweds—which they weren't. So perhaps they were more like the couples in the scary movies who find themselves in a large, dark forest and hear a deep rumbling from not very far away. In this case, it was Lucille being the hero, and Bobby Lee the nervous sidekick.

Betsy, trying to convince them she was not the big, bad wolf, said, "Sit down, please. May I offer you something to drink? I have Diet Pepsi, Diet Squirt, and raspberry iced tea."

"The tea, please," said Lucille.

"Pepsi, thank you," said Bobby Lee, his drawl more apparent than his wife's.

Betsy filled three tall glasses with chipped ice and poured the drinks over it—she selected the tea for herself, too. She gave them their drinks and sat down in her comfortable easy chair. "What do you think of the weather we're having?" Though it was warmer than yesterday, the high today had been only in the mideighties.

Bobby Lee grinned. "Feels like the middle of November to me."

"Doesn't it ever get cold in your part of Texas?"

"Oh, sure," said Lucille. "Late in December or early in January we usually get some frosts—once in a while, it even snows. But it melts the next day. We did have a bad ice storm a few years back, though it was worse just up the road in Oklahoma. I like it up here like it is right now. It's very comfortable."

"Just a little colder than back home this time of year," said Bobby Lee, mildly venturing to disagree.

"Well, yes," conceded Lucille. "But summer back home can be cruel. Some days my daddy used to say it was hotter than a goat in a pepper patch. I like this better; in fact, it's the oddest thing, how I feel kind of at home. Like I've returned after a long time away."

"Not me," said Bobby Lee. "People up here are as cold as the weather." He pulled up his shoulders as if bracing against a chill breeze.

Betsy said, "Bobby Lee, I know just how you feel. When I first came here from San Diego, I was really struck by how cool and distant people were. But after I'd been here a while, I realized they're just as kind as people are anywhere. They just don't make a show of it."

"It's what's called Scandinavian reserve, isn't it?" asked Lucille.

"Yes," said Betsy with a nod. "And it takes a while to get used to."

The pair were relaxed now, pleased to find a fellow traveler: Betsy was also—or had been—a stranger to these parts.

"Did you ever see so much water?" asked Bobby Lee. "I bet they have a flood every year. You can't drive ten minutes without coming to a lake."

Betsy said, "We get little floods when it rains too much, but big floods are rare. The land up here is used to dealing with water. I've been told the motto on the license plates—'10,000 Lakes'—is an understatement. Which is also typical."

Bobby Lee snorted in wry agreement.

Lucille took a drink of her tea. "This is delicious," she said.

But Bobby Lee put his soft drink down, indicating he'd

had enough chitchat. "Why did you want to talk to us?" he asked.

As usual, Betsy was blunt. "Because I'm trying to prove that Jan didn't murder her great-aunt. I've been poking around, and I've found out some things. Unfortunately, they don't fit together in any way I can make sense of."

"I don't see what we can do to help," said Bobby Lee. When Lucille seemed about to speak, he overran her with, "And I'm not sure we should interfere. After all, that police detective hasn't arrested her. Maybe he doesn't think she's guilty."

"Now, Bobby Lee, I told Betsy we'd do whatever we can to help. After all, Jan's a friend—maybe more than a friend." She turned to Betsy. "Does Sergeant Rice really think Jan is guilty?"

"I know he strongly suspects her, but I don't think he has enough evidence to arrest her."

"Why does he suspect her?"

"I'm not really sure. I'm not an authorized investigator, remember, so the people in charge don't have to tell me anything. That's why I'm grateful you agreed to talk to me."

"Well, I can't believe Jan's a murderer," said Lucille emphatically.

"Me, neither," said Bobby Lee, but more slowly.

"Have you met her mother?" asked Betsy.

"Nope," said Bobby Lee.

"No," said Lucille. "I want to, but I'm scared to. I think she may be my genetic mother, but maybe she isn't. What if she is, but when I meet her, I don't like her? What if she isn't? You know, what if the genetic thing is just some kind of coincidence?"

"Are you willing to undergo a genetic test to compare your genes with hers?"

Lucille took a deep breath. "Yes," she said, exhaling. "Because I have to know one way or the other."

"Has Sergeant Rice asked you where you were the night Edyth Hanraty was murdered?"

"Yes," said Lucille, "and we were in our cabin, just the two of us. Not much of an alibi."

"Do you have a set of double-zero Skacels?"

Lucille's eyes widened. "No. That is, I used to have them. I was going to try to learn to knit lace, but it was too hard. I don't remember throwing them away, so I suppose they're somewhere in my house, but I couldn't say for sure. I haven't seen them for months—but I haven't been looking. I do know I didn't bring them with me."

"Do you know how to pith a frog?"

Lucille's blue eyes widened, but she answered bravely, "Sure. I haven't done it since college, but it's not something you forget. I hated doing it, because you cut them open and their little heart is still beating and you don't know if they can feel what's going on. But it's what you have to do to learn what you need to know."

Bobby Lee said, "I used to do it for her—we met in a biology class. I didn't mind it." He made a descriptive movement with his hands. "It's not hard to do once you figure out where to stick the needle in."

"Bobby Lee!" said Lucille.

"Yes, please don't give me any details," said Betsy, hastily. She took a drink of her tea. "Have you been to see Edyth Hanraty's house?"

"No, of course not," said Lucille, surprised. "Why?"

"Susan gave me a tour. It's got some fabulous things in it. Edyth Hanraty was quite a collector of antiques and art. I wonder if that taste for collecting got handed down—have you been in Jan's house?"

"Yes, just once. It's nice—nicer than ours, but not as big."

"Oh, I think ours is plenty nice," said Bobby Lee.

"Did she show you the whole house?" asked Betsy.

"Oh, yeah, we got what she called the Nickel Tour. She is a collector, but it's charts; she has a whole filing cabinet drawer full of them."

"Have you met her husband?"

"Once. The three of them and the two of us went out to dinner one night. Hugs—isn't that a cute nickname?—he's real nice, and I like their boy, Ronnie, and we all got along just fine." She looked at Bobby Lee for confirmation, and he nodded in agreement.

"Hugs is all right," he said, "despite the nickname."

Betsy said, "Lucille, you share a whole lot of likes and dislikes with Jan—almost as if you were identical twins separated at birth. How many of the things you say you like that Jan also likes are real, and how many did you come up with after you met her?"

Bobby Lee stood up, but before he could say anything, Lucille told him to sit down. "How did you know?" she said to Betsy.

"Well," Betsy said, "Jan, she rattled on and on about how alike you are, and I began to wonder how two different women could compile two lists so nearly alike. You know, she was actually relieved to hear that you put some imitation bullet holes in your PT Cruiser, because she wouldn't dream of doing such a thing."

Lucille laughed. "I remember reading that fortune tellers just listen to their customers and repeat back what they tell them, and the customers think their minds are being read. So all right, I did a little of that with Jan. When she'd say she liked fishing, I'd let on how amazed I was that I liked fishing, too." She took a drink of her raspberry tea. "But there are some real things that we both do or like. We both love needlework, for example. And it's true that I always wanted to be a nurse like she is, but I couldn't afford the years of training. And I did always want a red PT, but we couldn't afford one."

"Are you driving a rental?" asked Betsy.

Bobby Lee swelled up a little and said, "I won it for her in a poker game."

Betsy got a glimpse of fear in Lucille's eyes, and a little light went on in her own head. She asked, "Bobby Lee, how long have you had a problem with gambling?"

"I don't have a problem!"

Betsy let that claim hang in the air. She sat back, sipped her tea, and waited.

Lucille looked near to tears but didn't say anything. Finally Bobby Lee said, "All right, maybe I do have a problem. But Lucille got on my case about it till I finally joined Gamblers Anonymous. I've been going to meetings, even up here. And I haven't been in a casino for almost a year. But not long back I got back into poker with some old friends. That's where I won the Cruiser, but Lucille almost made me give it back, she was so angry. Would you believe it was winning her that Cruiser that got me to quit gambling?"

Lucille said quickly, "That's true, it really is. All he ever talked about were the big pots he won, but all I could see was that there wasn't enough money to pay the bills. And I agree, somehow that PT Cruiser was the last straw. We each have a car—we have to with both of us working, and our jobs nowhere near the same place. My car was a nice little Kia, nothing to brag about, but reliable. Yes, I saw the Cruisers around and I wanted one—they're sharp and cool. But that was one of those 'someday' wishes, y'know? 'Someday I'm gonna have me a swimming pool. Someday I'll be able to hire a cleaning lady. Someday we'll take a trip to Hawaii.' We're still digging out of the hole he got us into with his gambling, so that 'someday' is a long way off. He won that car off a friend of ours, and I was ashamed to speak to him next time I saw him. But it made me madder and madder, and finally I just let it all boil over and told Bobby Lee I was leaving him if he didn't quit gambling."

"But you didn't make him give it back," Betsy said before she could stop herself.

"No. No, I didn't. Did you ever hear how to make a dog quit killing chickens?"

"I didn't know dogs killed chickens."

"Some do—the ones that live on a ranch. They think it's a game. Anyway, what you do is, you tie a chicken he killed around his neck and make him wear it till it rots off. He'll never kill one again."

Betsy looked at Bobby Lee. The look on his face was so pained she nearly cried out. He said, "I was so proud to give her that Cruiser, but she made me feel like a chicken-killin' dog. That was when I hit bottom and found the only way out was up." He smiled like it hurt his mouth. "I'd still feel like one, except Ham's wife made him join Gamblers Anonymous, too, and told us it was worth losin' the vee-hickle if it made him quit gambling."

"That was tough love," Lucille said. "Tough on both of us, but I'm proud of the way he came around. And in another couple-three years, we'll be out of debt."

Betsy said, "It may be sooner than that, if you really are Susan McConnell's daughter and in line for a substantial inheritance."

Lucille sat a moment thinking about that. Then she sighed deeply. "I almost can't think too much about that. It isn't what I came up here for, really it isn't. I just want to know where I came from."

Betsy said, "If you are her daughter, why does Susan McConnell deny it's even possible?"

"I wish I knew!" cried Lucille. She drew a deep breath. "Because maybe it isn't true. But the DNA links are real! Oh, I don't know what to think about all this!"

"When did you find out about the money?"

"Jan told me about it the second time we got together. She told me about the will her great-aunt wrote. We joked a little bit about how, if I really were her sister, I could claim some of the money. Only I wasn't joking. I was so surprised I didn't know what to say, all that money, and some of it could be mine, so I just went along with her joke. I don't know if she remembers that conversation—"

"She's aware that if you really are her sister, you have a legitimate claim to a share in the inheritance," said Betsy.

"Do you know how much money we're talking about?" asked Bobby Lee, trying to make the question casual.

"No," said Betsy. A thought struck her. "I don't want to unduly alarm you, but it occurs to me that if a member of the family murdered Edyth Hanraty for the money, he or she isn't going to be happy to find half of it may be carted off to Texas."

THE next morning, Jan was walking by her husband's office when she heard the phone ring. It was near lunchtime, and the clinic receptionist was gone. The other two nurses were helping Doctor with twin five-year-olds who were strenuously objecting to being given their school shots, so Jan stepped in and picked up the phone. "Young America Health Clinic," she said. "Nurse Henderson speaking."

"Just the person I was seeking!" said Stewart in a bright voice. "May I buy you lunch?"

This was different, Stewart offering to pay for lunch. "What's up?" she asked.

"You said we could talk sometime, and I was hoping today is the time," he said, still brightly.

Her heart sank. She wasn't feeling up to being the bad guy today. But she wouldn't feel like it tomorrow, or the next day, so putting it off wouldn't make it any easier. "All right; there's a cafeteria here in the Medical Arts building. Can you come at one?"

"Certainly! See you then!" And he hung up.

Stewart was waiting for her at the start of the cafeteria line. He waved one arm at her, smiling broadly. He was wearing an open-necked light blue shirt, navy-blue slacks, and white deck shoes. He looked like a retired cruise ship commander who had spent a lot of time in foreign ports. She smiled and waved back as she wove her way between the tables to join him. "You look beautiful," she said impishly.

"And you look like the wreck of the *Hesperus*," he replied—Stewart was fond of very old sayings—eyeing her faded scrubs and dirty walking shoes. "As soon as the estate finishes probate, you should quit that job and get yourself a new wardrobe."

"But I love my job! Oh, Uncle Stewart, you can't possibly think I'd give up nursing!" She was sincerely surprised at him.

He, in turn, was surprised at her. "Oh, come on! All those sticky, sick kiddies? I'd think you'd want to get into something more exciting, more fun! Something where you can wear stylish clothes." He cocked his head sideways as he looked at her. "You would look smashing—" another old term, though not as old as the shipwrecked *Hesperus*—"in a navy blue pinstripe, with a broad-brimmed straw hat kind of sideways on your head."

"You think so? But I couldn't go eye-to-eye with a three-year-old while wearing a hat that covers one eye. And trust me, there is nothing more fun than making a sticky, sick three-year-old smile through her tears. Or more exciting than helping Hugs find out what's wrong and how to fix it. Or more rewarding than telling a scared set of parents that their baby is going to be just fine."

"Oh. Well, all right, if that's what you truly want."

"It is. Come on, let's get something to eat. I can't stay away too long."

Shaking his head that someone could be happy in a job

that didn't reward snappy dressers or allow lengthy lunch breaks, Stewart followed Jan down the stainless steel shelf as she picked a bowl of fruit here, an egg salad sandwich there, and a bottle of cranberry juice at the end. He selected a ham and cheese sandwich, a bag of corn chips, a bowl of rice pudding, and coffee, black, with three sugars.

They found an empty table surrounded by empty tables—most people working here ate at noon—and sat down. He sighed deeply and began to tear open the papers of sugar and empty them into his coffee.

"Still like coffee syrup, I see," noted Jan.

"Yeah, but only when Terri isn't looking," he replied, wadding up the paper. "She's turned into a real Nazi about sugar. I can only get a taste of the real thing away from home." He looked across at Jan and smiled. "Of course, I've lost seven pounds since she starting cracking down, so there's good news with the bad." His smile broadened as he stirred his coffee. "You know, big money becomes you; apart from that singularly tasteless outfit, you look bright and shiny as a new quarter."

She smiled back and began to undo the Saran Wrap around her sandwich. "I don't have the money yet, but thank you. The lack of sugar becomes you. You're looking very svelte."

"Thank you." He watched her take a bite of cantaloupe and asked, "What's this I hear about you having a twin?"

She swallowed and smiled. "Who told you?"

"Katie. She says there's a visitor from Texas who looks enough like you to be your twin sister."

"Well, there is a woman here who actually claims to be a blood relative, possibly a sister. She says she has DNA evidence. But when I told Mother, she said she would be happy to take a DNA test to prove this woman was an imposter."

"What do you think?"

"I don't know what to think. DNA can't prove two people

are siblings, but that isn't what this is about. She has a symmetrical translocation of two genes and claims to have discovered the same translocation on my genes, and—"

"Hold on, hold on," said Stewart, raising one hand, palm toward her. "How did she get hold of a sample of your genes?"

"We both attended a conference in Houston, and when she saw me, she wondered if we were related, so she stole my hairbrush and had some tests run on the hair she found on it. She works in a medical testing lab, so that part wasn't hard."

Stewart had been looking more and more amazed at this account. "She sounds like some kind of nut!" he said.

Jan smiled. "No, she's not a nut. She was blindsided recently by finding out she was adopted, and she's trying to find out who her real parents are. Actually, I like her. We met at a knitting lesson, and we've become friends. We have an amazing number of things in common. The thing is, if she is related but isn't Mother's daughter, then where did she come from?"

"How old is she?"

"Four or five years older than me."

Stewart shrugged. "Not mine, then. I was in grade school when she was born." He ate some of his sandwich while he thought. Then his face lit up with amusement. "You don't suppose she's *Edyth's*?"

Jan choked on a strawberry and clapped a paper napkin to her mouth.

"Are you all right?" he asked, rising when he saw the deep red she was turning.

She waved her other hand at him to sit back down and nodded furiously, eyes watering, unable to make other than odd breathing noises for about a minute. "Urg!" she muttered at last, wiping her lips, "That was a *terrible* thing to say!" And she burst into laughter.

They both laughed long and loud at the notion of Edyth Hanraty ever allowing a man to father her child.

"But, but it's not possible, Uncle Stewart, you know that," Jan said and her laughter subsided into the occasional giggle. "It's beyond belief."

"I don't know," he said loftily. "Perhaps if she killed the father and buried him under a thorn bush after the deed was done . . ."

She laughed again, then said, "Hold on, hold on, that isn't what I mean. When Lucille was born, Aunt Edyth would have been at least fifty, and the woman who has a baby in her fifties is doing it with the help of some very modern medicine, which was not available back then."

"All right, all right, not Edyth's. And not Grandmother's, either, or she wouldn't have been given up for adoption. So whose?"

"That's what I asked you."

"How sure is this Lucille person that she's one of us?"

"Very sure."

"Do you want me to talk to her? Maybe I can help her see this is impossible."

"She wants to meet my family. And I'd like your opinion. How about I invite her and her husband to dinner, and you and Terri come, too?"

"All right, pick a night and let us know." He began to unwrap his sandwich. "If Susan is sure Lucille isn't hers—" He paused to look at Jan inquiringly.

"Mother is adamant."

"Then suppose it's David who's her father? You and Jason look like your dad, not your mom."

"Jason and I look like you, too—there's blond on both sides of my family. What ties her to Mother is that Lucille had a problem carrying babies to term, and so did I—and so did Mother. What's more, I suspect Grandmother did, too. You came a long while after Mother, and I know you had a sister who died young, just like Mother's daughter Julie. So if the link is genetic, it's down the female side of the family."

"Hmmm," said Stewart.

"Yes," nodded Jan. "I think your daughters should be tested for it."

"Katie had that amnio-thing, and her baby's fine."

"Amniocentesis doesn't test for the kind of problem I'm talking about. My two boys are fine, but I'm having them tested because they may carry the defect and hand it on to their daughters. And Katie may have the problem herself and was merely lucky with this first child. I'll talk to her, if you like, and the other girls. The test is expensive, but it can at least warn them of a possible complication."

Stewart frowned—he was never one to borrow trouble—but at last he nodded. "All right, if you think it's a good idea." He took a bite of his sandwich.

Jan picked up her fork, speared a chunk of pineapple, and turned her mind to the other problem. "Now, what did you want to talk to me about?"

"I have a business proposition."

She nodded. This was what she expected. "What kind of business?"

"Boating. Boating and fishing." He began to beam at her. "I know, doesn't it just finally make sense? The thing I love to do most, the thing I would do instead of working at my other businesses, should *be* my business: go fishing! Combine that with just cruising the lake, which I also love, and what a business! It's incredibly obtuse of me not to have seen the possibilities a long time ago! I think finding Aunt Edyth's boat was a sign."

"Now, Uncle Stewart," said Jan.

"All right, maybe not a real sign, but it's strange, because I've actually been thinking about the boat business for a while. Problem is, that sort of thing takes capital, the kind we just don't have. But now, with Aunt Edyth gone, the money is here—and what do we find going through her property? That wonderful old boat, the *Edali*! I really am halfway to thinking it is a sign, and from the old woman her-self, that she wishes me well, that this is the business I was meant to be in, this is the business where I can redeem my-self, take better care of my girls. I know what I am, a no-good loafer, been that way all my life. But it was never on purpose. It just seemed to happen, like I was born with a 'gone fishing' sign planted in my heart.

"But don't you see? That's why I chose the boat. It was like I was saying 'I understand' to Aunt Edyth. I can restore it and make it the symbol of the business, even offer to take special customers for cruises in it. Lure of the Lake, isn't that a great name? It's a *natural*!"

When Jan didn't respond at once, his smile faded into a worried look. "What's the matter? Can't you just see it?"

"Yes, I can," she said slowly. "And I agree, it would be a natural for you. But I can also see that this would take a large amount of money to start up. I take it you are hoping I will give it to you."

"Not give," he said. "Loan. L-O-A-N. I'll pay you back, with interest, I swear it. This is the best idea I've ever had. It's a sure thing. I know every square foot of Lake Minnetonka. I've been out on it since I was a little, little boy. I know all the best places to catch bass and walleye, the times of day when they're biting, and I can read the sky and water as well as any-one who boats on it. Remember how you and I were never skunked when I took you fishing? Or caught by surprise by rain? I'm a better weather forecaster for this area than any of those nimrods on television. I'd be the best guide for fisher-men ever! I know that lake, I *love* that lake like it was my own child. I'd never get tired or bored with this, ever."

Jan felt herself drawn into Stewart's enthusiasm. It seemed genuine—but then it always did. "Uncle Stewart, have you any idea how much starting up such a business would cost? You'd need property to build on, you'd need a building, you'd need boats—the cost would be *astronomical*!"

"Now, no, it wouldn't. For one thing, we already have the property. The land behind our house runs right down to the lake. And I've got a nice boat—and a second, spectacular one, too!"

"You mean, use your own house and yard for this? Does Terri know about this?"

"Not yet, not yet." He patted the air as if patting the shoulder of a weeping woman. "Now, now," he said, "once she sees how serious I am—and once I tell her I have the money in hand—"

"How much?"

"What?"

"How much money would it take to start this business up?"

He looked uncomfortable. "Not as much as you're probably thinking."

She asked again, more deliberately, "How much?"

He said with false bravado, "I'm not completely sure. Somewhere between five and seven hundred thousand dollars."

That was pretty close to what she'd been thinking he'd ask for. The interesting part was, she didn't think that was enough.

"Do you have another source for money?" she asked.

"What do you mean?"

"Did Mother change her mind and agree to invest in this?"

"No—why, did she tell you she did?" he asked eagerly.

"No."

"Oh. Well, no, I don't have another source for investment money. Why?"

"Because I don't think seven hundred thousand is enough. You'll have to put up a building and docks. You'll have to buy more boats. And restoring that powerboat is going to cost a whole lot of money."

"Aww, I can restore the *Edali* all by myself."

"Are you an aircraft engine mechanic?"

"Well . . . no."

"That's an aircraft engine—an *antique* aircraft engine—in the *Edali*."

He studied her, and a twinkle formed in his blue eyes. "Are you trying to convince me to borrow more than seven hundred grand from you?"

"No. I'm trying to convince you that this is not a business proposition. It's another of your impossible dreams. You haven't really looked into what it would take to build that business. You haven't got the facts and figures."

"I can get all that financial stuff any time you want it!" he said, with a dismissive gesture.

"No." She shook her head. "I'm sorry, Uncle Stewart, but no. I'm not going to lend you any money."

For the merest instant he looked sick with disappointment, then that smoothed away and he smiled a sad little smile at her. "I'm so sorry you aren't interested. I really could pull this off, you know. Return that money at no less than five percent interest. Ten percent, if you need me to go that high."

"Oh, I have no doubt of that. There are probably four or five of your previous ideas that could have turned out really well, made you a rich man. But somehow they went the same way as your ridiculous ones did. And with your three remaining daughters at or approaching marriage or college—or both—you no longer have time to build a company that could pay for those expenses. In fact, with Terri looking to retire, the last thing you need is a company that will be sucking every dime you have out of your pockets for the next several years, if not longer."

"Terri's not going to retire—"

"No, because she's the sole source of support for your family right now. But that means she can't afford to put any money into this new business of yours. Now Hugs and I, we're all right financially as we are, so even if Lucille—*and* her daughter, did I mention she has a daughter?—prove their claim to a share, we'll be all right. But that even more certainly means I can't throw seven hundred thousand dollars into a bottomless pit, because if my share gets cut from a half to a quarter, I might not *get* seven hundred thousand. There, see? I can see it in your face. You didn't do the math after that meeting with Attorney Weiner, did you? I did. *If* the estate tops out at nine million, which it might not, then after they deduct the percent going to the U, I'll get a million five. But if Lucille and her daughter prove their claim, I'll get half of that. I have no intention of dipping into our own funds to finance another of your schemes that will almost certainly go the same way as your previous ones. I'm sure you understand."

Stewart sighed and began, probably unconsciously, to stir his now-tepid coffee. "Oh, my dear, dear niece, you are going to be so sorry you didn't climb on board."

"I'll be the first to congratulate you if you manage to surprise all of us."

G ODWIN was listening carefully to Joe Mickels's proposition. The man was making good on his invitation to lunch, and Godwin was enjoying himself immensely, not least because he was correct in predicting the old man's motive. He wanted Godwin to invest in one of Mickels's deals. It wasn't a gold or diamond mine, it was lakeshore property up on Minnesota's North Shore. Minnesota looks as if it started out as a rectangle, but before the shape had set, it was buffetted by a stiff wind from the west, which blew the top eastward into an elongated arrowhead shape. This arrowhead runs along the top of Lake Superior and thus was dubbed the North Shore. That far north, the land is beautiful but rugged—a mix of chilled rock and pine trees, and a great hunk of it is a national park called the Boundary Waters.

But right along the Superior shoreline are many small towns catering to tourists, and between them are lodges and individual cabins owned by people who think that land under a year-round threat of frost makes for an ideal vacation spot.

"Property values keep rising in the state, and vacation property is especially on the upswing," said Mickels. "I've been investing up there, in a small way, for some while. Now I want to get in deeper—but when people find out it's me trying to buy a piece of land, they raise the price, because they know I can afford it."

"So you're looking for a front man," said Godwin, digging into his crab salad. They were in a very nice seafood restaurant in Wayzata.

"Not exactly, more like a partner."

"An equal partner?"

"That depends on how much you're willing to invest. I'll bring my own money to the table, in equal shares, and provide the expertise."

Godwin looked across the table at the little old man with the cold, shrewd eyes, and put his fork down to laugh gently. "You don't want me," he said.

"I don't?" Mickels raised his bushy eyebrows high.

Godwin enjoyed pranks, but this wasn't a prank. The man was making a real offer, not asking Godwin to be the cat's paw or sucker in some kind of underhanded deal. "I wasn't left a big chunk of money, Joe. What John did was set up a spendthrift trust. I get the interest from the trust for the rest of my life, and my monthly check is not big enough to invest on the level you're talking about."

Joe's eyes narrowed, and he sat back for a few moments. "You're telling me the truth, aren't you?"

Godwin nodded. "I was going to string you along, see how many great meals I could get out of you before you found out I was gaming you, but that was when I thought you were pulling a stunt of your own, trying to get your hands on my money for your own profit. Instead, you're trying to keep realtors from playing you for a fool." He chuckled uncomfortably. "I hope you're not mad at me."

Mickels was giving him a very cool look. But after a few minutes, he chuckled, too. "No, I don't think I am. It was worth trying. I should have realized John Nye was too smart to leave you a large chunk of change and just hope you didn't blow it."

"Would I have blown it investing in North Shore property?"

"I don't think so. But I would have done my very best to keep you from taking more than your share of the profits."

"That's why, even if I was left a 'large chunk of change,' I would not have gone in with you on this. You're too canny for me, Mr. Mickels." And he smiled a chilly smile of his own.

The two went back to their meal, each with slightly more respect for the other than when he arrived.

Eighteen

❖ ❖ ❖

"I'M glad to see you," said Betsy the next day when Jan came in. It was well after five—Crewel World stayed open till seven on Thursdays—but Jan had come straight from the clinic in her scrubs in answer to Betsy's call. "Have you talked to Sergeant Rice since he searched your home?" Betsy asked.

"No, why?"

"Because I'm having trouble getting in touch with him, and I have an important question. Maybe you'll have better luck."

"What's the question?"

"Ask him if the needle that was missing and is now back is a new needle or a used one."

"How can anyone tell which needle is the one that went missing and came back?"

"All right, ask him if any of the double-zero Skacels are new."

"How can you tell?"

"Scratches," said Betsy impatiently. "When you use

knitting needles, they rub up against one another, and they get scratched. If one needle in your set has no scratches, then someone bought it new and put it in there. If they're all scratched, then ask around. Someone borrowed it and brought it back."

Hope flared in Jan's eyes. "Yes," she said, "yes, that must be what happened!" She came to hug Betsy. "You're wonderful! I'll find out who borrowed it, I promise."

Released from the hug, Betsy went to the checkout and got the map out of a drawer. "This is the map I found inside your pillow. I'm assuming Edyth Hanraty stitched it."

A good soaking in Orvus had removed most of the smell and stains. The knit flag, being heavy yarn two layers thick, hadn't dried overnight and remained in Betsy's bathroom, stretched on a towel; so what Jan was looking at was just the map.

Jan, a true stitcher, merely glanced at the top and then flipped it over—real stitchers are at least as interested in the backs as the fronts. She made a critical face at the web of floss crisscrossing it. "Hmmm," she said. She turned it right side up again and took it to the front window to see it in natural light. "I don't see any initials on it," she said.

"I didn't see any either," said Betsy, coming to stand beside her, "but it was found inside that pillow, which was on the old boat owned by your aunt, so I was just assuming she stitched it. Was she a stitcher?"

"Not really. She could knit, and she did beautiful crochet lace, but embroidery or cross-stitching wasn't her thing."

"That might explain why the back of that map is so messy," said Betsy.

"Oh, I don't know. I've seen worse, actually; even Mother isn't fussy about her backs—though she never did anything this messy. But whoever stitched this knew what she was doing; these aren't just random stitches. Look, feather stitch, stem stitch, satin stitch."

"Yes, you're right. So okay, done by someone who knew what she was doing but was in a hurry. But why hide it? Was Edyth secretive? I mean, the sort to have buried something on the Big Island?"

"I . . . don't know." Jan smiled. "She never said." She looked at the map again. "But it really seems as if she's marked a specific place, and with a heart instead of an X. Isn't that odd?" Jan touched the spot on the map, which was draped over one hand. "What does it say?" she asked.

"Where her heart is, there's her treasure," Betsy replied.

"That's intriguing."

Betsy asked, "What did she love above everything else?"

Jan turned and looked at her. "I have no idea. It would have to be something small, wouldn't it? Something she could bury all by herself. And why bury something you love?"

"To keep it from being taken from her?"

Jan shook her head. "Aunt Edyth would never allow something she loved to be taken from her."

Betsy said, "Well, then, something that had died?"

"No, Mother said she buried her dogs on her property—and she didn't own any land on the Big Island. I wonder if Mother might know what this map is about. She spent all or part of just about every summer with Aunt Edyth until she went into high school, and until she married she was out there a lot. I'm sure they must have had some long talks."

"I wonder, when was it buried? It might date to a time before Susan was even born. Or a time after she no longer spent summers out there. Or to a time before Edyth owned the boat. I mean, didn't you say that boat was an old one?"

"Gosh, yes. It dates to the early twenties. Great-grandfather bought it from a bankrupt man in the early thirties. When he died, the house became Aunt Edyth's, and the boat with it. I'm not sure when it quit being used. Some time in the fifties, I think, or sixties. So it could date to any date in that spread. And you have to consider that maybe someone else made that pillow and gave it as a gift."

"Wait a minute. Did you look at the pillow before you brought it to me?"

"Yes, why?"

"Because there are forty-nine stars on the flag."

"Oh, that's right, I'd forgotten about that!"

"And 1959 was the one and only year there were forty-nine states."

"Oddly enough, I remember that. My father bought me a forty-nine star flag, and I foolishly threw it away when Hawaii became a state in 1960. So you're thinking this map was stitched around the same time as the flag was knit?"

"Maybe, though not necessarily. But the flag was not knit before the boat came into the Hanraty family."

"Okay."

"The question is, when was the map made—and why hide it inside the pillow?"

"Maybe so no one would find it?" queried Jan.

"If no one was to find it, why make it in the first place?"

"Maybe we're talking about two people here," said Jan. "One person made the map and mislaid it. Then someone else picked it up and used it as a liner for the pillow, not realizing it was a treasure map."

"Yes, that's possible. Any idea who either the stitcher or knitter might be?"

"No. I'll ask Mother. Of course, the really big question is, what's buried on the Big Island?"

"Are you going to go dig it up?" asked Betsy.

"Me? Why me?"

"Well, if not you, then the executrix of the estate. It's her responsibility to find all assets before making distribution of them."

"So you think whatever is buried might be of real value?"

"I don't know. Obviously the person who buried it

thought so. 'Where your heart lies, there will your treasure be also.' "

"I'm going to go ask Mother about this. May I take it with me?"

"Of course. It's yours. Do you still want me to restore the flag pillow?"

"Don't do anything till you hear from me."

"I think that's the name of an old song."

"It is? And anyway, I'm wrong. There is something you can do: Talk to Lexie—Alexandra—Stewart and Terri's second oldest daughter. I asked her if she'd talk to you and she said she would." Jan went into her purse with one hand. "Here—here's her phone number." She handed a business card to Betsy. "I said you'd take her out to dinner. She weighs about ninety-three pounds and adores cheeseburgers, the witch."

The business card had Terri's name and school phone number on it, with Lexie's name and phone number printed along one side. "All right, I'll call her right away. And wait, it's 'Do Nothing Till You Hear from Me.' Duke Ellington wrote it. The song, I mean."

Jan smiled. "You must be a whiz at Trivial Pursuit." She folded the map in half. "Do you have something I could put this in?"

"Of course." Betsy brought out one of the shop's paper bags, a flat affair with lavender flowers printed all over it.

"Thanks. I'll call you later if I learn anything."

"Me, too."

FRED Miller and Marjorie and Phil Benson were coming over this evening, and Susan was baking cookies. Summer was hardly the time for baking, but she was making just a small batch. The recipe was a bit complicated. She had begun yesterday with a sugar cookie recipe split into four equal parts. She had mixed instant Swiss mocha coffee into one, melted chocolate into two, and left the fourth one plain. They went into the refrigerator overnight. Today, she rolled the four doughs out long and thin, laid them one on top of the other, and sliced the resulting deck a quarter-inch thick. The cookies made like this were striped and very delicious. Her guests were coming to play cards, and she would serve the cookies with iced mint tea and lemonade.

She had just removed the second, last batch from the oven when the doorbell rang three times in fast rhythm: Jan's signal. She continued lifting the hot cookies from the sheet onto a wire cooling rack and, when the door opened, called, "In the kitchen, dear!"

Jan came up the half flight of stairs into the kitchen, sniffing and smiling. "Ribbon cookies!" she exclaimed.

"Don't touch," said her mother. "They're for company tonight."

"Awwww," grumbled Jan, but pulled her reaching fingers back.

"What's in the bag?" her mother asked.

"Something I want to show you. Maybe you can tell me something about it."

Jan went to the kitchen table and slid the folded cloth out. It was light tan, covered with colored stitching.

"What on earth—?" Susan asked, then stopped short. "Where—where did you get that?" and her own voice sounded like a stranger's to her ears.

Jan turned. "Mother, what's wrong? Are you all right?"

"Yes. No. I don't . . . know."

Jan grabbed a chair and pushed her mother into it. "Sit down. Take a couple of deep breaths." Susan felt a professional hand at her wrist. *She's taking my pulse*, Susan thought. *She thinks I'm having a heart attack. Maybe I am. I feel giddy, and I can't catch my breath.*

Susan said, "Mother, look at me." She did, looking into her daughter's frightened eyes. "Smile at me."

"What?"

"Smile at me. Come on, think of something amusing, think of—of Jason's first wife cooking Thanksgiving dinner."

The memory of that debacle brought the result Jan wanted, a smile. "That's good. Now, lift both arms over your head."

Feeling a trifle foolish, Susan obeyed.

"Very good. Now, repeat after me: It's a sunny day today."

Susan obediently repeated, "It's a sunny day today."

"What day is it?"

"Thursday."

"Good. Good." Jan looked relieved.

"I'm not having a stroke!"

"Yes, I know that, now. So what did happen?"

"I don't know. I've been cleaning the house and baking cookies. Maybe it was a little too much for me." But she couldn't help looking at the folded cloth on the table.

"That's what I came to show you," said Jan, misinterpreting the look, going to pick it up. Or was she aware and only pretending to accept her mother's explanation for the fainting spell? "Remember that pillow CeeCee found on the boat at Aunt Edyth's?"

I threw it away, so why is it here? "Yes," said Susan, drawing the word out as if not sure of her memory.

"Sure you do. You took it away from her and put it in a garbage bag."

"Oh, yes, I do remember."

"Well, I took it out again."

"Why?" Susan tried hard to make the inquiry casual.

"Because I could see that the front of it was handmade, knit in a flag pattern. I thought perhaps Aunt Edyth had done it, and I don't have any of her hand work, so I rescued it. I took it to Crewel World—Betsy does restoration work, did you know that?"

"Yes, of course; she does excellent finishing, too. I always have her finish my counted pieces."

"Me, too. Anyway, I brought the pillow to her. It was so smelly and dirty—"

"I know, that's why I threw it away. *Generations* of mice! I was surprised I could actually take hold of it. Ewwww, if something had jumped out . . . I just *hate* mice! They're worse than spiders—I don't know why you're afraid of spiders. They're not dirty like mice."

Susan was yearning to talk of something, anything, else, but Jan was determined to talk about the map. "Well, look what was inside it."

"I don't want to get near it, and I wish you'd take it off my nice, clean table!"

"It's clean. Betsy froze it for a couple of days to kill any fleas and then washed it thoroughly. Did you make it?"

"Make it?"

"The pillow. And the map that was inside it."

"No, of course not. What do you mean, map?"

"This." Jan touched the fabric, which she had not picked up off the table. "It's a map."

"It is? A map of what?"

"It shows this area of Lake Minnetonka: Gray's Bay, Excelsior Bay, Lafayette Bay. And the Big Island. It's a treasure map, we think."

"A treasure map? You mean like yo-ho-ho pirate's gold?"

"Mo-ther," sighed Jan.

"Well, after all . . . Let me see it." Jan held it out and Susan took it quickly, lest Jan see her fingers tremble. She turned away, toward the big kitchen window, to examine it in natural light. Not that she needed to. The colors were bright and had hardly run at all. The edges were ragged, the lettering that formed a frame was not really decipherable.

She turned it around twice, then asked, "What makes you think it's a treasure map?"

"Well, for one thing, the words around the edge seem to say, 'Where your heart is, there will your treasure be.'"

"Is that what it says?" She turned it around again, pretending to try to read it.

"Yes. And if you look close, at the Big Island, there's a tiny red heart. It's near the tallest tree."

Susan searched for a few moments. "Yes, here it is."

"The question is, what's buried there?"

"I'm afraid I have no idea." Susan turned and gave the map back to her daughter with a sad, forced laugh. "Sorry."

"What did Aunt Edyth love above everything else?" asked Jan.

Susan blinked, then frowned and thought. "Her independence."

"I mean something physical, some object."

"Well . . . I'm not sure. She really liked that motorcycle." Susan smiled, remembering Edyth's fierce joy in roaring over the winding roads around Lake Minnetonka.

"Did she ever say anything about burying something on the Big Island?"

"Not to me. Do you think she stitched this?"

"Well, who else?"

Susan shrugged. "I don't know. She didn't do embroidery, at least not that I remember."

"I know. Betsy wondered if the pillow was knit in 1959, because the flag has forty-nine stars. You would have been in high school and not staying out there anymore, right?"

Susan nearly leaped onto that but stopped in time. Big lies were never a good idea. "Of course I still went out there! But Aunt Edyth and I weren't as close anymore, because I was dating the young man who would become your father."

"You were awfully young, you know."

"Yes, but I was awfully sure." Susan smiled, remembering.

"Anyway, she wouldn't have approved of a millionaire college economics professor who could walk on water, if he was also a man."

"She didn't think much of Grandfather, either, I suppose?"

"No, she rather liked him—but she knew Grandmother needed someone to take care of her, and the one way she knew of making sure that someone stuck around was to join them in matrimony. Grandmother was old-fashioned that way. She had higher expectations of me. Why are you so interested in all this? You aren't thinking of going to the Big Island with a spade, are you?"

Jan laughed. "That does sound kind of crazy, doesn't it?"

"Yes, it does. Whatever the treasure was, I'm sure it's long gone."

"How do you know?"

"Well, my dear, it was a very long time ago when she would have been capable of going out there and digging a hole. I'm sure that whatever she buried decayed into dust decades ago."

"Decades? When did she use the boat last?"

Susan thought. "Early sixties, I think. Now, you had better be on your way. I've got a few things to do before company arrives."

"All right." Jan reached for the map. "May I have this?"

"Certainly." Susan could have bitten her tongue off for that too-quick response. She tried, and failed, to find a reason to change her mind.

"I'll call you tomorrow, all right?" said Jan.

"Fine. Maybe we can go shopping on Saturday, have lunch at Antiquity Rose."

WHEN Betsy came into The Malt Shop, a fifties-style diner in St. Paul, she saw a tall, light-haired young woman in a booth looking at her and lifting a hand tentatively. Betsy waved back—no one else in the place could remotely have fit the description Alexandra gave her.

The place certainly evoked places Betsy could remember from her early youth, with its red vinyl and chrome décor and poodle-skirted waitresses—well, except the jukebox was playing a Beatles song that would have been more appropriate in a head shop reeking of incense, whose customers wore tie-dyed shirts and bell-bottom trousers.

"Are you Alexandra?" Betsy asked, walking up to the booth.

"Yes, but call me Lexie. And you're Betsy, Aunt Jan's friend."

"Yes," said Betsy, taking a seat.

Lexie was nodding her head to the music. "Don't you think John Lennon's 'Imagine' is the most noble and true song ever written?"

"No," said Betsy.

"But you were alive when the song was written!" exclaimed Lexie.

"I'm not sure what that has to do with it."

Lexie chuckled. "You're right. I guess we tend to think of everyone from that era as being a flower child."

"It's not that I didn't love that song when I was your age," said Betsy. "It's that I've changed my mind. Anyway, thank you for agreeing to meet with me."

"I promised Aunt Jan that in return for a hamburger and a malt, I'd answer any questions you asked. So let's order, and then we'll talk."

Over their lunch—Betsy privately promised to work extra hard at aerobics next week—she asked, "Did your father talk to you about what you should choose from Aunt Edyth's house?"

Lexie hesitated, the pupils of her light blue eyes widening just a little. "Who told you that?"

"Your aunt Susan. She thinks your father did research on

the contents of Edyth's house so he could select the most valuable items for you and your sisters to pick."

Lexie asked, in a tone that betrayed her defensiveness, "Why would that be so awful?"

"Because she thinks he will ask you to sell your choices and give the money to him to start his fishing business."

This time Lexie's amazement was more genuine. "What a stupid idea! It's not true!"

"You picked the Navajo blanket, didn't you?"

"Yes, I think it's beautiful."

"Yes, it is. What are you going to do with it?"

"My parents will keep it for me until I finish school."

"And then?"

"I . . . I'm not sure. I'd love someday to display it in a home of my own."

"It would make a centerpiece of any room. But do you know what it's worth?"

"No. I'm assuming from what you just told me it's a lot."

"The best estimate I could find is a hundred and forty thousand dollars."

Lexie gaped at her. "No!"

Betsy nodded. "Yes. I talked to a gallery in California specializing in Native American artifacts, and its owner wants me to ask you if you're willing to let him be your agent when you sell it."

"Dad said it was more valuable than it looked, and if one of us liked it, she should ask for it." She looked thoughtful. "That's so much money. I'm going to have to reconsider keeping it. I could pay off my college loans and pay for the rest of my studies and have money left over to start a college fund for my own children, which I plan to have some day." She smiled. "Aunt Edyth would be horrified if she knew how many children I want."

Betsy smiled back. "Does your father know?"

"Oh, him. He thinks I should wait until I'm thirty-five

to marry and then have one child. But every time he says that, I can see in his eyes he wishes he'd had more daughters. One of his favorite song lines is, 'I am a man who's rich in daughters.'"

Betsy said, "Oh, I've heard that song! Doesn't it end with the man saying he's thinking about getting him another daughter?"

Lexie laughed. "That's the one. I hope Katie's baby is a girl. Dad would just dote on her."

"Maybe take her for boat rides, if he gets that business up and running."

"Yes," said Lexie, but her smile faded away.

"Do you think he could actually succeed in getting this one off the ground?"

"Sure he could!" she replied, too fast and too loud, then blushed. "I'm sure he'll do just fine," she reiterated, and took a hard pull at the straw in her malt. "It's something he loves, something he's always loved. And CeeCee is old enough now to take care of herself, so he'll be able to concentrate on business."

"Have you thought about going into a partnership with him?"

"Partnership?" she echoed, as if the idea were new to her, and the blush rose again.

Really, Betsy thought, life would be so much easier for the police if every liar gave himself away like this. "Yes," she said. "You could sell the blanket and invest the money in your father's business. Then when you finish school, you could be vice president in charge of operations or head bookkeeper or something."

She nodded, but didn't say anything.

"I have a feeling your dad's ideal day in the business would be to go out on the lake with the anglers, showing them the best spots. Or giving rides in the restored *Edali*."

Lexie's head came around. "Have you seen it?"

"Yes," said Betsy. "It's a beautiful boat, but I suspect it's going to cost a great deal of money to restore."

"Dad says he can do the work himself. He says the boat was famous in its day, lots of people knew about it and watched for it. Great-aunt Edyth would take it out and simply outrun any other powerboat on the lake. He says the sound of its engine is not like anything we've ever heard." Her eyes were sparkling now. "He says it can still go faster than anything on Lake Minnetonka, that the best seat is the one all the way at the back, with the spray coming up all around and the engine just roaring."

Betsy smiled. "I wonder how far in advance you'd have to buy a ticket for a ride on her?"

Lexie's smile broadened. "It really could be a successful business, couldn't it?"

"Yes—if he could find someone to do the hard parts: keeping records, paying taxes, doing upkeep, budgeting for advertising, all the boring parts."

Lexie grew serious. "Yes, those are the hard parts. And you know about them, don't you, since you own your own business."

"Yes. When it comes to owning your own business, what most people see is the pretty bird floating on the water—they don't realize that underneath, the bird is paddling like mad."

Lexie laughed, but sadly. "Yes, that's the part that trips people up, isn't it? Like that beautiful blanket I chose. What I saw were the colors and the pattern. What I didn't see was that it was a rare result of hours of labor that make it a costly souvenir."

SUSAN was a distracted card player that evening. She played two very bad games of bridge, explained to her guests that she had a headache, and sent them home early. Then she set her alarm for three a.m. and went to bed.

By three thirty, she was pulling into a driveway near Echo Bay. It was a long driveway, and the house it led to was hidden in trees. She unfastened the bungee cords that held her canvas kayak to the roof of her car, and carrying it over her head, threaded her way between the house and garage to the lakeshore. A dog two houses away barked briefly. She waited until it shut up, then slid the craft into the water and climbed into it.

Susan was almost as familiar with the lake as her brother Stewart. She had sold the motorboat a few years after David died—Stewart had one big enough for family outings, and Jason had a speedboat. But she'd kept the kayak. It was light to carry, easy to right if it tipped over, and a pleasure to paddle. She'd taken it up to the Boundary Waters a few years ago and come home a week later, satisfied that she could still paddle five days in a row, four hours in the morning and three in the afternoon.

And she had excellent night vision.

The night was cloudless, with a half moon well up in the sky. She paddled out a few yards, then sat still, moving her double-ended paddle only enough to keep her position in a light onshore breeze. In a few minutes, her eyes fully dilated and she could see the dark mass of the Big Island clearly against the starry sky. It was barely fifty yards away. She paddled for it, stopping a dozen yards from the shore to reconnoiter and find where she was in relation to the shore, then circled to the north. She made virtually no noise at all and rode low enough in the water that she could not be seen by a casual viewer.

As she came around to the northeast side, she slowed and listened. This place on the Big Island was a traditional gathering place for party boats—on summer weekends there were often so many boats that one could jump from one to another half the length of a football field with no difficulty.

But this was three a.m. Friday morning, and everyone was at home, resting up for the weekend to come.

She paddled closer to shore. There was a dock there—possibly the dock she remembered from so many years ago. She found it, went just beyond it and stopped to look at the shoreline outlined against the sky. There it was, the tallest tree on the island. Leafless—that's right, it had died a few years ago, she'd forgotten that. But its bare limbs still reached a dozen or more feet higher than the surrounding trees. She drifted along the shore, pulling in about halfway between the dock and the tree.

There used to be a narrow, one-lane road along here. Funny, it was gone, replaced by a path. She stepped off the path on the inland side, looking for the road, and nearly fell into a marsh. She had to sit down hard to keep from floundering into the cutgrass and mucky water.

"Whew!" she murmured, and struggled to her feet, rubbing her hip ruefully. "Getting too old to be gadding about in the dark," she muttered, then put a hand over her mouth to remind herself to keep silent.

Hanging around her neck was a short, waterproof flashlight, and as she got back to the path, she turned it on. The terrain had changed from when she'd been here last, many years ago. She walked up and down the narrow ridge, looking for landmarks, but the landscape had changed so much she couldn't find any. If it weren't for the little cottage back near the dock and the big tree, she might have thought she'd come ashore in the wrong place.

She went back to her kayak and climbed aboard, wincing at the pain in her behind from the fall, but well satisfied. The marsh had eaten the road, obviously, and the box with it. Even if Jan were so foolish as to come looking for it, there was nothing for her to find.

Nineteen

On Saturday morning Betsy was in the shop at ten with Godwin—the scheduled part-timer, Marj Fahr, woke up ill, and fortunately Godwin was available—and they were discussing a redesign of the layout of the shop over cups of tea.

"Well, I have a feeling the next emphasis in needlework will be on crochet," Godwin said. "So we need to get in some more books with crochet patterns, more crochet needles and threads, and maybe hold a class for beginners."

"Crochet?" said Betsy. "I haven't seen any increased interest in crochet. We've got a limited amount of space. I think we should change the layout again so our customers will walk in and have to relearn their way around, and maybe stumble on something new, but I don't see adding to our crochet stock. What do you think about tatting?"

"Tried it. Crochet is easier, and I'm bad at crochet. But I'm serious, I think it's going to be the coming thing."

The argument might have continued, but the door sounded its two notes, so they turned to see if they could assist their customer.

It was Jan, and she'd brought Jason with her. They both looked worried. Jan had a Crewel World paper bag in her hand.

"Is something the matter?"

"I'm not sure," said Jan. She went to the library table in the middle of the room and slid the map out. Godwin went immediately to it, unfolded it—it was backside up—and after a moment, turned it over.

"Say," he said, "this is part of a map of Lake Minnetonka!"

Betsy blinked at him. "Wow, it took me a while to realize that! You are *good*!"

"Yes, I know," he replied, not very modestly. "But what's the matter with it?"

"We think it's a treasure map," said Jan.

"Really?" Godwin eagerly began to study the map. He quickly figured out the lettering around the edge. "Where your heart is, there will your treasure be also," he said aloud after a minute or two of study. "I think you may be right." He looked the map over carefully, then found the red heart along the north shore of the Big Island. "There it is, a teeny heart—is that where you're going to dig?"

"Yes, that's it," Jan said.

He tapped it once with his forefinger, then looked up at her, eyes shining, and said, "When are we going?"

She hesitated, surprised.

"What do you mean, 'we'?" Jason asked in her stead.

Godwin gestured around the shop at Betsy, Jan, and Jason, then pointed to himself. "We, as in us. We'uns, us'ns, the people here present."

"Are you serious?" asked Jan.

"Why? Shouldn't I be?"

"Well," Betsy broke in, "the map was stitched by Jan's great-aunt, the late Edyth Hanraty, and was retrieved from the trash by Jan, so it belongs to her. She gets to choose who, if anyone, comes with her in a search for the treasure. If there is a treasure."

Jan said, "I'm pretty sure there is a treasure. But I think my mother stitched this map, not Aunt Edyth."

"Awwwww," murmured Godwin, obviously disappointed. "I thought it was a really old treasure map. More than a hundred years old. I've read for years about there being a treasure hidden on the Big Island, and I thought you had at last found a map to it."

"I'm afraid not," said Betsy. "This map was sewn as a lining into a pillow that was found on Edyth Hanraty's boat."

"This came out of *that* smelly old thing? Well, who would've thought!" He leaned forward and sniffed gingerly. "It sure cleaned up nice. But then I suppose you and your friend here—"

"He's my brother, Jason McConnell."

"Oh. How do you do?" said Godwin.

"Very well, thank you," said Jason.

"Are the two of you going to dig it up?"

"Maybe," said Jason, looking at his sister.

Jan said, "You see, there's this problem of ownership. I showed the map to our mother, and she almost had a heart attack. She pretended she had never seen it before, when it was perfectly obvious she had. So I'm sure she's the one who stitched the map—or at least she knows what was buried out there. In either case, it was clear she didn't want it dug up. But I talked with her on the phone this morning. She's fine with any digging we want to do!"

"She is?" said Betsy, surprised.

"So what's the problem?" asked Godwin.

"I suspect that when they go out there they'll find a freshly dug hole, or one freshly filled in," said Betsy.

"Exactly!" Jan said with a big gesture. "I think she snuck out there and dug it up."

"Oh, yeah, I can just see our sixty-five-year-old mother holding a flashlight in her mouth while she digs a big hole with a handy spade," scoffed Jason.

"She digs up her flower beds every fall to plant bulbs and every spring to plant annuals," said Jan. "She's a very competent digger."

"Why a flashlight in her mouth?" asked Godwin.

"Because she'd go out there in the middle of the night, of course," said Jan. "That's the best time to go sneaking onto someone's property to retrieve something valuable the owners don't know is there."

Godwin bent over the map. "You're right. This is on private property."

"How do you know?" asked Betsy.

"Because only the old Veteran's Home property out there isn't in private hands, and this isn't on Veteran's Home land."

"Let me see," said Jason, coming to the table.

Godwin turned the map for him to look at, saying, "See, the heart is on the other side of the Big Island from the Veteran's Home."

"You're right," Jason said. He looked up at his sister. "What'll we do, ask permission to dig?"

"Well, yes, I guess we'll have to."

"So you *are* going to go out and look," said Betsy.

"Yes," said Jan.

"Say, what if Jan's mother didn't go out there ahead of you?" said Godwin. "Can I come along? Please? *Please?* I *adore* the idea of digging up a treasure!"

"Well . . ." hedged Jan. "I was thinking of asking Betsy to come along, since she's the one who found the map."

"But I've got a strong back!" said Godwin. "Two of us digging"—he pointed at Jason, then himself—"are better than one." He bent his right arm to show the muscle that gently lifted the sleeve of his shirt.

"And what is to be the women's role?" asked Betsy.

"To wipe our sweating brows and stay us with flagons."
He frowned prettily. "Does that mean what I think it means?
To offer us cold things to drink?"

"Yes, I think so," said Betsy, laughing. She turned to Jan.
"May we both come along?"

"Yes, of course."

"One problem: we're open till five. It'll probably take a
while to locate the site, and who knows how long to dig it
up. Unless you want us to imitate your mother and dig with
flashlights in our mouths, we'll have to wait till tomorrow."

Jan said, "Meet us at the foot of Water Street at ten in the
morning. Okay, Jason?"

"Oh, yes, I've got some things to do today anyway."

"We'll be there, complete with flagons!" said Godwin.
"Gosh, what'll I wear? What does one wear to the digging
up of a treasure?" He went to refill his mug, mumbling to
himself.

Jason asked, sotto voce, "You don't think he'll turn up in
a bandana and golden earring, do you?"

Jan giggled. "Wouldn't surprise me in the least."

Betsy asked, "How do we get ashore over there? Is there a
public landing we can use?"

"Oh, no," said Jan, "we'll just pull up to a dock on that
side of the island, then knock on the nearest door and ask if
we can cross his land." She looked at her brother. "Your boat
or mine?"

"Mine has a bigger motor," he said.

"Good." She turned to Betsy. "It's a red fiberglass Chris-
Craft with an inboard engine."

Godwin came back with a steaming mug of tea in his
hand. "What if the owner doesn't want us to dig on his
property? What'll we do? Or what if he wants a share?"

"Well, what if he does?" asked Jason. "We may have to
give it to him."

"But what if it's not a very big treasure?"

"That's their decision," Betsy interjected. "You and I are not going to share in it."

"Maybe we can explain what we're up to, negotiate a fee or something with him," said Jan.

"I think we shouldn't tell him we're there to dig up a treasure chest," said Godwin. "Just tell him a relative of yours buried something on his property fifty years ago, and you want to dig it up to see what it is."

"Yeah," agreed Jason. "We don't know what it is. It may be a dead dog or a spicy diary."

"Oooooh, a *spicy diary*!" echoed Godwin.

"Yeah, written by a girl in her early teens," said Betsy dryly. " 'I kissed David three times at the sock hop Saturday afternoon.' Ooooooh, spicy!"

Godwin turned on her, his hands on his hips. "You take the joy out of things, you know that? Now I'm not all excited anymore."

"If that means you won't be singing a chorus of 'Yo ho ho and a bottle of rum' while you're digging, I'm happy," retorted Betsy.

"Heartless woman," sighed Godwin. "Jan, how about we bring the drinks and you bring the food, and we'll have a picnic? Then at least it will be *something* of an occasion."

"Fine with me," said Jan. "Come on, Jase, let's leave these two to whatever they were doing before we came in."

SUNDAY dawned reluctantly, daylight struggling through a thick layer of dark clouds. It started raining just before Betsy set off for the eight o'clock service at Trinity. The church was relatively new, of an elegant but severe and not very ecclesiastical design. Father Rettger, in green vestments and snow white hair, was a beautiful counterpoint to the dark gray walls and pale stone altar.

His sermons were edifying, the small choir well-rehearsed, the music traditional.

Martin Stachnik was in charge of Trinity's music. He had learned the organ at a very large cathedral full of echoes and so played rather slowly. Betsy liked that, because Martin, like her, was fond of Bach, and the deliberate pace of his music gave her a chance to better appreciate Bach's intricate braids of music.

She didn't stay for coffee but hurried home, ate a hasty breakfast, then changed into jeans and a long-sleeve shirt. She was in the kitchen when her doorbell rang. She went to press the release button that unlocked the door to the entrance hall downstairs. She left her apartment door open so Godwin—it had to be Godwin, who else would come out early on a rainy Sunday morning?—could come in and went back to the kitchen to bring out the bottle of wine and six cans of Coke and two big bottles of water from the refrigerator.

By the time he sailed into her place scattering gay hellos and sunlight in all directions, she had the potables and a set of plastic glasses loaded into an insulated bag with a shoulder strap. He was wearing army boots, chinos, a camouflage shirt, and a kepi hat. He was reeking of Deep Woods *Off!* "I thought of knee pants and a head scarf," he said, "but the mosquitoes on Big Island are a specially vicious breed." He reached into a capacious front pocket and pulled out a spray bottle. "Here, use this on yourself before we land. It's got DEET, which keeps most of 'em away. And re-apply as necessary when the rain washes it off."

"Thanks," she said. "But the forecast says it'll stop raining by ten."

And, in fact, by the time they were walking up the wooden planks of The Docks, the clouds were breaking up, and patches of blue were peeking through.

Jason's boat was one of those stacked models that are nearly as high as they are long. It was candy-apple red with silver trim and equipped with a powerful inboard engine. Jason, comfortable in old jeans and faded tank top, helped them aboard and told them to hang on. The boat burbled along quietly until they got out of the "no wake" portion of the bay, then began a baritone yell and smacked its way across the waves to the Big Island.

Betsy tried briefly to converse with Jan and Godwin but soon gave it up. They all three shrugged at one another and sat back to enjoy the ride. Every so often, one of the trio would go up to take a look at the progress but could only communicate satisfaction with a nod and a smile.

In about ten minutes, Jason slowed the motor back to its burble, and the bow of the boat came down enough that they could see they were coming along a low shoreline covered with trees and shrubs. Just about the place where it curved away into a shallow harbor was an old wooden dock, a single walkway about twenty feet long supported on poles. A green lawn came down to the water, shaded by two mature trees, and beyond the trees sat an old cabin fronted by a screened porch. It was a single story, cream-colored affair with a roof that sloped forward over the porch. There was no dog in the yard, so Jason maneuvered his boat up to the dock. Jan, re-splendent in yellow clam-diggers and matching shirt, hopped onto it, took the line Jason tossed her, and wrapped it around a pylon, finishing with a half hitch.

Jan said, "Betsy, come with me up to the house, okay?"

"All right," Betsy replied as she clumsily clambered out of the boat. "Do you know who lives here?" she asked, looking up at the house.

"No, do you?"

"No."

"Maybe it's a nice couple with a strong teenage boy who will help us dig," said Jan.

"Well, let's go see." Betsy waved Jan on ahead then followed up to the house. The screened porch didn't seem to have a door, so they went around to the side—which didn't have a door, either. The entrance was around back. No doorbell, so Jan knocked on the edge of the screen door.

After a short wait, an old man's voice called, "Who's there?"

Jan lifted her voice to reply, "Jan Henderson and her friend, Betsy Devonshire!"

After a minute or two, a wiry old man with wispy gray hair and suspicious gray eyes came out to peer at them through the screen. "What'd'ya want?" he asked brusquely.

"We'd like to talk to you about digging up something on your property—if your property runs along that way." Jan pointed to the east. "Past your fence."

"What are you, one o' them plant collectors? After a fern or somethin'?"

"No, sir. We found an old map and it says something is buried along the shore a little way up from here."

He began to laugh, just a few "heh, heh, hehs" at first, then more violently, until he had to lean on the doorjamb for support. Jan would have tried to interrupt, but Betsy touched her subtly on her waist, and they both waited until he quit.

"Who sold you the map?" he asked, wiping his eyes.

"Nobody. We found it sewn inside an old pillow."

Suddenly his eyes were keen. "Can I see it?"

"All right," said Jan.

"But only if you come out here," amended Betsy, backing away and touching Jan on the arm to get her to follow.

"Sure." He came out, a little old man in worn work pants and white T-shirt. Ancient moccasins encased his sockless feet. "My name is Randy Utterberg," he said, putting out a gnarled hand. "I've lived here for seventy-eight years. My granddad built this place, and my dad added the front porch.

I was born on the island, and I plan to die here. Which one of you has the map?"

"I do," said Jan. "We're not sure who stitched it." She went into a front pocket and pulled it out. She had run the edge of the map through her sewing machine to stop the raveling but had not cut off any of the loose threads.

"Stitched?" He took the map from her. "Well, I'll be dipped, it *is* sewn, like embroidery!" He laid it over an outstretched hand and slid it this way and that, studying it. "Yep, it's a map, all right," he said almost immediately, then went into a trouser pocket to pull out a shiny red metal tube about an inch in diameter and seven inches long. "Open that, one of you," he ordered.

Betsy recognized it and pulled it apart into two unequal lengths. Inside was a pair of small reading glasses. She unfolded the temples and handed them to him. He put them on and resumed looking at the map.

"Look for a small red heart on the north side of the Big Island," directed Jan, and he did.

"Sure enough," he said touching it. Then he walked out and around to the side of his cabin, looking up along the shore. "Somewhere between the big old tree and my fence line, I guess," he murmured, looking at the map, then the shoreline, then the map again.

His eye was caught by the shimmer of sunlight on Jason's boat, and he scowled. "Get away from there!" he shouted, gesturing at the boat. "Private dock!"

"No, they're with us," said Jan.

"Oh." He waved as if to erase the gesture and shouted, "Never mind!"

Jason, with Godwin beside him, waved back.

"They're our muscle," explained Betsy. "Going to dig the hole, with your permission."

"What do you expect to find?" Randy asked.

"We have no idea," said Betsy.

"The problem is," said Jan, "it's on your property, so legally, it's probably yours. On the other hand—" She reached out and expertly snatched the map away. "The exact location is known only by the owner of the map."

He looked at Jan a considering moment and then said, "I'll split it with you, sixty-forty."

"If we get the sixty, done," said Jan.

"If you'll do the digging, agreed."

"I'll go get the muscle," said Betsy, and she hurried down to the boat. "He says we can dig. Bring the spades."

Randy had an old pickax in a shed in back of the house, which he brought along as they started up the trail. "The map says this is a road," said Jan, looking around.

"Used to be," agreed Randy.

"What happened to it?" asked Betsy.

"Winters, ice, wind," he replied.

"I don't understand," said Jason, trying to smack a mosquito around the spade he was carrying. Godwin produced the spray bottle of Off! and began dampening Jason's bare skin, of which there was a considerable amount.

"The shoreline of the Island is always changing," explained Randy, coming to a halt and looking around. "The ice builds up along the shore and the wind pushes it, and the land retreats. Other times, it rains a lot, and the land washes down, maybe builds a beach. Then the ice comes along and pushes it up and builds dry land. Something's always happening to the shoreline. There used to be a one-lane dirt road along here when I was a boy, but it got squashed over a couple of hard winters, and now it's just this path."

"Interesting," said Betsy, looking around. "Godwin, stop it." The young man had finished spraying Jason and had begun on her.

"If the shoreline's changed so much, how are we going to figure out where to dig?" asked Jan.

"Well, let's see what kind of a mapmaker embroidered this map," said Randy.

They spread the map on the path and stooped to look at it. "Well, I'm guessing that old dead tree down there is the big tree on the map," said Jason, looking at the real tree and the stitched tree.

"Very likely," agreed Randy. "That was the tallest tree on the Island for as long as anyone can remember. It died about four years ago, and someone's going to have to take it down pretty soon, or it'll fall in a storm and do some real damage."

"Is there a house down there?" asked Betsy.

"Yes, on the other side of it, used as a vacation place by the owners a couple weeks every summer. The tree's on their property." Randy studied the map. "Here's my place," he said, pointing to the dock. "The treasure is closer to my place than the big tree—which is good, because my property ends about forty feet from where we are right now." The old tree was about sixty yards from them.

"Yes, but how do we figure out the exact place to dig?" asked Jan.

"Well, we probably won't get it right the first hole we dig," said Randy. "See, here's what's probably supposed to be a row of four bushes, but the swamp ate them years ago."

Godwin stood up, alarmed. "*Ate* them?" He looked over the side of the raised path, into a welter of tall marsh grass, black water, and shiny mud. "What lives in there, anyway?"

Randy looked up at him, amused. "Nothing bigger than a snapping turtle. What I meant was, the swamp shifts location, just like the shoreline does. It's about as close to the trail as I've ever seen it, though it's always been close. Problem is, it was a ways back when the treasure was buried. I think it's probably under water now."

Jan groaned. "That means we'll never be able to find it!"

Twenty

❖ ❖ ❖

"Now, now, don't get yourself all in a lather," said Randy. "Come on back to the house. I've got some things back there that may be helpful."

Betsy stood and looked around. "Are you sure you can't tell from this map where it is?"

"Yes, I'm sure. Come on, all of you."

Randy's house was small, shabby, and cluttered, but not dirty. There were a lot of bookshelves and cabinets, and they all were packed with books, photo albums, and scrapbooks. "I'm an historian," he said. "I know just about everything there is to know about Lake Minnetonka and absolutely everything about the Big Island." He had them sit down in his living room while he went around murmuring to himself, pulling out scrapbooks and albums and putting them back.

Jason said, "How about we eat our lunch now? Because if he finds what he's looking for, there's no holding us back to go digging."

The others agreed, and so he and Godwin went back to the boat to bring the basket of food and Betsy's thermal pack of drinks. In the basket were sandwiches, a jar of dill pickles, and individual plastic bags containing carrot sticks, cauliflower, and broccoli pieces. Jason, a gobbler, was finished with his lunch when Randy found what he wanted, which was an old map. He brought it to his kitchen table and unfolded it. "Here's the Big Island in 1933," he announced, and Jason, soft drink can in hand, went to look at it.

Randy continued his search. A few minutes later, he crowed, "*Aha!*" and brought another map to the table. "Big Island in 1960," he explained, and, a few minutes later, "Big Island in 1950." He opened a door and went into another room, probably his bedroom, since the rest of the house was pretty much open. He came back out with yet another map. "This is the latest map of this part of the lake. Who's got the embroidered map?"

"I do," said Jason, who had taken it from Jan. He spread it on the table, and the others gathered around.

"I hope your maps are all to the same scale," said Godwin.

"If it's close, we're good," said Randy.

Using the older maps, Randy and Jason came quickly to agree on where the treasure probably was located. They marked it on the 1960 map with a soft pencil, then taped the map to a sunny window. Then they put the newer map over the old one, aligning such features as they could find on both maps—and finding the scale was not identical, but close. "There," said Randy, tracing the circle on the old map onto the new one. "She's right inside that circle or I'm a kangaroo."

So it was back up the trail again, Randy in the lead with the modern map folded small, looking for landmarks only he could see. Finally, not far from where they'd stopped before, he paused and scraped a mark in the trail with his heel, walked half a dozen yards up the trail and made another scrape, then gestured to the landward side of the trail marked off with the scrapes. "Somewhere in here," he said.

"Here" was a swamp; there was no solid land anywhere.

"Oh, lord," sighed Jason, because he was the one wearing shorts. He went up to the first scrape on the path and stepped gingerly into the muck. He immediately began to sink and fell backward to grab onto the bank of the trail. This slowed his sinking, which stopped altogether about halfway up his thighs. The look on his face as he looked down at himself was a curious mixture of disgust and relief.

Jan had rushed to stand beside him on the trail, holding out a spade handle for him to grab onto if the sinking didn't stop. Her grin of relief was replaced by a cruel giggle when it did.

"Just walk along that edge at first," counseled Randy. "See if you can feel anything with your feet."

With extreme care, Jason began to walk along the mucky way. Green blades of grass sliced his thighs and lower arms, making him grimace. Facing the low bank of the trail, he held his hands at the ready to grab on should he step into a hole. Jan matched him step for step, ready to hold out the end of the spade to assist him.

On the fourth step, he went down far enough to wet the legs of his shorts, but the next step brought him up again—in fact, higher than he'd been at the start. "I'm standing on a flat rock," he said, thrashing one foot around to measure its limits. "Ouch!" he said, finding one. "It's got a point on that side!" He felt around some more and found the other side about a step and a half in the other direction. "Fatter on this side than the other," he reported. He stepped off the rock into thigh-deep mud, wincing as the marsh grass sliced thinly into his tender flesh. At the far end, Godwin and Randy helped him up onto solid land again.

"Whoosh!" he exclaimed. "Sorry, but all that's in there is that rock! Mr. Utterberg, can I go back to your place and sluice off? These cuts sting!" His exposed skin was covered with tiny red lines, some of which oozed blood.

"You sure you don't want to go out from the trail a bit and walk that line again?"

"I'm sure."

"Well, I've got a hose all hooked up on the east side of the house."

"Thanks." Jason walked off wide-legged, and Randy looked around at the trio remaining. "All right, who's next?"

"What, you want another one of us to go in there?" asked Godwin.

"Well, how else are you going to find the treasure if you don't go in there and look for it?"

"Drain the swamp?" offered Betsy hopefully.

Jan laughed, Godwin snickered, but Randy said, "What's the matter, don't you want to get rich?"

"Maybe we're already rich enough," said Jan.

"Who's got the thinnest shoes?" asked Randy. "You can feel around with your feet."

They all looked at their feet. Godwin smiled at his army boots, Jan smiled at her sports shoes, Randy held out one foot shod with an older, scabbier match for Godwin's boots, and Betsy sighed as she looked down at her thin tennies.

But at least the jeans and long-sleeve shirt would protect her from the cut-grass.

She allowed Jan and Godwin to each take a hand and lower her gingerly into the swamp. It came all the way up her legs. She sidestepped, pausing at every step away from the bank to feel around with one foot. The marsh quickly deepened the farther she went. After one step brought the level of muck to her waist, she elected not to go farther from the trail, and when her next step parallel to it brought the muddy water up to her bosom, she came close in again. "I'm sorry, but I don't want to sink out of sight."

A few side steps later, and she found the flat rock Jason had stepped up on. "You know, it's odd there being this one rock right here," she said. "The bottom all around here is just mush. What's it doing here? And what is it resting on?" She turned in a little circle, probing with one foot, then the other, finding the outline of the rock, by trying to reach under it with the toes of one foot. She could detect nothing underneath, so what was it standing on? It seemed to be coming out from the solid earth under the trail. She outlined it again with her foot. It swelled from a point out to a rounded top, and there seemed to be an indentation in the top.

It was as if a light went on. "I think this rock is shaped like a heart!" she shouted and raised both arms. "Lift me out!"

As they did, Jason came running up the trail, trailing water from the waist down. "What, what? Did you find it?" he called.

"No—well, maybe," said Betsy. "That rock you stood on, pointed on one side. It's rounded on the other."

"Yeah?"

"I think it's heart-shaped."

He stared at her. "Well, whadaya know! I didn't think of that—you could be right!"

"It's less than two feet down," said Godwin. "Come on, try to lift it up. I bet the treasure is under it."

"Hold on, hold on!" said Randy. "First, let's mark the spot."

So Betsy took the two spades and climbed back onto the rock. Standing on it, she pushed them into the muck, flanking the rock about eighteen inches away on either side. The blades went down, then the handles, until only the last fourteen inches or so were still in sight. Betsy pushed down a couple more inches and let go. The spades stood firm. Then Jason, swearing under his breath, climbed back in, and Betsy stepped off the stone and took two steps sideways.

Jason slammed the pickax into the water, causing the others on the trail to back off hastily. It took three tries before the point went deep into the solid ground of the bank under the stone. He began to lever it up. It resisted and resisted, and then suddenly broke free. Betsy grabbed at it, wetting herself to the chin. Jason yanked the pickax free and threw it up on the bank, then grabbed the stone from his side. The two of them lifted it until Godwin and Randy could grab on and drag it onto the trail.

About two and a half feet long, it was dark, wet, muddy and trailing silt and dead grass. And yes, sort of heart-shaped; one of the rounded lobes was nearly missing. "I think I did that," said Jason, pointing to the missing lobe. "I think the other part is stuck down there. It felt like it broke free."

"I think you may be right," said Randy, stooping to finger the shattered edge. "This looks fresh broke."

"Betsy, feel around," said Jan. "Is there something under where it was?"

Betsy padded around where the rock had been and said, "Not right under it. Wait, wait. There may be something way down there. It feels like there's something solid . . . it could be just another rock." She danced a slow jig over the place. "It's pretty far down, I think."

Jason pulled one of the spades out and stuck it down again as Betsy moved out of the way. Jason bent sideways, feeding the handle down almost to the end. It went smoothly, then stopped. "I think she's right," he said. "I think there's something down there. Doesn't feel like a rock—feels like wood."

"Oh? Oh?" cried Jan, excited beyond words.

"A *treasure chest*!" said Godwin, peering into the black water as if it were possible to get a glimpse of it down there.

"Yeah, but there's no way to dig a hole in this stuff," said Betsy, looking around.

"There's more than one way to skin a cat," said Randy. "I'll be back as fast as I can." He set off down the trail toward his cabin.

"Get us out," said Jason after a minute. "I'm starting to think about leeches."

"Ack! Ack!" cried Betsy, holding up both arms. "Out, out!" So they hauled her out first. She didn't go all the way back to the house, but rushed down the other side of the trail and into the lake, going out as far as the top of her shoulders and sloshing around. Then she came in to shallow water, sat down, unbuttoned her cuffs and inspected her arms as far up as she could pull the sleeves. She found nothing until she hauled at the legs of her jeans to inspect her lower legs.

There was a big splash as Jason joined her in the water. "Find any?" he asked her, moving his arms and legs briskly to clean off the mud.

"Y-yes," she quavered, pulling at a black thing on one calf. "No, wait, it's just a leaf."

But Jason found two, and grabbed a handful of sand to rub them off.

"They're not dangerous!" called Jan from the trail. "They even have medical uses."

"Oh, yeah?" said Jason. "Then how about you go in there and gather a few to take to Hugs?"

For some reason, Jan didn't take his suggestion.

It was nearly ten minutes before Randy came back, carrying two rakes—not the leaf kind, the garden kind, with heavy teeth. "Had to go borrow one," he explained.

"You expect us to *rake* the mud away?" said Godwin.

"No, son. We'll use the rakes to lift whatever's under there out. One on each side of it."

Betsy was adamant—she was not going back in. "It's not my treasure," she said, "and I'm not going back in there with those leeches."

"I'll dig," said Godwin, "but I won't wade in that."

"Well," sighed Jan, "It's my turn, I guess."

"I know how to do this, so I'll help you," said Randy.

So with eloquent faces, they stepped gingerly into the muck. Under Randy's guidance, they both pushed the rakes down, handles first, to locate and size the object Jason had felt. It appeared to be rectangular, about three feet long and two feet wide. It was at an angle to the trail.

"Now, turn your rake over and carefully go down the edges of the thing, on the long side, until you can slip the tines under it."

That struggle went on for fifteen minutes until both were satisfied they had all the tines under the object.

"Now ready? Lift up, as straight up as you can," ordered Randy.

The first thing that happened was both rakes came loose and had to be reset. It took less time this try, and the lifting began again. Jan's rake came loose several times, but at last the object broke the surface.

It was a wooden box, smaller than their first estimates—a little over two feet long and eighteen inches wide. And, by its heft, not empty. The lid was flat, nailed shut. It was very slimy, and their hands kept slipping when they tried to lift it. At last, Jason took one of the rakes and helped get it up on the trail.

"Now, let's go back to my place," said Randy. "I've got a chisel and hammer."

Back in the side yard, Godwin washed it off, then Jan took the hose and washed herself, groaning at the gray over-lay on her formerly crisp yellow outfit. Randy shut the water off, then went for his tools. "All right, everyone ready?" he asked.

"Yes, yes, get on with it!" said Jan, her hands clasped at her chest.

So Randy knelt and began prying the top off. The wood was old and soft. It didn't take long. The lid lifted at the front, then along one side, and at the back. He grasped the long edge and pulled upward.

There was a filthy wad of cloth filling the box. Jason turned the faucet until only a gentle stream came out of the hose and handed it to Randy, who played it over the cloth, washing away some of the filth. Then he reached in with one hand and began lifting the cloth away at one end. They all bent in to see as he played the stream over the pale gray-brown face of a tiny dead infant.

Twenty-one

JAN screamed and fell backwards, landing hard on her bottom. Betsy immediately knelt beside her, pulling her into an awkward sideways embrace. The others backed away from the box, their faces pictures of dismay and distress.

"Is that a real baby?" asked Godwin fearfully.

"Sure looks like it," replied Randy, leaning forward briefly for a better look. He still had the dribbling hose in one unconscious hand.

"It's so *little*," said Jason.

"A newborn, probably," said Godwin. "Maybe even a preemie?"

Betsy said, "Randy, was that place ever a cemetery?"

"No, there was never a white man's cemetery on the Big Island, and the Indians didn't coffin their dead. Besides, there was always a swamp over there, just smaller than it is today."

"Maybe—maybe it's a pioneer burial," said Jason. "You know, some poor mother lost her baby, and they buried it over there, back when it was solid land."

"No," said Randy. "It would be a skeleton if it was buried a real long time ago."

"What should we do?" asked Jason. "It's a dead baby, we can't just put it back."

"No, of course not," said Betsy. "We have to call the police."

"No!" said Jan sharply.

"What do you mean, no?" asked Betsy, so surprised she released her. "We have to report this."

"No, no, there must be something else we can do!" insisted Jan. "Don't you see? My mother buried that baby!"

"NINE-ONE-ONE, what is your emergency?"

"I just came home and found my wife! She's bleeding from her chest, I think, and her head! There's blood all over!"

"Is she conscious?"

"No. She's making funny noises when she breathes. Please send an ambulance right away!"

"Where are you?"

"In one of the Dove Cabins near the lake."

"What street? What city?"

"It's a town named Excelsior. The cabins are on Cedar Lane off of Third. Oh, God, please hurry!"

"WELL, that was embarrassing," said Jason, as he helped Jan put the basket back in the boat.

"Does that mean we haven't found the real treasure?" asked Godwin, waiting his turn to climb aboard.

"Beats me," sighed Jan.

"A *doll*!" muttered Jason, climbing up into the cockpit and flinging himself into the captain's chair. "We called the police over a stupid, crummy old doll!" He shot Betsy a venomous look, because she had insisted they not disturb the find any further and summon the police.

"Well, I'm glad it was just a doll!" said Jan. "I'm ashamed of the things I was thinking about Mother! Honestly, how I could jump to such a terrible conclusion!"

Jason thumped his fist on the dash. "When that cop pulled the blanket all the way back, and I could see it was just a dumb old doll, I wanted to go out and live on my boat—never go ashore again! Did you see his face? He just about gave himself a hernia trying not to laugh! I bet he's laughing now! I bet he'll laugh for a week! He'll tell all his friends, and pretty soon a TV camera crew will show up at my door! The final straw will be when we find ourselves in 'News of the Weird'!"

"Oh, shut up, Jason!" said Jan.

"You're being very quiet," Godwin said to Betsy, taking a plastic-wrapped bundle from her, then reaching back to help her climb into the boat.

"Yes, I suppose I am." She found a place on the bench seat along one side and sat down, frowning lightly.

"We're all aboard now," Jan said to her brother. "You can start for The Docks." The engine started to roar, and further conversation was impossible until they reached Excelsior.

Then Betsy asked, "Jan, are you planning on telling your mother about this?"

"Well, of course!"

"May I ask a big favor?"

"All right."

"Let me go with you when you do."

"What? Why? And anyway I was going to tell her on the phone."

"No, don't do that. Tell her in person."

"I don't understand."

"I think we did find the treasure. I think your mother buried that doll. I want to be with you when she tells you why."

A few minutes later, as Godwin was walking Betsy home, he asked, "Do you really think Jan's mom buried that doll?"

"Well, I have a theory now, and I'm sure that whoever stitched that map knew what was in the box."

Godwin sighed dramatically at the mention of the box.

Betsy smiled at him. "Poor fellow, such a disappointment! No gold coins, no ruby rings."

"And I was *so* looking forward to trying on the crown."

"Crown?"

"Didn't you ever read comic books? There's always a royal crown in treasure chests."

They were nearly at Betsy's apartment building when Godwin said, "Look, isn't that Phil Galvin?"

The old man was standing tall, looking around. When he saw Betsy and Godwin, he waved at them, urging them to hurry.

So they did. Coming toward them, he demanded in his too-loud voice, "Have you heard the news, about Lucille Jones?"

"What about her?" asked Betsy.

"She's in the hospital, hurt bad!"

"No!" said Godwin. "How, what happened?"

"Someone attacked her in her cabin. Maybe shot her. Her husband came home and found her."

"Where is she?" asked Betsy.

"HCMC, downtown," he said, referring to Hennepin County Medical Center in Minneapolis.

"Have the police arrested anyone?"

"Not that I know of. I only know what I heard over the police band."

"So this isn't on the regular news yet?"

"I don't know. I didn't turn on the TV or radio before I came over. I was in a hurry, y'see. I was thinking it might be a part of this business with old Miss Hanraty, and I know you're looking into that." He seemed anxious that she do something, right now.

The door to the upper apartments opened, and Doris came out. "What's going on? Who rang my doorbell?"

Phil, startled, turned around. "I did. I was trying to get hold of Betsy, and when she didn't answer, I rang your bell."

"Oh." She started to go back inside, but Betsy said, "Doris, perhaps you could invite Phil up. He's just brought me some important news, and now he's upset and needs to sit down before he goes home."

Doris looked as if she was about to refuse, then relented. Smiling, she said, "Of course. Come in, Phil."

Betsy said, "I have some things to do. Come on, Goddy."

Up in her apartment, while Godwin unloaded the left-over drinks into her refrigerator, Betsy dialed Jill's phone number. "Jill," she said, "can you find out about a patient at HCMC? It's Lucille Jones. Something bad happened to her, perhaps someone shot her, in her cabin."

"Oh, no, when did this happen?"

"Very recently. Phil Galvin heard about it on his police radio and was waiting for me when we got back from a trip out to the Big Island. It was Lucille's husband who called it in, I think. I'm going to call Jan, but I've got my cell phone, so call me back on that."

"Will do."

Betsy hung up and dialed Jan. "Jan, have you heard about Lucille?" she asked. "She's at HCMC with an unknown injury. I'm not sure of any details yet, but I wanted to give you a heads-up on this."

"Ohhhhhh," groaned Jan. "This is awful! What was it, a car accident?"

"I'm afraid not."

There was a little pause. Jan said, "You mean, someone tried to *kill* her?"

"I don't have any confirmation of details yet, only that her husband came to the cabin and found her, and she's at HCMC."

"What should I do? Should I go over there?"

"No, they won't tell you anything or let you see her, because you're not family. I mean—"

"Yes, I know what you mean. Oh, gosh, this is so awful!"

"Hold on, my cell phone's ringing." Betsy put down the receiver and pulled her cell phone from her purse. "Hello?"

"It's Jill. Yes, she's at HCMC, in surgery. Bullet wounds to the head and chest. I'm afraid she's listed as critical."

"Have they arrested anyone?"

"No. Looking at the husband, of course, but he's behaving appropriately, crying and angry. Sergeant Rice is there, but he's got Mike assisting—uh-oh, doorbell. Hold on."

"No, that's all I wanted. Thanks, Jill." Betsy disconnected and went back to Jan. "Jill says she's in surgery, that she was shot in the head and chest."

"Oh, my God! Who could have done this?"

"Well, not you or Jason."

"What? You couldn't think—oh, you're thinking like the police! We have *alibis*!"

"Yes. Jan, I want to talk to Susan right away, before that investigator, Rice, gets to her. I'll come and pick you up in a couple of minutes—I still need to change clothes."

"Y-yes, all right."

Godwin came out of the kitchen, eyes round, and said, "Shall I wait here and answer the phone?"

"Would you, Goddy? Thanks."

"Don't forget this," he said, handing her the plastic-wrapped bundle.

Ten minutes later, Jan climbed into Betsy's Buick. "What if Sergeant Rice is already there, at my mother's?" she asked, fastening her seat belt.

"He won't be. He's at the hospital, talking to Bobby Lee and waiting to see if he can talk to Lucille. But Mike Malloy's on the case, too. I don't know if the two of them have discussed Sergeant Rice's investigation into Edyth Hanraty's murder."

"Why would he do that?"

"Because you're involved, and so are the Joneses—and you're all living in Excelsior. Mike is going to be ringing your doorbell very soon." Betsy made the turn off Water Street onto Nineteenth.

"Will he be mad if I'm not there?"

"He'll be annoyed, but your husband can explain that you were out on the Big Island with me, your brother and several other people."

"And then he'll come to talk to Mother."

Betsy pressed down on the accelerator. "Yes, you're right."

They stayed on Nineteenth, winding among the bays of Lake Minnetonka through Shorewood, Tonka Bay, and Navarre to Fifteen, which went past Minnetonka Beach and Crystal Bay, in the greater township (well, city, in the lexicon of the lake) of Orono.

"Turn here," said Jan, pointing to Orchard Road, then immediately, "turn left," gesturing toward Fox Street.

Soon they were wandering in a development of townhomes. "Next left is Mother's," said Jan.

Betsy pulled into the driveway of a one-and-a-half level townhome that shared a wall with its mirror image. They were on a street of white twin homes distinguishable only by the annuals planted in their front yards.

"No strange car in the driveway, that's good," noted Jan, who climbed out and hurried up to the front door beside the garage. She pressed the doorbell several times, then opened the door.

Betsy, going into the back for the bundle, heard her call, "Are you decent, Mother?" She followed her to the door, but paused before going in.

Suddenly Jan was there, smiling apologetically. "Forgot my manners, come in, come in."

Susan McConnell was sitting in her living room, using the strong sunlight coming through the big front window as an aid to her stitching. But she had taken off the hanging magnifying glass and was putting her needle into the edge of her framed counted cross-stitch piece.

Though she had seen her dozens of times, Betsy was struck now by how much Susan was unlike her daughter. Susan was short, dark and slender, while Jan was tall, blond and sturdy—and so was her brother, Jason. Must take after their father, thought Betsy—and then thought of Lucille, who looked so much like Jan.

"Mother, we want to talk to you about something important. I'm going to let Betsy ask you some questions, all right?" Jan sat on the pretty couch and gestured at Betsy to sit beside her.

"All right," said Susan, looking swiftly between the two of them, trying to read the questions in advance. Her eyes stopped short at the bundle on Betsy's lap, which was just a big, black garbage bag wrapped around something and held in place with strips of duct tape.

Betsy said, "Mrs. McConnell, we went out to the Big Island this morning."

Susan nodded. "I thought that's where you'd go," she said to her daughter.

"Jan isn't sure, but I think we managed to find the treasure stitched on that map she showed you."

All the color drained from Susan's face, and she stared at the black bundle as if afraid it might grow teeth and bite her. But she managed a normal voice as she asked, "And what was the treasure?"

"This," said Betsy, beginning to pull at the tape.

"A doll, it's just a doll!" said Jan hurriedly, watching her mother's face. "A really old one, with a wax head, wrapped in a flannel blanket. Isn't that crazy?"

Susan looked at her daughter, astonished, and fainted, sliding out of the cream chair onto the pastel green carpet.

Jan was immediately by her side. "Here, now, what's wrong?" she said, pulling at her mother's legs to get her flat on the floor. Betsy handed her a crewel pillow from the couch, and Jan put it under her mother's feet. She took her mother's pulse, then chafed her hand gently. "Come on, darling, come on," she crooned. "Wake up. You're all right. Everything's all right."

"Does she need a blanket or something?" asked Betsy.

"No, look, she's opening her eyes now."

Susan's eyelids fluttered, and she made a soft exclamation. "What—what happened? Why am I on the floor?" The second question was asked more forcefully, and Jan smiled.

"You fainted, that's all. You're all right. You're going to be fine."

"Why on earth—? Oh." Memory returned, and color flushed into Susan's face. She looked around, saw Betsy, then looked at her daughter again. "Is what you told me true?"

"Yes, we found a wooden box nailed shut, and when we opened it, there was a doll inside, wrapped in a flannel blanket. It was under the muck and water of a marsh, so everything was wet and discolored. The blanket might once have been blue, but it was hard to tell."

"Where did you go looking for it?" asked Susan, now more in command of her senses. She rose to a sitting position, bending her knees, leaning her back against the chair.

"Right where it said to on the map," said Susan. "The marsh had expanded, and it took over most of the road."

Betsy, who had put the bundle aside, lifted it back onto her lap and began again to pull at the strips of tape. She said, "We found a rock first, shaped like a heart—" She paused when Susan gave a little exclamation, but Susan waved at her to continue. "It was under water. We found it by stepping on it. Jason pried it out of the side of the bank, and a couple of feet under it we found the box."

Susan fell silent for a little while, her face gone sad. Then, "Help me up," she ordered her daughter, and they had an awkward little struggle until she was on her feet. Jan sat her on the easy chair.

"May I get you something to drink?" she asked.

"Yes, please. I think there's a bottle of sherry in the cabinet over there. Just a drop or two."

Jan hurried over to the low cabinet, and soon the clink of bottle on glass was heard.

Susan looked at Betsy and said, "You said you have the doll with you?"

"Yes, would you like to see it?"

Susan stared at the bundle which now, with strips of duct tape pulled off, was beginning to unwrap itself. "All right. Wait, let me have my drink first. A wax head, you said?"

"Yes, a wax head and a kid leather body."

Susan said, "I've seen wax-headed dolls in antique stores. They look like miniature adults in those fancy old dresses."

Susan came to hand her mother a tiny cut-glass goblet half full of a red brown liquid. "I've seen them on *Antiques Roadshow*. It was the French who made the beautiful adult dolls. But I've also seen ones made in Germany. They're called 'character dolls' and were made in the early 1900s. Some were children, some even were babies."

Susan immediately swallowed half the liquid, then waved her hand in front of her face, mouth open. "I guess I needed that, but it's almost as bad as medicine," she said. She drank the rest, then handed the glass back to her daughter. "Thank you, dear," she said.

"More?" asked Jan.

"No, that's enough. Now I think I'm ready to see this doll you found." She sounded much more like herself, though the sherry had raised two bright spots of pink on her cheeks, and the rest of her complexion was still very pale.

Betsy pulled the last strip of tape off and unwound the bag. She let the bag drape over her lap, as the blanket enclosing the doll was still wet, if no longer dripping. The blanket was a dirty gray color.

Susan leaned forward as Betsy gently pulled it down to expose the gray-brown head.

Time had also done its work on the face. Probably once sweet-looking, now it was slightly distorted, the closed mouth pulled a little to one side, and one eye squinched almost closed. Susan put her hands over her mouth and made a tiny moan. Jan sat on the arm of the chair and put an arm around her mother. "Awful, isn't it?" she said, trying for a light tone. "We thought it was a real baby when we saw it. We even called the police. Jason said he was never so embarrassed in his life when we saw it was just a doll. The policeman had to try really hard not to laugh—though when he first saw it, he thought it was real, too, I noticed. I think he was laughing at himself, not us."

Susan slipped off the chair and came to kneel beside Betsy. Very, very gingerly she touched the tiny face. "Just a doll. It looked so real." She pressed her lips shut and sat back on her heels.

Betsy said, "I have some truly bad news."

"What?" asked Susan blankly.

"Something has happened to Lucille Jones."

"What?" Susan asked, with no hint she might know what it was.

"Lucille has been shot. She's in critical condition at the Hennepin County Medical Center."

"Shot—who on earth would do a thing like that?"

"The police are hoping she'll be able to wake up and tell them," said Betsy. Again, there was no sign of worry on Susan's face that Lucille might accuse Susan of the deed. "She really is your daughter, you know."

"Who is?"

"Lucille."

"No, I—" Susan stopped short, her mouth pursed to continue, but without any sound coming forth.

"That's right. You thought you buried your baby on the Big Island. Susan, please, tell us how that came about."

Twenty-two

❖ ❖ ❖

SUSAN sighed and leaned back in her chair. "It's the old, sad story, of course. I went to a New Year's Eve party with this upstanding young man. We'd known each other for nearly a year, since I turned fifteen. He was not quite two years older than I, which means a lot when you're just fifteen. He was very sweet, and my mother didn't like him, which helped a lot."

She smiled, and continued, "The party was at a friend's house, and he didn't tell us his parents wouldn't be home. And somebody brought a keg of beer. I had never had a drink before in my life, other than the one sip of wine at Thanksgiving my father permitted me after I turned thirteen, and I don't think David had, either, though he pretended he had. We didn't get falling-down drunk—which might have saved us, now I think about it. We just got drunk enough to lose our inhibitions, and six weeks later, I told my mother what had happened and why I suspected it wasn't a bad piece of fish the night before that had me throwing up that morning.

"This was 1959. The country was on the verge of social

change but hadn't crossed the threshold, at least not in St. Paul. Mother was furious, at me and at David. Father wanted a shotgun wedding, but Mother's dislike of David had only deepened over this mess. She won, and Mother told David and his family to stay away. I wasn't told about this, and I thought he'd abandoned me. I was only sixteen. Mother thought she was doing what was right. She wanted me to be at the very least a nurse, perhaps even a doctor. I wanted it, too—but I was carrying a baby, and that was a potentially ruinous condition, not just for me, but the whole family. An abortion was out of the question. I don't think it even occurred to any of us. But reputation meant a great deal back then, and a doctor could lose patients if it were known his daughter had a baby out of wedlock. And of course, if I kept the baby, I could not get into medical school.

"So we went to the old solution: As soon as I started to show, I was shipped off to Aunt Edyth—we were living in St. Paul at the time, and while there was some worry that Orono wasn't far enough away, there was no place else except a home for unwed mothers, and Mother absolutely didn't want me in one of *those places*—you know, where the young women were *those kind* of people. So our friends were told that Aunt Edyth had fallen and injured her back and was having trouble getting around, so I was going to spend the summer with her.

"Aunt Edyth was a peculiar woman all her life. She took me in and was kindness walking—except when I'd do something foolish or incorrectly, and she'd be so angry, it would set her off on a tirade. She'd berate me for a promiscuous fool and ask how I could be such a ninny as to believe love talk from a man. She was kind of a moody person, I decided. But now, looking back at the incredibly ignorant and opinionated idiot I was, I wonder if she wasn't justified in her disappointment in me. Either that, or she was suffering from cabin fever at least as bad as mine."

Susan chuckled, looking up at the ceiling but seeing

scenes from more than fifty years ago. "She must have hated having to pretend all summer that she was housebound with a bad back—she sure loved getting out and going places! She loved to ride that motorcycle on fine afternoons, and she loved to break speed limits in her automobile. She never kept a car more than two years, and she insisted on the biggest engine they came with. But of course that summer—" Her smile abruptly vanished. "God, I hated being a disappointment to her. She was so proud of me, of my abilities in school. She said it was like seeing herself in a better time, with more opportunities for women than she had. I loved her so much . . ." A tear formed and fell, then another, but she lifted her chin and blinked to stop them.

"She had told me that in my ninth month, she'd call one of those homes, and I'd go there the last couple of weeks and have the baby and sign the papers to give it up. At first, I was all right with that, but as my tummy filled and the baby kicked and moved, I started to fall in love with it. I asked her about keeping it, and she said no, positively no. I said she was a rebel, maybe I could be another kind of rebel, the kind that keeps her babies, even without a husband. That's when I found out that in certain respects she was extremely old-fashioned. She wouldn't hear such nonsense. My parents had high expectations of me, expectations that would be destroyed if I came home with a baby and no husband. What would people think? Alice and John would be held up to ridicule, trying to lie to the neighborhood about where I'd been. How could I think of doing such a wicked thing to them—and destroying my own future in the process?

"But I still thought about it. I couldn't let go of the notion that it could be worked out somehow, and I think she knew it, though we didn't talk about it anymore.

"And then, eight weeks from my due date, I got this terrific pain. My water broke, and I felt such pain as never in my life before. Aunt Edyth got me up to bed and after about twenty minutes of screaming, I had the baby. She wrapped it in a towel and took it out of the room. It didn't cry. I remember being very worried about that, because I knew newborns were supposed to cry right away.

"Aunt Edyth came back a few minutes later to see how I was doing, and I asked her about the baby, and she said she wasn't sure, but it was resting. I said I wanted to see it, and she said, 'In a little while.' She brought clean towels and made me comfortable, gave me something to drink, and went away again. And I fell asleep. I couldn't believe it. Even while I was falling asleep, I remember thinking how silly it was—I was frantic about the baby and I was still in a lot of pain, and I was falling asleep."

Jan and Betsy exchanged significant looks.

Susan, oblivious, continued, "When I woke up, it was dark out, and she was sitting beside me. She talked so softly and looked so comforting. She was in her nightgown, and her hair was in her long nighttime braid. And she told me the baby was dead. It was a boy, she said, but not completely formed, and it never took a breath.

"I thought I would never stop crying." She wiped her eyes with the fingers of both hands. "But I did when she said we had to figure out right away what we were going to do.

"We hadn't told anybody about the baby, of course, so no one would come looking for it. On the other hand, it wasn't a dead puppy, so I was totally against burying it on the grounds like one, which was her first suggestion. I wanted to look at him, hold it in my arms just once, but she said it was 'funny looking' and it would disturb me to see it. We talked some more, and I guess she was the one who remarked that the Big Island used to have many Indian mounds marking Indian graves, and that it was considered sacred ground even to the present time by the Indians. And we worked ourselves into deciding it would be a fine and natural burial place for the baby.

"She'd gotten an antique vase from an auction house a few days before, and she said we could use the walnut storage chest it came in. She wrapped the little body in a soft blue flannel baby blanket, and I named him David after the father. I got just a little glimpse of the face—it was such a wee, little thing, and I remember it had no eyelashes—as she put it into the box and took it downstairs. She nailed the top down . . ." Susan had to stop for a few moments.

"I have never, ever forgotten the sound of those nails being driven in. She never hesitated, just drove them in, one after the other, as if she were building a table or a gate . . ." Susan did stop then, to weep, and Jan moved to sit on one arm of the chair again and wrap her arms around her mother.

"Oh, my dear, my dear, darling Mother, how awful, how awful," she murmured. She began to stroke her mother's hair, as if she were a cat, repeating the gesture over and over while she murmured words of comfort.

"Oh, but this is silly. It was such a long time ago!" cried Susan, striving to stop crying. Then, suddenly, she grew very still. After a few moments, her still-streaming eyes came up to meet Betsy's. "And now you have the *audacity* to come here and tell me I did not lose that baby?" she asked in a low voice. "You're telling me Aunt Edyth *lied* to me?"

"Yes," said Betsy striving for a calm tone. Her own emotions were on a rave; she couldn't decide which was stronger— pity for Susan or anger at Edyth. "Where did you get the stone?"

Susan seemed about to refuse to answer, but finally said, still in that low voice, "It was something I'd found when I was eleven, part of a crazy-paving walk. Aunt Edyth had taken up the stones and piled them against the fence. The one I found had a kind of pink color to it, and it was shaped almost like a heart. I got a hammer and very carefully chipped away at it until it really did resemble a heart. I put it in the shed out back, thinking the next time we buried an animal, I would use it to mark the spot. I never did, but now I remembered it and insisted we bring it along.

"Aunt Edyth wanted me to stay behind, but I was absolutely positive I had to see where he was buried. She was so worried about that, sure I would get sick and die, and how would she explain what happened? But I said I didn't care if I died, I was coming.

"It was late July when we took the *Edali* out, a Thursday night—well, Friday morning, really. We went around the Big Island and found a place where the land ran down low into the water, and there was just this one cabin up a ways, with no lights showing.

"Aunt Edyth had a big battery flashlight and set it on the shore so she could see what she was doing, then got me ashore and made me sit beside it while she unloaded the spade, the coffin and the stone. There was a road along the shore then, just a lane, really, and I got up and walked a little way up it and saw three bridal wreath bushes in a row that I liked, though of course they were all through blooming by then, and I said that was the place. She took off the top layer of grass and weeds in front of the bushes and dug the grave." Susan paused.

"I think she was angry. I remember her pushing the spade in deep with her foot; and the way her head bent and arms moved said *angry, angry*. I sat on the ground and tried not to cry, because she scared me, and because she was taking care of me, and because of the enormity of what we were doing.

"I think she dug until she wasn't angry anymore. She put the coffin in. There was a little water in the bottom, it made a splash, and I said the Lord's Prayer and prayed for David's soul to go to heaven and wait for me, then we covered it up. She already said she wouldn't let me put the heart on top, for fear someone would see it and realize that something was buried under it, so I put the heart down when the hole was nearly full, and she finished and put the sod back and went and got the bait bucket and filled it a bunch of times to water it well. I was worried about that, but it rained the next afternoon, so I guess no one came along the lane before the rain and noticed that the ground was soaked in that one place.

"We came back home, and she put me to bed and made me stay there for seven days. When she wasn't looking, I stitched the map, and later I put it inside the pillow I'd been working on while I was waiting for David to be born. When I was ready to go home, we couldn't find the pillow." Susan fell silent then.

After nearly a minute, Jan said, "Is it possible that when Aunt Edyth brought you something to drink after the birth, there was something in it to make you fall asleep; and that while you slept, she took your baby to St. Paul, to the children's hospital there, and left it?"

"Why the children's hospital in St. Paul?"

"Because that's where Lucille was left."

Betsy asked, "What did you tell your parents?"

"I told them—and David—that the baby was a boy and had been given up for adoption."

Another silence. Then Susan asked, "You *promise* you found the box under a stone heart and this is the doll that was in that box?"

"Absolutely," said Jan. "The police officer said the tannin in the swamp water preserved it, like those 'bog bodies' they keep finding in England and the Scandinavian countries. Did you ever see a doll with a wax head in Aunt Edyth's house?"

Susan thought. "No. But that doesn't meant it wasn't there. The wax-headed dolls in the antique shop were very expensive—and Aunt Edyth was a collector with a fondness for expensive things. She might not have shown it to me for fear I'd play with it and damage it. Those wax faces must be fragile." She thought a bit longer, then said, "Remember that doll-size silk christening gown we found?"

"Yes," said Jan with a nod. "I am pretty sure that gown would fit this doll."

Susan heaved a lengthy sigh. "Why did she do that to me?" she asked.

"Because you were talking about keeping the baby," said Betsy. "She wanted to protect you and your parents from the consequences of your doing that."

"Yes, that would make sense to her. So, you believe this woman from Texas, Lucille Jones, really is my daughter, don't you?"

"Yes, ma'am, I do."

"But Aunt Edyth told me it was a boy."

"Because if something went wrong and you came to suspect your baby hadn't died and went looking for it, you'd be looking for a boy infant, not a girl."

"How very curious," said Susan. "I think I believe you, but I don't feel the least connection. You'd think I would, wouldn't you? I mean, now that you've halfway convinced me I didn't bury a son, but only mislaid a daughter? It doesn't seem real—it doesn't seem possible."

"I think that's shock, darling," said Jan. "I think in a little while, when it's all begun to sink in, then you'll suddenly want very much to meet her."

There was another long pause, then at last Susan spoke. "Who would want to shoot her?" she asked, in a strange, thin voice. She touched her forehead. "Oh, dear, I'm feeling very odd again. Not the floor this time; help me to the couch, Jan, please."

Betsy and Jan half carried her from the chair to the couch, where she lay down. Jan put the crewel pillow under her feet again. She was very pale. "I haven't told that story to anyone, not anyone, for nearly fifty years," she said, and tears began to spill. "It's hard to tell it at last and even *think* it was all a lie."

"But it wasn't a lie, not your part in it," said Betsy gently. "You had a baby, you took part in a burial of what you thought was your baby. Edyth Hanraty lied to you. It's not your fault that you believed her."

"Yes, that's true. So the natural question would be, if I buried a doll, what happened to my real baby? And you come to me with the answer already in hand. Is it possible that she grew up to be a laboratory technician from Texas named Lucille Jones?"

"I think we have good reason to investigate that possibility."

Susan closed her eyes. "What if she dies?"

"She's not going to die." Betsy said it fiercely, forcing belief on herself as well as Susan. It was too dreadful even to imagine, especially at the moment of reunion.

"But what if she does? What if she is my baby grown up, and she dies before I can talk to her? I don't know anything about her! Is she married? Are there children?"

Jan smiled. "Yes, she's married to an RN named Bobby Lee, and they have two grown children, an aircraft mechanic and a veterinarian. She herself is a medical lab technician."

"That's nice, that's nice. And now maybe I have two more grandchildren—and one's a girl. Yes, I want to meet her! I want to meet them all! Edyth wouldn't let me hold my baby. It wouldn't be fair not to get to hold her before she dies!" She began to cry again.

Jan said, "Hush, hush. Betsy's right, she is not going to die. Everything is going to be all right, don't get all fussed about it. Close your eyes and rest." When Susan obeyed, Jan said quietly to Betsy, "Come out to the kitchen. I want to talk to you."

"All right."

In the kitchen, Jan took Betsy by the arm and said, "Would you mind if I sent you away? I think Mother is working herself into hysterics, and she'd be embarrassed to death if you were here to see it."

"Can you handle her yourself?"

"Yes, we'll be fine. There are some pills in her medicine cabinet. I'll give her one in a little while, and she'll sleep."

"All right, I understand."

Betsy came back into the living room and said, "Susan, I have to go now. I have some things to do."

"Are you going to try to find out who shot Lucille?" That was as much a demand as a question.

"Yes, ma'am."

"Good, that's good. Are you here, Jan?"

"Right here, Mother."

"Hold my hand, dear, please."

Betsy slipped out the front door and got into her car. But she had to sit for a minute or two before she could pull herself together enough to start the engine.

SERGEANT Rice went to the Intensive Care Unit of Hennepin County Medical Center. The nurse's station was the hub of a wheel of rooms, a circular counter fitted inside with television monitors and computer screens as well as the usual medical detritus.

He walked up to the counter and said, "I'm back. How's she doing?"

A tall, handsome doctor with dark hair and eyes smiled at him. "Better. She's young, and her heart is strong."

"Is she conscious?"

"No, and she won't be for a while, which is fine. We're monitoring her carefully right now. If there's brain swelling, we may have to induce a coma to protect it."

"And if there isn't, when might I talk to her?"

"Possibly late this evening. But I'm sure you're aware

that when there's concussion there's pretty generally amnesia surrounding events before and after the injury."

"Yes, I know that, but maybe she can still tell me who hated her enough to do this."

Rice slouched away to a small office he had borrowed. Its tiny desk was covered with a computer, books, files and paper; a metal bookshelf screwed to the wall was jammed with file folders bulging with paper. How could someone work in such disorder? Never mind, the slob wasn't here right now. Sitting on a black-painted metal chair with a soft gray seat and back was Bobby Lee Jones, looking miserable and scared, which was appropriate whether he was responsible for his wife's condition—what if she woke up and told on him?—or not. He wore bright blue shorts and a non-matching blue shirt printed with palm trees and hibiscus flowers and faded red flip-flops.

Rice edged past him, leaning forward so as not to scrape his back on the shelf as he went past the desk, and sat down on the office armchair.

"When can I see her again?" asked Bobby Lee.

"In a while," Rice said. The truth was that he could go right now, but Rice wanted to talk to him some more first. "She's still unconscious but maybe improved a little, at least holding her own. The doc says her heart is strong, and they're satisfied she's doing all right."

"She cain't dah, she jest cain't dah," he said, his misery somehow strengthening his accent.

"I don't think she's going to die," Rice said.

"Are you lying to me?" Bobby Lee asked, hope and pain in his eyes.

"No, sir, it's not good policy for the police to lie to someone."

"Then that's good, that's good," said Bobby Lee. "I don't know what I'd do if she was to die."

"I want to talk to you while we're sitting here waiting," Rice said. "All right if I ask you some questions?"

"Yessir, go right ahead."

"First of all, about this business of your wife being the daughter of Susan McConnell. Do you think that's actually possible?"

"Well, sure it is! I would never've agreed to come up here if I didn't think there was a good chance it was true."

"Where were you before you came home and found—"

There was a shouted "Stop, stop!" from out in the hall, and Rice nearly knocked Bobby Lee over getting past him and out the door. He got the merest glimpse of someone in hospital scrubs disappearing into the stairwell at the other end of the hall, then turned to see one nurse bending over Lucille Jones while another was making some quick adjustment to the machinery at her bedside.

He ran to the circular nurses' station. "Call downstairs," he told the nurse there. "Maybe they'll catch her."

"Yessir, I'm doing that right now."

Next stop, Lucille's room. "What's going on?" he demanded.

"Someone was in here pulling out her IVs and resetting the equipment. I shouted, and she ran."

"Is Ms. Jones all right?"

The nurse nodded. "I think so. We got to her right away."

"Are you sure it was a woman who did this?" The person Rice glimpsed seemed tall for a woman.

"Well, no, I'm not sure. She walked like a woman but— I don't know. She was wearing scrubs and had a hair cover and a face mask."

"But you didn't think she was on the hospital staff?"

"No. First of all, I didn't recognize her. Second, there was no reason to be in there doing any procedure. And third, she

was doing too much, pulling out the IVs and resetting dials—
it was totally wrong. As soon as I shouted 'Hey!' she turned
and ran." The nurse frowned. "Or he."

"Could the selection of Ms. Jones be random?"

Another nurse said, "Oh, no. I saw him, too. He was
walking past the units, looking at the names. He was looking for Jones. Funny, we only have one Jones right now.
Usually there's two. Once, three."

Rice went back to the nurses' station, but no one matching the description—lousy though it was—had gone running out any exit. Great, thought Rice. Now there's another
jurisdiction involved in this mess. Too many cooks, definitely. At least this new department has the manpower to
spare a guardian for Ms. Lucille Jones.

Twenty-three

SO Jones won't talk for awhile, Sergeant Rice thought glumly, back in the little hospital office he'd used earlier. Bobby Lee was sitting next to his wife, determined to stay there until an armed guard arrived to sit outside the door. The incident had occurred while Jan and Betsy were on their way to see Susan, who could possibly have done it and gotten back home, just barely in time to be sitting calmly in her living room when they arrived. But he didn't think so.

And that meant the news wasn't all bad, because the timing eliminated Jan and probably Susan. Not that he hadn't sort of eliminated Jan anyway. Betsy had suggested that an examination of the double-zero Skacels in Jan's needle holder under a strong magnifying glass would find one of them without a scratch—knitting rubs two needles together, which puts tiny scratches on them. Betsy used that method when customers returned "unused" needles for a refund after finishing a project—the same people, she imagined, who returned dresses after wearing them to a wedding. If they all had scratches, then Rice should ask the teen in the Henderson house why he had taken a needle from his mother's collection. It turned out Ronnie had, in fact, "borrowed" a needle for a school science experiment in magnetism. He repeated the experiment for Rice, determining which needle he had borrowed by suspending a succession of them from a thread until one showed it was still magnetized by drifting around until it pointed north.

Rice began to feel he had the list of suspects whittled down to a manageable three.

B ETSY, faced with a dearth of customers, got out her knitting. Crewel World was involved in an ongoing project to knit tiny caps for premature infants in local hospitals. They were so tiny, and the patterns were so simple, that they worked up very quickly. Customers brought in leftover yarn, and Betsy added a few skeins of yarn too soiled to sell—after washing it, of course. Volunteers could take home the yarn and knit the caps. Every so often, when she got a bag full, Betsy would head off to a hospital with a care unit for these fragile babies.

She sat down at her library table and started on her cap. In barely two minutes, she had picked up the rhythm and felt the welcome settling and clearing of her mind. The humming coming from Godwin as he was getting out the Halloween charts and models barely made an impression on her.

While knitting away, she decided she needed to arrange events in chronological order.

First, there was this old woman named Edyth Hanraty with a great deal of money and a peculiar will.

Second, there was a medical conference in Houston, where Lucille met a woman who looked like her and from whom she stole a hairbrush. A genetic test revealed that the two were very likely related.

Third, Bobby Lee and Lucille Jones came to town seeking Lucille's genetic parents.

Fourth, Lucille and her possible genetic sister met and became friends.

Fifth, the old woman was murdered.

Lucille claimed she didn't know about the rich old aunt, but Betsy—hardly an accomplished surfer of the Internet—had found several stories about Edyth Hanraty, two of which mentioned Susan McConnell as her niece. A story about Dr. "Hugs" Henderson mentioned that his wife, Jan McConnell Henderson, was a nurse in his office. Betsy was sure that someone who really knew her way around the Internet could find the information that linked Edyth, Susan, and Jan.

Lucille had sounded very sincere when she said she did not know about the wealthy, childless Edyth Hanraty when she tried to connect with Jan. But she had tried to make the meeting here with Jan seem like an accident at first, hadn't she? She had seemed very sincere then, too.

There was still a step missing: DNA proof that Lucille was Susan's daughter. Betsy and Jan believed it; but belief is not proof. If Lucille was after the money, then the logical progression was, get the proof, then murder the old woman. Without the proof, there was no need to hasten her death—Edyth was an old woman. She might die of natural causes while they waited for the test results.

Nevertheless, right now, Bobby Lee was Betsy's strongest suspect—or would have been, if he hadn't been sitting with Sergeant Rice when somebody made a second try at killing Lucille.

Could Susan be responsible for the attempt on Lucille's life? The motive would be greed. Lots of people who seemed fiscally secure were actually treading on thin ice. Or maybe she feared the exposure of the secret in her past. Susan thought she had put that portion of her life behind her, until Lucille turned up. She had confessed the truth to Betsy and Susan, but maybe she couldn't envision making it more widely known.

Betsy put down her knitting and called Alida Dove over at the cabins off Oak Lane.

"Are you calling to tell me that yarn I ordered has come in?" Alida asked.

"I'm afraid not. Alida, I want to ask you something in strict confidence."

After the briefest of pauses, Alida said, "All right."

"You have a couple staying there, Lucille and Bobby Lee Jones."

"Yes, they're here until the end of the month."

"Did they have any trouble checking in? I mean with their credit card?"

The pause this time was longer. "Well . . . the first two credit cards they tried were close enough to their limit that they couldn't pay the rent on the cabin."

"Thank you. I was wondering about that. I like Lucille— she's become a good customer—but I don't know anything about her husband."

"I know he goes off by himself to Wayzata every couple of days, is gone for a few hours, and comes back looking like he's been to church, except he doesn't dress for it. Of course, no one does, any more."

"Are you sure he goes to church?"

"Well, he carries a New Testament with him. Or maybe it's a prayer book."

"Does Lucille ever go with him?"

"Nope, never. But she goes to Trinity, doesn't she?"

"Yes, that's right. Have you ever seen or heard the two of them quarrel?"

"No. They're sharp with one another on occasion, but mostly happy. I'd guess they're close, which is nice after being married so long. I just love their accents—and they say the cutest things! Just the other day Lucille was saying to her husband, 'That Stewart, he's all hat and no cattle.' Cute, huh?"

"Yes, it is. Thank you for the information."

"You're welcome. Bye-bye."

Betsy hung up. When, she wondered, had Lucille met Stewart?

And what about Stewart? Had he murdered his aunt in order to get the money for his newest enterprise, Lure of the Lake? He was described as greedy, lazy and feckless, a man with a very high opinion of himself. Betsy's introduction to him had done nothing to disabuse her of those acquired opinions, though she also had to agree that Stewart was very charming and amusing.

Had Katie done it in order to acquire the silver? By all accounts, she and her husband were struggling with a double burden of an incipient baby and college tuition. What might she do to win a prize of tens of thousands of dollars? But wait, Katie didn't know how to wield a thin, steel knitting needle as a murder weapon.

Or did she? Hadn't Jan said something about someone in the family pithing a frog? At the time, Betsy hadn't known what that meant.

But Bobby Lee did. Bobby Lee was good at it. He had done it for his then-girlfriend, Lucille, who was distressed to think a frog suffered during the procedure. There were too many medical experts in this mess.

And as for Bobby Lee going off to frequent church meetings, Betsy didn't think so. She had once been shown a copy of *The Big Book*, the text for alcoholics—also used by other twelve-step programs, such as Gamblers Anonymous. It was about the right size to be mistaken for a Testament or prayer book.

She sat back down and resumed her knitting. She went over her various conversations with Jan, searching for the memory she wanted—and there it was. Stewart, Jan said, had been interested in studying medicine until he had to pith his first frog.

Stewart had told Betsy that he wanted his daughters to have something of value, something he was unable to give them because of his lack of business acumen. Was that sufficient motive? Given his self-centeredness, probably not.

And if the same person who murdered Edyth tried—twice—to murder Lucille, that took Stewart out of the picture. Someone tried to murder Lucille because she was cutting into the inheritance.

The two-note bell of the shop's door sounded, and Betsy looked up to see Heidi Sweitzer coming in. She was struggling with a big cardboard box, and Betsy jumped up to go help. Heidi was Betsy's finisher, the person to whom Betsy brought needlepoint and counted cross-stitch pieces to be washed, stretched and/or blocked, and framed. The box contained all sorts of beautiful handwork: a lovely crewel piece, Angel of Autumn; a stunning "The Sangoma," a needlework portrait of a South African medicine woman whose braided and beaded hair was made of black yarn and real beads; a framed counted cross-stitch "quilt" of many squares, each containing a toy, basket, teapot, cat, rooster, or little motto ("To live well, laugh often, love much"); a needlework stocking painted by Liz of Tent Tapestry in the form of Santa riding a bentwood sleigh down the sky with a kitten in one hand and a puppy in the other; a reproduction nineteenth-century sampler stitched on uneven-count linen; and a square velveteen pillow with bands forming a sandstone-colored cross filled with a geometric pattern of squares and triangles in brown, green, and garnet. That last pattern had been in the September 2004 *Stitcher's World Magazine*. The stitcher was Doris, who became more adventurous in stitchery all the time.

Betsy compared the contents of the box to her master list and declared everything there. She wrote a large check to Heidi and then said, "You do a lot of restoration work, too, don't you?"

"Depends on what it is."

"I got a call from a Mr. Todd Warner who wants to know if I know someone who can restore a small antique Persian rug."

Heidi pursed her lips and blew lightly. "Afraid not. But maybe I can find someone. Todd Warner, you say? The guy that owns Mahogany Bay?"

"I don't know. Where's Mahogany Bay?" Betsy thought she knew the names of all the bays on Lake Minnetonka.

"In Mound. It's a store. He restores antique boats. I went there one time with a friend. I tell you, his prices lifted the hair on the back of my head like a Van de Graaff machine."

"What's a Van de Graaff machine?"

"Oh, you've seen them. They're like silver balls. You put your hands on it and you hair stands straight up."

"Oh, yes, I've seen photos. But hold on, he sells antique boats? What kind, like Chris-Craft?"

"Them, and Gar Wood and other famous boat builders. He had a little bitty canoe in his display room, a very simple but pretty wooden thing. He wanted ten thousand dollars for it. And people think my prices are high!" She laughed. "Well, if I find out about someone who can restore his rug, I'll let you know."

"Thanks."

When she sat down to her stitching again, Betsy thought about what Heidi had said. So Gar Wood was a famous name in old boats? She had never heard of him. On the other hand, she had never heard of Charles Craft or Susan Greening Davis, or Doug Kreinik before getting into needlework, and they were famous.

Hmmmmmm.

She went to her desk and found the phone number of Mahogany Bay.

"This is Betsy Devonshire of Crewel World. Is Mr. Warner in?"

He was, and he came to the phone sounding hearty and pleased to hear from her.

"Did you find me someone to restore my rug?"

"I'm afraid not—my finisher doesn't do that kind of work. But she promised to see if she can find someone. I'm calling for a different reason. Have you ever heard of a Baby Gar?"

"Sure I have. Why?"

"Well, there's an old, beat-up one sitting in a shed over in Orono."

There was a several-second pause. "Are you sure?"

"Yes. I've seen it. The finish is flaking off and bubbly, and it's sitting on a trailer with four flat tires—"

"*Four* flat tires?"

"Yes, is that significant?"

"Maybe, maybe. Is it an inboard or outboard, and is the motor on the boat?"

"The person who showed it to me says it's an old aircraft engine. And it's inboard, in the boat."

"Well, well, well. That's interesting."

"Is it? The current owner says it's not very valuable. He wants to restore it, see if he can get it running again."

"Has he started working on it?" Warner sounded dismayed for some reason.

"No, he hasn't taken possession of it. The boat belonged to Edyth Hanraty."

There was a little pause. "Is the boat the *Edali?*"

"Yes, that's the name on the stern. Have you heard of it?"

"Yes, it used to run all over Lake Minnetonka; I can actually remember seeing it when I was a little boy. I thought that old boat was wrecked years ago. How very interesting."

"I take it the boat is worth something?"

There was a significant pause; Betsy could almost hear Mr. Warner stroking his chin. "Well, that would depend on the condition it's in."

"Would you be interested in taking a look at it? I don't know when Stewart is coming to pick it up, so it would have to be fairly soon."

"Yes, I think I can break loose half an hour if you can arrange it."

"I'll have someone call you." Betsy hung up and immediately dialed Jan.

"Jan, this is very important. A man who sells antique boats almost swallowed his tongue when I told him the *Edali* was in a shed on the late Edyth Hanraty's property. He wants to take a look at it."

"He does?"

"Yes, and I think it might be a good idea."

"All right. When?"

"He says any time you can arrange it, he can find half an hour to take a look."

"Stewart is coming over tomorrow afternoon to pick it up. I think maybe we'd better do it before that. Problem is, we're booked solid here at the clinic. I'll bet Mother could do it. I'll call her. And we'd better get the estate lawyer in on it, too."

"I want to see it, too, all right?" Betsy felt it was very important to hear what Mr. Warner had to say about the boat.

Twenty-four

❈ ❈ ❈

THE next morning, Betsy watched while Marcia Weiner keyed open the padlock on the shed. The dining room table, its chairs, and most of the oddments that had blocked it had been moved back into the house in anticipation of the estate auction. Susan pulled open the other door so light could pour in and splash on the corroded red brown surface of a boat with an extravagantly long bow.

Todd Warner gave a very long, low whistle. He was a short man, muscular, with a craggy-handsome face, the sort who could be any age from thirty-five to fifty-five. He took off his Panama hat as if in homage as he approached the craft. He put a square hand on the side and pushed lightly. "How long has it been in here?" he asked.

"I think the last time it was on the water was in 1962 or '63," said Susan.

"Jesus, the original trailer and everything," he said, prodding a rotten tire with the toe of his shoe. He turned to them. "Did you know this is a car frame from a Pierce-Arrow?"

"No, I didn't," said Susan. "I do know it came with the boat."

He turned and started walking around the craft. He squatted at the stern to pull on a blade of the big bronze propeller—and, after a little effort, got it to turn. "Is the engine in it?"

"Yes, it is," said Susan. "Aunt Edyth said it's an aircraft engine—and certainly I remember it as very loud."

"Yes, it's a World War I Liberty V-12—if it's the original. Gar Wood bought forty-five hundred of them after the Great War as war surplus. He turned around and sold fifteen hundred of them to the Russian air force." He stood and again put a hand on the boat. "Some have four hundred horses, some five hundred horses—" He turned toward them. "You know what one of these boats cost new?"

They shook their heads.

"Eleven thousand, eight hundred dollars for the five-hundred horse engine. That was in 1927, when you could buy a brand new car for six hundred dollars! This was the top-of-the-line runabout. Only the richest men in the world could afford one." He stepped back to sight along the side of the boat, looking for evidence of warping. "Do you know who the original owner of this one was?" he asked.

"No," said Susan. "Someone who was hurt badly when the market crashed in 1929, because he sold it to my grandfather for three thousand dollars."

"The question I have today is, how much is it worth right now?" said Marcia.

"Can I look some more?"

"Sure," said Susan.

"Got a ladder?"

"Yes." She went to a dark corner of the shed and came back dragging an old metal stepladder.

Todd opened it, rocked it to settle it more firmly, then

climbed up to get into the front cockpit, ignoring the dust and dirt. "Dash looks all original," he remarked, running his hands over it. "Even the cigar lighter is still here." He looked over the side at them. "These fittings are made of German silver. All they'll need is polishing—don't let anyone talk you into replating them. Or worse, replacing them. That goes for the instruments, too. They were built by Elgin, and originals are rare and expensive." They heard his feet thumping on the floor. "Solid," he said, nodding, and poked the green leather seat with a finger. Stiff and dry, it didn't give. "Leather will need to be replaced. Make sure they match the color," he instructed them.

"All that space forward," said Betsy, lapsing into nautical terminology from her navy days, "what's in there?"

"Bracing and a watertight bulkhead, mostly," he said with a smile. "It's fourteen feet of *style*." He sat back in the dirty, cracked seat, chin up, one hand on the steering wheel, obviously seeing himself roaring across the water. "You know, there are only seven other Baby Gars in the world?" He grinned at them. "Three of the seven have passed through my hands—I have another one right now, fully restored."

"How much?" asked Betsy, and he looked at her. "I mean, how much for the other one?"

"I'm asking seven hundred thousand—and it's not the boat I suspect this could be." He stood and stooped to lift floorboards to check the inner planking and frames. "Sound, sound, sound," he murmured in satisfaction. Then he turned and, drawing a breath, held it and lifted the bifold doors over the engine compartment.

"Ahhhhhhhh," he breathed. "I was hoping, and there it is—five hundred beautiful horses, sixteen hundred and fifty cubic inches." He reached down and caressed something. "All four carburetors intact. Beautiful."

"My brother has claimed it from the estate," said Susan.

"He says that except for the engine he can do the restoration himself."

Todd looked at her, shocked. "No, no, no! Only professionals should be permitted to work on this wonderful old boat."

"What would it cost to have it restored by professionals?" asked Marcia.

He grimaced unhappily. "Well, okay, a lot. A proper restoration would start at two hundred fifty thousand. That doesn't include the engine. But it's worth probably a quarter million right now."

Susan gave a little gasp of surprise.

"And restored, how much?" asked Marcia, notebook in hand.

"Name your price," he said promptly.

"No, you name one."

He gave her a charming, slightly wolfish grin. "A million, if we could get it into a bidding war. Maybe more if it belonged to a famous person. P. K. Wrigley's is out at a museum in Lake Tahoe and is not for sale at any price. If this one belonged to James J. Hill . . ."

"I don't think so," said Susan, "or we'd know about it; that name wouldn't be forgotten."

All at once there was the sound of tires on gravel. Someone was approaching the shed. Susan and Betsy went out to see an SUV backing a big trailer toward them. Its engine shut off, and Stewart climbed out from behind the driver's seat.

"Hi, Suze!" he said, waving cheerily. "Hello, Ms. Weiner. I've come for my boat." Then he looked past them, and the smile died. "Who's that?" he asked.

Warner looked surprised. "You know me, because I remember you. My name is Todd Warner. You came out to my vintage boat store and talked to me, oh, last fall, I believe. You'd heard I had a Baby Gar for sale and you wanted to see it.

But you changed your mind about buying it because the instruments were replicas and half the planking had been replaced and it had the smaller engine in it. You asked me what I'd charge you for an all-original, fully-restored, bigger-engine Baby Gar, and you smiled when I said a million dollars."

Stewart's ebullience had melted away. He attempted a smile, but it was a travesty. He turned his back on them, heaved a big sigh, thumped the roof of the SUV. When he turned around again, he was looking assertive and confident. "Well, so what?" he said. "So what? I found the *Edali* in this shed, and I thought, by gum, here's something of real value, something I could treasure, something I want. Like Katie and that silver, just exactly like that, I want this boat. She's in love with the silverware, I'm in love with the *Edali*. But like that big old four-poster, I figured if you knew how much this boat could be worth, you'd never let me have it. So I resorted to—to subterfuge. And so what?"

"You knew about the *Edali* last fall?" asked Betsy.

"Sure. I was putting the dining room table and chairs out here—no way was I going to haul them up to the attic— and I saw it. I couldn't believe my eyes—the old *Edali*. Man, the great times we had on that boat, didn't we, Susan?"

"Yes, we did," she said, rather neutrally.

"And I told you the truth about her over lunch the other day, really I did. It was like my ship had come in—" He snorted a laugh, swallowed, and continued in a wheedling tone, "It was like a *sign*, Susan! Something I really loved— boating—something I've never gotten tired of! How could this not work if I made a business of it?" He wiped sweat from his forehead and turned completely around, hands uplifted, desperate to make her understand. "I talked with Aunt Edyth. I asked her about the boat, did she still want it, could I maybe buy it from her? I said I'd give her fifteen hundred for it. I told her it was probably not worth that, it was the sentimental connection that made me interested in it, just like I told you. And yes, I knew it was a lie, because I already talked to Mr. Warner over there. And you know what she did? She *laughed* at me! She said, 'There is not one item on my property I don't know the value of, from the china in my kitchen to that old motorcycle in my garage. I know the *Edali* is a Baby Gar, worth more than fifteen hundred, more than fifteen thousand, in her present condition.' Well, I pretended to be all surprised, and I said that I guessed I wouldn't be buying it from her after all."

He laughed, recalling the jest he'd made. He'd probably laughed just that way then, too, though the joke was on him. "And that was the end of it. I kept coming out, doing chores, running errands, until she died. I tried to talk her into leaving my daughters something in her will, anything, just as a recognition that they exist. But she didn't. And okay, I worked to get you to agree that everyone could choose one thing from the house, so my girls could have their own inheritance, and I could choose the boat. I just *had* to have that boat." He stopped talking then and just stood there with his head down, shamed.

"I understand," said Susan. "Oh, Stew, what are we going to do with you?"

"Well, you could give me the boat." He lifted his head to reveal a roguish smile.

"We can't do that. Mr. Warner, here, says that under no circumstances should an amateur attempt to restore this boat, that it's far too valuable to endanger it that way."

Stewart came closer. "You don't know who you're talking about, Mr. Warner. I've been around boats all my life. I think I know about as much as most professionals do about how to repair a boat, even a wooden one like this."

"Mr. O'Neil, this isn't just a wooden boat, it's made of African mahogany, which has special properties. You don't just scrape the old finish off and slap on a new coat of varnish. It needs special handling to ensure it looks like it did when new. The seats are Spanish leather, expensive, and dyed a very particular shade of green. This is a grand old boat, a national treasure, and it needs careful restoration."

Betsy smiled to herself. Warner was speaking with deep feeling. It was obvious he'd already formed an attachment to the *Edali* and was hurt to think an amateur might fool around with it and perhaps damage it. But this was not her problem to solve—it was Susan's.

"Stew," Susan said, "I'm sorry, I need to talk to Jan about this. I'm in favor of taking the boat away from you, but I'm pretty sure Jan is going to argue that we agreed you could claim anything you wanted, so the boat should be yours. I'll listen to her arguments—"

Marcia spoke up. "If there is evidence of fraud in this arrangement, then as protector of the assets of the Hanraty estate, I'll have something to say, as well. Mr. O'Neil, you have behaved, at the very least, very badly."

Again the shamed look, which Betsy thought not quite so well done as the first one. Perhaps sensing this, Stewart did not attempt to continue the discussion, but got into his rented vehicle and drove away.

A T two the next day, Jan and Susan were sitting in Betsy's apartment, looking wretched. "Oh, God, what if you're wrong, Betsy?" asked Jan.

"Then he will be acquitted at his trial," she said. "But I don't think I'm wrong. Neither does Sergeant Rice. Nor Mike Malloy."

"What made you sure?" asked Susan.

"The boat. I should have looked into that boat earlier. Why did he want it? It would take time and money to fix it up, and it wouldn't be suitable to take fishermen out in, so why did he want it so badly that he'd pass up things he could sell to get the money he needed to start his business?"

Susan shook her head. "But to *kill*, to actually kill some-one. I don't understand. I thought I knew him, my own brother! What kind of person was he to do that?"

"You told me yourself," said Betsy. "You said he was ambi-tious, greedy, and lazy. He wanted to be an important busi-nessman, but he wasn't willing to devote the endless hours it takes. He was incensed that you and Jan were to inherit a mil-lion or more dollars—when you didn't need it—while he, struggling and with four daughters to educate, got nothing. It wasn't fair. He probably was working on changing Edyth's mind when he discovered the *Edali* in the shed. Suddenly, he could see daylight. Oh, it would be nice to restore it and offer rides in it to select customers, but that notion only lasted un-til he found out that a restored Baby Gar was worth as much as a million dollars. That would even things up, if he could get a million just like his sister and niece!

"But Todd Warner told him that it's the restored Baby Gar that would be worth that kind of money—and that professional restoration of an antique boat would cost a great deal of money. Money he didn't have."

Susan said in a low, angry voice, "That's when he cooked up that deal with the girls, coaching them to choose very expensive items from the house so he could get the restora-tion money from them."

"No, I don't think so," said Betsy. "I think he genuinely thought he could do most of the restoration himself—he has an excellent opinion of his skills. By putting the girls for-ward as legitimate claimants, it made it possible for him to get the boat for nothing. But he really loves his daughters, Susan. That's why he tried to murder Lucille."

"Lucille? I don't understand."

"He was pretty sure he could talk Jan into loaning him some of the money she was to inherit. But she turned him down because she believed Lucille's claim was legitimate, which might bring Jan's share down to something even less than what he wanted to borrow. And he wanted to keep the boat."

"I never thought when I told him that . . ." said Jan, looking stricken. "Oh, no, *I* helped him decide that Lucille had to die!"

"No such thing!" said Susan. "I won't have you feeling guilty for something your uncle found out from you. He would have found out anyway." She sniffed back a tear. "Poor Lucille, walking into a nest of vipers all unknowing."

"One viper," corrected Betsy. "He was upset when his attempt on Lucille failed, but he still had Plan B, which was to tell Jan about the boat. If she loaned him just a hundred and fifty thousand dollars, she could have it back when he sold the restored *Edali*. He'd have enough left over to start his business."

"And fail," said Susan.

"Now, we don't know that," said Jan. "It really is a good idea, Mother. He loves to go fishing, and he knows every corner of Lake Minnetonka."

"Yes, but he doesn't like sitting in a cramped office doing sums and paying bills—and that's a great big part of owning your own business."

"It sure is," sighed Betsy, thinking of her poor, neglected shop.

"Not that he'll ever have a chance to find out," muttered Susan, who was using anger to stave off grief.

Jan looked at her watch. "Is it over yet?"

Betsy looked at her own. "Probably. Both of you will very likely have messages on your phone machines when you get home."

"That's why we're here," said Jan. "I couldn't bear talking to him right now."

"I can't believe it," said Susan. "When I thought the worst about Stew, I had no idea it wasn't remotely the worst. How could he? How *could* he?"

* * *

"DID he confess?" asked Betsy. She and Sergeant Rice were in a small conference room in the Excelsior Police Department building.

"Not yet," said Rice. "He's made some damaging admissions, however. How did you find out about that boat?"

"I got a call from Mr. Todd Warner, asking if I knew someone who knew something about restoring an old Persian carpet. I asked my finisher, and she told me Mr. Warner bought and sold antique boats. I called him back and asked him about Gar Wood, and when he found out I knew where the old *Edali* was, he was very eager to get a look at it. We managed to arrange that just before Stewart came by to pick it up—and discovered that Stewart had been talking to Mr. Warner about a Gar Wood boat last fall."

"I take it you didn't suspect him until then."

"Oh, but I did. Stewart was very near the top of the people I thought might have murdered Edyth Hanraty—except he didn't seem to have a motive. He wasn't in line for any of the inheritance, nor were his daughters. That is, until I found out that a restored Baby Gar is worth a serious fortune."

"I don't understand why you were looking at him at all," said Rice.

"A couple of things. He was among the people who didn't know Edyth Hanraty put her hair into a braid before going to bed. Jan did, and so did Susan. It might have occurred to Lucille—it's one of the things that turns up in women's literature and in old movies. But probably not Bobby Lee. They knew about Edyth Hanraty and her relationship to Susan and Jan before they came up here, so they were at the top of my list."

"How do you know that?" asked Mike Malloy.

"Because they couldn't afford this trip as a mere vacation," said Betsy. "Or even as a search for blood relatives. They are maxed out on their credit cards—I found that out from the owner of the cabin they're staying in. She said they had to try three times to find a credit card that would cover the rent. And Lucille told me that Bobby Lee is just getting over a serious gambling problem. Lucille wanted to come up here to connect with her blood relatives, but Bobby Lee wouldn't agree until he found out about Edyth Hanraty. If Lucille was a relative, maybe she was also an heir-in-waiting. If not, by making the connection now, while Edyth was still alive, she could work her way into the family and become one.

"Then Jan told Lucille about Aunt Edyth's peculiar will. If Lucille was Susan's long-lost daughter, she was, in fact, in line for a fortune."

Malloy made a noise in his throat. "Yeah, Mitch told me about that and how Lucille could be an heir."

Betsy nodded. "And the sooner they got the money, the sooner they'd be out from under the crushing debt Bobby Lee piled up while his gambling was out of control. Since they had never met Edyth, they had no reason to see her as anything but a will in their favor waiting to be sent to probate."

"What about the murder weapon, the knitting needle?" asked Rice.

"You can buy one in any store that sells knitting supplies. Bobby Lee had seen them in his house, Lucille had tried knitting with them. Worse, Lucille didn't know where they'd gotten to. Oh, yes, I was pretty sure Bobby Lee was the killer. He told me with some relish how he used to pith frogs for Lucille when they were both in the same biology class. It was the same method used to murder poor Miss Hanraty. But Stewart knew how to pith a frog, too."

"So how do you think he did it? Snuck up on her getting ready for bed?"

"No, she never would have allowed that—she locked her doors at night. He came over to do chores for her, just like he'd been doing for months, trying to get in her good graces.

He probably made cocoa, or coffee, or got her to make some, and when she wasn't looking, doctored it with sleeping pills. I know Susan has a supply of them. Jan told me about that when we showed Susan the doll we dredged up on the Big Island. Susan was extremely upset, poor thing, but Jan said she'd give her a pill. Stewart would have had any number of chances to steal a few, if he didn't have any of his own.

"Once Edyth was helpless, Stewart either killed her at the table, or got her into bed and killed her there. What I don't understand is why he left the needle there to be found."

Rice said, "The medical examiner said she threw her head back when she died, pinching it in place. So he cut it off close, but not close enough, and it was discovered."

"I understand that's typical of the man," said Betsy. "He has great ideas but isn't always good at carrying them out."

Rice said, "One thing I still need to check out is this DNA thing. I can't help thinking that a couple of coincidences and a faked test would explain a whole lot about Lucille Jones."

"It's authentic," said Betsy. "Jan told me Susan submitted a blood sample. Maternity is harder to prove than paternity, and the father wasn't able to provide a sample, so Jan did, too, since a full sibling is the next best thing. The test came back ninety-three point something probable that Susan is Lucille's mother. As soon as Lucille is up for visitors, Susan is going to see her."

Twenty-five

❖ ❖ ❖

LUCILLE had been moved from Intensive Care to a semiprivate room. She looked, as she put it, "like I was dragged through a knothole backwards," but managed a smile when she saw who was standing in the doorway.

It was a short, slender woman with silver hair and shining blue eyes, carrying a Chinese-red vase filled with red, white and lavender roses. Their fragrance came wafting before her.

"Please come in," said Lucille. "I think I know who you are."

"And I know you are my daughter," said Susan. She came in quickly, put the vase on the table, moved it aside, and bent to kiss the bruised face under its burden of bandages. "These are from my garden."

"They're beautiful," said Lucille, and immediately burst into tears.

"Here now, here now, none of that," soothed Susan. "You're still in recovery, and we don't want to complicate things." She picked up one of Lucille's hands and stroked it tenderly.

"Yes, yes, I'm all right. I'll be fine in a minute." Lucille sniffed and blinked. "There, see? I'm a good little Minnesotan, all over that now." The sobs had, indeed, stopped, but the tears still streamed, running out of the corners of her eyes to be soaked up by her bandages.

Susan pulled a Kleenex from the little box of them on the table and gently wiped her daughter's eyes. "Good thing you're all over crying. They charge about ten dollars apiece for Kleenex in this place."

Lucille choked on a laugh. "Isn't it scary how much things cost in a hospital? Oh, I had so many important things to say to you, and here we are talking about Kleenex!"

"The first thing I want to say is, I never stopped thinking about you. Every single day I thought about you—even when I thought you were a stillborn baby boy." Her smile was bittersweet.

"And ever since I found out I was adopted, I dreamed of meeting my genetic mama and daddy—I'm so sorry I missed seeing him."

"So am I. He was a very sweet man." She studied Lucille's face. "I think you have his eyes. But just like Jan and Jason, you have your grandfather John's big bones and fair coloring."

"Oh, I hope you have lots of pictures!" said Lucille. "And that reminds me, Bobby Lee brought the present I made for you to the hospital. It's in the closet over there, on the top shelf." She nodded toward a corner of the room.

As Susan walked over to the closet, she turned back to look again and again at the daughter she never knew she had. In the closet, on the top shelf, was a shallow box about twenty inches long and fourteen inches wide. It was wrapped in pink paper tied with a pink bow. Susan took it down and brought it back to the bed.

"What's in here?" she asked.

"It's for you," said Lucille. "Open it."

With swift economy, Susan pulled off the ribbon and undid the paper at one end. Out slid a white cardboard box. When Susan lifted the lid, she found a photo album with a cover made of white imitation leather. She lifted it and found an unframed counted cross-stitch piece done all in shades of brown on white aida cloth. About ten by eleven inches, it depicted a newborn's head and shoulder surrounded by her mother's face on top and arms coming up behind to cradle the back of her head.

"Oh, my," murmured Susan.

"I thought maybe you did that before you let me go," said Lucille. "I was so sorry to find out you never did."

"I have wished every day since you were born that I had gotten a chance to hold you. This is very beautiful."

"Do you like it? I sent all the way to England for it. It's called Tenderness. Vervaco's the name of the company. I never heard of them before, but I saw a model of it online and just had to get it to do for you. I had thought about a birth sampler, but that seemed kind of silly. I wanted something to give you, to make you think of me when I was just new." Tears threatened to spill from Lucille's eyes again.

"Thank you, my dear, it's exactly right. But what's in this album?" Susan turned a page and found a photocopy of Lucille's adoption certificate and beside it, a photograph of a baby in a woman's arms, a man standing proudly beside them.

And on successive pages, carefully reproduced, were photographs of Lucille through her childhood and teen years, with loving parents, birthday cakes, and rowdy friends. For the next hour, the two women went through the album, talking and laughing. In the later pages, one young man started showing up more frequently until he stood beside her in an ill-fitting tux, she radiant in bridal regalia.

On the last few pages were photographs of a boy and then a girl—the boy looking a great deal like his father, the girl like her mother—as infants, then children, then adults.

"Your grandchildren," said Lucille proudly. "Glen's the boy, Wanda's the girl—she's nearly finished with her internship as a veterinarian."

"What does Glen do?" asked Susan. By now she was perched comfortably on the edge of the bed.

"He's an airplane mechanic for American Airlines at Dallas/Fort Worth International. He works on the jet engines and is taking classes to be certified on the electrical wiring systems. He earns more money than I do, and he's going to get married next year to a wonderful girl," Lucille finished proudly. "Wanda wants to work with both large and small animals—she's crazy about horses. She never outgrew that horse thing some girls get into. But she's really good with cats. Her doctor says she can just put her hand on a scared cat, and it calms right down."

Hearing a noise, they both looked around to see a tall, thin man with salt and pepper hair and a bashful air standing in the doorway.

"Bobby Lee," said Lucille, "come in and meet your mama-in-law, Ms. McConnell."

"Call me Susan," said Susan, extending a hand.

The man came to take it in his own large, knobby one. "I'm pleased to meet you," he said, and then to his wife, "The doctor says he wants to take another X-ray of your head and chest. I think he wants to see how much of your brains have leaked out."

"Now, don't go teasing a poor, sick, weak woman," scolded Lucille, but without any sting to her words. She looked up at Susan, then again at her husband, then down at the album. "I feel as if a blank place in my personal history has been filled right up, and the story is good, even if there are some sad parts to it," she said. "I feel really bad about Uncle Stewart. I wish—"

"There's nothing that can be done about your Uncle Stewart," said Susan firmly. "Save your pity for his daughters."

"Is there anything we can do for them?"

"I don't know. Probably not right now. Stewart has sown the wind, and his wife and daughters are caught in the whirlwind. But the storm will pass, and maybe then we can do something."

Lucille looked up again into the clear blue eyes of her mother. *Lost—and found*, she thought. "We'll think of something, I'm sure. All of us, together."

Flag of the United States of America

Knitting Pattern by Denise E. Williams

Skill level: Enthusiastic Intermediate

A knitting pattern for an "anatomically correct" U.S. flag, with a suggestion of apple-pie top crust!

The Star Field is written as a graphed chart. A knitting chart is really a knitter's lingua franca—if you can read a chart, you can knit patterns from all over the universe!

This design uses one color, in pattern stitches to withstand pillow fights and dedicated lounging. The ambitious among us could add red, white, and blue to spectacular effect. Or, embellish the final piece with beads, ribbon, sequins . . .

Dimensions will vary, but the finished piece will be about 14" W × 22" L.

Monica Ferris

ABBREVIATIONS:

K = knit
P = purl
st. = stitch(es)
CO = cast on
P2tog = purl two stitches together

Moss Stitch = 1st row, K1, P1.
2nd row, K the Ps and P the Ks
Repeat these two rows.

Cable 2B = [P1, slip next 2 st. onto cable needle and hold in back of work, K2, K2 st. from cable needle, P1]

MATERIALS:

- 2 skeins Patons Decor worsted weight, pale taupe heather. Or substitute your favorite worsted-weight wool.
- Size 7 knitting needles, or size to get a comfortable gauge
- 1 cable needle
- 14 ring markers

PATTERN

CO 76 using your favorite cast-on method.

Rows 1-7: Moss Stitch.

Row 8: This row sets up the border and the thirteen stripes.

Moss Stitch 5 st., place marker.
P1, K4, P1, place marker. This will be a "red" stripe, in a four-stitch cable.

K4, place marker. This will be a "white" stripe.
P1, K4, P1, place marker
K4, place marker
P1, K4, P1, place marker
K4, place marker
P1, K4, P1, place marker
K4, place marker
P1, K4, P1, place marker
K4, place marker
P1, K4, P1, place marker
K4, place marker
P1, K4, Pl, place marker
Moss stitch 5 st.

Your piece should now have a five-stitch wide Moss Stitch border on either end and the thirteen stripes marked off in the body of the piece.

Row 9: Moss Stitch 5 st. K the Ks and P the Ps across. End Moss Stitch 5 st.

Row 10: Repeat row 8, slipping markers instead of placing them.

Row 11: Repeat row 9, slipping markers as you go.

Row 12: Moss Stitch 5 st. *Cable 2B; P2tog twice* repeat between *'s across body, end Cable 2B. Moss Stitch 5 st.

Row 13: Moss Stitch 5 st. *K1, P4, K1; P1 in front and back of next 2 st. *repeat across body. End K1, P4, K1. Moss Stitch 5 st.

Row 14: Moss Stitch 5 st. *P1, K4, P1; K4* repeat across. End P1, K4, P1. Moss Stitch 5 st.

Row 15: Keeping Moss Stitch border as established, K the Ks and P the Ps across stripes.

Now that the Moss Stitch border is established, the remaining instructions will assume five stitches of Moss Stitch on either side of the outermost markers. The instructions continue for the stripes only.

Row 16: *Cable 2B, K4* end Cable 2B.

Row 17: K the Ks and P the Ps across.

Row 18: K the Ks and P the Ps across.

Row 19: K the Ks and P the Ps across.

Row 20: *Cable 2B; P2tog twice* repeat across body, end Cable 2B.

Row 21: *K1, P4, K1; P1 in front and back of next 2 st. *repeat across body. End K1, P4, K1.

Row 22: K the Ks and P the Ps across.

Row 23: K the Ks and P the Ps across.

Row 24: *Cable 2B, K4* end Cable 2B.

Row 25: K the Ks and P the Ps across.

Row 26: K the Ks and P the Ps across.

Row 27: K the Ks and P the Ps across.

Row 28-87: Repeat rows 20-27. The instructions are much

more daunting in print than in yarn on needles in your hands. Basically, you will be twisting the cables every four rows, and drawing in and expanding the white stripes every 8 rows.

THE STAR FIELD

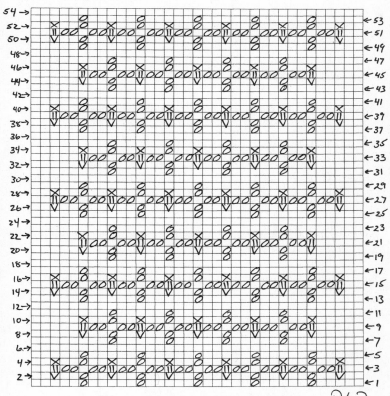

KEY   no symbol = knit on the back, purl on the front
O = purl on the back, knit on the front
V = K1, P1, K1 all in same stitch
$||$ = P3
X = P next 3 stitches together

Row 88: Moss Stitch 5 st. P across the next 36 stitches, removing markers and decreasing 1 st. so the Star Field totals 35 stitches. Place marker. Continue stripes as established. End Moss Stitch 5 st.

Your piece should now have the five-stitch wide Moss Stitch border on either end and the star field and remaining six stripes marked off.

Row 89: Keeping stripes and Moss Stitch borders as established, K across the Star Field.

Row 90: Keeping Moss Stitch borders and stripes as established, begin reading Row 1 of the star field chart.

Complete Row 54 of the star field chart. Decrease 1 st. toward the center of the piece to adjust the stitch count so that it will be in step with the Moss Stitch border.

Remove all markers, and Moss Stitch 7 rows. Bind off in Moss Stitch!